ACCLA

MW01504634

For *The Zero Dog War*

"…another audacious blend of genre elements. [A]n underlying sense of twisted humor…sardonic wit is on full display. …[A] breakneck-paced, action-packed, categorically cool, and utterly readable novel."

–Paul Goat Allen for Unabashedly Bookish

"Urban Fantasy meets hilarious sarcasm at its best…I had high expectations and The Zero Dog War didn't fail to deliver."

—The Geeky Lover for Book Lovers, Inc.

"I giggled so much reading this book, Keith Melton's humor truly shines!"

–Wicked Little Pixie for Writings of a Wicked Book Addict

"[A] hilarious tongue in cheek satire that pokes fun at the supernatural in [a] fast-paced action-packed storyline…filled with hilarious dialogue and some great inner monologue that kept me laughing throughout the entire book."

—Tori for Smexybooks

"Keith Melton writes an absurd mix of heavy-duty action and hilarious quips…I cannot wait for more books in the 'Zero Dog Missions' series."

—Danielle at Alpha Reader

~ LOOK FOR THESE TITLES FROM KEITH MELTON ~

The Zero Dog Missions

The Zero Dog War (Book One)
Dark Ride Dogs (Book Two)
"Red Dogs" (Book 2.5)

Thorn Knights

9mm Blues (Book One)

The Nightfall Syndicate

Blood Vice (Book One)
Ghost Soldiers (Book Two)

DARK RIDE DOGS

Zero Dog Missions Book Two

KEITH MELTON

etopia
press

Etopia Press
1643 Warwick Ave., #124
Warwick, RI 02889
http://www.etopia-press.net

DARK RIDE DOGS

Print ISBN: 978-1-947135-11-6
Digital ISBN: 978-1-939194-82-4

First Etopia Press electronic publication: May 2014

First Etopia Press print publication: May 2017

THE ZERO DOG ROSTER

Captain Andrea Walker — pyromancer, executive officer

Sergeant Nathan Genna — demon sergeant, second in command

Tiffany Sparx — scout, official succubus

Rafe Lupo — werewolf, health food jingoist, enthusiastic nudist

Gavin Carter — driver, possible empath

Hanzo Sorenson — medic, part-time ninja

Mai Tanaka — summoner mage, animal lover

Stefan Dalca — token vampire

Operation Dark Ride

Mission File:
010100110110101101111001011011100110010101110100001000000
100110001101111011101100110010101110011001000000101100101
10111101110101

Preliminary Report:

Paranormal mercenary team Rv6-4 "Zero Dogs" of the Hellfrost Group based in Portland, Oregon engaged hostile redcap goblins at the request of municipal authorities.

The following story takes place between June 7th and June 29th. Events do not happen in real time.

CHAPTER ONE
Lock and Load

Mercenary Wing Rv6-4 "Zero Dogs"
Border Inn Economy Motel, Portland, OR
June 7th

Zero hour. Go time.

We were weapons hot and cleared to use deadly force against murderous redcap goblins and being paid a pretty penny to do so. Usually this would be sheer bliss for a degenerate mercenary like me, but as I stalked down a back alley in the darkness I couldn't shake the feeling that something was about to go very wrong. And by "very wrong" I meant *more* wrong than night-creeping down an alleyway choked with litter, decorated with size-deluded graffiti of male genitalia, and featuring a reeking Dumpster crawling with flies as the *pièce de résistance*.

I'm Captain Andrea Walker, pyromancer and commanding officer of the paranormal mercenary team the Zero Dogs. The first bullet is always free, but after that you gotta pay.

I led my squad toward a breezeway that ran from the alley through the motel to the parking lot on the other side. The alley's foul stink and general filth was enough to make me wish I'd insisted on full-body hazmat suits. And to think some fools claimed the life of a paranormal mercenary was all glory, guns, and rampant hedonism.

We'd been contracted by the city government to hunt down and terminate a rogue group of homicidal redcaps. The hostiles had barricaded themselves inside the rooms of the Border Inn, a notoriously high-class establishment complete with peeling paint, hourly rates, and a purple coin-operated condom dispenser bolted to the wall outside the office.

I pressed against the cinderblock wall and raised my arm to the rest of the squad, clenching my hand into a fist, the signal to hold up. Alpha One halted behind me without a sound. The pre-combat stress hummed and snarled in my veins, but I ignored it and summoned magefire. Heat washed through me, shimmering from my skin, distorting the air around me in waves. Carefully, I lifted the Dumpster's plastic lid and peered inside, ready to ignite a burst of highly flammable vapor and incinerate any threats.

No redcaps hid inside the trash bin, waiting to spring out and stab me...though there *was* a disturbing llama-shaped piñata lying on a pile of garbage bags, glaring at me with a malevolent red eye. Also, the festering stench seared off half my nose hair.

I turned back to the breezeway, gritting my teeth and promising myself life was all sprinkles-side-up for my donuts. Creepy llama or no, I was roughly seventy-seven percent positive our dynamic assault would go off as planned. For the Zero Dogs, that percentage was as close to a sure thing as we ever came.

Sergeant Nathan Genna's deep voice rumbled over the radio, as hushed as he could make it, which meant he sounded like a highly pissed off Barry White trying not to be overheard in a restaurant. "Alpha Actual, this is Alpha Two. We are in position. Hostiles sighted. Ready to engage on your command, over."

"Roger that, Alpha Two," I said into the headset mike on my helmet. "Sit tight. Alpha One still *en route* to position, out."

The redcaps had already killed one person: a door-to-door salesman from Maximum Force Sales, Inc. who'd been lured into a motel room to his tragic end. According to Lieutenant Stone, the SWAT team leader who'd briefed us, the tiny bastards had stolen all of the salesman's Citrus Wonder solution to clean their iron-shod boots and then bathed their floppy wool caps in his blood.

Redcaps are nasty little shits, registering two notches past psychotic goblins on the New International scale of Fae douchebaggery. They sported huge, staring eyes with gray pupils the size of half-dollar coins, stringy, unwashed hair, sagging skin more wrinkled than wet jockey shorts stuffed in a car's ashtray, and they stank like sauerkraut. I didn't hate redcaps because they were ugly and smelled bad. I hated them because they wielded butcher knives, cleavers, pikes, hell, *pruning shears* and used them on the innocent people they lured into unsavory places. They murdered to keep the woolen caps they wore wet and red with blood. If those floppy hats dried out, the redcap would die. What these evil powries lacked in height they more than made up for in vicious disposition and abundant malice.

I slipped a small dentist's mirror around the corner of the gray stucco wall, turning it to scan the dark breezeway for threats. The corridor was empty save for a vending machine lying on its side with the front smashed in, bleeding shards of plastic and empty candy wrappers onto the concrete.

I drew the mirror back and glanced behind me at the rest of Alpha One. Tiffany Sparx, our succubus, wore combat fatigues and body armor. Black, bat-like wings sprouted from her upper back, and her slit pupils made a stunning face all the more memorable, like goat eyes on the Mona Lisa. She carried two SIG Sauer P226 Elite semi-autos, one for each hand, firing .357 SIG rounds—a helluva lot of fucking gun for a succubus who technically should've focused on charming things with sex magic.

Mai Tanaka stood behind Tiffany, one hand resting on the stucco wall. Mai proudly wore her body armor over a bright yellow summoner vest and silk robes, and she'd slapped a sticker of the blue Powerpuff Girl on the front of her helmet. Around her feet swarmed a mass of what could only be described as voles crossbred with Velociraptors and dyed lime green. The alien voles made miniature idling chainsaw noises. Their mouths brimmed with buzz saw teeth. Mai caught me looking and gave a thumbs up. The voles all turned their heads to stare at me as if I were an intriguing spicy chicken sandwich. I avoided eye contact and tried not to smell either afraid or like white meat.

Hanzo, our medic, brought up the rear. He wore ninja blacks and the lower half of his face was covered, but anyone could see that despite the name *Hanzo* he was not Japanese. His real name was Austin Sorenson. His healing magic could mend bullet holes, broken bones, and disembowelments with amazing skill, but he fancied himself a practitioner of the Way of Stealth, even with the red medical crosses I made him wear on his black pajamas.

"On me," I said and received nods all around. Even some of the voles nodded, chilling as that was.

I slipped around the corner and advanced down the corridor. The breezeway remained empty, without even a horror-movie-fodder cat to jump out and screech at the least opportune moment. Just more graffiti—stranger stuff than immense penises this time: "Edward Teach singed his beard but also burned the beaver" and "Red-nose Rudolph flies drunk"—

mixed with an alarming amount of ancient bubble gum stuck to the walls.

I used the mirror again at the next corner. No hostiles. The parking lot was mostly empty, but the street beyond teemed with police cruisers and officers, the SWAT team, and more news vans than you could throw granola and Birkenstocks at. The alternating pulse and flash of cruiser lights turned the night into a ghetto disco show. The air crackled with clipped police radio chatter, live news broadcasts, and the murmur of rubberneckers.

As I cleared the corner, I spotted Alpha Two strike team in position at room 117, waiting on us. I moved out, creeping along the dirty façade, getting spider webs in my face with every other step.

Alpha Two appeared good to go, stacked along the wall outside the door. The team consisted of Sergeant Nathan Genna, aka Sarge, a massive demon I suspected had sold his angel wings for access to high-powered military weaponry. Rafe, our werewolf who loved organic health food, fornication, and gratuitous public nudity…not necessarily in that order. Stefan, our debauched vampire, who pretended to be an aristocrat from some Eastern Europe mountain range, but was really only a rich kid from the Hamptons. Gavin, our official driver of all things vehicular, specializing in the heavily armored, heavily gunned variety. His file also listed him as an empath…though I nursed serious doubts regarding that bit of resume padding. For this mission, I'd shoved an MP5 and a grenade into his hands and told him to get his empathic ass in gear and go feel some pain, preferably someone else's pain, but I didn't have the time to be choosy.

We were in sight of the cops and crowds but not the hostiles as I led Alpha One into position, flanking the door to room 118, with Tiffany on the near side and me on the far side. After the close concealment of the breezeway, the openness here had my hackles up. I gave Tiffany a thumbs up. She grinned and nodded, but couldn't return the thumbs up because her hands were full of pistols.

Heat shimmered around my hands as I tapped my pyromancy again. Since the redcaps had murdered their only hostage for that repulsive blood-hat fetish, our contract with the city marked them as "Expunge with Extreme Prejudice" to be executed forthwith, care of yours truly and company.

I flipped the Heads Up Display on my helmet into position to check the view from the fiber optic cameras and listen to the audio feed from the mini microphones that SWAT had smuggled inside via the a/c vents. The HUD allowed me to switch views between the two groups of redcaps who'd turned this cheap motel into a half-assed evil lair for the malevolently height-impaired.

The HUD showed me the nine goblins in Room 118 first. Some of the wrinkled little bastards sat on the bed watching pay-per-view porn. Others ran around hacking and gouging the walls and furniture with their knives. Gleeful cackling mixed with erotic moans from the TV. The intertwined sounds made the hair on the back of my neck stand up, because some things were just plain wrong.

One odd redcap caught my attention as he paced on top of the table wearing a ringmaster costume that was entirely white: vest, jacket with tails, balloon pants, bowtie, all as colorless as vanilla icing. In contrast, his top hat appeared to be glistening bloodred felt that drooped on his head. His leather boots were bright crimson, and he carried a whip the color of shimmering coals. Oh, and he appeared to be wearing a bright red codpiece, God save us. Little droplets of blood rained from his hat, and his boot heels made *thock, thock, thock* sounds as he stomped back and forth across the tabletop.

The fretting, frustrated scowl on the ringmaster's face told me he was the leader. I knew that look well. He spun on his boot heel and frowned at a grizzled powrie using a bendy straw to sip from a fifth of Jack Daniels. The vanilla ringmaster had to shout to be heard over the evil giggling and porno moans.

"This is no thrice-damned *trap*," the ringmaster shrieked in the perfect key of knife-scraping-ceramic-plate. "None of those knobscobbing flail-monkeys have any hope of capturing me."

"Shut your yap-hole, fungus knuckles!" one of the other redcaps yelled back without looking away from the television. Apparently morale among evil fae ranked even lower than ours on any given payday.

The ringmaster's eyes bulged in outrage. "I'll shank you for that, Mosorg. I came over here to boot you sourblood femur-gnawing pus-packets into shape!"

He punted an empty liquor bottle across the room. It missed Mosorg and smashed against the wall. Mosorg flipped him off and still never took his gaze off the screen.

The ringmaster clenched his fists and executed a lively hopping dance of wrath before continuing his rant at the redcap sucking whiskey through a straw.

"Who loved the circuses more than I? Answer me, you slimy offspring of three blind hagfish. Who else yearns to rebuild the glory of the circus past? Those days when the road brought wonders instead of endless gas stations pushing three flavors of microwave burrito. And in repayment of my long struggle, you drink and fornicate with your own hands while watching shaved apes. As minions, you utterly fail!"

The grizzled redcap stared at him unblinking and slurped more booze.

I almost felt bad for the crazy little freak. Then I switched to the feed from the second camera and mike in room 117's a/c vent and unease fluttered through me. No trace of crazed revelry or distraction here. All was grim silence. These redcaps stood as motionless as demented garden gnome statuary, focused on the only two ways into the room: through the door or the front window. They clutched knives and cleavers. One of them struggled to balance an unwieldy pike and knocked over a lamp. Another powrie clutched a Phillips screwdriver in one hand and a standard screwdriver in the other. Each wore spiked iron-shod boots. Fae hated iron as a general rule, but redcaps branched out from the inbred goblin side of the tree and were not affected by the metal. Lucky us.

The sight of the salesman's corpse in the HUD viewscreen made my stomach clench and a snarl twist my lips. Murder most foul. Even annoying door-to-door salesmen deserved justice. Ripping through these knee-gnawing bastards would be a favor to the civilized world, and I planned to bring some serious payback...via Sarge and Alpha Two, because I was stuck assaulting the hyperactive rumpus room in 118 and it was too late to switch. Sarge had his work cut out for him against those grim redcaps, but it looked as if my Area of Responsibility would be a cakewalk. I'd buy Sarge a beer later for his trouble.

This close to the hostiles, I couldn't risk voice commands lest I tip the redcaps off. My rapid flurry of hand signals confirmed to Sarge and the rest of Alpha Two the number of hostiles I'd sighted in 118 and their deployment. Gavin eyed me as if I were having some type of seizure. No doubt he'd failed to study the Zero Dog dynamic assault handbook. Glorious flaming harpy shit.

Sarge nodded at my signal and turned to the dirty green door. His finger scored patterns of strange glyphs into the wood, leaving smoking purple lines that glowed with muted light. Rafe crouched below the window in werewolf form. His appearance resembled *The Howling* werewolves without the oversized bat-ears, rather than Lon Chaney's adorable furry wolfman. Rafe watched Sarge work, his canines bared, waiting for Sarge's spell to go off.

I pointed at Mai. She nodded twice then turned to her horde of vole-raptor half-breeds. At her command, the creatures formed up in a carpet-like mass ten feet from the door. Another glance at Alpha Two showed me Sarge had finished his spellwork. He gave me the double nod.

I took a deep breath, tried to calm my rapid heartbeat, and failed. "Execute! Execute! *Execute!*" I yelled.

Sarge's breaching spell went off with a rending crunch, crumpling their door into a wad of broken splinters. Next to me, the voles chirped as Mai ordered them to charge the door we were assaulting. They sprang off the parking berm and leapt at the doorknob/keycard reader combo. Each critter's wicked buzz saw teeth ripped out a chunk of wood before it circled back for another leap. I flinched when Rafe launched himself at the window and smashed into room 117 in an explosion of glass shards and a tangle of brown curtains. Sarge charged inside after him, MP10 popping off on semi-auto, followed by Stefan, with Gavin stumbling along in the rear, clutching his submachine gun and wheezing.

In less than six seconds, Mai's abominations had chewed away enough of the wood around the keycard mechanism for it to fall to the cement with a metal *clank*. They also gnawed through the wood around the swing bar door guard, though this was higher and resulted in more voles missing and bouncing off the walls with outraged chirps. Mai called them off.

I swung out in front of the door, ready to kick it in. A butcher knife thrust through the lower hole, sawing back and forth on the damaged wood. "Shaved monkey!" the redcap inside said and giggled.

I kicked the damn door in, knife or no. The thud and scream

brought a wicked smile to my face.

"Fire in the hole." I flung in my modified spell of super-condensed magefire and ducked behind cover.

Mai, Tiffany, and Hanzo looked away as my flash spell went off with a brilliant burst of light. When it was safe, I glanced into the room to see blinded redcaps flailing around and falling over each other. Others toppled off the bed. A couple of them accidently stabbed comrades, which sent off a flurry of hacking and slashing retribution, like cannibal mutant rats competing for a role in a slasher film.

I scanned for the ringmaster goblin, meaning to capture him first, but couldn't spot him in the chaos. We needed to capture at least one demented goblin for arrest, trial, and resulting media circus. Time to improvise.

"Tiffany!" I pointed at a redcap who came hopping out of the bathroom with his trousers around his ankles and a scrap of toilet paper stuck to one of his boots. "Charm that powrie!"

Tiffany stepped into the room and fixed her eyes on the redcap trying to simultaneously straighten his red floppy hat and pull out his cleaver. I felt the surge of her sex magic, the pheromone flood crashing toward the hapless male creature, who instantly plunged into both love and dismayingly obvious desire for the succubus.

"Love you, cat-eye girl!" the charmed redcap bellowed. Then he buried his cleaver in the floppy hat of a comrade who'd had the misfortune to stagger into his strike radius. The hat was sheared in half and fell to the stained carpet. The goblin skull was likewise notched and the creature followed his hat to the ground.

The charmed redcap scrambled toward Tiffany, still dragging his pants and the scrap of toilet paper, all drooling and doe-eyed, reminding me of my date for the senior prom.

"Love you, queen of my hat!" The charmed powrie almost

collided with another of his stumbling mates still dazed from my flash spell. The charmed redcap's eyes narrowed and he began to hack at the other goblin. "Make beautiful fucky fucky—"

Tiffany shot him in the head with both pistols. What a .357 round will do to a goblin skull at close range might best be compared to dropping a hand grenade into a jack o' lantern filled with oatmeal and red wine. So much for charming a redcap to throw to the media sharks, and goodbye to my appetite for the next three days.

I pushed deeper into the room, searching for the goblin in the ringmaster gear, still hoping to take him alive. The redcaps had regained enough of their sight to present a growing danger. The air rang with gunshots, growls, curses, erotic moans, giggling, and the happy chirping of the Velociraptor voles.

A glowing pinwheel of energy appeared in midair near the television, bursting into existence with the tortured shriek of a car squashed in a compactor. The cold backwash of partially consumed energy raised goose bumps along my skin. A spinning pattern of glowing filaments spread from the center of the pinwheel. The view of the wall behind it shimmered and distorted. The filaments shot further out, flattened, widened, and sealed together, creating a circular portal that wavered in midair.

I cursed and scanned for the goblin who'd opened the portal. Creating wormholes and Veil jumping were far more powerful and complex undertakings than standard goblin magic could handle. The distant dirge of a calliope reached me, along with the smell of buttered popcorn and corndogs.

The ringmaster darted from beneath the table and launched his small body onto the bed. "Flee! Flee, you red-knickered drool-nozzles!"

"This hovel has bedbugs, not *fleas!*" the redcap with the

bendy straw and the Jack Daniels bellowed, spraying whiskey. He swore, wiped at his face, then shouted: "And they made *you* chief? Hah!"

"Tiffany!" I yelled again. "Charm the goblin in the balloon pants!"

Tiffany's magic surged once more. The charm spell hit the ringmaster and he staggered, toppling off the bed. I hurried toward him, hoping to secure him before Tiffany changed her mind and began shooting him instead. The ringmaster stared at Tiffany with lustful mooncalf eyes, but her spell hadn't hit with the same effectiveness as before. The ringmaster clambered back onto the bed. He screamed out, "You'll be mine, sex demon!" and shuddered as if he'd been hit with electric current. Then he belly flopped through the portal before I could grab him.

Damn it. The flashing images inside the portal unnerved me: funhouse mirror distortions, dark roller coasters, and screaming clown faces. I edged closer anyway. I hoped to snatch him back before the portal closed, then drag him in front of the cameras by his bow tie. Before I reached the portal, another redcap flung himself off the nightstand at me. He gibbered and slashed with a broken pair of scissors. I dodged aside. The portal snapped closed, cutting off the circus soundtrack.

I cut loose with my magefire, blasting a horizontal column of fire at Mr. Scissors. A burning floppy cap drifted to the carpet with the slow grace of an autumn maple leaf. The remainder of the scissor-swinging bundle of goblin hate had been incinerated. The television screen exploded exactly as the chorus of moans reached an orgasmic crescendo. The wall behind it caught fire.

Shit. Not again. Why did everything burn so easily?

Mai's small army of carnivores seemed to enjoy their goblin meat raw. Witnessing the carnage, I realized I wouldn't be comfortable with those things coming within a five hundred mile radius of my person ever again. The air stank of burning plastic and blood, spilled liquor, sauerkraut, and the strange clove-like scent of the voles.

Tiffany continued to fire on the redcaps, more demon goddess of diabolical retribution than sexy sex symbol. I watched my chance of taking prisoners steadily evaporate into arterial spray. Ever since the night zombies had overrun our house, Tiffany seemed to take a little too much pleasure in shooting bad guys into pulpy red messes.

A goblin slashed at my shin. I kicked him in the stomach with my combat boot, punting him so hard he bounced off the wall, knocking down a hideous oil painting of Nantucket. Hanzo slashed with his katana at the redcaps battling him with chef knives. The voles chewed on everything that wasn't a Zero Dog, including pillows, telephones, and lampshades.

My headset radio crackled. A transmission filled with werewolf snarls and measured, unhurried gunshots blasted over the com. I overheard Stefan in full auto bitch-whine mode complaining about the taste and consistency of goblin blood.

Before I could tell Stefan suck it up like a man—or at least a man-like vampire—my headset speaker distorted with a wild, ripping blast of submachine gun fire. Had to be Gavin, because Sarge never shot with such uncontrolled gusto. An instant later Gavin screamed words in the high-pitched shriek of a man who'd lost both testicles in a horrible canning accident. "Suck on explosive death, you ankle-biting freaks!"

A grenade blast roared simultaneously in my headset and rattled our window. I scorched a redcap trying to bite Tiffany's ass cheek, then yelled into the mike, "Status, Alpha Two!"

Gunshots. Growling. Incoherent profanity. Screams from the redcaps. Then Gavin yelled over the radio. "Chew this, pus-eater!" More gunshots. "How you like a *man's* boot in your ass?" Erratic gunfire. "And floppy hats are for fucking *nimrods*!"

"Room clear," Tiffany called out near me. She paused to blow on both smoking gun barrels, managing to make rampant killing seem disconcertingly sexual. Hanzo kicked down the bathroom door. The shower curtain's metal rings jingled as, from the sound of it, he slashed the hell out of everything inside before confirming the bathroom was clear.

I concentrated on the radio transmissions from Alpha Two, praying they were all right. "Alpha Two, this is Alpha Actual. I repeat: what's your status, over?"

"Alpha Actual, this is Alpha Two," Sarge said over the com. "Room 117 clear. Hostiles neutralized, over."

"Then what the hell is Gavin doing?"

"He's a little keyed up. I took away his gun and put him in time out."

"Christ." I closed my eyes for a second and took a deep breath…then nearly choked on the smoke and reek inside the room. The air also smelled vaguely of honey-baked ham. I didn't know whether to enjoy the scent or toss my cookies.

"All rooms clear," I finally confirmed. I knew I'd come to regret that little circus bastard's escape. His strange thaumaturgy must've given him the resistance needed to throw off Tiffany's charm magic long enough to flee through the portal. I switched frequencies on my radio to the band SWAT used. "Overwatch, this is Alpha Actual. One hostile rabbited through an interdimensional portal and escaped. All other hostiles neutralized, over."

"Copy that, Alpha Actual. One suspect rabbited, unable to locate." Lieutenant Stone's voice dripped with *schadenfreude*. Our newly renegotiated contract with the city of Portland let the Zero Dogs take the first crack at "paranormally enhanced criminal elements," which didn't sit well with Stone or the rest of SWAT. "We'll run a BOLO for the escaped suspect. Element incoming to your position, over."

"Roger that, Overwatch. Alpha Actual, out." I turned to the rest of my team. "All right, saddle up and move out. Leave everything for the cops and coroner. Nobody steal any towels." I paused, frowning. "I mean it about the towels. They're probably infested with very scary things."

I escaped outside with the rest of the crew, reveling in the blessedly cool night air, free of the smoke and the stink. SWAT, in full tactical gear, swept past me into the room. Two fire engines roared into the parking lot. Fire fighters leapt out and began hooking up hoses.

I watched them, but from a distance, because fire fighters never loved a pyromancer. My hands shook with the aftereffects of adrenaline-dump. I crossed my arms and trapped them under my armpits. Black and gray smoke billowed into the sky.

Mind numb, body all jittery, I suddenly felt lonelier than I had in weeks. I wished Jake were around to crack a joke—hell, to put his arms around me, because even battle-hardened mercenaries needed a hug once in awhile. No dice, though. My favorite Green Beret was on a Special Forces op. So I sucked it up best I could and stared at the column of smoke, wondering where that portal led and worried about the havoc the ringmaster would plot next.

* * *

Most of Alpha Two team had formed up at the other end of the motel's parking lot, giving the lookie-loos an eyeful to gawk at and record on camera phones. I dutifully headed toward the fire chief's truck as the rest of Alpha One trooped over to Sarge. My people appeared a bit rough and worn, but good on the whole.

I paused, yanked off my helmet, and swiped a forearm across my face. Of course, the sweat I'd missed immediately trickled down and stung my eyes, making me grimace and blink. As usual, I stank of smoke and yearned for a shower, but I allowed myself a moment of quiet relief. Mission accomplished, the Ass of Evil Kicked (AOEK), and no Zero Dog casualties. I couldn't ask for more than that, even though one of the goblin bastards had escaped justice. Damn shame we couldn't have brought the hammer down on the murderous redcaps sooner, before the salesman had been killed. The life of a door-to-door salesman carried some heavy-duty risks when trying to close the deal and meet quota, but this was still nothing but a tragedy. If I remembered right, there was a famous play about that kind of thing—*Death of a Sales Professional* or something to that effect.

The flashing lights of the cop cars and fire trucks strobed the front of the motel in alternating colors. I caught a glimpse of a homicide detective named Miller headed into the motel, but I didn't want to talk with him right now. Let him wait for the After Action Report. I sought in vain to locate the fire chief, who wasn't at his truck after all. The guy probably hid from me on purpose. My stomach growled, protesting my neglect. Fighting monsters, even snack-sized ones, made me hungry. To hell with it, I'd check in with the fire chief later. The firefighters had their hands full saving the motel anyway. I didn't even need to find Norville Ford, a paper-pusher from city hall who hated my guts, and fight with him about signing off on our work because, thanks to my Homeland Security connections and a new liaison with the municipal authorities, it was all auto-bill easy these days.

I keyed on my radio. "Zero Dogs, pack up and prepare to roll out. We'll give our After Action Reports at Zhong Kui's—food and drinks on me."

A cheer went up over the radio. I smiled because the promise of Chinese food and beer made even the tedium of

AARs bearable.

My stomach growled again as I cut across the parking lot back to my crew, weaving through the cops, firefighters, and paramedics. I felt strangely joyless, and couldn't stop wondering about the salesman, who he'd been, how many people would miss him. Jake would've understood. But he wasn't here.

Tiffany saw me coming, smiled and waved at me, bouncing on her toes and predictably drawing the gaze of the male masses. I put on a smile for my mercs that felt like a lie with teeth. Sarge leaned against a cop cruiser, his MP10 slung over his shoulder, a cigarette dangling from the corner of his mouth. He'd started smoking about three weeks ago, claiming that, as a demon, he needed a few self-destructive habits to continue pissing Heaven off. I knew his boyfriend hated it, but I was wise enough to keep my mouth shut. Mai was kissing each Velociraptor vole on the head before letting it scamper through a portal to the alien world from which she'd summoned them.

Rafe stood naked, having shifted back into human form but making no attempt to cover himself. He reveled in exhibiting his muscular, over-tattooed body. His newest piece of body art showed two cows piloting a UFO and abducting an alien via tractor beam. Beneath the picture scrawled the word *Payback*.

So much for my smile, I could feel my eyelid twitching as his naked ass mooned me and all the gathered civvies and news crews. Damn werewolves. "Rafe. Your clothes. They aren't on your body."

"Yeah, Captain. I thought I felt a draft."

"Rafe. Your clothes. They *should* be on your body."

"And cover up a work of art? You see anyone throwing clothes on Michelangelo's *David*? Not even a fig leaf to conceal the bait and tackle."

"Rafe…"

"Fine, fine. I'd happily get dressed, Captain, but those little green furry mokes stole my underwear."

I looked down at the final handful of alien voles who happily played tug of war with an article of intimate apparel. "Is that…a tiger-striped g-string?"

"It cost a ton of money, which is why I think underwear is a complete scam. The price of underwear is inversely proportional to the amount of underwear material—the skimpier the skivvies, the more pricey the lingerie. Bitter truth, Captain. We should ban underwear completely."

I felt a headache coming on with the force of a derailing freight train. "Since when is a tiger-striped banana hammock a regulation-approved part of a Hellfrost mercenary uniform?"

Rafe scratched at his five o'clock shadow, considering. "I'm really a boxer man myself, but Nikki is an ass girl. She loves a tight gluteus maximus." He turned around to show me. "And these aren't just buns of steel, Captain. They're buns of *titanium*. See?" He began to flex his glutes, alternating left ass cheek, right ass cheek, and I readied my ass-kicking combat boot for immediate deployment.

Instead of punting, I took a deep, steadying breath. When I was calm enough to speak, I shouted: "Get your ass covered, merc! Yesterday! You're corrupting little old ladies!"

I was ready for an entire bottle of Captain Morgan. Or cooking sherry. Whichever I found first.

Rafe scrambled to get dressed. Gavin laughed, but I fixed him with such a withering stare that he clamped his mouth shut on his tongue and cursed. Just then an egg sailed through the air and smashed into the cop car next to Hanzo. Hanzo drew his katana and glared around with narrowed eyes, standing protectively in front of Mai.

I turned toward the crowd, boiling with annoyance. Another egg flew out of the gathered gawkers. I pointed and the egg exploded in a burst of flame. Burning yoke rained to the asphalt.

"Mercenary whore!" a man screamed.

The crowd around the man edged away and left him standing alone. He was Portland-artsy-typical. Soul patch and ponytail, a slew of ear piercings. Sandals and black socks. Even exposed, he didn't back down, and for his bravery I gave him due respect.

"Murderers! Mercenary whores! Fascist tools of the oppressor!"

Clearly some breed of activist. *Fascist tool of the oppressor* was not an insult you yelled at someone who cut you off in traffic. Activists weren't exactly rare in Portland, but I sighed anyway. Right now I didn't have the patience for this crap. Still, I tried on a winning PR smile for the hell of it. "All whores are mercenary. Nature of the business, my friend."

Mr. Activist replied by chucking another egg from the carton he held. I blasted it out of the sky with a thin stream of fire. A fried egg flopped to the asphalt.

Frying his egg seemed to enrage him further. "How many helpless creatures you kill tonight? How much blood stains your greedy hands, you fascist whore?"

Sarge moved toward him, a huge mountain of muscle and eggplant-purple and sunset-red skin, a shaved-bald head sans horns, and burning crimson eyes. I raised a hand and waved him off before he did something painful to the guy. Sarge halted, but didn't look pleased. I didn't want the activist hurt for talking shit and being offensive. I believed in freedom of speech the same as any other Constitution-loving American.

And there were cameras around.

And lawsuits were expensive.

"What special interest group *du jour* are you from?" I asked. "The egg farmer's union?" I snorted at my own joke. The crowd stared at me. No one laughed.

Humor-challenged barbarians. I made a mental note to train my mercs to laugh on cue so I didn't sound pathetic at key moments.

The activist sneered. "SETNONHP. Society for the Ethical Treatment of Non-human People. The blood of the oppressed and downtrodden is trapped beneath your filthy, ragged fingernails. You…you racist, *species*-ist murdering wh—"

"Whore. Yeah, I get it." Annoyance flashed to anger. "Go take your outrage and explain it to the salesman murdered by your *downtrodden* and *oppressed* tonight."

The problem I had with bleeding hearts was not their outrage or empathy—that was far, far better than the opposite end of the spectrum, those bloodthirsty people who cheered killing as if it were ever a good thing. No, the problem I had was how conveniently these fringe bleeding hearts forgot or ignored the victims of the so-called oppressed they championed. No matter his crimes of annoyance and transgressions of trespass, that door-to-door salesman deserved better than death at the knives of monsters who wanted to dye their woolen caps in his heart blood. A crime had been done, and we'd brought hard justice in fire, fang, and bullets. This was the law of the urban jungle. It wasn't pretty. It was never nice. And I didn't like it. It was simply the way the game went down.

Mr. Activist wasn't having any of it. He steamrolled right into his rant with fiery rhetorical flair. "They kill because they're confused, oppressed by tyrannical capitalist governments, fronts for corporate excess and unending greed. Those poor creatures were misguided. Provoked. They strike out *because* they suffer, and you and your ilk are the attack dogs of their oppressors. How dare you render judgment like a god, bringing death? An eye for an eye leaves everyone—"

"You know what? I agree with you."

"You...what?"

"I wish everything was sparkletastic unicorns and singing suns and happy endings you never had to pay for. I wish rain tasted like kiwi-strawberry lemonade. I wish the DMV didn't exist, and there was no money, and infinite food for everyone, especially meat—" I held up my hand before the guy could launch into a fresh tirade— "meat that didn't come from actual living creatures, but grew on trees like...fruit meat. Trees that grow bacon."

The guy stared at me. I pressed on anyway.

"Nobody good gets off on killing." Which was a complete lie, because I loved killing zombies. "But I'm here to save people's lives, so I do what I have to do."

"Lying bitch!" He shoved a hand into his coat pocket and yanked out a can of red spray paint. He scurried toward me, raising the spray can. "Killer pig whore!"

Shit, he had to go there. We couldn't simply hurl insults and inflammatory rhetoric like good Americans on either side of a complex issue. I used pyromancer magic—just a shred—and heated the metal of the can, but not enough for it to explode. He shrieked in surprise and dropped the spray can.

He staggered backward, glaring at me with hate and fear. He hadn't lost any fingers, wasn't even bleeding. Bastard should count himself lucky. Still...the whole sorry scene further pulled my mood down toward black.

"Everybody suffers," I told him, seizing onto my anger again. "But if you kill an innocent, then I'll roast your chestnuts for Christmas. There's a line, and you damn well know it. Cross the line and you'll find this demon bitch breathing fire down your throat. Now get the hell out of my face before I lose my temper."

Nothing like winning an argument by degrading into

murderous threats. Christ on a motor scooter.

The activist drew himself up and pointed at me. "Life will make you pay for the black karma you've earned. Don't pray to escape, because you can't."

He turned and pushed his way through the crowd. I didn't feel any triumph, seeing him retreat. I only felt sick to my stomach, my heart thudding away, my mouth dry. The crowd watched me warily, as if I'd mutated into the demon bitch I'd been yelling about. Sarge walked up and stood beside me.

"We're not loved," I said. It didn't make me sad. It just made me tired. And I was fucking hungry.

Sarge gave a half-smile and shrugged. "I have someone who loves me. You have someone who loves you. We have exactly what we need. Greed for more will only make us soft."

"Guess you're right." Although I wasn't sure I believed him. I *wanted* to be greedy. I wanted everything perfect, wanted a steady paycheck, wanted the press and public to love us, and wanted Rafe to stop losing his underwear in public. Damn, did I ever miss Jake, who could be counted on to spit out some kind of half-assed quip to make me laugh. But my lover was off on assignment in Tunisia, and I hadn't talked to him in a week. I had to stop thinking about him all the time.

I pulled the plug on the emo-fest and turned to the rest of the Zero Dogs. "All right, show's over. Pack it up and let's roll out for food and beer."

Grins all around from my mercs…except from Stefan, who was an insufferable snob about food, even though he didn't eat and relied on blood-fortified energy drinks and wine coolers.

I took one last glance at the burning motel. The emergency lights still flashed in bright blues, ambers, and reds, spinning and horrible in their raw color cheer. Smoke spilled and twisted into the dark clouds of the night sky. The glow of flames painted everything orange and reflected in the eyes and on the faces of everyone around me. The forceful hiss of spraying water and the constant roar of fire warred for dominance.

A smoke-shadow of doubt crept at my heels and continued to whisper that this wasn't over as I walked away. I was afraid the activist had been right about there still being karma to settle. My mouth tasted of ashes. I kept remembering the activist's furious eyes. That, and little burning red hats.

Everyone else seemed jazzed about the prospect of beer and Chinese food, but I left the scene thinking about karma, murder, and mercenary whores.

CHAPTER TWO
Fortune Cookies Can Kill You

Mercenary Wing Rv6-4 "Zero Dogs"
Zhong Kui's Chinese Restaurant and Bar
June 7th

We'd swung by the house to clean up, gathered our significant others from across Portland and Beaverton, and then crashed Zhong Kui's with a rapid deployment. The hostess's eyes had bugged out as we'd piled through the door, loud and laughing and on the hunt for food and alcohol.

Now I sat on a swivel stool at the bar, sipping a BridgePort India Pale Ale while eyeing a Chinese painting on the wall. The painting depicted a pissed off Chinese guy with a blackened face and hyper-bushy beard who looked ready to rip out someone's eyeball and eat it. I'd tasted that kind of fire earlier, but now I merely felt tired and down. Even perfect beef curry and pork fried rice couldn't salvage my mood.

Also, the nine fortune cookies I'd eaten and the nine bad fortunes they'd given had done nothing to help. The cryptic fortunes brought back the same feeling that had haunted me as I'd stalked the alley behind the motel — the uneasiness of spotting storm clouds gathered on the horizon set to rain poisonous frogs. When the mission had been a success, I'd wanted to believe the premonition of things going very wrong had only been the jitters of pre-combat stress. But the feeling hadn't left. And now these evil fortunes...

I pulled out my cell phone and dialed Jake's number. He didn't carry a cell with him in the field, but I clutched at the hope he'd be back at barracks by now.

My call went straight to voicemail. "Captain Sanders. Leave a message."

For a moment I couldn't talk. Hearing his voice sucked all the air out of my lungs. Then I forced myself to draw in breath and spit out words. "Jake...just Andrea. Uh. Calling to see how things are going..." God, I was so bad at leaving coherent phone messages. Heat crept up my neck and ears. I had so much I wanted to say, but now that the chance had arrived, the words dug into my throat with grappling hooks. "Just wanted to tell you about my day. Goblins. Ass kicking. Kicking goblin ass, I mean. *We* didn't get our ass kicked, are you kidding me?" That sounded pathetic as hell. I hesitated, not wanting to babble into the echo-chamber of voicemail, but doing so anyway. "Pick up some milk from the store on your way home—don't forget." Even more pathetic. I likely wouldn't see him for another two months at least, and my joke fell directly from my lips to the floor, landing on its face. My throat clicked when I swallowed. "Keep yourself safe. Give me a call when you're done top-secretly saving the world. I miss you. I—"

The voicemail cut off. I disconnected and stared at the cell phone as my pulse pounded in my ears, then I shoved it back in my pocket. Sipping my beer, I watched as the seconds slipped by on the wall clock, knowing that with each passing minute the hope I'd nursed that Jake would immediately call back faded further away. The accusations and, more than anything, the *hostility* of that activist guy kept reverberating in my head, making me feel even worse when piled on top of my unease and the tragic murder of the salesman. I stared at the crumbs from all the fortune cookies. The desire to simply pack up and go home ached in my chest. But I was paying the tab for the team and couldn't leave.

The rest of my crew were living it up, drinking and laughing. Zhong Kui's had a full bar in a room behind the main restaurant which featured karaoke, so Rafe was on stage, shaking it for all he was worth while enthusiastically maiming an Aerosmith song. His current girlfriend…Nikki, if I remembered her name right…cheered and stuffed dollar bills down the front of his jeans. Jeans I'd ordered him to leave *on* his body in their *standard* position, ruefully remembering the last time he'd creatively interpreted the standing order by wearing jeans and jockeys on his head.

Sarge sat with Shawn at a booth, both of them leaning their heads together to hear one other over the music. Sarge held Shawn's hand across the table, a small smile on his face. There were two times I could bank on Sarge being happy: when he was shooting guns or when he was with Shawn.

Gavin slouched in the corner at his own table, writing in a battered journal, empty beer bottles clustered around him. I'd tried to talk with him earlier, but he'd dismissed me with a curt "I'm in a creative phase," and continued to scrawl unmetered lines of poetry in spiky handwriting. Tank driver. Empath. Wannabe writer. He'd given up on becoming a romance novelist a couple months ago, claiming you couldn't throw a happily ever after without hitting another budding writer these days. I suspected this was sour grapes because he'd failed to find anyone interested in his work.

"Poets get laid more often," he'd assured me. I'd nodded as if I hadn't believed he was a hopelessly unhinged wingnut with the maturity level of a thirteen-year-old. He'd grinned back as if

I'd encouraged his madness. So much for his empath powers.

Our degenerate vampire Stefan was still trying to pick up a Goth girl at the far end of the bar. Earlier I'd had the misfortune of walking past him and caught an earful of his routine. " — it really does sparkle, I swear before my ancient vampire sire. Are you curious? Don't worry. I never bite…unless you *like*."

Hanzo was rambling about a movie he'd loved called *Alien versus Ninja*, trying to impress Mai as he waved his hands around as he reenacted various scenes with a fork instead of a sword. Mai ignored him and fed lo mein to one of her mutated voles that she apparently hadn't sent home with the others. Tiffany sat with them, but she seemed focused on her cherry soda, staring into the glass as she swirled the ice with two straws. I frowned, momentarily forgetting my own woes. Two studs had tried to pick her up already. Succubus pheromones and otherworldly beauty were a bitch — though, as she still wore combat fatigues and had cinched her hair into a ponytail, she'd done nothing to provoke attention. The men had lingered longer than decorum allowed, forcing Hanzo to interrupt his inspired monologue and make threatening motions toward his sword, finally driving them off. I'd smiled, because he'd handled it better than I would have. I would've lit somebody on fire by now.

Watching Tiffany made me think of Jake again and ripped that hole inside me — that place he fit and made me happy — even wider, leaving it aching and empty. I wanted to cheer her up, but didn't have it in me right now. So I failed her and turned back to my beer and my fortune cookies, feeling like shit and not knowing how to make things better for anyone.

I sipped beer and glared at the cryptic fortune cookie fortunes collecting by my elbow. Nine little white pieces of paper amidst a layer of cookie dust. Normally, I loved fortune cookies. Something about having a cookie, a breed of food-type thing that I cherished, dispense obvious advice or vague fortune innuendos amused me every time. But these cookies sucked. Each fortune had been more disturbing than the last. I arranged them around the wet ring from the bottom of my beer. The first read:

A heavy heart drowns the strongest swimmer. Well, I could agree with that one at least.

Accept fate before fate accepts you. Standard fortune cookie crap.

Answer not clear, ask again later. Some guy at the bakery was a smartass fond of his magic 8 ball.

Competence like yours is undervalued! That one was a hundred percent true facts.

Ghosts of the past haunt the future. This fortune only made me remember the ghost jellyfish that now haunted our rebuilt mansion, which sent a shiver of revulsion wracking down my spine.

This cookie contains ingredients known to cause cancer in the state of California. Troubling. Very troubling. Especially after I'd just eaten nine of them in a row. But because I wasn't currently *in* the state of California, I maintained hope I was safe.

Don't confuse stupidity with confidence. Not a problem. The Zero Dogs had both in abundance.

Every flower blooms. Every petal falls. Lucky numbers 217, 0, 1.618, 9, 23, 9413. I could barely keep my cactus alive in its little sombrero pot. This fortune mocked me to my face with its dark metaphor.

You will die, but a last hope approaches.

This final fortune bothered me the most. It didn't seem like advice you'd hide in a cookie. The little slip of paper sat there half-curled on the bar. Cryptic. Likely meaningless. And yet, I couldn't help but wonder if the universe had fired some kind of metaphysical shot across my bow. Should I have taken the activist's parting shot about karmic payback more seriously? Or was this connected to the redcap ringmaster who'd escaped? I'd studied the lore and intelligence dossiers. Redcaps had access to a bastardized version of *nurata*, goblin hedge spells, but weren't supposed to have interdimensional portal-hopping capabilities.

Or was I over-thinking this? These were the type of suspicions I usually entertained at two in the morning or after downing a few too many absinthes. Two a.m. was hours away and I didn't feel drunk. I took another swig of beer. A very mild buzz, nothing more.

Gavin wandered past me, clutching his composition book and chewing on his pen as if it were a cigar. Our gazes met. He veered over and plopped onto the stool beside me. "Hey, Captain. Drowning your sorrows again? Don't worry. No one judges you."

"How's the poetry? You still trying to find a rhyme for the word *silver* in your epic unicorn poem?"

Gavin rested a hand on his composition book as if fearing I'd light it on fire. Perhaps he knew me too well. "It's free verse exploration of existential suburban despair. You want to hear some?"

"No. I just ate a bunch of cookies and I'd prefer them to remain untossed."

"Everyone's a freakin' critic." He picked up the last piece of paper, fortune number nine, and eyed it sourly. "Nice, this one says you're going to die. Looks like *my* fortune cookie was correct about an imminent promotion."

"Does this fortune seem a little...I don't know, weird to you?"

"Nah, I had one once that said, 'Help, I'm trapped in a Chinese bakery!' Those fortune cookie writers are always bustin' someone's balls." He swiveled back and forth on the stool and threw a glance toward Tiffany. "Let me ask you something, Captain. Me and Stefan were talking. So Tiffany's a succubus, right?"

My hackles went up and my eyes narrowed. "So you finally noticed," I said carefully. "You're about that age when you might start noticing some changes in your body and you may begin to feel differently about girls. Don't worry, it's called puberty and it's all a part of growing up."

"Hilarious, Captain. With you, the yuks come twenty-four seven, three sixty-five. So *is* Tiffany a demon? As in fallen angel, eviction notice from heaven, spawn of Lilith, 'I fornicated with the archangel Samael' and all that crap? Because Stefan said a succubus is only a kind of crude vampire that feeds on passion and the lust of people bumping uglies. But *I* always heard a succubus is a demon who turns a man into a mindless horny tree frog with an erection that lasts way more than six hours, before she devours his soul." He shrugged. "We have a bet on it."

"Strange that none of my fortunes mentioned something like: *You will soon incinerate two of your employees.*" I turned on my bar stool and leaned toward him. "You're very close to a line, Gavin. She's my friend."

"Fraternizing?" He waggled his eyebrows, though the look in his eyes was sharp, almost challenging.

I took a deep breath and willed myself calm. "I'm not going to respond to that. You're a good driver. You suck as an empath, but you can steer things around like nobody's business. So I'm going to ignore your behavior here tonight, choosing to believe it's the beer talking. But don't you dare mention your stupid bet to Tiffany. Ever. Keep your mouth shut or I'll staple your testicles to the apology card I'll make you send her…with a poem begging forgiveness, written in your own blood."

He raised his hands and shook his head. "Whoa, *whoa*, Captain. Threatening a man's yam bag is a bit aggressive, don't you think? We all care about her. I wouldn't hurt her feelings or anything."

"The fact that you and Stefan made that bet tells me all I need to know." I had problems enough with the fortune cookies and brooding about the escaped redcap, with zero patience left over for juvenile idiocy.

"Don't be like that, Captain. I'll be discreet and ask Sarge. He'll know the ins and outs of demonology." He smirked at his innuendo, and I barely refrained from smacking him with my beer bottle. "But speaking of bumping uglies, I could use your advice on a little something something."

My scowl deepened. Gavin paid no attention. Instead, he stared down the bar toward an auburn-haired woman who sipped a margarita and played with the salt on the rim.

"You think that chick loves poetry?"

"Classy segue as always, Gavin." My dislike deepened. Gavin and I had a rocky relationship, and tonight he was doing it no favors. I waved the bartender over for another beer. Widmer Hefeweizen this time. I studied the woman in question as I tipped the bottle back. She looked far too intelligent for Gavin, far too refined. Then again, ninety-six percent of breathing females were too intelligent and refined for Gavin. "Tell her you drive tanks. That might impress her. But for God's sake, try being a gentleman for once in your life."

"Hmm. Drive tanks. Write poetry. Man in uniform, or sensitive artist? I can't tell what she'd go for. I don't want to screw up my only chance." He chewed on his pen. "What about pilots? Don't forget, I also have my wings. Chicks love pilots."

"Just don't tell her you're qualified on our new armored assault moped. That'll cost you all your man points, sadly depleted as they already are. And don't call her *chick*." I peeled off the bottle's label and used it to hide that last fortune cookie paper. I couldn't shake the feeling that the fortune was somehow aware of me. That it watched me, ticking off prophetic seconds until I died. "I don't know why I'm helping you. You're an empath. Empath something. Ask her if she likes otters."

"Who the hell likes otters? That doesn't even make sense." He stared at the woman while rapidly tapping his pen against his teeth. For the first time I caught a glimpse of the indecision and nervous—almost desperate—tension that twisted around him in python coils. I gritted my teeth against any twinge of sympathy after he'd acted like such an ass, but I was too soft for my own good.

"Go on. Give it a try," I said after a long moment, focusing on rolling the neck of my naked beer bottle between my fingers, anything to keep my hands busy and my eyes off him. "No guts, no glory."

He frowned at me again, but he finally climbed off his stool. "The poet in me yearns for the day you steal a few inspirational quotes that ping a little lower on the cliché meter."

I smirked and let that one slide, coming from a guy who wrote about endless, soul-rending love, stock car racing, and heart-trampled Yuppie despair.

He picked up his composition book and headed toward the woman. I drank beer and arranged my collection of fortune cookie fortunes in different patterns while trying not to watch him in case he crashed and burned. My armpits were damp. My skin felt too warm. God, it was bad enough that Jake was out on some mission while I was here alone and under threat of evil fortune cookie doom, but did I really have to vicariously experience the stress of hitting on strangers in a bar? Completely unfair.

"Think he'll score?" Shawn asked from behind me, making me jump and almost knock over my beer. Sarge loomed behind him, appearing terrifying without even trying, with his skin all various degrees of red and eggplant purple, a dying sunset look, and his eyes unnerving with their black irises and red pupils. No demon wings or horns, cloven hooves or pointy tails, but he sure as Hell didn't need them to broadcast his badass status to the world.

I motioned for them to sit down. They each took a seat flanking me.

"Depends," I said, rearranging the peeled beer label. Had that fortune crawled out from under it to eye me again? Damn, I thought it had. "A girl likes to be approached by someone classy, respectful, and genuinely interested in her as a person."

Shawn grinned. "Because this is Gavin we're talking about, your answer means no."

"He's an empath. He'll be fine."

Both Sarge and Shawn stared at me.

"All right, all right. He's toast." I drank more beer and found the bottle empty. Dammit. I saw a pattern forming here. "So what can I do for you gentlemen?"

Shawn caught the bartender's attention and ordered me another beer. He played the cello in the Oregon Symphony. In his late twenties, with scruffy two-day beard growth that I knew was carefully cultivated, dressed in slacks, dress shirt, and an electric blue tie only slightly rumpled this late in the day. "How's Jake?"

"Jake's off saving the world, fighting evil while playing in the sun."

"Good soldier." Most of Sergeant Nathan Genna's pronouncements came out in deep bass rumbles, and this one was no different. "When's he due back in the world?"

"Not soon enough." Truth was, I didn't know. Because he was Special Forces, he could be out in the bush for another month or six. Me, I was only a mercenary. I didn't have access to US Special Operations Command mission info, and it drove me nuts. To not be in control. To always be waiting, but unable to influence anything. I hated being helpless more than anything. But no one said this thing Jake and I had would be easy.

Time to change the subject and avoid a maudlin beer-flavored soliloquy. Luckily, Gavin chose just that moment to get shot down. The woman stood and stormed out of the bar. Gavin slumped on the stool, chewing on his pen and trying to look as if he'd meant for that to happen.

None of us said a word. After a moment, I lifted the piece of paper that held the cryptic legend I'd come to think of as Fortune #9. "What do you think about this?"

They both leaned in to read it. Shawn shrugged. Sarge only frowned, watching me out of the corner of his demon eye.

"You don't think this is some type of real prophecy, do you?" I laughed to show I wasn't serious.

"In a fortune cookie?" Shawn said. "It's just some pseudo-philosophical fun. Read and then toss."

I nodded, reassured.

"I've seen stranger things," Sarge said.

I considered banging my head on the bar and barely managed to hold myself in check. "You've had accurate fortunes from a mass-produced cookie before?"

He nodded and scanned through the rest of my fortunes, brushing away some of the crumbs. He arched a black eyebrow at me. "Hungry?"

"They're *cookies*," I replied, as if that explained everything.

"I've heard stories about prophecies showing up in strange places," Sarge continued. "Tea leaves are standard, but also coffee grounds or the sludge from hot cocoa. Tarot, of course, but standard playing decks as well. Crystal balls and car rearview mirrors. Palms…and there was this imp in Topeka who read people's toenails."

"That's disgusting." Shawn said. "I need another beer just to wash that image out of my brain."

"I don't believe in prophecy." Unfortunately, I didn't sound as confident as planned. I tried again. "I *don't* believe in prophecy. I don't believe in fate. I hate them both. I believe in free will. I'm the master of my destiny. Me. No one else. Anything else is too horrible to consider."

Sarge slapped a hand on my shoulder. "Try not to think about it then, Captain. Especially how prophecy can be self-fulfilling."

He and Shawn headed off together, leaving me to wonder if he'd meant I *shouldn't* think about the half-assed prophecy from a fortune cookie and thus avoid it being self-fulfilling, or if he'd really meant that last bit as a warning that I *should* give it more thought or I'd inadvertently spark my own death. God, I was turning neurotic.

I crumpled all the pieces of paper into a ball and shoved the ball down the neck of an empty beer bottle.

Fuck you, prophecy.

CHAPTER THREE
Even Buddhists Get the Blues

The Last Representatives of the Funtastic Redcap Rousties
Silk and Suds Laundromat
June 7th

Quill discovered that remaining calm and unflappably Zen was a challenge after a portal burst open in the Laundromat and dumped Chief Gorsh onto the MaxiLoad washing machine. Chief Gorsh thumped off the washer, screamed "Fairy tits!", and crashed to the speckled linoleum tiles.

Quill scrambled out of his lotus position perched on the orange plastic chair near the dryers where he'd been meditating and waiting for the machine cycles to end. His saffron-colored kasaya robes crackled with built-up static electricity. "Are you hurt, Chief?"

"Of course I'm hurt, you simpering lemming-pellet." The chief shoved himself to his feet and adjusted his soggy red top hat, which had made a half-circle splatter on the linoleum. He brushed at the dirt on his ringmaster costume. "I fell on my magnificent codpiece and scuffed the polish on my fucking boots."

The chief wasn't yet capable of stringing together more than three sentences without inserting an insult, gratuitous profanity, or some tirade about the death of the circus, so Quill had long since forgiven him the failing. Fortunately, the Laundromat was empty, save for them. "I didn't expect to see you crossing the Veil, Chief. Our laundry isn't done yet. I have fifteen minutes left on the dryers and two dollars left on my swipe card. Then I have to fold—"

"Three sharks for the filthy laundry," the chief bellowed. "All the boys were wiped out! You hear me, you worthless peace-fobbing gremlin? All of them! *Gone!*"

"I'm truly sorry. I—"

"Shove your puerile bleatings. I escaped by the width of a sasquatch's crotch hair." Chief Gorsh began to limp back and forth in front of the laundry carts. "A powerful ghost summoner like me sent running with his ears slapped. A spiritmaster diabolic, a ringmaster for the ages, a worshiper upon the altar of the Circus Maximus—*me*, forced to flee like a whipped puppy who piddled on the rug."

"When I'm humbled, I consider it a chance to—"

The chief wheeled around and hurled a box of dryer sheets at him. The box hit the window and bounced onto a chair. Chief Gorsh clenched his fists, grinding his teeth so hard Quill heard it over the monotonous hum and tumble of the driers. His teeth sounded like two pumice stones rubbed against one another.

"Never interrupt an evil monologue, Quill! Not only is it extremely *verboten*, it's *hakel morodie*—heaping three shades of shame upon your ancestors forever. There's no point in megalomania if you can't pig-swiving *talk* about it without fear of preachy interjections! Now where was I...? So of course I had to abandon my minions and escape. I must survive to realize my dream of the Grand Show Phantom Circus Magnifique. The greatest show this side of the spirit world!"

"When a dream consumes, it becomes a nightmare—"

"A *nightmare* is the first intelligent idea you've yarped all night, you three-legged ruminant." The chief paced faster, chewing on a yellow fingernail. "I knew bringing the carnival to this city was a mistake. Newman, that cheap bastard, sending us ahead to post flyers and secure permits like worthless peons. Now my ghost summoning has failed and all my lackeys are dead or dying, all because we needed to wet our caps."

Quill settled into the lotus position on another hard plastic chair. He smoothed his robes and sighed. It grieved him to hear that the other redcaps had been slain, and grieved him more that wetting the caps meant some innocent person had been killed. He used pig's blood to keep his own cap red, and that stained his soul enough, spending the life of another living creature to sustain his own.

He struggled to find his focal point and concentrate again, seeking a state of compassion and empathy. The dirty Laundromat was not an ideal place to quest for insight and tranquility, even without the chief's constant ranting. The buzzing fluorescent lights, humming dryers, and sloshing washing machines threw out a constant screen of noise, but if one couldn't find right mindfulness in such a place, one didn't deserve to take refuge in the Three Jewels. Quill started to chant the *Pancasila*, because repeating the Five Precepts always calmed him, centered him with its simple and insightful code of ethics. Soon his loathing for his bloody cap and his sorrow for all the death became both disconnected and yet more profound.

"Shut your piety hole!" Chief Gorsh glared at Quill with one bulging, enraged eye while squinting the other nearly closed. "Or so help me by stone and by blood, I will end you and use your skull for a codpiece."

Quill stopped chanting. The chief seemed fixated on codpieces and violence tonight, feeding on his own rage. Unfortunate and disappointing. But he held on to his faith that the chief would someday walk the path to enlightenment and stop his obsessive plans for creating his Grand Show Phantom Circus Magnifique. Or, as the chief liked to call it after consuming tequila, his Eternal Malevolence Carnival and Incredible Show of Evil.

"Remember, Chief, 'hatred does not cease by hatred, but only by love; this is the eternal rule.'"

The chief snarled and threw a laundry basket at him. The basket missed and hit a vending machine before clattering to the floor. "That for your blabbering quotations, you son of a three-boobed mannequin. This is no time for feeble blathering. I haven't had a thrice-damned setback like this since Norkul doused himself in rut-musk to lure out that were-moose and ended up trampled to death. Fleeing Alaska tasted damn bitter, but this...*this* is a bloody powrie circus tragedy."

Chief Gorsh resumed pacing back and forth in front of the large industrial dryer that tossed socks and tumbled jockey shorts. Quill hid his disappointment behind a serene mask. The achievement of harmony and the ritual shaking-loose of the chains of suffering seemed the furthest things from the chief's mind. His negative energy crashed against Quill in waves. The fear and rage made meditation far more difficult than any noise from the Laundromat.

"I almost didn't make it," Chief Gorsh continued, sounding shaken for the first time. "Some huge-mammaried vixen cast a love hex on me, and all the blood rushed out of my brain. I still feel the pull of her ménage-a-magic. Likely she zeroed in on my colossal codpiece. They tell me it's a curse." The chief wheeled around and pointed at him, glaring. "Don't even open your mouth and start squeaking. We've got three tons of other problems. I might've escaped the warm clutches of that delicious minx, but what lie can I spit at that officious bastard Newman, now that we have no permits? He'll give us the bloody boot for sure."

Mr. Newman was the "Monsieur Loyal" who owned the Funtastic traveling carnival that employed them. Despite the elaborate white and crimson costume, Chief Gorsh was not the ringmaster, and that pricked his pride something awful. A ringmaster wasn't necessary anyway, because the traveling funfair show didn't have anything resembling a big top, acrobats, or circus animals. It was nothing more than mobile rides and vendor booths.

The chief sagged against a folding table as all the fury poured out of him at once. "Without the Ochre Calliope running, I've no hope of bringing more than a triad of ghosts across the Veil. You see? You understand the cascade of calamity those devil dog freaks unleashed upon us?"

"'It is better to conquer yourself than to win a thousand battles,'" Quill quoted, seizing the perfect moment to teach. "'Then the victory is yours. It cannot be taken from you, not by angels or by demons, heaven or hell.' So says the Buddha."

Chief Gorsh alternated between bunching his hands into fists and hooking them into birdlike talons, clawing at the air while shaking his head, exactly how Quill suspected a T-rex choking on a Stegosaurus would appear. Instead of attacking him, the chief wheeled away and resumed his agitated pacing. His boot heels *thocked* back and forth on the linoleum. The rim of his top hat was bent, and his straggly white hair hung in irregular, greasy clumps.

"Thrice damn their mercenary meddling," Chief Gorsh spat, making more clawing motions. "If I lose this job, I lose the Ochre Calliope. If I lose the Calliope, the world will never end in ghosts. Those bloody-handed mercenary dogs! Iron nails pierce their eyes, and scissors snip the bottom of their tongues. Damn them beneath my heels *three* times."

"Seek your calm center, Chief." Quill used his most

soothing voice, speaking from the center of himself, completely at ease in his lotus position. The hardness of the plastic chair beneath him didn't matter. Neither did the stink of sauerkraut, fresh blood, or cloying fabric softener. The weariness that had etched its way across his bones in a seeping acid stain after he'd hauled countless loads of laundry also didn't matter. These were passing things, inconsequential. "Join me. Remember what the Buddha taught. 'Holding on to anger is like grasping a hot coal with the intent of throwing it at someone. You are the one who is burned.'"

"This for your thrice-damned *calm center*! You make a piss-poor goblin, Quill. You should be more like me, ready to chew someone's spleen. If you didn't have a slice of *nurata* spelltouch I'd have wrung out your cap long ago." Chief Gorsh yanked at a strand of greasy hair, viciously twirling it around his finger. "If only that knee-gnawer Mokor hadn't loitered under the hot air from that restroom's hand dryer and dried his cap... Now instead of evil glory, we're fodder for the twenty-four hour news cycle."

"The news is always full of suffering. Consider what this means."

"Shut your yap-hole or I'll consider what *you* mean to me, which is less than nothing!" Chief Gorsh rubbed a hand across his face, then glanced at a battered, graffiti-scarred public pay phone in the corner. "No...no, on second thought, you're absolutely right, Quill, my bleatingest minion. Perhaps I'm seeing this entirely the wrong way. Perhaps those thrice bloody merc pigs have challenged me to escalate and *achieve*. There's an opportunity looming for a few iron-shod bastards such as ourselves that we can't afford to miss. What am I doing *pretending* to be a ringmaster, under that miser Newman's penny-pinching scrutiny? Chief Gorsh is no lackey! Even if, in one hour of grim trouble, I worked for him as merely another disrespected roustie peon who smelled of caramel and wet straw, that hour is past! As of *this* hour, I work for no man or beast, ghost or monster! It's time I call in the crimson hat boys from Corvallis, and we'll speak with Newman, oh yes. This is a most fortuitous turn."

Quill frowned, but quickly forced his face back into a serene mask. The crimson hat boys from Corvallis needed to seek compassion and serenity even more than the chief. They were redcaps of a particularly nasty turn, dealing meth to senior homes and stealing suitcases from baggage conveyor belts. They suffered, and suffering, they brought more pain into the world. He would have to meditate on the best way to guide them to greater enlightenment. He only hoped he was up to the task.

Chief Gorsh stomped to a halt in front of him. "Damn your third eye, don't you want to know what the opportunity is?"

"We should concentrate our minds on the present moment. Opportunities are like snowflakes, as unexpected as they are fleeting. You may as well beseech the clouds for snow as curse them, each is equally futile."

"Such a pathetic excuse for a goblin." This time the chief sounded disappointed instead of enraged. "I can't believe I promised your mother I'd watch out for you, all because she could suck coconuts through a straw. A talented mouth like that could draw promises from any creature requiring a codpiece."

Quill struggled to meditate until his desire to kick the chief in the teeth with an iron-shod boot passed back into tranquil calm.

It was not easy.

The chief grinned. "The time's come to charge the Ochre Calliope to maximum and unleash my spectral circus de fantastique."

"But I thought the calliope was broken—"

"There's a crimson hat boy by the name of Valco who's so

handy fixing the mechanical that you'd swear he was a three-armed gremlin. Maybe his mother *was* a three-armed gremlin... Never mind, now where was I? Ah, yes. This is the hour I seize the title of spiritmaster as my right and create the circus of my secret dreams. This is an opportunity that will that'll keep us in meat and blood; hats wet, knives sharp."

"I won't help you harm others," Quill warned. "Hasn't there been enough harm done already? Why are you so eager for more?"

"Curse your bloody hat, you bald little worm. You need to keep your cap red, same as the rest of us, you filthy slither-scamp. We'll dispense triple the bitter vengeance for our slain brothers like...like an ice cream truck of cold retribution. My hour is at hand! Listen close, you porcupine-molesting son of a three-tongued manatee, because you're part of this too." Chief Gorsh placed his hands on his hips and flashed a sadistic grin. "Tonight's setback was nothing more than a birth pang, and behold, the world will soon witness the unveiling of my Grand Show Phantom Circus Magnifique!"

The serenity Quill had sought to embrace shattered into jagged ceramic shards. All his *samatha* meditation, all his seeking of harmony and truth, all helped him endure and overcome the plain fact that he hated carnivals, especially the carnival where he worked. Worse still, he'd loathed the circus since he'd been a wee powrie. He found the sly barkers odious and intimidating, abhorred and feared the clowns, shivered at the squeaking of balloon animals, hated the vomit and the dirty straw and the creaking, clanging rides and the rolls of tickets and the tiny bowls of over-priced nachos stained with angry yellow cheese lying two feet from the trash bin in obscene little piles that seethed with ants.

Hated it all, and in turn despised himself for his own weakness, his own failure to free himself from the chains of this hatred. Now Gorsh would expect him to help unleash his twisted vision on an unsuspecting world which still believed the circus a source of wonder and fun.

Chief Gorsh must've recognized the torment on Quill's face, because he threw back his head and laughed.

CHAPTER FOUR
Prophecy Redux

Mercenary Wing Rv6-4 "Zero Dogs"
The Zero Dog Compound
June 17th

I'm not a saint.

Ask anyone in the Zero Dogs and every single mercenary tongue will happily tell you a different tale of Captain Andrea Walker's scorched halo. Hell, that douchebag who'd thrown eggs at me would wholeheartedly agree. I'm a pyromancer, and proud of it. No pyromancer had ever burned at the stake, because, well…the irony would probably cause the world to implode. But not being burned as a witch still put me quite a few miracles short of canonization.

Thus, having established my lack of sainthood, when the doorbell of our supposedly locked-down-and-secure-for-the-night facility chimed Greensleeves, I stomped to the front door growing angrier with every step. No one ever bothered to answer the damn door except for me, and what colossal breed of assclown would dare bother us this late?

Not another zombie horde, that's for sure. Zombies didn't ring the doorbell, and the last necromancer we'd tangled with was either dead or disappeared. The only other action we'd seen had been ten days ago against the redcaps, and we'd rolled those little bastards hard. True, the odd ringmaster had escaped, but why would he ring the doorbell even if he could get past the security gates? Too late for pizza delivery. Too dark for door-to-door evangelists...unless I was dealing with vampire Jehovah's Witnesses.

Shit.

Heat shimmered around my hands as I reached for the flat screen monitor mounted on the wall next to the front door. I hesitated and forced myself to calm down or my pyro magic would fry our security electronics and melt the plastic.

Still, a vampire Jehovah's Witness could be bad.

When the residual heat had dissipated to safe levels, I turned on the monitor to scope out who lurked outside. We had an old school peephole of course, but I'd paid a ton of money for high-tech security after our mansion had been overrun by zombies, so I was going to damn well use it. The security cameras showed me a high-resolution color image of the porch, our worn *Go Away!* welcome mat and a man standing on top of it, ignoring its message. He shifted his weight from black cowboy boot to cowboy boot. Not a vampire, at least. He appeared human, although his religious affiliation remained open to question.

He couldn't have been more than twenty-two, twenty-three years old, but he had a long face that seemed older when the shadows cut across its sharp angles. He was tall and lanky...nearly skinny. His skin appeared pale, almost unhealthy, but maybe that was just the cast of the security lights. He wore a black three-piece suit with more wrinkles than string theory had dimensions. His black tie hung crooked from his neck. A backpack dangled over one shoulder, and he carried a battered guitar case in his left hand.

A singing Jehovah's Witness armed with a guitar was even

worse than a vampire. Either that or the guy was a rabid fan of Johnny Cash and had walked *way* the hell off the line to show up out here. I cycled through the rest of the camera views to the ones watching the defense wall at the bottom slope of our property. All the security lighting blazed away, illuminating the Zero Dog compound in a flood of white brilliance. There was the upside-down jet-ski Hanzo and Gavin had crashed into the hedges. And yes, there was the main gate standing wide open. *Dammit, Rafe.* That werewolf was notorious for leaving things unlocked.

I returned to the screen showing Mr. Guitar and frowned. The unease that had taken days to shake off after the motel assault and the fortune cookies started to smolder in my mind again. I had that same feeling I'd had in the alley — that my little red sports car of life was about to veer off the yellow brick superhighway of Good Times and slam into the concrete pylon of Fucked Up Beyond All Recognition.

I began to hope it *was* some hyper-motivated guitar-slinging evangelist and nothing more. We lived in the hills west of downtown Portland, on a winding asphalt driveway curving past the Pittock Mansion, with a great view of skyscrapers, hills, and Mt. Hood in the distance. Occasionally we got a lost tourist or an activist of some breed or another, but that was about it. We fired live ordnance and had military-grade hardware tearing around our property, which frightened off visitors.

The man rang the doorbell again. I punched the intercom button and started to machine-gun words. "Not sure why you're out evangelizing this late, but if I joined your church you'd kick me out in a week for being incorrigible devil spawn. Or I'd be shunned, and shunning really pisses me off. So, while I sympathize that it's tough knocking on the doors of rude, impatient people all day long, getting mauled by attack dogs, tripping on children's toys, being drenched by sprinklers, etc,

etc, amen, I *don't* want a copy of your tiny magazine that tells me what a debased sinner I am. Thank you. Go forth, forthwith."

The man leaned toward the intercom. His voice was so quiet and unassuming that I had to strain to hear it through the speaker. "I'm here because of a prophecy —"

Prophecy. I threw the bolts, chains, locks, and ripped open the front doors. An avalanche of stifling hot summer air collapsed on me, but I scarcely noticed. My heart was pounding so hard, echoing in my head, that it felt as if I had 12-inch woofers mounted in each of my temples. The guy's eyes widened and he stepped backward.

"Who are you?" I demanded.

"If you don't hire me, you will die."

Magefire flared to life around my hands, licking up along my arms. Showy as hell, but still a delicate trick that required precise control to avoid igniting my clothes. "That a threat? Because I turn away applicants who include death threats in their resumes."

He stared at me with morose brown eyes, his face grim. I prepared to cut loose with fire if he made a play for me. Adrenaline rode the lightning through my veins.

"I'm not making a threat, Captain Walker." He kept very still, as if sensing my readiness to scorch off his eyebrows.

"You know my name." I shouldn't have been surprised, and yet it unsettled me.

"I was given a message. Captain Andrea Walker would fall into mortal peril if she didn't hire me. It was foretold that I would save you, but only if I fought beneath the banner of the Zero Dogs."

"You said *prophecy*." In my mind, I could see the image of those damn fortune cookie fortunes arranged on the top of the bar, mocking me with their vague, cryptic incoherence.

"Prophecy, not message. I heard you."

He nodded slowly. "A prophecy from a great seer. Please, I know how it sounds."

"Good, because it sounds rabid-batshit-crazy."

"I'm not crazy, and this is no prank. I've come all the way from Minnesota." His stomach growled, a sound shockingly loud in the night's quiet. He blushed. "Please, just hear me out."

It was the blush and the stomach growl that did it. No assassin I'd ever known blushed or did a job hungry. He'd fishhooked me with the word prophecy, so I didn't slam the door and release the metaphorical hounds. Yeah, he still might be completely unhinged, but I downgraded his threat level to medium-rare and shut the feed on my magefire.

"Are you qualified to be a paranormal mercenary?"

"I'm a berserker. My name is Erik Cantrell."

I'm a berserker isn't a phrase I'd heard often from hungry people skulking on my front porch. Depending on who you talked to, berserkers either fought like rabid wolverines suffering meth-induced delusions or like psychotic badgers raised on a diet of steroids and horror movies. When their rage magic kicked in during a fight it gave them superhuman strength, reflexes as fast as a vampire's, and shielded them from pain—though not from damage. You could kill a berserker, but pulling it off was messy as hell.

"Why would I let some strange berserker into my house?" I'd learned a lesson after I'd once allowed a severed zombie head inside and barely survived the resulting chaos. Some shit you just left outdoors.

"What did the fortune cookies say?" Erik asked.

I darted forward and grabbed him by the lapels. "You *know* about the cookies?"

He gave me another grim nod. "The seer who sent me, she said you'd be expecting the fulfillment of prophecy. That you'd been sent messages to prepare the way—"

"That's bullshit."

"I'm here. I knew about the fortune cookies."

"Prophecy can bite me."

He continued to watch me with those sorrowful brown eyes and didn't reply. It was like being trapped in the room with a chronically depressed greyhound whose stomach kept growling.

"Tell me who sent the damn cookies. How'd you make sure they'd end up with me at Zhong Kui's?" I started to sweat. And I began to feel really stupid talking about cookies in my *Don't Fuck With Me Or I'll Melt Your Face* voice.

Erik shook his head. "I had nothing to do with it. All I know is what I was told by the oracle about the prophecy. You will die if you don't hire me. The prophet said I can't let that happen because you're important."

"Damn right I'm important," I hedged, starting to feel even more uneasy. Other than the fact that I was rather fond of myself, I couldn't think of one indisputable reason why I was important. "Fine then. Who is this psychic? Not that damn Jersey oracle in Newark, is it? Monsieur Philippe? 'Cause I hear that guy's a real prick. And *wrong*."

"Mistress Patel gave me the prophecy in Minneapolis. At my psychic reading. She was very specific. She said the Tarot cards were as ominous as she'd ever seen. The Tower. The ten of swords. The three of swords. Then she showed me the book."

Oh. Shit.

"Mistress Patel…the woman who wrote the *Omniphaelogos*? She showed you *that* book?"

Erik shifted his guitar case to his other hand. His stomach growled again. "That's her, and that was the book."

No wonder those cookies had ruined my night. I'd seen Patel on Oprah once. A stylish thirty-something lady who'd supposedly predicted all sorts of calamities—the Great Recession, hurricanes, worthless social media stock IPOs, the Illuminati's control of *Dancing with the Stars*. The *Omniphaelogos* was where the creepy woo-woo factor revved into overdrive. The grimoire was said to be full of random words and incoherently cryptic passages that rearranged themselves depending on who had opened the book to read, yielding all manner of disturbing and reader-specific prophecies. No two readers ever read the same text. People claimed the prophecies from the book were eerily accurate, but no lottery numbers or Triple Crown winners, which would've been the first things I'd have tried to find.

"I guess you'd better come in," I said and stepped aside to let him into the house. "Maybe together we can figure out how far up shit creek I am this week."

* * *

I sure as hell didn't need this, not now, not ever. Worry and vexation made me rush through the halls. Erik had to rely on long, rapid strides to keep up.

Why me? I was a woman of simple wants. I wanted my people safe and I wanted easy, profitable jobs: guarding bubble-wrap factories or fighting monsters made out of construction paper while rescuing the grateful heir to a massive fortune. I wanted Jake. I wanted a heated toilet seat. I wanted a camouflage Snuggie and hot cocoa spiked with scotch or brandy—I wasn't picky. That's it. Well, that was a good start anyway. But prophecy…what a crock. And yet, I was afraid to disregard it. I led Erik through our mansion toward the conference room, my thoughts taking an increasingly dark turn. I risked small talk when his silence and my inability to think positive began to grate on my nerves. "Is there really a guitar inside that case? Or is it a concealed machine gun or some kind of hidden rocket launcher?"

"A war axe."

I gave him an arch look. "Is that musician lingo for electric guitar during battle of the bands?"

"It's a literal axe. Blade. Spike. Haft."

I grinned. For the first time I considered what bringing him onto the team would entail, instead of simply dismissing the idea as insane. I preferred my people to have some type of ranged attack if possible, but maybe berserkers couldn't shoot worth shit when all zerk-raging around a battlefield. His strength would be a definite plus in hand-to-hand...unless he lost control and attacked friendlies. I wouldn't commit to signing him, cryptic warnings or no. Even big axes didn't impress me much. Besides, could a berserker follow orders when all keyed up? I didn't need a loose cannon, or loose axe in this case, deep-sixing missions or getting my people hurt because he couldn't follow commands.

Still, that prophecy...

We entered the living room, and I silently cursed the disordered state of our mansion. An arrow pinned an empty beer can to the wall at about head-height. William Tell eat your heart out. A large cardboard cut-out of a sasquatch hid between two huge plastic potted plants, both decorated with twinkling Christmas lights and empty yogurt containers. A damn tire mark slashed across the ceiling—I didn't even want to know about that one. The typical scattering of food containers and wrappers were strewn across every flat surface: pizza boxes, Chinese takeout, Quiznos, etc. Every maid and cleaning service I hired quit after only a month because we were filthy animals.

Erik paced along beside me, his gaze roaming from sight to sight, but his long, thin face remained inscrutable. If he wanted to work for us he'd better get used to the mess. Maybe he could go all berserker with a vacuum and toilet brush. If so, the man was as good as on the roster.

The Zero Dog compound was huge, built to hold six or seven times our current number. We'd reached the hallway leading to the conference room when we had to stop to let Squeegee the three hundred pound mutant housecat saunter past. The huge calico looked up at me and rumbled her chainsaw purr, hoping for food.

"Big cat," Erik said.

"That's not a cat, it's a rhinoceros with fur. She answers to Squeegee. Wait, I'm wrong. She *is* a cat. She doesn't answer to anything."

Squeegee stopped purring, sat and began to lick her tail, displaying typical cat disdain. I frowned at her. She really needed to start a diet. Gavin couldn't keep feeding her bacon cheeseburgers and jalapeno poppers or she'd turn into the Jabba the Hutt of felines, and that just wasn't healthy.

I petted Squeegee until she purred again, then we edged around her and continued down the hall. Music drifted from behind the closed conference room door. Why the hell was the conference room *always* taken when I needed it…and was that bad dance jazz?

Erik glanced at me, perhaps noticing my eyelid twitch. Inside the conference room, someone chanted, "And three, and four, and five, and swing that pelvis like you're Elvis, and eight, and nine…"

God help me, I opened the door.

Rafe was naked in the middle of the conference room floor, dancing…or exercising, or having a very rhythmic epileptic seizure while standing up. I couldn't quite tell. Werewolves were not shy about shedding clothes due to the requirements of shifting from one form to another. Rafe took a lack of modesty to an entirely new level.

He was currently in human form, and I've mentioned he's not a bad sight when he's clothing-impaired, which is all too often for any Comics Code censor's peace of mind. He was muscular and handsome enough, except for the roughly two and a half million tattoos all over his flesh canvas. Terrible tattoos. Horrible, crime-against-humanity tattoos. Tattoos of jet fighters and naked cat women, obscure majica symbols, and all kinds of random phrases and designs.

Before I could retreat from my interruption of Rafe's naked step lunges, he glanced away from the conference room television (currently showing a mass of people in bright leotards flailing about) and noticed me.

"Hey, Captain," he called over the jazzy music. "Want to join me? I'm doing Jazzerbo!"

I tried to block Erik from witnessing Rafe flop around as he swung his pelvis just like Elvis. Yeah, first impressions. The Zero Dogs excelled at making them memorable…or at scarring people for life, depending on one's point of view.

"Why are you naked?" I asked, very calmly.

"Nude Jazzerbo is very liberating. It's an entire order of healthy above standard exercising. My sweat evaporates faster. No restraints, no restrictions, just freedom from the oppression of spandex and leg warmers."

The conference room table had been flipped on its side and shoved against the opposite wall. No chance of merely kicking Rafe out and taking over the room now. I'd be forced to reassemble the place before I could use it, and it already stank of testosterone and sweat.

"Liberating," I repeated. Not a question. More of a plea for God to Rapture me right then. Either my math had failed to determine the official evacuation day for the devout, or I was still not on God's quick pick list.

"Exactly. My balls must breathe free." Rafe jumped and

punched and executed kicks to jazz. "Don't worry. I shaved."

Erik averted his eyes and stared out the large windows that gave a view of distant downtown Portland. Windows...

"You're cavorting in the conference room with the blinds *open*?"

"No one's gonna see me, Captain. Except you and that guy." More rhythmic kicks and punches. "What happened to Jake? This a little taste of sugar on the side?" He waggled his eyebrows at me. Like werewolves everywhere, his eyebrows were aggressively bushy.

I rubbed my temples, trying to massage away the building headache. "This is Erik Cantrell. He wants to join up, but he probably just changed his mind. And what the hell is Jazzerbo?"

"Jazzercise meets taekwondo. It's really getting popular. Look Captain, Jazz-hands!"

I finally realized I was in Hell. I'd died years ago and been trapped here ever since, suffering my eternal torment, now new and improved with a grating jazz soundtrack.

"All right...I guess we'll just...go to my office. Because you're in here. Naked. Jazzerbo-ing. Oh, and by the way, if you leave the security gate open again I'll turn you into a pelt. Got me?"

"Sorry, Captain." For a moment he seemed almost abashed, then he broke into a wide grin. "Maybe this will help." He stopped punching the air in time to the music and turned his bare ass to me. "Look! M-O-O-N, that spells moon!" And he howled.

I half guided, half shoved Erik out of the room and slammed the door behind me. The music, diminished but not silenced, continued to fill the hallway. Erik looked at me. I looked at him.

"My office is safer," I said. "I swear."

Erik's expression was that of a man who'd broken into a

mental asylum and discovered that getting in was far easier than getting out.

* * *

The mess in my office was nothing compared to the creeping disaster that spread downstairs in the common areas like demonic kudzu vine. Just files, folders, paperclip chains, and a scattering of pens. Some of those pens were dry, some brand new, but they were all intermixed, making it a gamble which I'd get when I picked one up, a kind of bastardized Russian roulette with writing utensils. Still, I could never get around to throwing any of them away. My cactus sat in its little sombrero pot perched on the window ledge, a Christmas bow pierced by its needles, and December long gone.

The new computerized intercom-slash-PA muzak system I'd had installed after the previous fire had gone psychotic again, like HAL's musical little brother, and was now playing *Putting on the Ritz* on continual loop. I sighed and cleared off a chair for Erik, piling all the assorted invoices and UPS boxes on a file cabinet with enough flat surface to risk the towering stack. Erik set his guitar case against the wall beneath my motivational poster of a sloth passed out in a scattering of empty booze bottles.

After Erik took a seat, I plopped down in my swivel chair and slammed my feet up on my desk. "Tell me why I'm going to die if I don't hire you."

His stomach rumbled again, sounding exactly like someone drowning in motor oil while trying to sing the Star Spangled Banner. After stumbling upon naked Rafe, I didn't want to risk tromping through the house again to get him something from the kitchen, so we both did our best to ignore his stomach thunder.

"Your death was foretold by Patel the prophet and by the arcane stochastic processes of the *Omniphaelogos*." His expression was earnest, despite his words which sounded strained, rehearsed, and stuffed with melodrama. He didn't even crack an ironic smile. "Probability distribution yielded your future. If you don't hire me, your doom is sealed."

Doom. *Sealed*, no less. "Ninety-eight percent of the time prophecy's pure bullshit. The other two percent is dead on, which makes telling the difference really damn hard. What did the prophecy say? Exact wording matters."

He closed his eyes and started to recite. "'Lo, when he who is capped in crimson becomes the ringmaster of ghosts, spectral clowns will exult, and the flame-dancing dog will be thrown into mortal peril. Life and mission will be forfeit unless the axe bearer fights beside her."

"Sounds as stupid as the standard prophetic crap. About as clear as pond scum and riddled with pompous blather to make it sound authentic." I made a show of scowling, but a chill had iced my insides. The *capped in crimson* thing might well refer to those psychoblade redcaps. The one who'd escaped had been dressed as a ringmaster. Exulting spectral clowns though? Give me a break. And I sure as hell didn't flame *dance*. "So you're the axe bearer then? Isn't that just as cute as a kitten in booties?" I thumped my heels back on the floor and leaned toward him. "I hate kittens. *And* booties. Wait, axe bearer... You sure this seer wasn't yapping about the Tin Man from *The Wizard of Oz*? Or maybe a dwarf? I'd hire any dwarven axe-slinger in ten seconds flat. Those dudes know how to chop."

He stared at me without even a strained joke-pity smile. Strike One. When I told jokes, I expected people to laugh, whether it was funny or not. Perks of command.

"I am the axe bearer," he said grimly.

"You claimed the prophecy came from Patel *and* the

Omniphaelogos. Were these prophecies *exactly* the same?"

"Exactly."

"Was she reading over your shoulder?"

"I was alone with the book. The words were unmistakable."

I didn't like the sound of that. The *Omniphaelogos* belonged to a small group of infamous tomes, and the only one whose text changed with each new reader. Supposedly it had been created in the late 1800s, making Mistress Patel well over a hundred years old if she were the true author and not simply another charlatan. Charlatan had my vote. On television she'd appeared in her thirties at most, though perhaps the makeup artists on the show were really damn good.

According to legend, there were only seven copies of the prophecy book still surviving in the entire world. Mistress Patel owned one, said to be the original. The British Museum and the Library of Congress both had copies, but the Bibliotheque nationale de France had returned their copy for credit, and it had ended up with some private collector. Another copy, won in a bet over a game of beer pong, was locked in the rare book section of the Hannon Library at Southern Oregon University. A water-damaged version remained at Miskatonic University, and rumors whispered of a final copy with a stripped cover floating around Southeast Asia.

"Well, shit," I said.

"You *must* hire me, Captain Walker. Please."

"At least throw me some viable reasons *why* I should hire you." I paused. "Aside from the fact that my life depends on it, which is hard to quantify for Human Resources. What skills do you bring to the crew?"

Erik turned toward the window and recited his combat history to my cactus, only occasionally making eye contact through wary glances. He'd done some freelance work, mostly dungeon crawling and slogging through stormwater systems in the Minnesota-St. Paul area, hooking up with people in adventurer guilds and hardcore Society for Creative Anachronism members who wanted to take it to the next level. Some convoy escort duty in both North and South Dakota. Pit fighting in Columbus, Ohio.

"Paranormal pit fighting's very illegal." Strike two. "Not sure including criminal activities on your resume makes me eager to bring you onboard."

"I'm being honest. And I hated it. Every moment of it. But I had to eat. There was nothing else."

I hesitated, because I wasn't a voyeur and had no desire to make him re-bleed any tragic, hidden past. A good many people joined Paranormal Action Teams to escape shady personal histories. "Ever fight zombies?"

"No."

"I hate zombies. Long story. Long, ugly, stupid story." I sat back in my chair and folded my arms. "Let me tell you a bit about the Zero Dogs and see if that scares you off. We're a Paranormal Action Team—and never use the acronym PAT in my presence. Rv6-4 is our official designation, a wing of the Hellfrost Mercenary Group for the Pacific Northwest. We work for money, not to propagate peace and love in the world. Nuns might be meaner, but we're better armed."

No laugh. No smile. And he was languishing at two strikes already. Still, I realized that part of me *wanted* him to do well in the interview. The same way I always cheered for the underdog or for those idiots on *American Idol* who sang like peacocks being flayed alive, which made me deeply embarrassed for them even though I should've been pointing and laughing along with everyone else.

I pressed on, reciting some of the general info found on our brochure and website, pay rates and jobs we'd pulled off and so forth. My usual hiring schtick. I hyped up the action, adventure, and swag procurement, but also included the part where we routinely ran low on funds and faced impossible odds. Then I rambled about the contract until his eyes glazed over. "Those are the basics. Still, interested?"

That caught his attention. "You must hire me to save your life."

"Yeah. I remember. There's a standard trial period, should I decide to sign you up. Also, lots of paperwork—"

"No. Tonight. It must be tonight, Captain Walker."

Pushy. Strike three. I was sorry because I liked the kid. He was earnest as hell, and seemed wound so tight he was apt to start spitting clock springs at any second, but he carried a battle-axe in a guitar case. That had style.

"Even if I were inclined to bring you on board this instant— and I'd want to see you in action first as a minimal requirement—I can't because of contract issues. I'm sorry. I really am. Give me a business card or a resume and I'll be in touch."

"I'll sign anything." His hand clenched.

"Look, I'm not scheduled for a mission and we have no jobs on the horizon, so there's no chance of me dying at the hands of any ringmaster crimson ghost or whatever. My horoscope warned against making rash decisions, but mentioned nothing about death by carnies."

Normally, not having any clients paying for our destructive expertise would drive my stress level into the stratosphere. After all, we'd already burned through a decent chunk of the money we'd earned on our last mission for Homeland Security, and the redcap job had been a pittance compared to that. But for once I felt grateful to have nothing on the schedule, in case Mistress Patel the Minnesota psychic had given Erik a rare two-percenter prophecy.

One would've thought I'd verbally abused a puppy in

French to see Erik's face when I refused him. "Captain Walker, I'm begging you. You must hire—"

"—me tonight. Yes, I get the hint. But the chances of me hiring you tonight are zero and trending downward. I won't be rushed, pushed, or coerced into something stupid." I ignored the fact that I was regularly rushed, pushed, or coerced into all manner of stupid things on a day-to-day basis as captain of the Zero Dogs. "The answer's n—"

His stomach grumbled again, louder than ever.

We stared at each other.

"All right, dammit," I snarled, cursing myself for the worst kind of sucker. "I'll think about it. *No* promises. Now c'mon, let's get something to eat."

Erik's smile was entirely too grateful. Right then I knew I was going to regret this. Some hardass mercenary I'd turned out to be.

I led him down to the kitchen and heated up some leftovers. It had been Tiffany's night to cook and she'd made a pasta casserole with baked ziti. Erik barely let me finish heaping it onto his plate before diving in. He shoved food down his throat so fast I wondered why he even bothered with the fork. He caught me staring and choked, coughing.

"You all right?" I asked.

"It's just...so good." He resumed his frantic eating pace. Then he ate all my food after I'd lost my appetite watching him attack his meal with the gusto of a shark ravaging a seal. I didn't say anything more until he pushed his empty plate away, leaned back in his chair, and closed his eyes.

"You can stay here tonight in a guest room," I said. "We'll fill out paperwork tomorrow and I'll get a background check started. You're on probation, nothing more, so don't get excited. Step out of line in the slightest and I'll boot you out of here, cryptic prophecy or no. Because you're an unknown, you'll have to sleep in a secure room. If you can't handle that, you'll have to leave."

He nodded as if my caution and lack of trust didn't concern him in the least. "Is the food always this good?"

"Um. No." Tiffany's food was decent enough, just like mine was decent. The only really good cooks we had were Mai and Rafe. We never allowed Stefan to cook. As a vampire, his taste was atrocious. Sarge burned everything. Gavin had mastered toast and ramen noodles and that was it.

Erik cleaned up his plate, even washed it, all without being asked. A definite notch in the plus column. I was curious what the other Zero Dogs would think of him. "Ready to meet the rest of the crew?"

"I guess so... Is that naked guy gonna be there?"

I grinned. "With us, that's not even the worst thing you'll see. C'mon, I'll introduce you around."

He followed me as I led the way to his first trial by fire. I drew up short before heading into the game room where I could hear the rest of my mercs laughing, mocking each other, and shooting the shit.

I paused with my hand on the doorknob. "I want to do a little constructive visualization before I take you to my people. Imagine bacon left on a hot skillet for an hour and a half."

Erik stared at me and slowly nodded.

"Keep that image in mind, because if you hurt any of my mercs, I'll slag you so hard it'll leave charcoal on Santa's boxer shorts all the way at the North Pole. So. You planning on hurting any of my people?"

He shook his head.

"Good deal." I dialed back a little and tried a non-threatening smile. "I might as well give you the rundown on a few things, try to sand off some of the edges and give you a chance to better integrate with the rest of the misfit toys."

I waited for a laugh, a smile, *something*. Erik only stared at me in silence. An evil and petty part of me hoped that famous psychic in Minnesota got scabies.

"Sarge is second in command," I continued, undaunted. "He's easy to ID cuz he's huge and a demon. Do everything he says, and double-time unless it countermands a direct order from me, which it won't, because me and him are like a two-headed hydra."

Rambling again, but I rolled with it because I didn't get to do this part of the job often enough. "Don't give Sarge a reason not to like you. One time there was this redneck making homophobic slurs, so Sarge tossed him through a plate glass window, then walked out and stole the dude's snakeskin cowboy boots. You don't want to fuck with a guy who'll steal a pair of cowboy boots off the scumbag he left bleeding in the gutter."

"True," Erik said quietly, appearing more uncertain. Good. Uncertain would keep him frosty.

"We use acronyms and jargon to separate out those in the know from the civvies. If you don't know all the acronyms flying around, don't worry. Simply act as if you do. Maybe make up a few of your own to fit in. In fact, I just coined one tonight. FPD—Fucking Prophetic Doom."

Erik nodded again, this time far more warily, as if I were a rabid talking lemur spitting out dirty limericks.

"Oh, and before I forget, just a little aside. Don't go up in the attic. Ever. It's haunted by a ghost jellyfish."

"Ghost...jellyfish?"

"Yeah. I know. Most of the time it stays up there, but trust me, if you wake up in the middle of the night and feel anything tickling your feet, don't open your eyes or turn on the light. That goddamn ghost jellyfish has some freaky foot thing going on. I'm gonna smoke that sneaky bastard as soon as I can."

"I'm not…I…can I make a phone call?"

"And miss introductions? No can do. This is standard operating procedure for all potential recruits." I gave him a wicked grin and marched into the game room. Taking my fear of Fucking Prophetic Doom out on him wasn't fair, but I was tired, irritable, and worried about those damn fortune cookies. Besides, I couldn't get at that crazy prophet lady from the land of the ice and snow.

Everyone looked over as I entered with Erik. Seeing my people steadied me a bit. Command had plenty of downsides, but instant attention had always been a plus for the ego.

The entire team was here except for Rafe. Stefan and Sarge huddled over the billiards table, a game in progress. Hanzo stopped his martial arts routine using one of the cue sticks as a bo staff in his continual quest to impress Mai. Meanwhile, Mai sat in her beanbag chair and peered at me over the top of a book. Shrill screeches and hoots came from the pile of hot pink and black creatures gathered around her, creatures which resembled a mix between a quail and a garbage disposal, only fuzzier and swarming all over her body. Tiffany was playing one of the arcade games, a gory one where you shot off pieces of zombies with a light gun. Gavin slouched at the wet bar running the far end of the game room, drinking a bottle of beer while he wrote longhand in a notebook. More poetry. At least I'd be free of his verse if FPD came crashing down on me.

Sarge straightened from his pool shot. "Everything all right, Captain?"

"Sort of. We're not under attack yet, if that's what you're wondering—"

"Who is the man with you?" Tiffany's voice was quiet, almost cold.

I glanced her way, surprised. As a succubus, Tiffany's voice was usually soft and sultry. I assumed men believed those aural tones hinted at scorching heat between the sheets and the promise of all sorts of wicked things. She didn't do it on purpose to get a rise out of anyone—and I should score points for that pun—but that was simply the way she was built: like a sexpot Ferrari. But now she stared at Erik with an intensity that seemed a shade short of hostile.

"This is Erik Cantrell. He's applied for a job with the Zero Dogs."

"Lobotomy victim?" Gavin asked.

I ignored him, watching Tiffany and Erik closely. Many males, meeting Tiffany for the first time, gaped at her as if they'd just had a pornographic religious experience which would send them straight to Hell and drag the rest of us along for being in the same room. Instead, Erik bowed to her. His face was grim and in bad need of a shave, his suit disheveled past the point of no return, but somehow the bow worked. If Stefan had tried to pull off the same bow it would've come across as pretentious and forced, done for calling attention to himself. Erik bowed as if he wished to honor her.

Tiffany blushed, but she didn't look away. I had a bad feeling about that. In the *abstract* it was good that Tiffany was finally showing interest in someone. Because maybe I'd made myself obsessed with her non-existent love life, especially after my own love life had gone from imaginary to engines-racing reality, and seeing her lonely had always cut me deep. But in the *specific*, Erik did not have the Captain Andrea Walker stamp of approval. I hadn't even completed the background check yet.

"Erik Cantrell's a berserker." I did my best to keep my smile bland and my attention off the two of them. Soon as I could, I'd explain to Erik that if he broke her heart I'd have to murder him. Slowly. With fire.

"Erik the Berserker." Gavin sipped his beer and frowned at us. "Stupidest thing I've ever heard. Don't hire a 'zerker,

Captain. Bad rage mojo."

My stomach twisted up like a wrung out shammy. Gavin had given boorish voice to my fears. Erik only stared at him, his face carefully blank. Score one for keeping the old temper.

"We can insult him all we want after he's officially joined the team," I said with forced cheer. "He's gonna crash here tonight, show us what he's got tomorrow. He's really eager to join on. I like that enthusiasm."

"That's because he's a fucking loon," Gavin said. "Berserkers always turn on you, Captain. That's truth."

I favored Gavin with my Evil Eye of Authority (or EEA). "I suggest you shut your blowhole and focus on doing your own damn job, merc."

"Why start now?" He grinned, then shook his head in disgust. "It's your ass, Captain. But this is gonna make one helluva tragic, yet completely kick-ass epic poem. 'Beowulf' meets the 'The Waste Land' with a few bawdy ballads thrown in for off-color spice."

I reminded myself that Gavin was one of the best drivers of all things vehicular I'd ever known. I reminded myself how I didn't hire mercenaries for their personality. I reminded myself that I had to set a good example. I still wanted to plant a boot in his rear quarter, but mostly I was afraid he might be right.

No turning back now. I put whip-crack in my voice. "Make him feel welcome, mercs. That's an order."

The Zero Dogs gathered around him, peppering him with questions. I caught Sarge's attention and cut a sidelong look at the berserker. Sarge gave a curt nod. I knew he'd keep an eye on the stranger in our midst, make sure the guy was righteous. If the guy wasn't, well, demons weren't very forgiving.

I turned to go. Right now I wanted to call Jake. More than anything, I wanted to hear his voice and shake off some of this lingering unease. As I walked out of the room, I caught one last glimpse of Tiffany. She was staring at Erik, a guided missile with a target locked.

Death prophecy. A foretelling of redcap circus madness. A Fucking New Guy, and worse, a FNG *berserker* of uncertain loyalties and temperament. And my shy succubus friend finally expressing some kind of interest in a male.

I left in a hurry, escaping before the mental breakdown that hunted me even knew I was there.

* * *

No breeze outside on the deck. It was late and I was tired, but I had to make this call before bed. I leaned against the railing, feeling the day's heat still hiding in the wood like a nymph, warm against my forearms. Portland had seen a hot spell of late and the days had sweltered. The overcast sky trapped the warmth like a thick, wet blanket smothering a feverish man. I started to sweat and immediately considered marching my ass right back inside where the miracle of central air conditioning ruled.

I promised myself I'd eat ice cream and fall asleep under the blast of cold air from an a/c vent after the call. But I couldn't sit inside where it was cool and comfortable and talk to Jake. Not when I knew he was off in some African desert choking down MREs and iodine-treated water in temperatures that made Portland's hot spell seem a mild Spring day.

I lifted my phone to dial his number, and my cell started to blast its Talking Heads ringtone, startling me so badly I almost dropped it. The ringtone song was the one about burning down houses, picked by a certain wiseass Special Forces captain and set before he'd gone on deployment. Some superstitious part of me believed changing the ringtone he'd chosen would tempt fate, invite bad luck. I forced my hands steady and looked at the cell screen. The number made my heart beat combat-fast and turned my stomach all fluttery.

Jake. The only man who could turn this spitfire mercenary into a soft serve ice cream. I took a deep breath. Steadied my voice and answered the cell. "Speaking of psychic, I was just about to call you. How weird is that?"

His slow baritone came back over my phone speaker, made me press it harder to my ear as if I could get closer to him that way. "I didn't realize we were speaking of psychics, but it's damn good to hear your voice. I've missed you something wicked, Andrea."

I loved the way he said my name. As if it were important. As if it were worth taking the time to say. I grinned as wide as a shark tripping on ecstasy. "You missed me, did you? How much? Feel free to stroke my ego. It's been neglected."

"I'll show you exactly how much when I see you again," Jake said, and I could hear the smile in his voice and feel the heat in his words. "No part of you will feel neglected then. I promise."

"How long?"

"Can't say. We wrapped something up and just got back to the forward operating base. I got your message as soon as we crossed the Hescos. The only milk we have around here is goat's milk or dehydrated. I'd pick some up, but we're headed out again tomorrow."

The wheels of my mind spun mud without gaining traction. Then I realized he was referring to the sad joke I'd made in one of the voice mail messages I'd left. I almost blurted out the forbidden questions: where was he, what he was doing? I snapped my mouth shut so fast I clipped the edge of my tongue.

We were both professionals. I couldn't help him in whatever mission he was prosecuting. Knowing details would only make me want to run and fight by his side. When he was actively deployed we were trapped in two different worlds. I couldn't deny it was hard. Nobody promised life would be all cheesecake and the smell of clean babies.

"Forget the milk," I said. "Guess I'll just have to bore you with *my* day. You have time for this?"

"For you? All the time in the world."

The grin reappeared on my face. I was so going to reward him for that when I got my hands on him again. I stared at the low gray cloud ceiling that hovered over the skyscrapers, the ache of missing him a deep squeezing pain in my chest, making my grin falter and fade. Few things repulsed me as much as sounding weak and needy, especially when nothing could be done about it, so I stared at the skyline until I knew there'd be no catch in my voice. From these hills, downtown seemed at once so distant and so very close, as if I were a god pressing my face to a fishbowl, watching people swim about in the artificial lights of their streets and buildings and streaming lines of cars.

"So, it's been business as usual. The PA system broke again. It's playing *Putting on the Ritz* at the moment, but for a week it wouldn't play anything but *Muskrat Love*."

"That's a lot of muskrat love."

"That's what I said. Let's see, what else? Somebody gouged the hell out of our best non-stick pan with a fork. Of course nobody will own up to the crime. Oh, and get this, a berserker showed up on our doorstep slinging a battle axe in a guitar case like the Viking version of Johnny Cash."

"A berserker?" His tone was flat. Guarded.

"He told me I gotta hire him so he can save my life from ghost clowns. Apparently, I'm the victim of a drive-by prophecy."

I laughed. He didn't.

One of the things I loved about Jake was how he well he listened — on the phone anyway. If he was watching a Mariners game, all bets were off. I knew I had a problem, a small tiny infinitesimal challenge that might involve loving the sound of my own voice, but Jake rarely gave off the bored vibe. Not the way my brothers did two seconds after starting to talk with them.

This time he remained strangely, *intensely* quiet. He seemed to be listening so hard it unsettled me.

"You still there?" The thread of unease wormed its way deeper into my chest.

"I had a dream about you."

Back in high school, when I'd been young and at least ten percent stupider, I'd gone skiing for the first time. During my virgin run down the slope I'd plunged straight into a snowdrift. The sudden icy shock of cold, the explosion of white powder, ice crystals flashing as my breath was knocked out of me and the weight of the snow pressed down—that was how I felt now as his words traveled from his phone, through satellites and cell towers to my phone, to my ear, and plunged me into freezing cold. Dreams. Fate. Part of me knew that, whatever Jake was about to say, it wouldn't be good.

I attempted to play it off anyway, dropping my voice, trying to make it sultry. "Oh, one of those kinds of dreams? You *do* miss me."

He didn't take the bait. His words were flat, uninflected, and that frightened me even more.

"You were walking down this hallway that stretched on forever," he said. "You left footprints behind you—the footprints were on fire, burning, but with no smoke, and they didn't die out. You carried this huge book, reading as you walked. An old book—it gave off this aura, this psychic stink of…not evil, but danger maybe. Threat. The ceiling was glass. There were clowns crawling all over the ceiling, peering through like it was a window, as if you were in a lobster tank and they were watching their food."

"I had no idea you had a thing for clowns." I managed to say it without my voice shaking. Points for me. But my heart still revved like mad, and adrenaline dump made my chest feel compressed, my muscles turn jittery.

"The glass started to crack," Jake continued. "I wasn't there…I was floating—disembodied, I don't know—tried to yell a warning but couldn't make any words. You didn't notice or didn't care, just kept walking. The ceiling broke and all the clowns…all these evil-looking things straight out of a Stephen King novel fell on top of you in a rain of glass." He took a deep breath. "I woke up, but I was in the field, freezing my ass off under a poncho and couldn't call you. I told myself it was nothing. Just some stupid acid-trip joke my subconscious was playing because it was bored and missed you. But now…"

"That's really strange." I swallowed, hearing my throat click. My mouth was desert-dry. "First the perfectly timed phone call. Then eerie, messed up clown dreams. Maybe we share some kind of psychic connection." I laughed to show how high this scored on the universal stupid scale. My laughter sounded feeble and forced, so I stopped. Jake stayed silent.

"But there's nothing to worry about," I continued quickly. "I kept the berserker around as a temporary measure, just in case. If there *are* ghost clowns—and that prophet wasn't just making shit up to sound more *legit prognosticator* and less *lying hack*—I'll melt their greasepaint smiles and emerge victorious as the heroine of my own epic tale of glory."

He still didn't respond to my verbal smokescreen. I waited him out this time, watching the dark, darting shape of a bat catching bugs near one of the exterior flood lights. This new silent Jake was unnerving. Part of me wanted to ask him what he thought about prophecy. Those words gathered into questions inside my brain, but my lips wouldn't spit them out.

Jake seemed to choose each word carefully. "Who gave the prophecy and sent the berserker?"

Lying to him was tempting, because my fears suddenly breached surface again. What if he ended up killed in whichever backwater corner of the world he was running amok in because he was distracted by worry for me? Not sleeping. Losing his edge. In the wilderness, exhausted, unable to help me, but unable to stop fretting about me. I'd never live something like that down.

Then again, I didn't want secrets between us. I didn't *want* to lie.

Yet, on the other *other* hand, he kept all kinds of secrets from me about classified Special Forces operations. I'm sure some of his missions would've turned my hair white with worry for him if I'd have known the details.

So what was right?

I told the truth, because I believed my dad would've done the same, and that was how he'd tried to raise me. That was a corny-as-hell answer, but sometimes schmaltz and a shrug was all you could throw back at the world.

Sometimes it was all the world deserved.

"Mistress Patel gave the prophecy," I finally answered. "And it showed up in a semi-famous book."

"I've heard of her. Wrote the *Omniphaelogos*."

"Bingo. If you ask me, there's more money in self help books than soothsaying. You ever read *The Secret*? What a rip off. Every morning I visualize myself turning into a giant red dragon and it never happens."

"Do you trust this berserker?"

"Not at all. He'll be locked in guest quarters for the night, under surveillance until I find out more about him. Sarge is watching him now." I remembered how Erik's stomach had growled all through his attempt to convince me he was righteous. That, more than anything, had lowered my guard enough to give him a chance. Oh, and also the fact that this flame-dancing dog didn't want to die any time soon. "You have any experience with 'zerkers?"

"Yeah." He didn't sound pleased. "They're erratic. They get keyed up and they'll chew through the walls to get at an enemy, but they're also not known to be discriminating when it comes to targets."

"You know I'm careful. I mean to find out everything I can about him before jumping one way or another on this prophecy business."

The absurd lie about being careful aside, I was thinking about Tiffany again and how she'd watched Erik so intently. I considered mentioning the fortune cookies to Jake, and didn't. Lies of omission didn't count. Besides, that shit was too crazy and would worry him for sure.

I could feel his disapproval through the connection, seeming to freeze its way inside my ear canal and into my mind. I leaned against the railing and slowly massaged my temple. "So. What do you think? Was it a mistake to let him through the door?"

"The undaunted, devil-may-care Captain Walker is asking for advice?"

"Jake. Don't."

"You're right, I'm sorry. Look, I don't like it. This berserker's an unknown, and I don't like unknowns. They get people killed." The distant rotor chop of a helicopter stuttered through the phone. He spoke louder to compensate. "But Patel is legit, far as I know. I don't see how you have any other choice but to keep the berserker around if he's tied to a prophecy. Any jobs on the table?"

"Just so happens we *are* planning a trip down to Circus Circus—"

"I'm serious, Andrea."

"No. Nothing."

There was a long pause on the other end of the line. I heard the rumble of a diesel engine over the phone.

"Will you take a job, if one comes up, and bring this berserker along?"

"Not if it involves ghosts or clowns or redcaps. Tempting fate is for heroes. I'm mercenary to the bone."

"Yeah, right." The concern in his voice was easy to hear. "You know I'd be there to watch your back, but I can't get to you right now because of this other shit." The rotor chop sounded louder now, an insistent chattering roar. "Promise me you'll be careful. I mean it."

"I'm always careful," I lied again. "It's like I'm permanently encased in bubble wrap and walking on streets paved with feather pillows and air bags."

"Remember my dream. Don't risk shrugging off this prophecy."

"Okay, okay. I'll keep frosty and watch my ass. Promise." I took a deep breath. "Promise me you'll be careful too."

"Always. And watching your ass is my job, because nobody enjoys it more. I just need to take a rain check for now, but I'll damn well collect soon."

"Oh yeah? Then stop dreaming about clowns."

He finally laughed, sounding more like his old self. "What about rodeo clowns? Fair game?"

"No clowns!" But I was grinning again.

"I have to go," he finally said. "Duty calls, and so on and so forth."

"No joyriding in tanks and blowing up bridges for sport. You hear me? Saving the world should be hard work."

"Keep your promise," was all he said and disconnected.

CHAPTER FIVE
Upwardly Mobile Through Murder

Redcap Crew
Funtastic Carnival!
June 23rd

"I'm going to teach you how to be evil even if it drives nails through my eyelids," Chief Gorsh growled at Quill as they hurried along the asphalt toward Newman's office trailer. "Shame your father was murdered by those dark elves after he stole their grog. If your mother hadn't been one of those wickedly flexible gals who could bend into all sorts of tantalizing positions, I never would've agreed to drag a hopeless case like you along. If *I'd* been your father, you'd swing some real goblin balls!"

Quill took a steadying inhale as he reached for his calm center. He was pristine water. Raindrops rippled his surface, but could not disturb his depths. So too were the Chief's constant insults and insinuations about his mother. Raindrops, nothing more.

He followed Gorsh as the chief stomped across the asphalt toward Newman's office trailer. All around them, rousties unloaded trailers and set up rides, assembled booths, and erected gates and rail queues. The air trembled with the rumble of diesel engines and generators, clacking ride motors, and clattering cars. One thing that had disappointed Quill about working for a travelling funfair carnival had been the discovery that the rousties didn't sing bleak songs as they did in the movies. Rousties here merely cursed a lot. They cursed the rides, the bosses, each other, told raunchy jokes, and played profanity-happy hip hop over buzzing speakers. At least there were no scary pink elephants on parade anywhere to be seen.

He didn't want to be here. More than that, he really didn't want to be a part of Chief Gorsh's imminent confrontation with their boss, Mr. Newman. His chest tightened down, a fifty-pound stone of fear crushing his sternum. He took another deep breath and released it slowly, exhaling all his worries and tensions, blowing the fear out of his body and calming his mind.

"Stop snorting like a drunken water buffalo," the chief warned, hopping over the unsecured cable snaking this way and that. He wore his freshly laundered ringmaster regalia, bleached a pristine white that seemed nearly incandescent. "I can't abide a mouth breather, all snorty-grunt-whoosh breath. Now that I think of it, your mother made sounds like that when I used to—"

"Chief, I don't care for you mentioning my mother with such disrespect."

"That right, you soggy little pork rind? I'd ask what you meant to do about it, but I know you'd only twist your panties into a pretzel and *ohmmm* over it for three hours. Lucky I swore a solemn oath to your mother I'd paint your heart in malice before I kicked off."

"All your hopes that I'll turn to evil are in vain. All your desires that I'll use *nurata* spellwork to do harm are futile. Please consider what this means."

"Flash your wicked ju-ju or triple your abject failure," Chief Gorsh said, shaking his head in disgust. "Either way, you're a damn poor substitute for a ghost."

They were close to Newman's trailer now. Chief Gorsh dragged Quill behind a half-erected fish taco stand. Two Corvallis redcaps clomped past and tossed mats on the electrical cables so people wouldn't trip. Mr. Newman either hadn't noticed or hadn't cared that the goblins he'd sent to Portland to secure permits and stir up buzz for the carnival hadn't been the same ones who'd returned.

Gorsh grabbed Quill's robes and spun him roughly around. When he spoke, his tone was reverent. "There it is. A device so terrible, the world will shiver in its booties. All shall behold the Ochre Calliope and wallow in unmitigated anguish!"

The Ochre Calliope stood on four large wagon wheels, and the shadow that spilled from it spread toward them, black as a tar pit. Quill made sure he kept well clear of the shadow, because for a moment he'd been sure it had been moving against the path of the sun. The steam whistles were ochre-colored, as was most of the framework, reminding Quill of baby food. Baby food that might've been sweet potato apricot or maybe vegetable turkey dinner, but either way, would taste cold and foul. Ornate scrollwork decorated the frame with spirals and whorls and complex patterns that resembled eyes. Sly eyes. Angry eyes. Slitted demon eyes. Eyes that watched him with a speculative malevolence that raised every hair on his arms. He knew, without the slightest doubt, that this steam organ's song would be a desolate thing. The haunting music of dying hope.

Chief Gorsh settled his red whip onto a hook on his belt and cracked his knuckles. He began to chant in goblin-tongue, flinging his arms around as if addressing an invisible crowd. The calliope began to pipe a minor key dirge-like rendition of "Stars and Stripes Forever."

Gooseflesh crawled across Quill's arms and up his neck.

"You got it to run?"

Chief Gorsh stopped his chant and leered. "Brought a cappie named Valco onto the crew. He's a goblin knacky enough with a wrench to torque the pipes of that infernal steam organ wide open. Now stop interrupting your betters, you pox-licking son of a mollusk."

Quill bit back an uncharitable reply. The grinding calliope music made his teeth hurt, as if he'd started chewing aluminum foil again, a habit he'd broken as a child. Between the constant insults and the creepy music, he really wished he'd hidden in his trailer and pretended to have food poisoning instead of answering the chief's summons.

Chief Gorsh nodded his head in time to the calliope and began to chant again. Three swirling patterns made of something viscous and translucent began to spin in the air nearby. Quill watched, dazed, as his arm stretched toward the churning substance, moving of its own accord. He couldn't tear his gaze away from the goo. It spun faster and faster, forming into two rough humanoid shapes and a round blob. His finger brushed the edge of the substance, and he jerked his hand back with a surprised hiss. The stuff was freezing cold.

"Ectoplasm," the chief grunted. "Colder than a polar bear's left testicle. Now watch and learn."

Low, anguished moans filled the air. The sound deepened, distorting, becoming inhuman and at the same time stronger, vibrating in the back of Quill's molars and in his kneecaps. The roiling ectoplasm slowed its spinning until it congealed into three shapes with vivid, horrifying detail.

The secret of existence is to have no fear. Quill struggled to follow that precept and failed.

Two ghosts and...a ghost fish floated silently over the asphalt, draining the heat from the air, sending a shiver wracking through his body. He wanted to back away, but it was if his boots had frozen to the pavement.

"Don't gnaw your bleeding little heart and piss yourself because I remade these phantoms into more suitable minions," Chief Gorsh snarled. "I am finally come into my own. Call this goblin *chief* no longer. I am a spiritmaster, ringmaster to the dead!"

A clown ghost floated bare inches from the ground to the chief's left. A flower sprouted from the faintly translucent top hat perched on the clown's head, writhing and trembling without any breeze. Luminous greasepaint covered the clown's face, giving off a sickly pale glow. Two black-iris eyes pondered Quill with eager malevolence. Its bright orange pupils smoldered like droplets of molten steel. Its too-wide mouth brimmed with darkness and bristled with nail-shaped teeth. The clown's shirt was spotted with washed-out polka dots, the huge floppy shoes on its feet appeared bleached to a bleary yellow, and its checkered suspenders were dull and faded. The ghost made no noise, but its unsettling gaze seemed sly and cruelly amused.

The other ghost resembled a carnival barker, with a shriveled-peach face and one gloved hand gripping a hooked cane. The barker's red and white striped jacket and red bow tie appeared faded, the colors drained away to near nothing. His round, banded straw hat was cocked to the side, and his eye sockets were the same black pits with orange sparks. The barker's mouth continually moved as if forming words in one non-stop chatter session, though with zero sound. Quill couldn't read lips, but he felt certain the barker was not discussing the Noble Eightfold Path.

"Are they not beautiful, you holier-than-thou pig-bleeder?" Chief Gorsh slapped Quill on the back so hard his cap almost flew off his head. "They represent a brighter, more hopeful time. A time when clowns made us laugh with madcap antics involving fire, cream pies, and tiny dogs. When barkers opened the eyes of the innocent and the rube-ish to games of chance, then *gave* us the chance to gawk at freaks of nature for a negligible fee. A golden age of circus festivities, grand entertainment unparalleled, and a dog and pony show of classic magnificence. An era of bootstrap-pulling and brash moxie, all to the smell of caramel, wet straw, animal shit, and frying doughboys. This is a day of revival. Witness the birth of the Grand Show Phantom Circus Magnifique!"

Quill had rarely heard the chief sound so impassioned. So nostalgic. So halfway coherent, and with half the rage. He hesitated before pointing to third ghost. "A…phantom sea squab?"

The ghostly pufferfish, fully inflated, drifted around them, a spiky balloon with vacant round eyes and a gently swishing tailfin. The puffer's body shone with the pale green luminescence of a glow-in-the-dark sticker. Its lips opened and closed as if sucking in non-existent water. It floated to the ghost clown and tried to land on the top hat, fascinated by the wobbling flower. The clown snapped at the inflatable fish with its nail-teeth. The puffer floated out of range and drifted in serene circles above the fish taco stand.

Gorsh hocked and spat into the taco stand's bin of plastic forks. "Thrice-damn worthless ghost of a Tetraodontidae. When a spiritmaster as powerful as myself travels beyond the Veil, he finds himself attracting all manner of restless beings, even the souls of departed marine life." He cracked his knuckles again. "Now where was I, you milk-drinking, pouch-slouching marsupial? Didn't I fopping warn you about derailing an evil monologue? Let's see. Ghost clowns. Animal shit. Doughboys. Golden Age. Ah, yes. The hour has come to place a powrie as master of the three rings."

Chief Gorsh turned on his heel and marched for the owner's

trailer. The clown and barker floated along behind him. The pufferfish drifted in the wind and ended up inside a popcorn maker, smearing ectoplasm along the glass and butter-dispenser before squirming free and bobbing in slow pursuit. Quill prayed for guidance as he hurried after Gorsh. He had to do what he could to stop the chief's explosion of enthusiasm from hurting anyone.

The chief tried kicking in the trailer door, but because it opened outward, he ended up leaving a boot print on the panel before rebounding backward off the metal steps. Quill helped him back to his feet.

"Did you see that?" Gorsh dusted himself off with dramatic slaps. "My massive codpiece got caught on the door. Threw me down with its titanic weight."

The two circus apparitions floated nearby, staring as if they harbored secret phantom fantasies of dining on goblin meat hors d'oeuvres.

"Chief—"

"That's *spiritmaster*, you pus-chugging son of a goat-nurse!"

"Spirit...Chief, um, do ghosts hunger?"

"Of course!" Gorsh grabbed the handle and yanked the door open. "They hunger to wreak bloody vengeance upon the living! But let's keep that a surprise." He motioned for the ghosts to stay, then stomped into Mr. Newman's office trailer. The barker continued his silent spiel. The clown started to juggle fiery purple balls. The pufferfish drifted through the air like an untethered balloon. Quill hesitated, but because fear was the enduring enemy of a thousand cold, grasping hands, he squared his shoulders and followed Gorsh into the trailer, mostly because he didn't want to be left alone with the ghosts.

Mr. Newman sat on the edge of his desk, grinning sharkishly at a middle-aged man who, from the look of his sharply pressed slacks, spotless dress shirt, and silk tie, appeared severely out of place at the carnival. The man gripped a clipboard and binder as if they were weapons he was considering using on Mr. Newman. Sweat beaded along his scalp at the edge of his thinning hair, and the lenses of his glasses flashed in the light from Mr. Newman's lamp. Neither of them threw more than a cursory glance toward Quill and the chief.

"There are no permits." The man shook his clipboard in accusation. "Not even a record of Funtastic Amusement Services *applying* for a permit this year. Furthermore, every ride and every food booth needs to pass inspection. You can't operate until the permits are approved and everything passes safety review."

"Two reasonable men like us can work through a bit of minor bureaucratic inconvenience." Mr. Newman's smile flashed wider. Their boss was a man who often bragged about working his way up from the ranks of rousties to the very top, and he still sported the callused hands and heavy shoulders to prove it. A steel ring choked his long brown hair into a ponytail that dangled halfway down his back. His eyes had the same flat, lusterless gaze as a dead bluefish, but someone who didn't know better might've believed the smile on his lips genuine.

"You don't seem to understand, Mr. Newman. I'm recommending this event be shut down and a hefty fine levied. You can appeal the fine, but this carnival *will* remain closed until all civil and OSHA complaints are addressed."

"Are you sure you don't want Blazers tickets?" Mr. Newman asked. "Primo seats. Or maybe a concert coming up at the Rose Garden? Name one. It's yours."

"You're not listening. This carnival will not open to the public until these issues are resolved."

"The gates open in three hours, buddy. I already have crowds lining up. A delay will cost thousands. That's a helluva handful of lost tax revenue your city will never see."

"This is a safety issue. I have a court order mandating the closure. If you don't comply, I'll have sheriff's officers enforce the order."

Mr. Newman wiped both hands down his face, stretching his heavy features into a mask of dismay. "I can't believe I'm hearing this. I sent an employee here over a week ago to pay the damn land use fees and taxes and *more* fees and get the damn permits. There's gotta be a mistake on OSHA's end." His gaze slid over to Gorsh, and he stabbed a finger at the chief. "Explain to Mr. Kaiser how this is all a misunderstanding and you got the permits locked down like I sent—what the *fuck* are you wearing?"

Gorsh straightened the lapels of his ringmaster outfit. "I'm here to unleash the Grand Show Phantom Circus Magnifique, a dazzling show of ghosts for the ages. Such a performance requires no permits or bureaucratic skullduggery and I piss on them."

"You didn't secure the permits? You rotten little bastard. What'd you do with my goddamn money?"

The safety inspector threw a wary glance their way. "You still can't operate until the permits are approved. You can't take in money. You can't allow people on the rides. This place stays closed."

Mr. Newman raised a hand to the inspector, giving him the *yeah-yeah* nod, and glared cold murder at Gorsh. "You're fired. You hear me, you demented Shriner wannabe? *Fired*!"

"Do you believe in ghosts?" Chief Gorsh toyed with the end of his whip and stared at the ceiling.

"You crazy little piker. Get out of my trailer and go sober up. Take that stupid-looking mini-monk with you. In fact, take all the those worthless powries and get out. You're all fired. Mistake hiring the rabid lot of you. Get! *Out*!"

Gorsh grinned. "First answer the thrice-damned question. Do you believe in ghosts?"

The safety inspector surprised Quill by answering first. "Ghosts are created by infrasound. The feelings of dread. Optical illusions due to resonant frequency. Your eyeball resonates and sends phantom images to your brain."

"I was hoping someone would say that," Chief Gorsh said. "C'mon, boys. I want you to meet the old boss, who sure as fairy turds ain't the same as the new boss."

The ghosts floated through the trailer wall and into the room. The clown still juggled. The barker spun his cane. The pufferfish circled the water cooler and made surprised fish faces at the tank.

The inspector dropped his clipboard and staggered against the wall, thrusting his binder out like a shield between him and the specters while making panting, gasping sounds. Mr. Newman darted forward and grabbed the chief by the front of his white ringmaster jacket. His biceps and forearms bulged as he hauled Gorsh clear of the ground. The chief's legs kicked madly as he struggled to break free.

"You think your third-rate illusions scare me, you miserable shit?" Mr. Newman said. "Since you won't leave nicely, I'll take repayment out of your check *and* your hide and bounce you myself." He hurled Gorsh at the metal file cabinet.

"Bollocks!" the chief screamed before he hit the file cabinet with a resounding *bong* and crashed to the floor.

The clown and barker glided closer. Quill glanced at them, unsettled to find the clown staring at him with eerie speculation in its disturbing, inhuman eyes. It flicked a black tongue over its vicious teeth. Black shadow-drool seeped over its lips and stained its white face. The ghost pufferfish floated over and landed on the clown's top hat. There was a brief squabble as the clown tried to catch it before the puffer again drifted serenely out of reach.

Yet the puffer's distraction gave Quill his chance. He jumped between the chief and his ex-boss, struggling to keep his face calm as Mr. Newman loomed over him like a Kodiak bear in no mood to dance. "Please stop," he said. "Violence will only injure you both."

"So far it's injuring mostly *me*, you squab-sucking noodlecock!" the chief bellowed from where he rolled on the floor, clutching his head.

Mr. Newman smirked at Quill, cracked his knuckles, and shrugged. "It's a chance I'm willing to take."

"I...I should really leave," the inspector said and edged toward the door. "Get you started on the appeal process. You're perfectly right. Reasonable men can work this out. I—I'll be calling you very soon—"

Chief Gorsh struggled to his feet, leaning against the file cabinet for support. He whispered to Quill, "Pull your knives, you peace-shabby bunghole!"

"I've never carried knives," Quill whispered back helplessly. Sweaty patches had dampened his armpits. *Show no fear. Show no fear.*

"No wonder your mother was always weeping." Gorsh unhooked his red whip and began to slide it through his hands. The whip coils made a snakelike hiss against his palms. "Never mind. The show goes on." He flicked a hand at the ghost barker and pointed at the inspector. "Don't let that one leave, but don't kill him just yet."

The barker floated over and put his wizened face inches away from the inspector, staring into the man's eyes as his mouth moved nonstop, forming silent words. The inspector pressed against the wall as far from the ghost as possible. He shivered and his teeth rattled with the clatter of shaken dice.

Mr. Newman advanced on Quill and Gorsh with his fists

bunched, ponytail swinging, and every footfall as loud as a cannon shot, vibrating up through Quill's boots.

"This attack is called Unleashing the Trouser Snake!" Chief Gorsh yelled. He cracked the whip and knocked over the water cooler. The blue jug rolled out of the base and began to spurt water onto the cheap carpet with a *glub, glub, glub*. Gorsh spit a curse. He gestured to get the clown's attention and pointed at Mr. Newman. "Make that man laugh until he screams."

The clown sailed forward eagerly, dropping the fiery balls it had juggled. They splattered to the ground and vanished, leaving the floor scorched. The clown's fingers blurred and twitched as they reached for Mr. Newman. Its eyes blazed ink black and neon orange, the unnatural pupils leaving snail trails of light shimming in the air behind it. Mr. Newman hesitated.

Quill tugged at the chief's sleeve. "Ghosts can't really hurt people."

"*Mine* can," Gorsh said.

Mr. Newman turned to run, but the ghost clown gave chase and brought him down behind the desk. What followed involved very little laughter and a good deal of screaming. The inspector huddled against the wall and sobbed. Quill's stomach did a slow, sickening somersault in his abdomen. His hands shook so hard that when he lifted them up to hide his face he ended up only staring at them in sick fascination, watching them tremble. He grimly fought off the urge to vomit.

"You look like you're about to blow donuts, you pebble-stoned pansy," Chief Gorsh screeched. A mad light gleamed in his eye. "This'll put evil hair on your gonads!"

But Quill, still trembling from cap to boots, knew this was it. This was the moment. His goblin chief could not be saved. Not by Quill at least. There was no hope of turning his fellow redcaps to the Eightfold Path, leading them to enlightenment through example and gentle exhortations. He should've known.

Truly the Buddha was right. *No one saves us but ourselves. No one can and no one may. We ourselves must walk the path.*

Too late to save Mr. Newman. He could only hope to prevent the same thing from happening to the inspector or to anyone else. Quill closed his eyes, smelling the reek of blood and terror in the air.

From this hour forward, he would walk another path.

CHAPTER SIX
The Call

Mercenary Wing Rv6-4 "Zero Dogs"
June 23rd

I chewed on a pen, my feet up on my desk, and stared out the window at the dark trees that sagged, limp and wilted, in the hot night air. Erik shifted in his seat, trying to find a comfortable position in my office amidst all the stacked boxes of files, piles of books balanced in erratic towers, and snow drifts of printed paper. A heaviness lingered in the air, gathering mass in the silence between us. Erik waited for me to tell him the bad news. I could read it on his face.

We'd trained for three days with Erik. His skills were impressive; he knew enough small unit tactics to keep pace, and he took orders better than most of my Zero Dogs. All the same, I'd been doing research on berserkers. What I'd read hadn't exactly quelled my concerns.

I pointed the teeth-marked pen at him. "Did you know that a berserker with the Snakkur mercs in Iceland went all rage-crazy and killed one of her teammates and seriously wounded two others?"

According to After Action Reports, they'd deployed to terminate a Gryla who'd been sighted in the mountains. Gryla were, as best I could tell, rare but hideous descendants of an anti-Santa Claus-style monster. They sported three heads, goat horns, overstretched earlobes, and a highly criminal proclivity for stuffing naughty children into sacks around Christmas time. The Snakkur had destroyed the Gryla, but a berserker named Svana who wielded a Viking sword in each hand had gone all battle frenzy and kept right on killing even after the intended target was dog food.

"I heard that once." He lowered his head, staring at his boots.

"You ever see the video with that berserker who attacked a drive thru when they couldn't get his order right? It went viral all over the Internet."

Erik nodded, frowning, still not meeting my gaze. My curiosity got the better of my discretion. "Why don't you look at me when I'm talking to you? I mean, I'm not your mother, so I won't put you in time out for it, but it bothers me."

He met my gaze. "I make people nervous when I look at them." He shook his head. "So I try to seem unthreatening. Better than the alternative."

The fear. He didn't like when people feared him. He didn't like this conversation, and maybe he didn't like me for forcing it. I sighed and leaned further back in my chair. I had a half dozen other instances of groups and armies that had experienced problems working with berserkers. I tossed the papers onto my desk, didn't want to read them anymore.

"You don't need to do that around me. I'm too stupid to be scared by anything." I tried out a smile, and a quick return smile flashed on Erik's face. Score one for the team.

"You did well today, training with the crew," I continued. "You take orders, and I appreciate that."

"Thank you, Captain."

In truth, he soldiered so effectively he'd shamed a few of

my mercs into working harder during the drills. We'd practiced mock assaults on our course behind the house. He watched his sectors, cleared corners, kept on mission, never bitched. If not for the battle rage mojo, I'd have hired him in an instant.

And then...Tiffany.

I'd assigned them different teams because they couldn't seem to exist in the same room without saturating the air with pheromones. After the drills, he'd offered her a drink from his water bottle, and though there were roughly three hundred unused, ice-cold water bottles in the cooler, she'd accepted. He'd watched her as she tilted her head back and drank deeply. I'd recognized that thirst in his eyes.

I chewed on the pen again, eyeing him. "What are your intentions toward Tiffany?"

His face flushed red. "I really like her. She's very..."

"Sexy? Tempting? Sensuous?"

"She's very quiet. She makes me feel quiet inside."

"That's different. Most men just want to screw her."

The flush in his face deepened, but for the first time he seemed angry. "I have noble intentions."

"You don't want to screw her? Because I smell bullshit."

"Captain. You're provoking me."

"That's right, I am. Deal with it. She's *my* friend. I care about her a helluva lot more than I'll ever care about you. And it looks to me like my friend is trending toward making a mistake with a man who goes all rage red and loses his mind as a superpower." I leaned toward him. "Do you think I'd feel right, letting something like that happen?"

He didn't answer.

"You roll in here uninvited, claiming that I have to bring you on board or I'll die. Well, I'll admit that's a bit of a kick in the ass. But I'm responsible for keeping my people safe, so I have no desire to bring a viper into the nursery. You a viper?"

Again, he didn't reply. I reached for the folder with all his background information. I'd paid a very pretty penny to have the info unearthed on such short notice. He had nothing in his records that was any worse than could be found in Sarge's or Mai's dossiers. Then again, Mai had once overthrown puppy mills in Lancaster County with a horde of alien battle dogs and led some type of farm-country canine revolution.

"No," Erik finally said, an instant before I spoke.

"No?" I'd forgotten what the question had been, imagining Mai, the Joan of Arc leading an army of rampaging puppies.

"I'm not a viper. I won't hurt anyone here. Never her."

"People say all kinds of things. Can you prove to me you'd never hurt any of my crew?"

"No. I can't. You'd have to trust me."

"If you hurt her..." I gritted my teeth, swallowed the emotion lodged like a stone in my throat. "If you did anything to her, I'd come after you. And I'm not very nice."

He nodded. We watched each other like lions over the carcass of an antelope. Here was the Erik that he kept hidden behind the quiet, deferential façade. This Erik was a warrior. Someone worthy of the axe he hauled around in a guitar case. Still...I was going to let him go. True, there was still the matter of the annoying death prophecy, but I intended to refuse any jobs that had anything to do with evil fae or anything vaguely circus related. That should keep my bacon from burning. Fucking Prophetic Doom avoided.

"Erik, I hate to do this, but I don't think I have a choice—"

The phone rang, cutting me off with a jangling blast that startled us both. I fixed the cordless handset with the same stink-eye I gave to live grenades and Rafe running nude with scissors. A telephone brought the bad news home and stabbed you in the ear with it.

Slowly, I lifted it off the base. For a moment the bright

supernova of hope flared inside me that it might be Jake again. Just as quickly, the hope caught flame and burned to ashes. Jake always called me on my cell phone, not the business line.

When I finally spoke into the receiver, my voice seemed to come from very far away, wavering in unstable radio signal shivers. "Zero Dog mercs. Captain Walker speaking."

"Andrea, this is Jim Houston. I have a mission for you. Hope you like carnivals."

My heart jumped off the turnbuckle of my interior wrestling ring and body-slammed my stomach. Jim was Oregon's new Special Crimes Interfacer for the northern half of the state, from Eugene up to Portland. Now here he was with a new job and all the proof I needed that the universe hated my guts.

"You still there?" Jim asked. "The connection drop or something?"

"Jim, the answer's no."

"Listen to you, busting my beans," he said. "Because if the answer really was no, there might be a few things like breach of contract to discuss and words like *you'll never work for this city again* to be bandied about. And that's just an ugly conversation."

Damn it. I lowered my head and rubbed my eyes. Dodging prophecy was like dodging bullets at close range. FPD.

"There are no redcaps involved, are there?" My voice didn't even tremble. Score one for the professional. "Because if there are, our prices just tripled."

"Always with the jokes, right? Good thing I appreciate it, because it seems the redcap threat wasn't as expunginated as we'd marked down in triplicate on those official forms. Seems our *unimportant* escapee happened to be a spiritmaster who joined up with some vicious Corvallis-bred goblins and a Buddhist. Yes, I said Buddhist. They took over one of those fly-by-night traveling carnivals at the fairgrounds by murdering the manager with — and this is according to preliminary information at the scene — ghost clowns. Then they took a hostage. The OSHA inspector who was there to safety-check the rides."

For a moment the room spun and I couldn't breathe. Instead of wrestling moves, now my heart pounded with the force of .357 recoil, as if I'd swallowed the gun and my appendix gleefully pulled the trigger.

A mission. Carnival. Ringmaster. Capped in crimson. Axe man. Ghost clowns.

Shit.

"Hostage rescue?" The smooth calm in my voice caught me by surprise. "You should call the FBI. They've got a premiere hostage rescue team. Or Delta Force. They'll do it. Hell, they'll do it and won't even talk about it afterwards. Those guys are good."

"The goblins are making demands," Jim continued. "They want the Zero Dogs and they'll let the hostage go. I know this isn't ideal — "

"Ideal? That's about as fucked up as oral sex with a shark. They'll control the grounds and all the choke points, waiting to chew us to pieces because we have to go in weapons tight due to hostages. The place could be rigged top to bottom with booby traps. They'll have every tactical edge. And it's a damn *carnival.*"

"Fine. The city will pay double your standard contract rate. And, the hostage they've got…Howard Kaiser, he's a good guy, Andrea. He has a family. Kids."

I might not be a saint, but I had a big time soft spot for innocent Joe and Jane Shmoes caught up in dangerous paranormal circumstances. I sucked in a deep breath, closed my eyes, and exhaled slowly. In the end, what choice did I have? Our contract with the city, which I desperately needed, was at risk. Far more importantly, a person's life was in danger. All because I'd allowed that crazy circus redcap to escape, trying to capture him when I should've just smoked him, and now he had a hard-on for vengeance.

"All right, dammit, we'll quick deploy. But the universe is gonna owe me big time."

"Anything you say, Andrea."

I could hear the relief in his voice, and that dampened my fires a bit. If the civilian authorities hadn't used SWAT or the FBI Hostage Rescue team it could only mean this would be a nasty slice of paranormal urban warfare. Jim and I sorted out the remaining details, and I returned the cordless phone to its electronic charger-womb with numb fingers. My hand trembled a little, clattering plastic on plastic. Had Erik noticed?

I turned to him, very aware of the cold dread in my chest, seeming to dig icy knives into my lungs. "I could really use a magical battleaxe right about now."

The eagerness on his face might've been amusing, if it hadn't been so fierce. "My axe blade was forged of magic and metal mined from a meteorite crater in ancient Mesopotamia and blessed by a high Sumerian priest, then, much later, counter-blessed by an Irish Cistercian monk from Greyabbey. The haft was cut from a hickory tree that sprouted in the lee-side shade of a rowan following a bitter winter. *Carthage* was the name bestowed upon the axe by the hero Merrick Lithe, who became the bane of unholy darkness and oppression. The weapon was once wielded against unclean spirits in '30s Chicago."

No one ever seemed to own a melee weapon without a name, and it was never a name like Fred the Sword or Helen the Holy Halberd. No, it had to be "Carnage Fang" or "Stormslice." I couldn't tell if Erik were making some kind of obscure joke about alcohol and ghosts and Prohibition there at the end of his little speech, because Mr. Straight-Face Berserker wasn't exactly standup comedian material.

Didn't matter, though. Not if that thing worked against ghosts. "Soooo, we're talkin' plus one, maybe plus two points against the undead?" I looked him in the eyes, very aware of the knot of dread yanked tighter in my guts. "You're hired."

He didn't smile at the news, but then again, neither did I.

CHAPTER SEVEN
All Hands

Mercenary Wing Rv6-4 "Zero Dogs"
The Zero Dog Compound

I slammed my hand down on the large Code Red Maximum Alert button I'd had installed after the last zombie attack. It was the new Defense Condition One signal for the Zero Dogs to suit up and grab the jockstraps and the guns. The alarm button clicked...but there was no accompanying Klaxon, air raid siren, or flashing red alarm lights. Instead, our PA system belched static, switched songs and started playing Jimmy Buffett.

I glanced at Erik and flashed my best grim, hardass stare, trying to look as if I'd meant for our DEFCON ONE alarm to sound like "Margarittaville."

His expression indicated he didn't buy it.

Not at all.

* * *

Sarge and I had the team assembled and loaded in vehicles and applying rubber to asphalt in less than fifteen minutes. Almost a new deployment record for us. We'd hauled along

DARK RIDE DOGS 107

every Ectoplasm Disrupting Round we had in stock, plenty of shooting iron, and every other ectenic force-effective tool we had. We were a bit low on EDRs, but we had enough to rock and roll.

Still, the entire time that I rushed around snapping out commands and squaring away loose ends, I couldn't shake the feeling that I'd committed to a horrible, irreversible mistake.

We rolled out from the compound in loose formation. The road allowed me too much time to think as we raced toward the carnival in our vehicle caravan. The longer I brooded over our current SNAFU, the deeper the unease sank its fangs into my mind.

Everything came back to those fucking cookies.

It was possible I'd been set up, the fortune cookies and their dire prophecies planted to manipulate me into taking a berserker onto our team with only a cursory background check and a couple of interviews. Perhaps Erik wasn't here to save my ass from some big time FPD after all. Perhaps he was an axe-slinging double agent assassin. I'd only have myself to blame if he painted his face with my blood while screaming a Valkyrie war cry.

Also, what was Mistress Patel's angle? I couldn't get my head around the game she played. Call me a cynical, paranoid bitch, but I didn't believe in altruism from total strangers, not something this abstract anyway. If she *was* on the level, and Erik was righteous, then at some point they'd want the debt repaid.

And what would they demand then?

Heavy thoughts for the road. Thankfully, traffic trickled at a minimum, and the herds of feral cyclists who plagued Portland had thinned with nightfall. We drove in loose formation. Soon we slipped past the gigantic inflatable purple octopus lounging on the roof of a barbershop as we headed for the narrow Sellwood Bridge leading across the river to the fairgrounds. My humiliation gauge usually redlined every time we rolled out in public these days. Maintaining a hardcore mercenary front while driving a minivan in a convoy of "technicals" was not for the timid. Technicals were civilian vehicles modified with weapons and armor, basically half-assed Mad-Maxed cars and trucks, with heavy emphasis on half-assed. We'd lost our Bradley Fighting Vehicle when a disgruntled necromancer had blown it into a million smoking shards. Desperate for wheels, I'd picked up our current rides at a bank repo auction.

I had the wheel of our minivan—a sun-faded Chevy Venture painted with an urban camo pattern. I glanced in my rearview mirror. Behind me sat Erik and Tiffany. I hadn't witnessed so many awkward and telling silences since reading that Amish romance novel. I'd almost ordered Tiffany to ride with Gavin and Rafe in one of the trucks. I still hadn't figured out why *this* guy? Mysterious stranger syndrome? A bad boy kick, romanticizing berserkerism? And if berserkerism wasn't a word, it damn well should be.

As usual, there seemed to be no good answers. Did I keep Tiffany where I could keep a protective eye on her, which meant close to Erik, because of the prophecy? Or did I split them up and risk having her start sneaking behind my back? Either way, I knew I couldn't win this war, and I had no time for these distractions anyway. My slog-through list was already too long. Shit to kick, people to rescue, money to make, and a grim fate to dodge. Cupid could kiss my ass.

The only other person in the minivan was Sarge. He sat in the very back, the demon on the mounted .50 caliber M2 machine gun, riding strapped into the leather executive chair sans wheelbase that we'd bolted to the floor, creating our favorite hillbilly weapon platform. Sarge hadn't said anything since we'd left, that wasn't his way, but once I'd noticed him watching Erik with a hard, measuring stare.

The rest of the Zero Dog caravan was not much better than our road warrior minivan. Gavin drove a beat-to-shit '70s era Ford truck, indifferently spotted in primer and brown paint. He always rode point in the column because he claimed he had a flawless GPS system lodged inside his head. He certainly had something lodged somewhere. The truck had a Mk 19 grenade launcher mounted on a swivel stand on the bed with Rafe at the trigger, and huge speakers attached to the roof and sides of the cab. Part of Gavin's psy-war attack: blast music during full frontal somewhat-mechanized assault to demoralize and confuse the enemy. Exactly like a white trash version of the *Apocalypse Now* helicopter attack.

Stefan drove the newest of the vehicles I'd picked up, a long bed Silverado truck that guzzled fuel with more gusto than a tornado making love to a trailer park. Mai was on the M203 ARC gun in the back, a happy little weapon that shot lightning bolts. The truck bed seethed with her army of alien quail. Those alien quail appeared ready to quick deploy and peck through steel or crap corrosive bird shit or whatever it was quail-shaped monsters were good for.

Last in the convoy came Hanzo, our medic, riding on a Vespa. I hadn't wanted to bring the damn Vespa. One couldn't maintain a shred of dignity when one charged into battle on a scooter. Even though our Vespa had smoke grenade launchers, a paint job of flames and shark's eyes and teeth, a 250cc engine modified for nitro and a M249 SAW awkwardly mounted on the handlebars, it didn't matter.

Scooters got no respect.

But Mai had seen the scooter at the auction and had exclaimed over its inherent cuteness, so Hanzo had bought it with his own savings. Our banner streamed from the back of the scooter above his med kit. People in traffic gaped, pointed and laughed at our hillbilly armor. I kept my eyes locked on the road and concentrated on keeping formation as we crossed the Willamette River. The carnival grounds were close now, and my embarrassment had nearly reached its end.

Then Gavin turned on the music.

A song about piña coladas and being ambushed by rain blared from the external speakers. Rafe started to dance in the back of the truck, barely hanging on to the mounted grenade launcher and madly shaking everything he had to the rhythm. The sight of Rafe dancing brought back the horrifying memories of Jazzerbo I thought I'd repressed.

We slowed some as we approached the police barricades. As carnivals went, this one sure as hell wasn't the Portland Rose Festival. This was a cheap, slap-dash funfair carnival, sprouting like a weed on an empty asphalt lot and gone again just as quickly. Even the chain link fence bordering the lot had wheels and could be disassembled into sections and loaded on a truck. Darkness drowned the entire collection of rides and booths in varying depths of shadow tide. That darkness added an air of haunted, brooding menace to the place, all the more disturbing when layered over the primary colors, pennants, and crudely painted artwork marring the funhouse and game booths.

No bright flashing lights. No riot and noise of a carnival in full swing. I suddenly appreciated how the lights and loud music helped conceal the creepy, joyless, furtive decrepitude of an empty carnival. Lights, music, and *lots* of beer in red cups.

The police had the carnival's perimeter locked down. Cruisers with flashing lights blocked the only access road, but the officer waved us through after I told him our business and he radioed his superiors. He seemed rather unimpressed by us. I tried not to hold his lack of faith against him.

We rolled past more barricades and swung around the cluster of news vans from every local channel and from CNN and Fox. The speakers on Gavin's truck now blasted the song

"Stray Cat Strut." One Fox cameraman filmed Rafe pole dancing with the grenade launcher mount as we drove past. Could I get an ad for a replacement werewolf up on one of those job sites by next Monday? It'd be close.

Portable flood lamps blazed away along the police perimeter, throwing back the darkness with stark white floodlight. A slew of fire trucks were positioned on stand-by, thanks to the impending arrival of yours truly. Three ambulances. Dark sedans with state government plates. The fire marshal's truck. A bunch of vehicles from Portland General Electric. Noise and chaos and heavily armed cops everywhere. My kind of scene. Looked as if we were fashionably late for the party.

Our convoy parked near the SWAT team van. SWAT didn't like us, but we knew them, had even bought each other cases of beer on occasion. We were comfortable working with them, even if SWAT believed they ranked a thousand times higher than a bunch of mercenary freebooter scum.

I climbed out of the minivan, stretching my legs and ignoring the snickers and insults about our wheels. Sarge unbuckled from the gunner position and walked up beside me. By some unspoken psychic agreement we both turned to stare at the haunted carnival.

"Why can't it ever be a haunted hot spring?" I muttered. "Or maybe we could assault a bakery for once. Fresh, warm bread. Pies. Cinnamon rolls. Soft pretzels. *Pies.*"

Sarge grunted. "And miss the funhouse? You know that place will give us grief."

"Bring the explosives and RPGs. I'll start the fires. We'll blast the funhouse to smithereens, never set foot inside."

"Hostage, remember?"

"Dammit."

Sarge grinned and headed off to assemble the Zero Dogs,

but I lingered for a moment more, finding the silent carnival more disquieting the longer I stared at it. The jumbled words of Erik's prophecies chased themselves through my mind.

Beyond the bright white ring of floodlights, the booths and rides crouched in black gloom, waiting. I scanned for targets, but saw nothing move. The shadows transformed the Tilt-a-Whirl into a slanted mass of hard angles and pooling darkness. The unlit Ferris Wheel loomed high overhead, brooding over the center of the tents and rides, struts and cars cutting blacker shapes against the low clouds. Anything could be hiding in those buckets, and with our luck it'd be a nasty surprise. Flesh-eating thaumaturgical gastropod mollusks had my vote. Cables snaked across the ground, covered here and there with mats. A carousel hunkered near the funhouse, the horses, unicorns, and wolves frozen in mid-stride, all watched over by a gigantic leering clown-face of dingy white greasepaint and mad cartoon eyes. A large sign arched over the main entrance—which was nothing more than the gap between the eight-foot chain-link fence encircling the lot and the ticket booth. The sign showed the disembodied head of another laughing clown as it peeked over fat, multi-colored balloon letters proclaiming: "Funtastic Carnival!"

"I'll say this is certainly *fun*-fucking-tastic," Gavin said from behind me. I flinched in surprise and cursed. He lifted his hands in a placating gesture, raising his eyebrows. "Didn't mean to scare you, Captain. Don't burn me."

"Then don't tempt me." I turned my attention back to assessing assault vectors and possible ambush sites inside the carnival. "And who the hell is scared? I'm pissed Jake's not here to win me a huge teddy bear on the midway. Besides, you talk too loud, you know that? Disrupting my highly focused concentration at a critical moment of command-tactical decision making."

"Yeah. It's okay to be afraid, Captain. SWAT guy over there says the place is crawling with psycho ghosts and killer goblins. How many you think are in there? Two, three thousand?"

I shook my head, scowling. I hadn't been briefed yet, so I had no idea. For all I knew, we might face a hidden army once we passed the fence.

Gavin scratched his chin as he stared at the rides. "I say a couple hundred at the very least. Carnies make me nervous. Ghost carnies can only be worse. And carnivals...creepy as fuck. That's all atmosphere right there."

"What's wrong with you, Gavin? Fall off the merry-go-round when you were a wee lad? Did a sad clown steal your cotton candy?"

"Fuck clowns. I never went to these places—carnivals and circuses and fairs. I went to Disneyland. Good Americans go to Disneyland. It's a patriotic duty, like registering with selective service. Mouse ears all the way, *oorah*!"

"Time for you to confront your fears." I grinned and slapped him on the back. "That's why I'm sending you in there on a scouting mission. Alone. Good luck, merc. Try not to die." I strode off to check on the rest of the Zero Dogs, ignoring Gavin's curses. I wanted to make certain the crew would be okay if I left them alone for fifteen minutes so I could find the command center and learn the current situation report. The Zero Dogs were like toddlers in a way. Dangerous, foul-mouthed, smartass toddlers armed to the teeth, some of them armed *with* teeth, and non-stop trouble all around.

A wonder I didn't have an ulcer.

My mercs were seeing to their gear, checking weapons, adjusting armor, combing Brylcreem into their hair—or at least that was what vampire Stefan was doing in between inspecting his fangs in the truck's side mirror. Rafe had shifted into werewolf form. He crouched, muscular, dark gray, menacing, on the hood of the truck, his claws *screeling* on the metal when he moved, an arresting image silhouetted against a police spotlight. Some foreign tourists were taking pictures of him with digital cameras while he stared menacingly off toward the dark carnival and occasionally growled for effect. If I didn't get Rafe something better to do and quick, he'd end up howling for them. The civvies adored werewolf howling. The kids always howled along.

Tiffany stood next to Berserker Erik, watching as he undid the clasps on his guitar case and withdrew his battleaxe. The blade and spike had been powder coated or enameled with crimson at some point, and had jagged, slashing glyphs etched in the steel. I frowned as she cooed over it, and then both of them blushed furiously, all awkward glances and restless silences. Had I been that pathetic with Jake in the beginning? Definitely not, because even in love I was a kick-ass, eat-pins-and-shit-out-paperclips hardcore mercenary. And even if I *had* been that pathetic, being said style of kick-ass mercenary meant no one would dare bring it up again.

Mai busied herself marching her alien quail around in formation. The quail moved with admirable military precision, although occasionally they would shiver and utter unnerving whirring sounds. Sarge, now cradling the ARC lightning rifle detached from the truck's gun mount, headed toward me. His eyes glowed an eerie red in the darkness, and his face appeared relentlessly grim, even for a demon. Not a good sign.

"Problems," he grumbled.

"Already? We just got here."

"The police commissioner. He wants SWAT to go in and clean this up, not us. Said we'd already fumbled the ball at the motel."

Commissioner Hagel. Nice. He wasn't exactly one of my biggest fans, and I bristled at the comment. "Nobody bothered to mention to us that the weird ringmaster was a damn portal jumper. How was I supposed to guess he'd dodge through the employee entrance to the Twilight Zone?"

Sarge only grunted.

The beginnings of a headache twinged in my temples. Although, bright side: if we packed up and headed home there was no way the prophecy could come true...was there? This was the perfect out.

"I'll go sort this shit out," I told Sarge, starting to feel better than I had since I'd answered that damn phone call. "Make sure the teams are good to go, just in case."

He nodded, and I stomped off to find the command center to find out exactly what the hell was going down. Hopefully I'd find myself back at home sweet home in an hour, sipping a cocktail and sending my recently hired berserker back to Minnesota to tell that seer to shove her visions up her oracle.

CHAPTER EIGHT
Clowns and Command Decisions

Mercenary Wing Rv6-4 "Zero Dogs"
Fairgrounds

I joined the usual suspects around a folding table near another SWAT tac van. Portable light stands running on generators blazed away, throwing down harsh white light that simultaneously faded shadows to almost nothing and multiplied them like crazy. Three men huddled over the table, staring at papers and photos and maps while radios filled the air with squawking police chatter. A fourth man stood off to the side, holding coffee in a paper cup and staring at the dark carnival.

"Gentlemen," I said, "what's the sit-rep?"

Police Commissioner Hagel was burly, balding, and wore his full dress parade uniform for some reason I couldn't fathom. The medals and stripes glinted in the flood lamps when he moved. His mustache bristled with disapproval, as threatening as a pissed off porcupine.

"Fill her in, Lieutenant," Hagel said and petted his facial hair. "She might as well know what she's missing."

Lieutenant Ken Stone was SWAT leader. We knew each other in passing from other engagements, most recently our assault on the motel. He hated my guts, but was professional about it. I tried not to rub it in when we were sent to mop up a monster-swarming mess instead of SWAT. He refrained from reveling in the fact that the city only used us because we were both expendable and independently licensed and bonded, which meant if we died in the line of duty the city wouldn't have to pay our heirs a cent.

Stone pointed to a street map, but the third guy — decorated in all corporate-robot stylings: impeccable suit, clean shaven, short hair, and clutching an iPad — cleared his throat and interrupted.

"Commissioner, I thought it was agreed. Third party contractors would handle this and save the city from exposure to extensive liability."

Great. Another suited bastard who wanted our umbrella organization, the Hellfrost Group, to take the hit if we left the place a smoking crater. I tried not to glare. "Who are you?"

"Ted Clark of Solidarity Mutual United, insurance and underwriters. We represent the interests of Funtastic Amusement Services."

Lieutenant Stone cut a contemptuous glance at the guy, but spoke to the Commissioner. "We're good to go on this, sir. Already deployed, ready to roll. We'll keep the place in one piece."

"Jim Houston sent us down here to clean this mess up," I said carefully. "But I hear you tasked SWAT instead. True?"

Hagel's mustache prickled when he scowled, making me wonder if that monstrous 'stache fed off the food he shoveled toward his mouth like some furry mutant version of a remora fish. "That's right, Captain Walker. Is that a problem?"

A problem? A problem that I was going to do an end run around the Fucking Prophetic Doom and win by bravely sitting on my ass and letting someone else tackle the dangerous job?

"No problems here. I'm still charging the city by the hour for showing up, though."

Commissioner Hagel grunted and eyed me with the revulsion of a man who'd noticed a sea cucumber forging a slime trail across his Baked Alaska. I disliked him just as much, so that made us even.

The fourth man who'd been standing off to the side watching the carnival turned toward us. I recognized Detective Miller. Not a bad guy, worked Robbery-Homicide. Good-looking, dark blond hair, in his thirties, with hard lines around his mouth and deep crow's feet at the eyes. A victim of the cop squint—the hard, narrow-eyed stare. He wore a surprisingly decent suit that had no wrinkles and fit him well. His tie even matched. Score one for fashion and Robbery/Homicide glamour.

Miller saluted me with his coffee cup. "Captain Walker."

"Detective. How's the dead body business? Slow, I hope."

"Never slow enough, especially with you guys around. You plan to leave me someone alive to arrest this time?"

"Looks like I'm warming the bench on this one. Talk to Stone."

Miller only smirked, as if he knew something I didn't. That smirk made me nervous.

The insurance guy cleared his throat. "Excuse me for interrupting again, but I have word from a certain...let's say, an important government official...indicating it would be preferred if the Hellfrost contractors were used in place of conventional civilian authorities."

My stomach plunged into freefall. Who was so damn gung ho to have a bunch of expensive mercenaries go in and why?

Commissioner Hagel frowned. "That means jack shit on a cream cheese bagel to me, Tom."

"*Ted.*" He gave a quick, nervous smile and fiddled with his tablet computer. "They are independently licensed and bonded with their own liability concerns. I really think you should consider the request carefully. An election year fast approaches."

Lieutenant Stone clenched his fists as if he entertained visions of making Insurance Guy swallow his own teeth. Commissioner Hagel, a political mammal to the core, hesitated, eyeing the man warily. "I want authorization. I'm not being left to hang by the balls for this."

"A moment, please." Insurance Guy pulled out a smartphone and turned away from us, rapidly tapping the touch screen. My philosophy was simple. Never trust a guy with too many high-end electronic gadgets on his person.

Detective Miller returned to staring at the carnival, while Lieutenant Stone tossed me a look I couldn't read. I shrugged, playing it nonchalant, but my pulse boomed in my ears. The cold trail of a sweat droplet carved a river down my back. No escaping that damn prophecy after all.

Insurance Guy talked for a bit, then handed his smartphone to the commissioner. Hagel took the phone and wiped it on his sleeve before putting it to his ear. "Who is this?"

He listened and his face paled. He walked a distance away so we couldn't overhear, which left us dangling in an intensely awkward silence.

"So how about those Blazers?" My voice sounded brittle and too loud. No one answered. A long moment later, the Commissioner stomped back over to us. I watched his mustache for signs of mentally unhinged twitching.

"The Zero Dogs are lead on this," the commissioner growled at Lieutenant Stone. Stone wore the expression of a man who'd spontaneously shit kittens, but he managed keep his silence professional. Detective Miller didn't react, standing there sipping his coffee and watching the empty rides.

I clenched my teeth as a cold snake of dread writhed in my guts, thrashing and twisting. There were few things I hated more than my own fear. I wanted to incinerate it, wanted to watch it burn as it screeched and flailed. I took a deep, steadying breath and forced myself to remember two things. First off, fortune cookie number nine said I'd die, but a hope fast approached. That hope, according to a certain oracle in the Midwest known for writing terrifying books of prophecy, turned out to be a berserker who carried a war axe in a guitar case. Second, there was a man's life on the line. I wasn't about to let those psycho redcaps murder another innocent person to keep their hats soggy.

"This comes from the top," Hagel continued. "No municipal assets are to be risked unless the Zeroes screw the pooch."

"All this faith makes an adorable little soldier of fortune like me feel all tingly inside," I said. "So here we are, right back to square one. I need a detailed rundown on the situation. Tactical deployments. Status, et cetera."

To his credit, Lieutenant Stone didn't let his disappointment in being pulled off lead interfere with supporting the mission, although it gave him yet another reason not to love me.

"No new developments in over an hour and fifteen minutes." Stone glared down at a satellite photo of the empty lot. "We don't have good look-down images of the carnival's layout. It appeared too recently. No sign of hostiles moving around the perimeter so far, but the interior areas are full of ghosts and goblins."

As a team, we weren't a hundred percent weapons effective on ghosts, so I'd have to be careful. Pyromancy could incinerate ectoplasm, but fangs and claws would be useless. Sarge's ARC rifle would work, and we'd brought all of our "ghost killer" Ectoplasm Disrupting Rounds, so it would be all guns and magic this time out.

Stone gave me a grim smile as he continued. "The limited intel we have suggests the redcap you failed to kill or capture at the motel is a spiritmaster."

I nodded. That explained the portal through the Veil and the specter infestation. "What do we have on him?"

"Not much. Goes by—lemme see..." Stone scanned his notes. "Spiritmaster Gorsh the Exalted Ringmaster of the Grand Show Phantom Circus Magnifique. Yeah, with capital letters. Our negotiator talked with him on the phone and gave us a rundown. Standard MO for these types. The guy's sixty-three ounces short of a Jumbo Soda, dresses like a circus ringmaster, summons and shapes ghosts, and wears women's underwear."

"You're telling me the flavor of a suspect's undergarments is priority intel for SWAT guys?"

"Just playing the probability game. These megalomaniacal freakbags are all weirdos to the core."

I decided to leave that conversation alone. "Location on the hostage?"

"Unknown."

"Sniper teams?"

"Team one is located on the roof of that skating rink beyond the fence. Sniper team two is on top of the van, so he doesn't have great elevation. We're hurting for good vantage points. No other tall buildings close by."

I stared at the largest structure around. "If the hostiles have someone on top of that Ferris Wheel they can spy everything we're doing. How are the assault teams deployed?"

"Near the entrance and behind the carnival, ready to make a move. We have the area surrounded and sealed off. Until now, Portland SERT was the primary element, ready to go. Gresham SWAT units as back up, to our northwest, near the river."

SERT stood for Special Emergency Response Team—the

standard SWAT team operators. "Good. Any demands yet?"

"Nothing sane."

"Feel free to elaborate, Lieutenant Stone." I tried to keep the annoyance out of my voice and failed.

"First the negotiator made contact with a suspect called 'Quill,' who rambled about the harmful effects of violence and hatred and pleaded for a peaceful resolution, at which point the suspect identifying himself as Spiritmaster Gorsh, *et cetera, et cetera,* took over the phone call. He demanded we leave the area or they'd ice the hostage. When we didn't comply, he demanded we send them the people responsible for something he called the Great Motel Slaughter or he'd unleash the Ochre Calliope or some such bullshit. Yeah, capital letters on those words too. Gorsh then ranted about a succubus he apparently has a hard-on for. And look at that, here you are. Propagators of the Great Motel Slaughter."

Nice. This Gorsh was still revved over Tiffany's charm spell and now he wanted vendetta hour. Nothing spiced up my life more than a good old-fashioned blood feud with a bunch of deranged, knee-high monsters.

Commissioner Hagel petted his mustache. "Whole thing's highly irregular. According to the employees, the carnival company was legit, just another run-of-the-mill funfair show. The goblins apparently worked for the owner, a guy named Newman. According to Quill, Newman was murdered by clowns. The homicide is the primary reason Detective Miller's haunting us."

Miller didn't turn, didn't reply. His reticence was making me nervous.

"Near as we can tell," Lieutenant Stone continued, "they killed the owner and took an OSHA inspector hostage some time this afternoon. At approximately six-thirty p.m., the OSHA office contacted 911 Emergency because their inspector had never returned and couldn't be reached. A unit was sent out to investigate. The redcaps must've seen the cruiser and panicked. They powered down all the rides, killed the lights. A whole heap of ghosts appeared, chasing people around, cranking the havoc knob to eleven."

"Casualties?"

"Most people ran. Some injuries. Broken bones. Bruises and abrasions. A few people transported to emergency rooms. No deaths. Aside from the owner, that is."

"Thank God. But only one confirmed hostage?" I cast my thoughts back to the call with our liaison. "The OSHA inspector. Howard Kaiser. No others?" More hostages meant more bargaining power. If the powries were only interested in keeping their caps soaked in blood, a single unfortunate government employee wouldn't last for long.

"He's the only hostage confirmed. According to Kaiser's boss, the owner didn't get his paperwork in proper order before opening for business, and the rides weren't inspected prior to operation." Stone scowled at the insurance guy. "Kaiser threatened to shut the place down."

"At this point, we don't know details," Insurance Guy said quickly. "So perhaps we should refrain from speculation on irrelevant and non-established issues. Captain Walker, I implore you to do as little damage to structures, stages, rides, and stands as possible. There's a significant monetary value attached to this policy."

His disregard of the hostage in favor of a bunch of equipment only made me want to light everything afire out of sheer spite. "Obviously you haven't heard of the Zero Dogs. We're an act of God waiting to happen. We're the destruction equivalent of a hurricane full of rabid wolverines or an earthquake in a nitroglycerin factory. I could go on, but I'll spare you the dirty details such as cost and collateral damage."

The man kept his tablet computer between us like a high-tech shield. "On the contrary, I *have* heard of you. You are quite…well, notorious, is such a strong word."

A savage grin spread across my face. "I'm on to your little scheme. Your *warning* is just mandatory hot air. If we rip up your little carnival, per standard Zero Dog operating procedure, you'll sue Hellfrost to cover your liability for all the people hurt by the ghosts and goblins. Goblins that Funtastic employed. That how it goes, Todd?"

"*Ted.* And I'm not authorized to speak about potential legal action, even in a hypothetical sense. But I'd say rescuing that hostage is the most important thing, wouldn't you?" He gave me a sickly smile.

"I know my job, buddy. So go fondle your fortuity principles and finite risk calculations and shut the fuck up in the presence of professionals."

Using the hostage as a pawn to manipulate me into charging in all gung ho? This guy was total pond slime. No matter my anger or disgust, I'd still go and my people with me. A man was in danger. I'd prosecute this mission no matter who'd been on the phone to change the commissioner's mind for whatever nefarious reason. Never mind that I'd caught a nasty case of Fucking Prophetic Doom that dangled over my head like the sword of Damocles. Some things were simply worth the risk. Saving people was at the top of the list.

I turned back to Lieutenant Stone, who was smirking, and Commissioner Hagel, whose face had folded into the stern disapproval of an origami nun. Detective Miller remained quiet, but now he was watching me instead of the distant carnival. I guess I put on a better show.

"So in conclusion, business as usual," I said. "We blaze in hot, save the civvie, apply the boot to enemy backsides, and roll out for home. Anything else I should know?"

Hagel blew a gust of air through his aggressive facial hair. "We have the recording of the call between the hostage negotiator and the suspect identifying himself as Spiritmaster Gorsh. According to triangulation from the cell towers, it came from one of the trailer rides. The funhouse."

The funhouse. Because *of course* it had to be the damn funhouse.

"Lieutenant, play the call for her. She should know what she's up against."

Stone pulled out a digital recording device and pushed play. A raspy, guttural voice growled from the speaker. "We who have wandered, dust storms blowing across these states, now face your thrice-damned and ever-endless regulations, your limitless persecutions, and your everlasting petty tyrannies. That some nameless bureaucrat hagfish, a supposed servant of the people, that one so *insignificant* can bring a halt to the music of the calliope, stop the horses upon the carousel, grind to an end the eternal spin of the Ferris Wheel…that, *that* is a tragedy born of a hundred thousand miseries."

The hostage negotiator's voice came back online, gruff and all business. "Is Howard Kaiser alive? Does he need medical attention?"

A long silence, then the gravel-flecked voice spoke again. "Listen to my voice. The voice of a spiritmaster is the sound of wind through overturned tombstones, a broken oboe playing a catchy dirge. Yes, you liver-lipped babbler, yes, the government lackey still breathes. He's watched over by my spirits, my entourage of the *circus de mystique*, and they entertain him with shows of ages past. Why do you care, you testicle-deficient mealy bag? He's only good for keeping a few caps wet."

"We need to be certain Mr. Kaiser is okay. Will you put him on the line?"

"Don't distract me with trifles when I have greater things to teach. Tell me, where have the true fairs, the unadulterated sideshows, the burlesque, the carnivals of yore gone? They've vanished. The foreign oil despots have sucked our heartblood dry for the price of a drop of fuel. The insurance parasites have festered within our guts, leeching our nutrition until we starve. The bleeding hearts have turned aside and closed down the bearded lady, the freaks and sideshow attractions, shaming us for our curiosities, declaiming our honest urges and desires to see — "

"You weren't kidding," I interrupted. "What a fucking wingnut."

Stone grunted. The commissioner rubbed a hand across his lips, and his mustache made the sound of a street sweeper brushing against a curb. The Insurance Guy rocked on his heels, smiling a smile I couldn't decipher. But Miller...Miller said more nothing.

" — gone the days when a funfair could command the attention of a town or a city, now lost in the digital blizzards of the Internet and its ubiquitous degradations, misspellings, Viagra peddling, and constant, unending, omnipresent *bickering*."

The negotiator cut in. "We're prepared to do whatever you want to secure the release of Mr. Kaiser. You're in control here. Tell me what you need."

"Need, you leaky little blood bag? *Need*? Can you bring back the golden age, when a roller coaster could draw the worship of thousands? My spirits, my specters, my *ghosts*, are formed from the distant ages of grand circuses past. Clowns, acrobats, jugglers, fire eaters, and trapeze artists, proud performers all. Damn your eyes with iron. Can you return them their respect? What are your words, that I should listen?"

The negotiator: "Ah...so what should I call you?"

"Name me Spiritmaster Extraordinaire, Ringmaster of

Desolation and be done." Grating goblin laughter followed, scoring at least an eight point five on the batshit crazy scale. "Or, if you aren't done, call me Spiritmaster Gorsh the Exalted Ringmaster of the Grand Show Phantom Circus Magnifique. All caps."

"See?" Lieutenant Stone threw me a look.

The negotiator pressed on. "Um. How about something shorter?"

"Your modern attention span tells again, human. If you dare enter, this carnival will be a place of despair and horror for an age."

"As if they weren't already," I quipped. Nobody laughed. As usual I was surrounded by killjoys and the humor-impaired.

The negotiator: "We'd like to send in some EMTs to examine Mr. Kaiser—"

"Your wishes mean less than nothing. Attack, if you dare. Send in your mercenary puppies so we might apply the rolled newspaper of vengeance to their backsides. Send the succubus goddess so that I might teach her the true meaning of carny carnal caramel. We've already wet our caps in the blood of our ex-boss. Charge to your doom, chattering lemmings. All shall stand in the never-ending queue, the eternal line, the wait infinitum."

Lieutenant Stone turned off the digital recorder. "He goes on like that for a long time. Verbal masturbation. That puppy comment made me smile, though."

"There's a chance he's just screwing with us," I warned, looking up at the low dark clouds as I mulled it over. "That his head is really locked on tight and he's running that babbling bullshit to throw us off. Provoke us into underestimating him. Because, honestly, who the hell talks like that?"

"He's a madman," Commissioner Hagel said. "Clearly deranged. That was the last direct contact we had with him.

After he terminated the call, one of the redcaps tossed a teddy bear prize over the ticket booth." He pointed to a nearby police cruiser. A large pink bear lay on the hood, covered in splashes of red, like a casualty from a toy box war.

"Is that blood?"

"Cherry syrup. We found a note pinned to the bear's chest with a knife." He handed me a wrinkled and hacked piece of lined paper. Words had been slashed across one side with sparkling red glitter Magic Marker, probably stolen from some vendor stall.

"*Send us the mercenary dogs and their bitch leader or the human will be used to wet our caps in blood.*"

I handed back the note. "Glitter makes everything more ominous."

"Those demands are the only reason Jim Houston called your sorry asses," Lieutenant Stone said. "Think you can manage to finish the job this time around, Walker?"

"Zero Dogs eat this stuff for breakfast. We never leave a job unfinished."

Except for that sasquatch hunt in Happy Camp, California. Oh, and that haunted Nevada brothel infested with inter-dimensional Peeping Toms also known as shadow people. And maybe one mission in the ruins of Nothing, Arizona, that decaying ghost town on route 93 consisting of collapsing buildings and a bunch of severed mannequin heads which dangled from a billboard and wore strange hats. I couldn't remember that desert mission without a shudder of revulsion. But other than those, we ran about a hundred percent completion rate.

"Yeah," Stone said. "Just make sure you save that hostage before burning the place down."

"Ah," Insurance Guy said. "That leads me to another important stipulation. You cannot use fire in any way, shape, form, or manifestation. For safety and insurance reasons, of course. Attacking with flames presents an unacceptable risk to our insured assets. All policies will be null and void if fire is used, and the Zero Dogs assume all liability."

"No fire," I lied, straight-faced. As if I'd ever pull one of our best cards out of our hand before we even played the game. "But if the *bad guys* should happen to light things on fire, or something should, say, spontaneously combust, I want it on the record that we weren't responsible."

The insurance guy opened his mouth to protest, but I gave my most charming smile, a double thumbs up, spun on my heel, and started back toward my troops.

Detective Miller called after me. "Take some prisoners this time, Captain Walker. I like to make arrests."

I mock saluted without turning around. All I could think of was Fucking Prophetic Doom all the way, and now some asshole didn't want me to use fire.

CHAPTER NINE
Behind the Lines

Quill brought the can of soda to where their hostage, a rather nice man named Howard, had been bound with hundreds of feet of duct tape and tossed inside the seat of an out-of-service roller coaster car. He'd been hidden in the maintenance section of the carnival funhouse, inside the back service area the public never entered. The sight of the OSHA inspector mummified in all that gray tape made Quill's soul grieve. It wasn't right to hold another being captive against his or her will, and removing all that tape was going to sting something wicked.

"Are you thirsty?" Quill lifted the soda can so the man could see it.

Howard only stared at him with fear easily readable on his face and in his too-wide eyes. He looked to be in his thirties or forties, with some gray in his hair, and his glasses duct-taped askew on his face. Sweat ran down his forehead and cheeks, and beaded where he wasn't bound with tape.

Quill hesitated, wondering if peeling off the tape over his mouth quickly would hurt more than pulling it off slowly. At least it would be over fast. He reached out and ripped it off with one quick jerk.

"Ow!" The man grimaced and licked his lips. Then he spat,

probably because of the glue residue.

"I'm sorry. Are you thirsty? I have soda. Would you prefer diet or regular?"

"This some trick?"

"I won't trick you. You have my promise."

"Why...why are you being nice?"

"Because it's the right thing." Quill lifted the can again and tried a warm smile, but Howard paled and looked away. Perhaps a redcap smile wasn't as nonthreatening as he'd hoped. A helpless feeling washed through him, followed by a surge of hate for his bloody red cap. He closed his eyes and inhaled deeply, struggling to find inner calm again.

"What are you going to do with me?"

Quill lowered himself next to the roller coaster car, settling into the lotus position where the man could still see him. "This place," he swept a hand around, "it teems with negative karma, fruit developed by unenlightened creatures. Action and result—*karmaphala*—and these deeds will sow unwholesome crops yet to be reaped."

Howard stared at him as if he'd lapsed into speaking the goblin tongue.

"Ah...let me explain. At first my chief desired to murder our boss and realize his dream to become an evil ringmaster and have a long title attached to his name. It was unfortunate you were there when very bad things happened. Now my chief is using you to lure those he sees as enemies to this carnival so he can extract three-fold vengeance. And there's a bit about a succubus and his codpiece that I'll spare you the details. Then you will be murdered and your blood used to wet the hats of my brethren."

"Oh God..." Howard's teeth chattered. Quill could see him shaking against the constraint of the duct tape. He wanted to get the man a blanket, though there were none around. He didn't dare leave the man alone to risk a search. Too many ghosts loose. "Please…I was just doing the inspection. Come on, *please*. I didn't do anything to you. Come on, I got a *family*."

"I know. My heart is heavier than a stone. Please, meditate with me. We'll leave suffering and worldly cares behind us. If you show fear to those who wish you harm, they will only feed upon it, then use it as nourishment to distract from the pangs of their own suffering."

"Why don't you just let me go? I won't come back, I swear."

Quill closed his eyes against the sight of the man's desperation, which ripped at him in harrowing cat o' nine tails slashes. "Every particle of my being wishes to set you free right now. But this isn't the moment. You'll only be killed, and me with you. Don't struggle. I sense portentous things in the wind."

Howard didn't answer. Quill was about to try teaching him the path of meditation for tranquility when the door to the maintenance area crashed open.

Chief Gorsh stomped into the room, iron-shod boots booming on the floor, followed by the clown and barker ghosts. The temperature plummeted by at least twenty degrees. Quill stood slowly, turning to face Gorsh and the ghosts, who glowed against the swath of black night and the motionless amusement park rides beyond.

Gooseflesh rippled up and down his arms. He yanked his cap lower, down to his eyebrows. He hated the damp stickiness of the hat clinging to his forehead, but he felt safer with it low. *The secret of existence was to have no fear.* But he struggled to embrace that precept now.

Spiritmaster Gorsh sauntered over to them. He glared at the soda can. "What are you, fraternizing with the enemy, you conniving son of a mule?"

"I didn't want Howard to be thirsty."

Chief Gorsh's face went red and his eyes flashed dangerously. He opened his mouth to speak, but the ghost pufferfish floated through the ceiling and landed on his hat. Gorsh swiped at it, cursing. The pufferfish drifted away, flipped over, and circled the room with its belly to the ceiling.

Gorsh stomped to the roller coaster car and loomed over Howard before turning his accomplished stink-eye back to Quill. "Swallow all that feel-goody unicorn shit! This fool has caused us enough trouble. A brilliant plan derailed! Unforgivably reckless. Why did I listen to your bleating and begging to keep him alive? A man on official business who would be missed. If your mother hadn't looked so tantalicious in garters and paisley stockings I'd punt a runt to the thrice-blasted curb!"

"But Chief, this man is innocent."

"That's *Spiritmaster*, you pig-sticking nutter-boots!" Chief Gorsh began to pace. The ghost pufferfish floated around his balloon pants as if caught in fascinated love. "Even the Corvallis Boys didn't realize this hagfish human would cause such a ruckus. He's a government worker, for Lorr's sake! Who ever misses those thrice bloody bastards? They're like census takers or those fools who dance on the corner dressed as the Statue of Liberty to lure you into using their tax preparation service—scorned, disregarded, ignored!"

"Perhaps there's some way we might make it right," Quill suggested. "Setting him free. Maybe a ritual of atonement—"

"Be a goblin for once, you spineless invertebrate! My dream of a carnival of souls is threatened by an army of crazy stork-legged-milk-sop law enforcement bastards. I need enough volatile negative energy to charge the Ochre Calliope again. Without it, I can't hold open a portal for more than a few seconds."

"But you escaped from the motel—"

"I said nothing of escape! The circus knows no retreat. You and the Corvallis Boys and all the ghosts will fight those thrice-damned mercs when they finally grow stones enough to creep inside. After the glorious bloodletting, the calliope will rend a hole big enough for an *army* of ghosts to cross and finish wreaking assorted vengeance upon those who seek to destroy my Eternal Malevolence Carnival and Incredible Show of Evil."

"I thought you named it the Grand Show Phantom Circus Magnifique?"

"Changed the billing to suit the show. Keep up, you poxy laggard! Now scuttle out of here and use your *nurata* the way goblin magic was meant to be used. And that's *to bring death* if you're too stupid to realize."

"I won't be part of that. I'm a creature of peace."

"I see," Chief Gorsh said quietly. He stroked the soggy end of his cap. "Your mother will forgive me for this, I'm sure." He motioned the ghost clown and the ghost barker closer. "I hear pacifists taste like chicken." He pointed at Quill. "So eat him."

For a moment Quill found himself unable to move. The two ghosts floated toward him with evil, hungry smiles.

He took a step backward, and then another. "Eating me will injure you more than me."

"Those are some idiotic last words." Chief Gorsh gave a nasty laugh.

The ghosts surged forward, snatching at him, their mouths gaping wounds in their distorted faces. The pufferfish floated along placidly behind them, its fins swishing in the air, its mouth making fish kisses.

Quill couldn't think of a single thing to say or do that would derail the train of hurt and suffering racing his way. So he turned and ran.

CHAPTER TEN
Go Time Part Two

The ticket booth sat beneath the hideous, overly amused clown painted on the Funtastic Carnival sign. Alpha One team advanced into position at the carnival's entrance. We crouched under the clown's feverish stare as we prepared our assault. No matter how much I hated that clown picture, I couldn't light it on fire because we were too close to witnesses.

I tried to calm myself by remembering how things could always be worse. Yeah, the carnival was dark and haunted by ghost carnies—but it might've been dark, haunted with ghost carnies, and *raining*. This was Portland, after all. Or a meth-addicted dragon could've been tear-assing around, crushing cars, lighting stuff on fire, and pushing all the gold into huge piles to make a pricy, yet uncomfortable bed. Hell, that vampire IRS agent could've been stalking my accounting books again, flashing his fang-filled grin every time I assured him our trip to Vegas *actually did* qualify as a business expense.

Now that I considered it, naming off the ways things could be shittier never did make me feel any better. Screw it. I had a hostage to save.

Rafe, in werewolf form, had point because I needed his keen sense of smell to scent out the hostage. He sniffed the air cautiously as we secured the ticket booth. A dispenser roll had spun out a long tongue of generic red tickets. One hand-lettered sign read: "You cannot bring your own food or beer!" A glance inside the booth showed me a tipped over mega-cup of soda and an empty cash box with loose change strewn across the counter, the floor, the chair, and submerged in the soda puddle. More disquieting: a stuffed penguin prize, all glassy-eyes and gaping beak, with a pair of scissors shoved through its forehead, pinning it to the backrest of the office chair. A drift of white stuffing dribbled from the hole like cotton brains. Only a triple-A-rated sicko would deface a stuffed penguin.

We kept tight formation as we pressed deeper into the carnival. Rafe led the way, while Gavin brought up our six. I held position behind and to the right of Rafe. Then came Berserker Erik. He gripped his huge battleaxe in both hands as he trailed me and scanned the darkness for threats.

Tiffany, decked out in combat armor and packing dual pistols, moved alongside Erik. I'd been prepared to assign Tiffany to Sarge's team, but one look at her pleading slit-eyes silently begging to stay with us and I'd caved. This wasn't the time to confront her fascination with our new hire because we were weapons hot and prosecuting a mission inside a damn haunted carnival. Besides, at this rate of distraction I'd do something stupid and get myself killed, turning this whole charade into one twisted self-fulfilling prophecy.

"Alpha Two, this is Alpha Actual," I said into the radio headset. "What's your status, over?"

"Alpha Actual, we are five by five," Sarge said. "Through the wire and on active hunt, over."

"Roger that. Weapons tight until hostage is secure, over."

"Copy that, Alpha Actual. Weapons tight until hostage secure. Alpha Two, out."

We'd deployed in two teams instead of advancing in one large force. That meant splitting our firepower and taking greater risk, but we could cover more ground and do it faster with this recon in force. Once we located the hostage, we would assault the place he was being held from two directions at once, upping our chances of securing him before redcaps or circus ghosts could kill him. I didn't like taking greater risks, especially with my people on the line, but saving the hostage had to be our priority. Smaller, nimble strike teams were better suited to achieving mission objectives using scouting and maneuver, especially because no one had any idea what this goblin spiritmaster brought to the game.

Alpha Two team consisted of Sarge, Stefan, Mai, a hundred or so demonic quail, and Doctor Ninja. On my orders, they'd circled around to the east, near the rides, and sheared through the chain link with bolt cutters. Both teams would approach the funhouse from opposite directions, keeping things fluid, reacting on the fly. Again, I didn't like it. Any soldier worth her salt wanted solid intel about the enemy's deployment, strength, and movements. I'd been given little choice but to work with next to nothing.

The reek of burned popcorn, corndogs, and grease saturated the air. We passed a kiddie ride with purple dragon-shaped cars on a circular track. Near it stood a trash can with a drift of food wrappers and a crushed Styrofoam cup lying wounded at its base. Farther out, as if trying to achieve escape velocity from the trashcan's questionable gravity, a cardboard cone from cotton candy rolled on the asphalt as a breeze kicked up, and a Twinkie sat in a tuft of weeds, swarming with ants.

Rafe drew up short. I had to dodge aside to avoid crashing into his back.

"What is it?" I whispered. "Ambush? Mines?"

"That's a *fried* Twinkie." He punctuated his sentence with a snarl.

Gavin keyed his radio. "Hold up, people. We got a Twinkie

sighting." He aimed his pistol sideways at the Twinkie, gangsta-style.

"Are fried Twinkies bad?" Erik asked. I could read the uncertainty in his eyes. I was guessing that uncertainty wasn't about the Twinkie, but about the band of heavily armed asylum escapees he'd fallen in with.

"Hell, yes!" Rafe said. Werewolves were hard enough to understand as it was. Although they kept their human voice box, they had a lot of teeth, a muzzle, more tongue, and plenty of predator growl, which made speaking clearly a challenge. Rafe managed to get his point across. More or less. "They're amber crème-filled *death*. And fried, they are death exponential, tempura batter and oil sacrilege, empty calorie abominations, profaned by powdered sugar and saturated fat—"

I walked over and stomped on the Twinkie. It went *splat* and spurted crème filling in a rather disturbingly sexual way that I didn't want to think about and hoped no one else had noticed. "When this fine city is attacked by a fucking demon-possessed hundred-foot tall snack cake from the third circle of Hell then, and *only then*, will we worry about sonuvabitching *fried Twinkies*. Until such time, I want us to focus. On. The. Mission!"

Rafe had the good sense to appear chagrinned, and his tail even drooped a bit. Gavin only made laser-beam noises—*pew, pew, pew*—at the smashed Twinkie remains and muttered, "I'll bust a cap in yo spongy ass, motherfucka."

Screw professionalism. I surreptitiously kicked Gavin in the shin. Nothing brought back focus like a boot to the shin.

"*Ow*, Captain! Like the priest said, what the frock?"

"Get your head in the game, merc." I glared around at each of them. "All right, we all have our listening ears on? Good. Now move out and keep sharp. These little bastards could be anywhere. They'll bone you like a fish and wet their tiny caps in your heartblood. Then they'll stomp on your spleen with their miniature iron-shod booties and chortle with deranged powrie glee. And don't get me started on the ghost clowns."

Erik hefted his axe. Tiffany cocked her pistols and sidled closer to him, peering around at the shadowed gates, abandoned booths, and empty rides. Far off, I heard the echoes of deranged giggling...though I couldn't tell if the hair-raising sound came from a speaker as part of the funhouse ride or was an insane redcap gleefully sharpening a can opener. An old-school can opener—not those stupid clamp-and-turn versions which were near impossible to use for murder.

We resumed our advance. The glow of city lights painted the clouds overhead. Stark blasts of white from the searchlights at the police perimeter threw crazed and distorted shadows across the carnival, deepening some pockets of shadow, turning others into monstrous, twisted shapes.

Twenty meters in, we entered a pseudo-courtyard nestled between stands, trailers, and tents. On the right stood a bouncy castle with patches on its base and the faded, hand-painted words "Brinca, Brinca Bounce House" above the netting. The gasoline-powered air blower rumbled and growled to itself. Across from the castle slouched an abandoned Hit the Bell game with all the prizes—stuffed animal monkeys, dolls with staring, horror-filled eyes, and strange paper-stretchy hats—strewn about the ground, while the bell tower itself leaned off-balance to the side. Other booths and food stands huddled close around us in an erratically shaped wall. The air stank of soda and vomit.

I turned to my team. "Clear those booths—"

A clown car raced onto the midway. It made no sound as it swung straight for us, not even a whisper from its fat tires as they rolled along the asphalt. Ghastly green light poured from the headlights—a diseased green that brought to mind molds and mildews and various disgusting slimes growing in drains.

When the light cut across me, I felt a wash of bitter cold prickle along my skin. I struggled to breathe, and my hands trembled. The car was packed with clowns. The gears in my brain slipped and ground as I tried to remember the last time I'd come across a situation like this. One involving a phantom clown car packed full of grease paint, red honking noses, eerily luminous hair, and the grinning clowns to which those belonged. I kept coming up with the same answer.

Never.

"Contact!" I yelled, breaking through my paralysis. "Cover!"

Alpha One scattered, but I held my position and faced the clown car alone. I summoned my magefire as the ghostly car bore down on me. The clown car was a Volkswagen Beetle, slathered in neon colors that writhed and shimmered on the frame. The huge, madly grinning cartoon face painted on the hood leered at me and winked.

Heat distortion shimmered around my hands as I lifted them. Fuck my promise to that insurance agent keyboard-humper. Magefire incinerated ectoplasm as if it were gasoline. The right tool for the right job, that's what Grandma always said.

Erik stepped to my side, hefting his axe, and staying clear of my field of fire. His sudden presence caught me by surprise, but I didn't order him to back off. I had the prophecy to consider. Then Tiffany moved beside Erik, raising her twin pistolas. On my other side, Rafe drew up alongside me and crouched to leap, showing a wide crescent of wicked teeth and growling. The only Zero Dog who actually obeyed orders was Gavin. He ran to the bouncy castle and threw himself inside, shrieking: "Here come the clowns!"

The clown car slid to a stop thirty or so feet from us, leaving stripes of luminous tire tracks smeared across the ground. The car shimmered with an unearthly spectral glow, then faded and distorted, a projector image thrown against an unstable surface. The driver door swung wide with the shriek of a rusted nail being pried from a plank.

A floppy, bloodred clown shoe thrust beyond the door and slowly settled on the asphalt. Next came a white-gloved hand, wrapping around the edge of the door. A lanky white-faced clown pulled himself free of the car. He wore green-checkered pants with suspenders, ruffled sleeves on a paisley shirt, and those huge damn shoes. The clown turned to us and hunched forward, grinning a cunning painted smile. His eyes glowed the same diseased green as the headlights.

A gunshot rang out—the booming blast of something large caliber and very near my head. The clown's face swirled like mist disturbed by the wind, becoming a twisted mess of distorted features that spun clockwise where the EDR had hit. Energy crackled in green-blue arcs. The clown's body shivered and shook before exploding into purplish vapor and dissipating into nothing.

I glanced at Tiffany, who stared along the sights of one of her P226 pistols. My ears were ringing, despite the high-decibel hearing protection of my headset. "I applaud the enthusiasm, but wait until I give the order to open fire before blasting everything, 'kay?"

Tiffany blushed and lowered her pistols. "Sorry, Captain."

The radio headset in my helmet crackled. "Alpha One, this is Alpha Two. What's your status, over?"

"Alpha Two, this is Alpha Actual. Contact with tangos on the midway. Engaging now."

Lieutenant Stone's voice broke in over our com. "Alpha One and Two, this is Overwatch. Be advised, our spotters have sighted multiple hostiles incoming to your positions. It's starting to look like 'Night on Bald Mountain' out there, over."

Shit. "Copy that, Overwatch. Thanks for the heads up."

The clowns continued to climb out of the car, unfazed by the first ghost's ectoplasm disintegration. Standard clown car routine: an obscene amount of clownflesh packed into an excessively tiny vehicle. Large clowns. Small clowns. Some sported top hats, and others wore tutus. Then there was the mostly naked clown with a strategically placed rubber ducky. I decided to destroy that clown first, because that was a terrible place to wear a duck.

"What do they want?" Erik asked.

"I don't know," I replied. "But they look way too happy to be sane. Keep frosty."

My radio clicked and Gavin whispered, "Tell me when they're gone."

I glanced at the bouncy castle. I didn't use IR goggles or nightvision because my pyromancy blinded those devices with huge flares of light and heat, so I couldn't actually see Gavin cowering in the dark beyond the castle netting. Still, he was useless. Absolutely useless.

The clowns continued to pour out of the clown car—well over fifty strong now. I'd have been impressed by their packing ability if they hadn't been incorporeal, which seemed like cheating. The clowns began to march around the car in a circle, formed into a loose column sometimes as wide as five across. Weird enough, but their heads rotated on their shoulders to maintain eye contact with us, turning around 180 degrees when they showed their backs, like refugees from an Exorcist movie in grease paint and multicolored pantaloons.

"Why are they doing that?" Tiffany spread her black, bat-like wings to their fullest extent behind her and, because she stood so close to him, over Erik as well, making a type of wing umbrella of protection. Erik didn't seem to notice because he focused so intently on the threat in front of us, but I saw it. Yes I did.

"Let me ask," Rafe said. He drew himself up to full height and let out an earsplitting howl. The clowns only continued their creepy circuit around their car, heads swiveling to always keep us in view. Every so often one of them would lift a gloved hand and honk a red bulbous nose. Instead of a honk or a squeak, a human shriek of utmost torment would rend the air and fall silent again when the clown stopped squeezing.

Sacred Cow of Fucking Perdition, I hated ghost clowns. Rafe loosed another howl of challenge. The clowns only circled and honked their noses, venting hideous screams, while their eyes glowed in haunted green or black with glowing orange pupils. The tension in the air twisted tighter as the echoes of Rafe's howl died.

"Maybe they don't speak wolf," Tiffany murmured.

Rafe's lip curled. "Heathens."

I took a step toward the circular parade. "Hey all you clowns! Get on the ground and place your hands behind your...wigs. *Now!*"

The clowns honked their noses and circled.

Flames burst to life around my hands as I summoned and cycled the flammable vapor that formed the core of my magefire, psychically directing it in currents around my palms.

"Well, this has been a real fun show, but it's time to light 'em up." At the sound of my voice, one clown raised a squeaky horn and squeezed. Instead of a honk, the horn made the intermixed sound of a crying baby and a braying donkey. The sound drained all my bravado away. "God, that's just *wrong*. Anybody see any sign of the hostage? Stuffed in that car maybe?"

A chorus of negatives answered my questions.

I lifted both hands for pure Hollywood effect, flames

writhing around them, and cut loose with a stream of fire. The horizontal column of flames raked the clowns. They didn't burn so much as evaporate into luminous smoke as the fire incinerated their ectoplasm. The clown car roiled and distorted, stretching in a running smear of vibrant colors before vanishing.

I shut down the feed of flammable vapor and my magefire died, the roar cutting off as abruptly as if someone had slammed the door on it. A few weeds still burned. Scorch marks spread in wide fan patterns across the asphalt. No sign of the ghost clowns or the clown car. Not even a mess of charred ectoplasmic goo.

"Strangely easy." Erik sounded disappointed.

I cracked my knuckles. Paper tigers. How I loved to singe them. Although that sustained blast of fire had taken a big bite out of my reserves. My body felt as if I'd just sprinted half a mile, but I was careful not to let it show. After I notified Alpha Two of our status, I turned to the bouncy castle. "Gavin, you can stop hiding. The bad clowns are gone."

"I'm not hiding," he yelled from inside. "I'm prepping an ambush."

"Make sure you include that in your epic war poem," Rafe said. "The medal of honor-quality valor you showed while storming an undefended bouncy castle."

Gavin crawled out and dusted himself off with sharp slaps at his Kevlar vest and Hawaiian shorts before glaring at the werewolf. "Hey, Rafe, your breath stinks like another dog's ass, you know that? I'm a *driver*, not a grunt. If we had a tank, I'd have dealt with that fucking clown car."

"All right," I said, hoping to cut off the bickering before it devolved into the usual kindergarten hour snipe-fest. "We have a limited supply of EDR rounds, but magefire gets rid of them easily enough. I'll take point from here out, since Rafe can't eat them."

"Has the fleabag ever tried?" Gavin grumbled.

"None of them were clowns of the female persuasion." Rafe's wolf ears twitched. "I wouldn't deny the freaky girl clowns the pleasure of Rafe's tongue. Rafe Lupo doesn't hold back the passion, because clowns need love too."

Tiffany blushed. Erik cleared his throat and looked away. Gavin made disparaging noises filled with sparkling profanity.

I closed my eyes and massaged my temples. "People. *Focus.*" I took a deep breath. "Rafe, stay next to me, I still need your nose. Erik, I want a hundred and ten percent of your attention locked on keeping me safe. Tiffany, you charm any goblins we run across. Don't just shoot them in the head, got me? It's a waste of expensive EDR ammo, and we need live perps for the cops to arrest." I glanced at my driver and class 2 empath. "Gavin, stick close and try not to get killed."

"Why am I the only one you're warning about getting killed?"

Everyone stared at him.

"All right, fine, dammit. I'll stick and try not to get killed. Happy?"

"Ecstatic. Everybody on me. Move out."

I hadn't taken a step when a shrunken figure in a white ringmaster circus outfit appeared on top of the fish taco and churro food booth. I recognized the powrie from the motel melee.

The redcap cracked his crimson whip and bowed. "Welcome to my *circus de mystique* and to your imminent death, you pus-sucking sons-of-dogs—"

"Suck this!" I yelled as I shot a wave of magefire straight at him.

CHAPTER ELEVEN
Broken Arrow

T he wave of flammable vapor ignited into a crescent of flame and engulfed the booth's hand-painted sign of a happy cactus eating a taco, then lit the roof on fire. The rest of the flames passed straight through the ringmaster's body. His form flickered and re-solidified. His outraged glare could've bubbled paint.

Flames had no effect, so he wasn't the real thing. Not a ghost either. He must be some kind of astral or psychic projection. His limited trick meant he could look but couldn't touch, and the same went for us.

My headset radio cracked. "Alpha Actual, this is Overwatch. Our spotters just sighted a fire. Be advised, you are not cleared to engage with pyrokinetics, do you copy?"

"Overwatch, this is Alpha Actual," I replied, making distortion noises into my headset microphone. "Did not copy your last. Transmission's breaking up, over."

"Jesus Christ," Lieutenant Stone snarled over the comm. "Can you be any more predictable, Walker?"

Predictably, I didn't bother to answer, too busy staring down the spiritmaster. The light from the burning taco stand didn't illuminate him, but the billowing smoke partially obscured his small form.

"You missed the show, chuckles." I grinned. "The famous clown car act got called on account of flames. Now release the hostage and surrender, and I promise no harm will come to you. Fail to comply, and we'll bring down an inferno the likes of which will make Hell shit fire in its infernal boxer shorts."

"Nice one," Rafe growled.

"Thanks. I practiced."

The ringmaster's voice sounded both in my ears and inside my mind at the same time. "The simpering fool tried to shut down the Greatest Show in Multnomah County. Gods and demons know in holy heart and damned soul that the show must go on and ever on."

"Fuck yeah," Gavin said. "A whack job. My favorite."

A wide column of black smoke snaked up from the fish taco stand behind the redcap, obscuring him completely for a moment. The air stank of charred salmon and burned churros. The smoke cleared enough to show the ringmaster staring at something behind me. "I see you brought the sex goddess who tried to enslave my codpiece and failed, to her bitter woe. She yearns for me, I can tell—"

Two large handguns fired in rapid succession, so loud they made me flinch. The bullets did nothing to the astral projection, since it wasn't physical and wasn't ectoplasm. I glanced at Tiffany, who stared down the barrels of her pistols again, her face very unamused.

"Tiffany. Charms first, bullets later. Remember?"

"Sorry, Captain. But he was lying so I had to shoot him."

The spiritmaster didn't seem pleased either. "You're supposed to let me give my spiel. We engage in witty banter and taunts of violence and mayhem inflicted upon each of our persons. You brutish, three-knuckled thugs keep going straight to the violence, forsaking the satisfying build up!"

"Yeah, yeah, we're a pain in the ass," I said. "This is your last warning. There's only two possible ways for this to end. If you let the hostage go, I'll get the commissioner's office on the phone. You can complain to the city council, the mayor, hell, to your congressman, about code enforcement in that special rambling way of yours. Have a ball." I gave him my best hard-case stare. "Or you can refuse. Then we take your ass down."

"We ghostify you," Gavin yelled. "Spec-terminate you. Shade-ominate your creepy ass. Um. *Menace* your phantom…and shit."

"Gavin. Stop."

The spiritmaster adjusted his bloody top hat. "Your threats are three times as laughable as they are pathetic. Welcome to the funhouse. Thrill to a dark ride you shall never leave."

I waited politely for mad laughter, which usually followed those types of pronouncements, but the spiritmaster just fondled his whip and stared at us — or, more precisely, Tiffany.

"Why can't we ever fight some super-hot female world-conquering villain?" Rafe asked, his voice growling like a cement mixer packed with two tons of lava rock. "Why must my alpha swagger constantly be wasted upon the sausage-class? Just think, I could show how love conquers war and carnal lust conquers hatred and how lube conquers chafing."

Gavin sneered. "There's 10W-30 motor oil back in the truck. Why don't you try it out on that whip-wielding weirdo? I'll write your Penthouse letter for you, since you can't spell."

I cleared my throat and used my death glare on them both. A muscle in my cheek twitched. Violently twitched.

Rafe shrugged. "Just thinking aloud, Captain. Don't get your g-string in a knot."

Erik stared, his face very still. I'd forgotten he was new and unfamiliar with how the Zero Dogs stumbled around insulting each other and blowing stuff up until we either won or went home. I felt sorry for him, and almost embarrassed. Tomorrow

I'd drill my teams until we spent *less* time making with the quippy banter and *more* time with the rampant killing for money.

"I swear before Lorr, you'll suffer three times for ignoring me." The spiritmaster began to coil his whip with slow, smooth motions. "I wished to look upon the beaver-fleecing face of my enemy, but now I must go to prepare the way. This time, I won't stop with wetting my cap. This time I'll dye my *socks* in your heartblood."

The spiritmaster's form flickered and vanished from the top of the taco stand inferno.

"We have met the enemy," Rafe said, "and he is an idiot."

Gavin snorted. "We're evenly matched then."

"We still have a hostage to save, people," I snapped. "On me. Move out."

A lightning bolt cracked to the east and a bright flash painted the rides in that direction with brilliant blue-white. Sarge's ARC rifle.

Alpha Two had made contact.

* * *

Two more lightning bolts flashed and cracked, followed by gunshots echoing across the carnival. I'd scanned that sector but could see nothing beyond the close-set wall of game booths, abandoned food vendors, and churning smoke. I keyed my radio. "Alpha Two, this is Alpha Actual, what's your sit-rep, over?"

Another lightning bolt crack, chased by staccato gunfire. Then Hanzo yelled over the com: "Running from ghosts!"

"This reminds me of a *Scooby-Doo* episode." Gavin pointed toward Rafe. "We even have a massive dog with a speech impediment."

"*And* a munchies-craving slacker who runs away," Rafe snarled back.

"Quiet, dammit!" I slipped a hand beneath my helmet pressing the earpiece against my ear, concentrating on the noise coming through the headset. "Alpha Two, do you require assistance, over?"

"Broken arrow! Broken arrow!" Another lightning crash, followed by strange keening and a pulse of light. A tremor shivered through the magical ether, enough to raise the hair on my arms and the back of my neck.

Broken arrow was the code that a unit was in immediate danger of being overrun, usually a desperate ground unit call for air support. My heart smashed against my ribcage like a 'roid raging bodybuilder trying to punch through a wall. "Alpha Two, what's your location, over?"

A blare of static across the com. Hanzo answered, panting heavily, "Running toward the Ferris Wheel. Ghosts and mimes everywhere!"

A pause, then static followed by a pulse of bright purple and deep blue light to the east. Magic for sure—demon magic? Sarge loved guns, but he was no stranger to fell thaumaturgy. Hanzo had borrowed a Glock nine loaded with EDRs, owing to his katana being worthless against phantoms. I had no idea how effective Mai's quail abominations were against spirit world minions. Since Stefan scorned firearms, he'd be generally useless. Same old, same old.

"Alpha Two, we are en route to your position, over!" I sounded calm, despite a thousand thoughts and fears careening around in my head like nitro-fueled bumper cars. I turned to the rest of my squad. "Move out! Rafe, take point and track Alpha Two by their scent. Watch for ambush. The hostiles could be luring us into a killbox."

Rafe set off, loping along in that peculiar gait that wasn't quite a human sprinting or a wolf running but a strange mixture of the two. The rest of us ran along behind him in loose formation. We passed close to the Tilt-a-Whirl. The ride came to life with a shudder and a groaning rumble. Crazy, upbeat music blasted from overhead speakers. Multi-colored lights flashed on and off in a spinning kaleidoscope that momentarily dazzled me. Tiffany shrieked and opened fire with her pistols, capping off three or four rounds into the spinning seats before we all realized the ride was empty. It had started on its own.

Not the only one either. All across the carnival, rides powered up and started to run. The Ferris Wheel began to spin, the lights on the long spokes flashing. The carousel went round and round, filling the air with creepy calliope music.

Rafe scented the air as he led us onward. I saw another flash of purple-white light and felt the thrumming charge of magic. A bumper car spun through the air and smashed into a line of blue Porta-Potties. We kept running.

I caught sight of movement at an open booth with helium tanks and a brightly colored sign that read "Balloon Joy!" The sudden piercing squeak of twisting balloon plastic made me wince. A ghost mime stood beside a helium tank. His white-gloved hands expertly twisted and shaped a long red balloon into something…perhaps a doggie or centipede.

I hated mimes, almost as much as I hated elves. I'd had the misfortune of meeting a zombie mime once, and that white-faced son of a bastard still haunted my nightmares. This ghost mime shone with pale spectral illumination. Even his beret glowed. His mime make-up made his face seem perpetually, almost slyly surprised. Mockingly, evilly surprised.

The mime let go of the red balloon shaped like a miniature schnauzer. The balloon floated along the ground, charging toward us while making angry squeaks. The ghost mime immediately began to fill, tie off, and shape another balloon, all the while staring at me with that surprised mime "O" face.

I skidded to a stop and summoned magefire. Before I could cut loose with an inferno, Erik loosed a deafening battle yell and hurled his battleaxe. It spun end over end, and though it was not a throwing axe, it still managed to shear its blade through the mime's head instead of only smacking him with the haft and embarrassing us all. The ghost mime dissipated into a watermelon-green smoke bomb and vanished.

Erik hurried over and wrenched his axe free of the booth's support post. He glanced at me and smiled almost apologetically. "You should save your fire for when it counts."

I sucked in breath to boast that I had infinite fire and more besides, but a goblin popped out from behind the balloon stand, armed with a pair of bolt cutters.

"I'll nip off yer chestnuts, blood bags!" the redcap screeched. "Aiieeee!"

Tiffany opened fire with two-fisted, two-gun action, emptying both clips into the murderous goblin ankle-biter. What was left of the redcap would've fit into a freezer bag with room left over for his hat.

"It's like fucking Whack-a-mole around here," Gavin said, glancing behind him nervously. "Little bastards jumping out left, right, and sideways."

"Remember, Tiffany," I said, very patiently. "A little less Rambo and a little more irresistible sex queen who charms people over to our side, okay?"

"Yes, Captain, sorry. I *would've* charmed him, but he wanted Erik's chestnuts and so I had to kill him."

"Next time, try not to use so many of the EDR bullets that cost three hundred dollars apiece." I heard a strange balloon-rubbing screech sounding over and over again. Please not another damn ghost mime. I turned to find Rafe staring down at the balloon dog the mime had created and set loose on us. It was humping Rafe's leg.

Gavin laughed. "There's your alpha swagger at work, dog-face."

Rafe cocked his head and peered down at the balloon dog. "I kinda like this little guy. He's got spunk."

Not literally, I silently prayed. Rafe put the balloon dog on his head, between his wolf ears, where it glanced around happily with its blank sausage-plastic-section face. Good lord, he was *not* taking that thing home with him.

"Rally on me, be ready to move out!" I hit my mike, going to a secure channel as everyone scrambled back into position. "Alpha Two, this is Alpha Actual. What's your status, over?"

A blast of static came over the com. Then Sarge's deep voice said, "Alpha Actual, this is Alpha Two. We are on the carousel, in heavy contact. I've set down spellwork to wall the ghosts off from storming the carousel, but we're pinned and can't maneuver."

"Roger that, Alpha Two. Casualties?"

"Negative on casualties, over."

A wave of relief flooded through me, so intense it made my knees weak. "What's the status of hostiles, over?"

"An entire circus tent full of ghosts. Clowns, trapeze people, contortionists, jugglers. We engaged and destroyed several redcaps. We're holding for now, over."

No more pincer movements or flanking maneuvers. We were too heavily outnumbered. I wanted to merge with Alpha Two. We'd cover less ground, but we'd be stronger, and I'd know they were safe. "Sit tight, Alpha Two. We're incoming to your position, over."

"Roger that, Alpha Actual. Alpha Two, out."

I killed my mike and signaled for the team to move out. Slowly swirling smoke wreathed the section of the carnival where the booth had burned. The night was filled with blaring music, a cacophony of bells and whistles and insanely merry tunes, brilliant with thousands of lights. We set off again, advancing toward the grinding, off key dirge of the carousel's calliope music. I prayed we wouldn't arrive too late.

CHAPTER TWELVE
The Carousel

Quill scurried beneath a pushcart that sold cotton candy and balloons as a lightning bolt shot past and exploded the ghost chasing him on a unicycle. He edged to the wheel and risked a look. War raged all around him. Lightning bolts cut jagged lines across the midway, hitting ghosts and blowing them into particles of ectoplasm. Bullets cracked through the air. The soldiers of fortune that Chief Gorsh hated were defending the carousel as if it were a brightly lit, garishly painted, fully musical Alamo. The demon mercenary blasted lightning from a strange gun, and a ninja with medic insignias shot at ghosts with a pistol, an incongruous sight that had Quill's brain reeling. Stranger still, quail-like creatures flocked here and there, spitting iridescent venom that repulsed the phantoms.

He debated breaking from cover and trying to surrender to them, but froze when a vampire mercenary snatched a Corvallis redcap that had been sneaking over to backstab the woman leading the quail. The vampire drained the powrie of blood, then nicked his blood-soaked cap and wrung it into his mouth. Running to the mercenaries suddenly seemed akin to leaping from a burning ship into kraken-infested waters.

He struggled to find his calm center, but fear turned his

thoughts into drowning rats, biting and clawing each other. Some Buddhist he'd turned out to be. He couldn't even master his own fear enough to help poor Howard the OSHA inspector. He was an utter disgrace. His terror and his craving for safety made him cower, uncertain, his vows to follow the Noble Eightfold Path abandoned.

Creepy, out-of-tune calliope music blared from the carousel as it started up and began to spin, nearly throwing the ninja off the side. The ninja grabbed a carousel horse and barely managed to pull himself out of the reach of a huge clown with a gaping bullfrog mouth and painted tears on his white cheeks. As far as Quill could see, the main thing keeping the ghosts at bay was the demon with the gun that shot lightning. But his shots grew wilder after the carousel jerked to life and started to spin. One bolt clipped the top of Quill's hiding spot and filled the air with the stench of scorched cotton candy.

Something bumped his leg and he screamed. He scrambled away, fetching up against the far wheel, straining to see what had touched him. A vision of a madly grinning mime trying to yank him into the open danced silently into his mind.

The ghost pufferfish bobbed in the air a few inches from the ground, goggling at him side-on with one wide eye. It made fish-puckering faces and drifted, placid and serene. He stared at it. It stared back. Another bolt of lighting lit up the area in a brilliant blue-white flash, followed by a boom of thunder that shook the cart.

Quill tore his gaze away from the phantom blowfish and looked back toward the carousel, which swarmed with ghosts of all kinds. Juggling clowns, contortionist specters that crab-walked in painful-seeming poses, roustabouts swinging mallets, acrobats sailing through the air in spinning flips, clowns riding tiny motorcycles, and other clowns with packs of tiny ghost dogs. Far too many to shoot with the demon's lightning gun or the ninja's pistol. If Quill didn't do something, and quick, they'd be overrun and ripped apart by the chief's spectral legions. That would mean several very bad things, including a huge crushing rebound of *kamma* onto the chief, because bad actions yielded terrible, inescapable results.

Also, the mercenaries were his only hope of saving Howard. Quill couldn't rescue him alone. He wasn't strong enough, wasn't brave enough, wasn't *vicious* enough. He needed help, and they were the only option the universe had provided. Though they'd attacked Chief Gorsh and the others at the motel, Quill bore them no malice. All of them, goblin and mercenary, had been trapped in a brutal spiral of violence. He'd wanted to escape it, but before there'd been no chance because Chief Gorsh had dragged him back into the mire again. Now, though...now he had Howard to consider.

He reached out and snatched a singed string from one of the decorative balloons destroyed by stray lightning strikes. Then he hexed the string with *nurata* — the goblin magic he often struggled with, sometimes denying it was even a part of him — so the string would remain impervious to ectoplasm. He wrapped it around the tail of the ghost puffer and tied it in a knot. The sea squab watched him impassively, fully inflated, making fish faces and waving its fins.

When the puffer was secured to the string like a balloon, he crawled out from beneath the pushcart. The other ghosts didn't notice him right away. They swirled around the carousel, maddened by the calliope music. A clown wearing a cone-shaped hat spotted him first. It stopped its floppy-shoe-shuffle and waggled a pink, corkscrew-shaped tongue. It floated toward him. Its giggles seemed to echo, not in Quill's ears, but inside his mind, all shivery and gleeful.

He stood his ground, clutching his pufferfish balloon. He sucked in a deep breath and yelled. "Hey all you unfortunate dead clowns and dead ride jocks and dead sideshow individuals! I turned your fish into a balloon!" He yanked the string. The phantom sea squab, bound by the hexed string, jerked down and floated back up, tethered, staring wide-eyed into space while making fish lips. The puffer seemed to care not one whit about the abuse.

A few ghosts turned to peer at him as if he were a juicy specimen they wanted to drain of life energy and discard as a fun-sized goblin husk. Quill took a step backward, then steadied himself. He chanted, "The enemy is fear. Fear is the enemy. The enemy is *fear*." Then he yelled at the ghosts who hadn't heard him the first time, realizing he was going to have to get nasty.

"Hoy! All you dead circus freaks! Your master told you to eat me! So, *eat* me!" He grabbed his crotch and gave a most un-Buddhist-like hip thrust.

The ghosts stopped. They peered at him in eerie silence. Then every ghost came for him at once in a glowing wave, all lifeless eyes, back pit mouths, and twisted teeth. Quill's bladder nearly let go. He spun on his iron shod heel and ran. He ran as if he were the gingerbread man escaping from Hell while mainlining performance enhancing drugs.

More cracking lightning and gunfire, picking off ghosts here and there. A shimmering sheen of iridescent light burst from the carousel, but Quill had no time to investigate. He was too busy running hard, weaving around generators and booths as ghosts chased him, squeaking their noses and screeching as they tried to grab him.

The ghost of a juggler burst out of a nearby garbage bin and hurled a bowling pin at Quill's head. He yelled in surprise and threw himself aside. The glowing pin missed his head by inches and hit a clown on a tricycle with an ectoplasmic *smack*. The tricycle clown careened into a ping-pong ball/goldfish bowl game booth.

Quill ran faster, his robes hiked up above his knees, as mad, exhilarating terror quaked through him. The pufferfish sailed behind, dragged along at the end of the hexed balloon string. Quill started to gasp high-pitched chants in Vrardish, the language of the goblin kin, desperate for some *nurata* hex to keep the ghosts away.

Lightning bolts crashed through the air one after another, striking ghosts and blowing them into glowing green bits that rained to the asphalt like radioactive Tic Tacs. He cut back toward the trailers, hoping to hide from the spectral tornado he'd provoked. A clown riding a tiny motorcycle screeched around in front of him, its glowing tires leaving eldritch slime in a huge comma-shaped skidmark. Legends claimed it was impossible to outrun a redcap, but the legends mentioned nothing about tiny phantom motorcycles. The clown seized him by the front of his robes, jerking him off balance. It dragged him toward its gaping mouth, filled with jostling square teeth. He could only scream as the mouth grew ever closer, as wide around as a toilet.

A bright stream of fire seared through the ghost clown. The tiny motorcycle and the clown suit burst into flames. A wave of incredible heat broke against Quill. He wrenched himself away from the burning clown, tumbling to the ground to smother the flames that had spread to his robes. The world spun wildly as he rolled. Lights flashed. Something rumbled a chipper-shredder snarl. He beat out the last of the flames and pushed to his feet, his robes singed and smoking, scorch marks on his boots.

A woman in body armor and military gear shot streams of fire from her hands at the attacking ghosts, incinerating them. They burned away faster than paper, drifting toward the ground and shedding parts of themselves in fiery snowflakes.

Around her swarmed more mercenaries. A wolf-humanoid hybrid loped along the asphalt, trying to bite the ghosts and not having much luck, while a tiny balloon dog raced around his heels, squeaking with joy. A man with a huge axe slashed his way through the ghost clowns and phantom acrobats who stood in his way. The axe must have been enchanted to disrupt the ectenic force ghosts used to touch and move things because it destroyed them with ease. A stunning woman with black wings sprouting from her back opened fire with pistols at one of the Corvallis Boys who'd been watching the battle from the Ferris Wheel and throwing knives. The gunshots were so loud they made Quill cringe and his ears ring. Her bullets punched through the metal side of the Ferris Wheel bucket. The redcap knife-thrower toppled out and plummeted to the asphalt. Quill looked away quickly.

He had no choice but to hold tight to the floating pufferfish and sprint away from the chaotic fight before someone shot him, incinerated him, blasted him with lightning, or tore him apart with tooth and claw. The violence made him sick to both stomach and heart. He was deeply ashamed to have been a part of it, even as a spectator. He'd run in a complete circle around the carousel and spotted the damaged cotton candy pushcart again. He scurried back underneath, smelling the burned sugar and avoiding the puddles of melted plastic where the balloons had fallen.

He pulled his cap down low, reeled the balloonfish in close, and watched as the mercenaries finished routing the ghosts. Puddles of burning ectoplasm smoked on the asphalt, sending up greasy, foul-smelling clouds as they vanished. The last ghost clown raced away on a tiny motorcycle, screaming toward the funhouse. The clown's red-painted, white-mouthed face was turned down in sadness. A column of fire shot out and enveloped both ghost and motorcycle, while a lightning bolt from the demon's rifle struck with a boom at the same instant, yielding instant phantom obliteration.

The thunder echoes finally died out. The carousel kept turning and playing "Camptown Races" as the mercenaries abandoned it. Quill huddled under the pushcart, restraining the pufferfish who seemed eager to investigate the mercenaries.

"Good timing, Captain," the big demon said, changing some kind of huge battery in his gun.

The pyrokinetic woman in the armor and helmet answered him. "Would've been here sooner, except we were busy bickering like Kindergarteners." She cut a frowning glance at the werewolf and a human wearing a Kevlar vest over a T-shirt and Hawaiian shorts.

The beautiful woman with the wings strolled to where Quill hid behind the cart's wheels. She was gorgeous enough to make him mourn his vows of celibacy, especially when she squatted down to peer at him with blue cat-like eyes, and he noticed the way her fatigues tightened against her body. Even the pufferfish seemed eager to float closer to her.

"Here's one, Captain," the woman said in a hesitant, yet sultry voice. "Should I charm him? He looks so scared and harmless..."

The demon walked over. Quill drew further back, trying to compress himself into a tiny, non-threatening, very pacifistic bundle. Conversely, the demon was massive. Muscle packed on muscle tacked to a wall of muscle. His face was stony, hard to read, and his red pupils seemed to shine with infernal light.

"This one helped us out."

"What?" the woman who'd answered to *Captain* said. "Why?"

The demon shrugged.

The captain eyed the sea squab tied to his hexed balloon string before meeting his gaze. "Hey you, come on out. We won't hurt you." She looked around at the others. "Hear that? Don't hurt him."

No choice now. Quill slowly crawled out and stood. All of them were so tall, looming over him and the pufferfish that bobbed around his head. The small balloon dog scurried over and started to hump his iron shod boot. He recognized it—one of the ghostly mimes made those possessed animal balloons. Still, if they hadn't destroyed the little balloon dog outright, maybe there was some hope of talking peace with these soldiers of fortune.

"I'm Quill. This is Puffer the spirit fish. I want you to help me save a man trapped in the funhouse."

"Had to be the funhouse," the captain grumbled. "The shittiest place here."

"Except for the Porta-Potties," the man with the Hawaiian shorts said.

The captain ignored him and fixed Quill with a hard, no-nonsense stare. "Why should we trust you? We've been icing redcaps left and right."

"I'm a Buddhist." He pointed to his singed robes and hoped they didn't look too hard at his blood-soaked cap. Even though he used pig's blood to keep it wet, and loathed it and the harm done pigs, the mercenaries might misunderstand. "I want this horrible violence to end. I promised to help Howard. I had to run because of the hungry clowns, but I mean to do everything I can to save him."

"Those fucking clowns," Hawaiian Shorts said. "They freak me out. Ninety-eight percent of the population has coulrophobia, the fear of clowns."

The werewolf picked up the balloon dog and put it on the top of his head, where it proceeded to start licking between its legs, making little squeaks. The werewolf didn't seem to mind. "That's not a disorder recognized by the Psychiatric

Association, you moron."

"Yeah? Ever hear that song about how you can't sleep or the clowns will eat you? Alice Cooper *knew*."

"Whiskey Tango Foxtrot, guys," the captain said. "The bickering. It stops. *Now*." She glanced toward the funhouse. "A Buddhist redcap? That's a bit like being a virgin porn star, isn't it?"

Quill risked a small smile. "Closer to the old 'honest politician' joke."

The captain snorted. "I like this guy... More than most murderous powries, anyway. Hey, Erik. Anything in that stupid prophecy about scoring help from a goblin?"

The grim man seemed to consider her words as he stood very straight, the axe head planted on the ground between his feet, resting both his hands on the end of the haft. He shook his head and said nothing else. Quill had no idea what they were talking about, so he kept quiet and tried to keep the pufferfish from floating into danger.

The winged woman, who Quill realized was a succubus wearing more clothing and armor than he would've guessed, walked over to stand close to the axe-man. She had a kind face though, and as tempting as the fantasy might be, things would never work out between a succubus and a redcap.

The captain eyed Quill for a long moment before turning her gaze back to the funhouse in the distance. He realized she was impatient to get there, but he also knew his life hung in a delicate balance, on a scale he did not fully trust.

"All right, we'll use you for intel. If you're on the level, it'll go a long way toward mitigating any crimes you've committed. I want the hostage, and I want him safe. That's priority number one. Can you help me with that?"

"Yes." The relief that flooded through him made him want to kiss them all in gratitude, though they probably wouldn't appreciate the gesture. He'd be able to make good on his word and help Howard, perhaps even bringing an end to all this bloodshed and madness.

The power suddenly shut off again. Floodlights and ride lights died. The Ferris Wheel and Tilt-a-Whirl went dark, and the carousel slowed to a stop as the music warbled and died. The heavy silence only lasted a few seconds, because over the PA system speakers, Chief Gorsh began to sing. The words were a Vrardish lament, so only Quill could understand the verses about codpieces, murder, and the merciless cap-drying sun. However, there was no denying that, despite his grating speaking voice, his ex-chief did have one beautiful tenor.

CHAPTER THIRTEEN
Fun Times at the Fun House

S trange bedfellows and all that. I was a believer. How else to explain our new travel-sized ally?

"Keep scanning your sectors," I said into the headset mike as we approached the funhouse along a section of the midway. "Eyes out for ambush."

I followed behind the redcap, careful to keep an eye on him, in case he really wasn't a Buddhist and decided to burn us. I expected it, and sooner rather than later, but I was certain we had the force and firepower to deal with any goblin betrayal. After all, we'd handed the spiritmaster's forces two stinging defeats so far.

I'd been dragging ass for a while now, struggling not to show my exhaustion or hint at the headache thudding in my skull. Too many pyrotechnics and too little rest, and the big show was still to come. But I had to keep up a hard-charger front for the troops.

Alpha One and Two teams covered opposite sides of the midway's approach to the funhouse. Quill claimed the hostage was duct taped inside the funhouse's maintenance section. I meant to assault the maintenance area with Alpha One. Alpha Two would strike through the ride's entranceway, creating a distraction that would give us cover and surprise.

The midway was eerily empty, dark booths, silent rides. No more ghosts…except for the pufferfish that trailed after Tiffany as if in love, though the hexed string kept it tethered to Quill's wrist. Even the balloon dog perched on Rafe's head stayed quiet.

Lieutenant Stone's voice crackled over my headset. "Alpha Actual, this is Overwatch. What's your sit-rep, over?"

"Overwatch, this is Alpha Actual. Multiple hostiles KIA. Proceeding to primary objective. Estimated contact in five zero minutes, over."

"Be advised, snipers report movement inside the funhouse. Something Fox Mike is going down, over."

Fox Mike meant *fucking magic*. Great. "Roger that, Overwatch, Alpha Actual out."

The funhouse languished in shadows, the queue deserted, and the madly grinning mouth of a huge painted clown forming the entrance. More goddamn clown art, though garish haunted house paintings and green and black hypnotic spirals also decorated the sides.

"Alpha One, on me," I said quietly into the mike. "Alpha Two, stack on the entrance."

"Copy that."

Sarge hurried to the front of the funhouse and pressed against the wall, covering the doors with the ARC rifle. Hanzo moved next, pistol in hand. Stefan glided over and lounged against the wall, picking his fangs and looking bored. Mai took up rear guard. She'd taken a chance, with my go ahead, and sent back the alien quail and summoned a handful of demon bunnies she claimed would eat ectoplasm. Each bunny was pitch black, had a burning tail of orange-red flame, needle teeth, and white, pupil-less eyes.

Sarge gave me a thumbs up to show Alpha Two was ready. I double-nodded and followed Quill around the side of the funhouse to an iron fold-down stair and a single door with a sign that read: "Employees only!" I took point and edged toward the door in a crouch, tapping my pyromancy. Erik stayed close on my heels, followed by Tiffany, the Buddhist goblin and his pet pufferfish, Rafe, balloon dog, and, finally, Gavin.

No windows for a visual or infrared scan. No way to feed a fiber optic camera or microphone past the door without breaching it first. The door opened outward, so there'd be no kicking it in. I set my ear against the metal of the funhouse trailer and flinched away. The metal was icy cold. If there'd been more moisture in the air, frost would've covered the entire surface.

Quill, grim-faced, pulled his arm out of the folds of his robes and pointed at the door and mouthed the words "in there."

A little late with the heads up. With my luck, I'd probably lose my ear to frostbite. I cycled through my options for gaining entry and came up with dismayingly few. Gavin had Primacord, but I couldn't risk blowing the door without knowing the hostage's location inside the room. That left brute force.

I signaled Rafe. He handed the balloon dog to Gavin, who threw it into a trashcan. The balloon dog started to squeak. I glared at Gavin until he pulled the balloon dog out again and set it safely on the ground, where it immediately started to get busy with his boot.

Rafe took position beside me. I readied my flash spell, brighter than a flashbang but without the concussion effect. It took me longer than usual to build the spell's core. I had to clench my fists to stop my hands from shaking. A wave of nausea swept through me, but I fought it off, then kicked back the exhaustion until I had myself and my magic under control again.

Quill seemed unsure what to do and retreated from the door. Erik set a hand on his shoulder and stopped him. I nodded my approval to Erik because I wanted the redcap close in case he nursed any thoughts of betrayal. I wasn't naïve. This could still be a trap, and I didn't trust goblins as far as I could dropkick them.

The distraction almost gutted my spell. I struggled to control my breathing and shake off the weariness as I keyed my radio. Go time. "Execute, execute, execute!"

Rafe leapt forward and seized the door. With a loud snarl, he tore it from its hinges and threw it. The door hummed as it spun through the air and smashed into a weight guessing booth, knocking the whole thing over. At the same time, a burst of light and resounding boom came from the front of the funhouse. Alpha Two breaching the entrance.

Rafe dodged aside from the open doorway. I spun out from behind the doorjamb, fired off my spell and ducked back out of sight again. The blinding flash went off, and I grabbed Quill by the back of the robes and hauled him along as I charged through the doorway. Quill gave a surprised "Gah!" when I seized him, but didn't struggle. He also didn't seem surprised to double as my personal goblin-sized shield.

Unfortunately, I'd forgotten the pufferfish string was tied to Quill's wrist, so it came along for the ride, bouncing along at disturbing proximity to my ear.

The maintenance room was near pitch black. I dodged clear of the entryway and summoned more magefire, cycling and burning it in a spinning wheel of flame near the center of the room to throw light around. The simple spell made it a struggle to move fast, but I forced myself anyway. A flickering wash of orange-red light revealed no hostage and no hostiles. The reek of machine oil and mildew hung in the air. A few tools and other odds and ends lay scattered around the room. Spare cars for the dark ride. A litter of empty cardboard centers from rolls of duct tape. Extra parts for the funhouse displays. Large fake spiders. Plastic skeletons. Black lights and wiring and cardboard boxes.

The rest of my squad followed me inside, spreading out to clear the corners. I kept my attention on the closed metal door leading deeper into the funhouse.

"This is Alpha Actual," I said into the radio. "No visual on hostage. No contact, over."

"Copy that, Alpha Actual," Sarge radioed back. "Alpha Two inside the perimeter, no contact, advancing."

I glanced down at Quill. The little redcap's wizened face and gray eyes appeared terrified. After a moment I realized he was terrified of me, probably thinking I'd immolate him because he'd given bad intel. I gave him a smile I hoped came across as reassuring. Bad intel was SOP in this business.

The funhouse burst to life around us, making us start and dash behind cover. Screams, creepy laughter, scary music, howling wind and wolves competed with hooting owls, thunder, and clanking chains as the dark ride cars clattered along the tracks. Standard haunted house noise that almost drowned out the generator's rumble. When there was no counter attack, I signaled for the rest of my team to form up, making certain Erik remained close. No sense in getting blindsided by a death prophecy at the finish line.

I approached the interior door, pressed against the wall, and yanked it open. I stepped into a long hallway with flashing strobe lights, shaking skeletons, plastic severed limbs dangling on fishing line, and a long row of curved mirrors throwing back distorted images. No sign of hostiles. The cars traveled down the center of the corridor on a slowly rolling track.

We advanced along the hallway, staying to the right of the

empty rolling cars, moving past undead pirate mock-ups and a fake iron maiden that burst open as we walked close. A screeching corpse lunged out. Erik swung his axe in a short arc. The blade slammed into its skull, slicing clean through the extending struts holding the corpse in place, then shearing through the iron maiden before finally lodging in the wall. Sparks burst out in a blue spray and sizzled on the floor. The recorded screech died into a pathetic warble. Erik wrenched the blade free and shrugged.

I gave him a thumbs up, because even though the corpse had been fake, he was paying attention and enthusiastic about destroying stuff. Both were a win in this situation.

"Captain," Gavin whispered from the back of the squad. He was examining himself in the distorted funhouse mirrors.

"What is it?" I snarled, because clowns didn't seem to be eating him at the moment, and I was damn-well busy.

"Do these shorts make my ass look fat?"

"Gavin, goddammit, we are *on a mission*!" The bastard was going to get me smoked because he wouldn't stop screwing around. "I am going to murder you and blame it on the goblins if you don't shut your Twinkie hole and get your rear in gear!"

"Sorry, Captain." He snapped off a half-decent salute and even managed to look a bit ashamed. "I'm completely squared away now."

I took a deep breath. Let it out slowly. I scanned around to make sure an ambush wasn't about to vomit death upon us while I engaged in mid-operation tongue-lashings, but the funhouse corridors remained clear of ghosts. The air was warm and close, while the halls reeked of mildew and sweat.

We advanced again, breaking to the right at the end of the hallway. Optical illusions and flashing lights made movement tricky. The next corridor was darker and filled with alcoves. I sent the fire ring floating on ahead of us. Erik started after it, keeping his axe ready.

The sudden crack of the lightning gun made me flinch. Smashing and crashing sounds echoed somewhere deeper in the funhouse. Sarge's deep voice rumbled over the com. "Alpha Two in contact. Engaging."

"Copy that—"

A ghost floated through the ceiling, some kind of spectral acrobat, and flew straight for me. Before I could lock in and light it up, Erik sliced off the acrobat's ghostly head with an axe swipe that buried the blade in the opposite wall. Cold ectoplasm sprayed me across the face and helmet. I stepped back, cursing and wiping it away. Gavin grinned at me and opened his mouth to make a comment, but I only pointed at him and he snapped his mouth shut again.

The noise of battle added a savage undertone to the ride's looping screams and howls and mad laughter. Calliope music suddenly blared from deeper inside the ride, thrumming through the walls. "Camptown Races" again, because apparently calliopes were incapable of playing "Ode to Joy." The music didn't come across the tinny, crackling speakers. It sounded as if it came from a real steam powered calliope— which was madness. Where the hell were they keeping it, and why the hell had they turned it on?

We charged down the hall toward the music, entering a bigger room with a creepy fortune teller theme. Howard Kaiser sat duct taped to a metal folding chair at the table of an animatronic crystalmancer peering into a quartz ball. He stared at us in absolute terror. My heart leapt in triumph, and I started forward, eager to secure the hostage. Then the ghost of a bear in a cone-shaped hat charged through the wall on my right flank, dancing from leg to leg as it barreled down on me.

For a critical moment I hesitated, not wanting to cut loose with pyromancy with the hostage so close. The ghost bear loomed over me and swiped with a huge paw.

I dodged, but not fast enough. Its claws ripped into my body armor and smashed me backward. My breath left my body in a wheezing rush. I slammed into a plastic coffin and tumbled onto a cheap skeleton, crushing them both. The bear's slash had torn across the Kevlar and scratched along the trauma plates in my armor, but hadn't penetrated to my chest.

Everyone started to yell and move at once. A bowling pin-shaped ghost clown seized the chair with the hostage and dragged him to the passing ride cars. I rolled to my knees, gasping. I wouldn't have believed a ghost could generate enough ectenic force to lift the hostage off the ground. Wrong again, because the clown heaved him into one of the passing ride cars, wedging the chair inside. The car rolled onward, hauling the hostage away. The clown waved a cheery goodbye and floated after him. I couldn't reach the hostage because the damn dancing bear was in my way, cavorting closer, stretching its claws and eyeing me with ursine malice. What a way to die, murdered by a spectral bear.

Erik bellowed—a sound louder than any bear roar. Everyone looked at him, including the bear. Erik's muscles were rigid, tendons tight as steel cables beneath his skin. He gripped the large battleaxe in one hand as easily as if it were a hatchet. His eyes were wild, enraged, and power swept around him like magnetic fields. He leapt at the bear, swinging his axe, and the bear danced to meet him.

I was momentarily distracted by the brutal man-on-bear violence, but caught a glimpse of Quill darting across the room. He dodged past the fight, yanking the ghost puffer along with him on its string. He scrambled over the cheesy fortune teller's table, knocking the milky crystal ball off its stand. It rolled off the table and broke on the floor. Quill vanished through the doorway deeper into the funhouse where the ride car had transported the hostage.

Gavin shocked me by yelling, "Let's do this!" He ran across the room, kicked over the fortune teller table, and charged through the doorway after Quill. I was torn between admiring his gung ho charge and wanting to kick his ass back to barracks for a psych eval. His mind must've snapped at the sight of the dancing bear, but at least he wasn't hiding in a bouncy castle.

I clawed my way back to my feet. Tiffany and Rafe made short work of the few remaining redcaps that tried to hit us from behind. Berserker Erik finished reducing the bear to firewood-sized pieces that slowly dissolved into ectoplasmic goo. Balloon dog ran around in circles, squeaking.

Which left me to storm after the hostage, Quill, and my suddenly heroic and likely unhinged empath. "Zero Dogs!" I yelled. "Rally on me!"

I didn't wait to see if anybody followed orders. I darted through the doorway into the largest room I'd seen in the dark ride.

Fog machines sent drifts of gray vapor curling across the floor. Strobe lights and speakers tried to simulate a thunderstorm, but were drowned out by the screaming calliope. The ride tracks cut straight through the center of the room. On either side stood cheesy animatronic zombies, moving in jerking little starts and stops. The zombies were threatening an animatronic woman and man who'd apparently wandered into a graveyard at night, during a storm, where one usually didn't find 24-hour convenience stores or ATMs. I'd faced down a real zombie assault. This theme park undead crap didn't hold a candle.

The car with the hostage had already crossed half the room. Quill was trying to chew through the duct tape binding the hostage to the metal folding chair. He gnawed with his sharp teeth but there was a *lot* of duct tape. The pufferfish was either fighting with the clown or trying to use its head as a landing strip, I couldn't be certain. Gavin shot the clown ghost, hitting center of mass, and the EDR round destroyed it. He took position on the moving track opposite Quill, holstered his pistol and started sawing away at the duct tape with his combat knife. I drew my own knife and ran to help them.

The car track shuddered and groaned, then came to a creaking stop. The sudden change in motion threw Quill off the car and sent Gavin staggering. I slowed, holding my knife and stalking forward warily. My heart pounded, and sweat ran down my face, soaking my helmet straps.

The funhouse soundtrack blared a shriek of static through the concealed speakers and cut out. The deafening calliope music died with a whistling wail.

The animatronic zombies shimmered as if with heat distortion. My lips peeled back from my teeth in a silent snarl. Fire burst to life around my free hand. Ghostly shapes began to push out of the zombies. The ghosts had been hiding inside the robotronic undead, waiting to spring their trap. Twenty of them at least. How they'd all compressed inside I had no idea.

This wave of ghosts was comprised solely of clowns, as if they massed in vengeance for the clown car holocaust I'd inflicted. All of them had unknowable faces, ravenous smiles, gleaming sparks for pupils, and every last gaze was fixed on me.

"Quill!" I yelled. He glanced at me. I underhand-tossed him the knife, praying it wouldn't tumble and cut him. He nimbly snatched it out of the air and joined Gavin in slicing through the thick layers of duct tape.

I faced the clowns alone. I had to buy them time. The calliope started again, grinding along. The music was a strange, joyless dirge like nothing I'd heard before.

A ripping, rending screech sounded behind me, even louder

than the music. I recoiled and wheeled around. A spiraling series of glowing red filaments twisted in the air, radiating outward from a central point in the middle of the doorway I'd come through. The space between the filaments distorted and bulged as if my image of the world were a two-dimensional sheet suddenly being pushed into three dimensions. Those filaments, like floating red-hot wires, spread toward the ride car that had stopped and partially blocked the doorway.

Erik and Tiffany appeared beyond the doorway, hurrying toward me.

"Watch out!" I shouted. I had no idea what those air-dancing strands would do to a person if they were touched.

They pulled up short just in time. The expanding wires reached the car and sliced into it with the merciless precision of a laser beam.

Erik locked eyes with me. I knew we were both thinking about the prophecy.

"Stay back!" Erik warned Tiffany, right before he vaulted the ride car and swung his axe at the interlacing red wires. The enchanted blade sheared through them. As it cut the wires, a shriek blasted out, the screech of train wheels braking hard on a rusting track. A blinding flash threw sparks as bright as an electric welding arc.

His axe blade sliced open a hole. But even as he cut the wires away, they started to spread again, moving to seal the gap. Erik hurled himself through the hole, twisting past the glowing red wires and through the bulge-like distortion of the light. My breath caught in my throat. One of the wires kissed along the edge of his hair, slicing it, filling the air with the stink of a burning handlebar mustache. Another severed his narrow tie and cut the heel from one cowboy boot. Still, he made it past, spun and tucked in mid-air like a high diver. He hit the metal floor on his shoulder and rolled into the room.

Tiffany stepped toward us, brandishing her guns, her face stricken. The calliope music blared in one long, discordant note. The wires flashed, and the center of the bulge burst, ripping open a tear in the fabric of reality that shimmered with light distortion and sheared away the metal walls and floor. The portal obscured Tiffany and the rest of the arriving Zero Dogs, cutting us off from them completely.

"What's your status, Captain?" Sarge's voice came over the radio, heavy with tension bordering on fear, which nearly sparked off panic in me. Sarge always kept his cool.

"Heavy contact. *Hurry.*"

Erik stood by my side, battleaxe in hand. His face was grim, all hard angles and Clint Eastwood squint.

The ghosts watched us. They hovered around the room, leering, thinking evil clown thoughts, but they didn't strike. Their silent restraint was more unnerving than an actual attack. Quill and Gavin relentlessly sawed away at the duct tape.

"How you guys doing?" I asked them quietly.

"Almost there…" Gavin replied, not looking up, for once not even spitting out a smartass comment.

Spiritmaster Gorsh stomped through the opposite doorway, clambering up and over a stalled ride car. He shook his whip loose and it snaked along the floor. He spotted Quill and Gavin slicing through the duct tape and his expression grew enraged. With a flick of his arm he made the whip crack. "Quill! You filthy three-pronged son of a traitorous goat! Your mother—"

I threw fire at him. Gorsh flung himself aside, spitting out goblin gibberish and sweeping his hand through the air. A strange cold pulse of magic flared to life. A glowing will o' wisp appeared in the air, made of shivering blue-green flame. The wisp flattened like a shield an instant before my fire broke against it. I felt the battle between the spells, sensed the warring understructures of energy that supported them, and could feel the link of magic to each of us. The clashing, interlocked spellframes wrenched our auras and mind-spaces close enough to one another that I snagged a glimpse of his jumbled thoughts — *strong, bitch is strong, dig deep, dig triple deep* — as we struggled, facing off as if glaring over crossed swords.

Then his spell prevailed with the suddenness of breaking ice, shunting aside my magefire bare inches before it would've charred him. A strange hum reverberated through the room, making my teeth hurt. The calliope wound into a grinding screech of discordant notes. My deflected flames licked against the walls and the ceiling. They left scorch marks and charred streaks but didn't catch. I stumbled, barely catching myself. Weakness and nausea washed through me and left me shaking.

"Clowns!" the spiritmaster screamed. "Rend them! Rip them! *Ravage* them!"

"'Kill them' would've worked just fine," I panted to Erik, struggling against the exhaustion that threatened to drop me to my knees.

Berserker Erik didn't laugh. He fixed his grim stare at the ghost clowns that pressed in from every side, floating ever closer. "I have to go battle rage, Captain. Give myself to *berserkergang*. I don't want Tiffany to see me like this."

My mind spun, my lips unable to form the words he wanted to hear. Prophecy or no, I hoped Tiffany and the rest of my crew got here ASAP and saved my ass from a personal clown apocalypse.

Erik didn't look at me, didn't seem to expect an answer. He closed his eyes.

Then Erik got angry.

CHAPTER FOURTEEN
Their Answer to Violence is Yes

Erik Cantrell's battle cry made my ears ring, my heart pound, and sent new adrenaline racing through my veins. The scream seethed with fury and frenzy. His face transformed into a mask of rage: lips drawn back to show his teeth, his eyes burning, maddened. It was a war cry of pure anger and defiance and battle joy all intermixed. Wordless, it still thrummed with power and magic. My heart lifted, and my exhaustion fell away. I felt like a warrior ready to charge into combat and hew down my enemies, to trample the grass of battlefields and stain the blades red.

I wanted war.

The ghost clowns hesitated. Our utter lack of fear seemed to confuse and dismay them.

A red, writhing curtain of energy swirled around Erik as he gripped his battleaxe in two hands, hunched over with his stance deep, still bellowing his war cry. All his muscles were taut. The cords stood out in his forearms and neck. Veins throbbed in his forehead. A stray thought flashed through my mind — that I'd never in my life screamed anywhere near as loud. My voice box would tear itself out of my throat and I'd cough up both lungs.

Erik hurled himself at the clowns. He swung his axe so fast

the blade blurred in vicious arcs. The clowns swarmed him. He bellowed again, slashing, spinning, hewing, hacking. Such was his ferocity that in seconds half the attacking ghosts had been cut into dissolving piles of ectoplasm and fading magnetic fields.

The spiritmaster cracked his whip. The coil snaked around Quill's knife hand as he cut through the last of the duct tape. Gorsh yanked the whip and jerked Quill away from the hostage.

"Three times the shame, you simpering pus-licker," the spiritmaster yelled. "You infernal traitor of the third kind! I'll use your skull as a bedpan instead of a codpiece!"

Quill wrenched his arm back, pulling Gorsh off balance. He slashed with the knife and severed the whip. "I quit, Chief! I quit the circus forever!"

"You can never quit the circus! Not even in death!"

I shunted aside my fatigue and charged the spiritmaster. A clown swerved in front of me, cutting me off. I seared away its painted face, scorching the orange tufts of hair and melting its red, bulbous nose. It flailed about, burning and giggling.

Utter exhaustion slammed into me with the force of a sledgehammer. I staggered and fell, my body shaking uncontrollably. I managed to stay on my knees, but only barely. The room spun, and all the sounds of combat were tinny and distant.

Losing it. Dammit, I was losing it. The fear crept in again, driving away the battle high given by Erik's berserker yell. Weakness sank leaden fingers deep into my muscles. I closed my eyes, gathered every last bit of strength I had, and levered myself onto my feet. Seemed as if I'd been staggering back to my damn feet all damn night.

Some of my strength returned once I started moving, and I realized I was pissed. Fucking *furious*. No one murdered door-to-door salesmen on my watch. No one rolled into my town and duct taped innocent fathers to carnival rides. No one swaggered into my personal Hallmark movie and abused Buddhists with whips. And no one, absolutely *no one*, put me in the sights of Fucking Prophetic Doom and got away with it.

My kick caught the spiritmaster in the chest, knocking him into the wall and leaving a dirty boot print on his vest. "Get the hostage clear!" I yelled to Quill and Gavin.

The hostage was still partially cocooned in duct tape, though he was free of the chair. They half led, half dragged him toward the unobstructed door opposite the portal where the cars would've traveled through the rest of the ride if they'd still been running. The hostage stumbled, falling, but Quill and Gavin caught him. They did their best to keep him steady as they hurried him along.

Gorsh staggered to his feet and made a move to stop them, chanting strange goblin words. I wheeled toward him, dragging in the very last of my energy to charbroil his face, but a ghost clown flew straight for the hostage, grabbing for his throat. I incinerated the clown before it touched him, blasting it into burning pieces that rained to the floor.

The world spun wildly again, grayed out, and then rushed back with black dots growing and bursting in my vision. My knees lost all strength and buckled like overstressed bridge struts, dumping me to the floor. I squinted, clutching my head as jagged knives of pain stabbed my brain. I gagged and shivered. My hands shook so violently that, if I hadn't known better, I'd have suspected I was doing it on purpose. I struggled to get control of my body and was horrified to discover I couldn't.

My final jet of flame had provided enough cover for Quill, Gavin, and the hostage to escape through the far door before the spiritmaster finished whatever magic he was attempting. I felt a snarling smile break across my face. If fate decreed I must be eaten by ghost clowns, at least I'd die knowing we'd freed the hostage. Part of me wished I could see the homecoming scene when he was reunited with his family.

Gorsh stopped chanting and cursed. He edged toward the portal he'd ripped open as his gaze skipped from Erik to me and back to Erik again. I lifted my shaking hand as if I could actually throw fire again. A pathetic bluff. Yet he seemed to buy it.

Erik was busy slaughtering clowns with frantic, frenzied gusto, slashing, spinning, leaping from the walls, whipping his two-handed axe around as if it weighed nothing. The blade hissed as it sliced the air and hummed as it sliced ghosts. Ectoplasm splattered the walls. It fell in rains of glowing green goo the exact shade of radioluminescent lime gelatin. The ghosts couldn't touch him. He was a mad-eyed whirling dervish of destruction. Any specters that tried were eviscerated, de-limbed, and expunged.

I tried to warn Erik that the spiritmaster was escaping but couldn't manage more than a wheezing cough of words. He never would've heard me over the calliope dirge or his savage growls and battle screams. He'd become more snarling, fighting jaguar than man. The sight of a berserker in full battle rage made a dark flower of fear bloom in my chest.

Gorsh must have felt the same because he ran and flung himself into the portal. I watched in sick frustration, unable to stop him. The portal's glowing edges stretched and rebounded as if they were made of elastic, wobbling back and forth with the force of his passing. Beyond the portal's surface I glimpsed blasted and jagged rock surrounding a massive stepped pyramid, far larger than anything humanity had ever built of stone. Each step of the pyramid was filled from end to end with big tops, booths, and amusement rides. Then the calliope stopped playing and the music shivered into echoes. The portal folded back on itself, the red glowing threads tightening and drawing together, collapsing into the center and vanishing.

Erik leaped over me. He loosed a scream of rage at the vanishing portal. He raised his axe far behind his head and slashed where the portal had been. The axe blade flared a shimmering, shifting crimson. It carved through the metal walls on either side of the doorway. He slashed again and again, reducing the doorjamb and the closest ride car to twisted chunks of metal.

Sarge burst through the doorway with Rafe and Stefan a step behind. I didn't want my people to witness me lying on the ground and shaking, so I made up for my failing strength with grim, bull-headed determination and dragged myself to my knees for the umpteen billionth time tonight. I was careful to stay clear of Erik's axe as he continued reducing everything around him into tinier pieces.

There were no more clowns. Only spatterings and puddles of ectoplasm that dissipated back into eddies of ectenic force and disappeared. I had quite a bit of the stuff on me and on my hands from when I'd fallen. The ectoplasm felt like cold oatmeal, but it was vanishing even as I stared at my fingers in disgust.

Tiffany ran into the room, pushing past Stefan. She had her pistols out and aimed, but there was nothing left to shoot. She spotted Erik and stared, her eyes wide, her face very still.

A mix of dismay and dread sank through my body, starting in my chest and then pooling in my stomach. Erik hadn't wanted Tiffany to see him in full berserker mode, caught in mindless battle rage. I opened my mouth, but had no idea what to say. I didn't know how to fix this.

Erik stopped shredding the walls and the ride cars. He stood there, hunched over and panting. Sweat streamed from his face, and his skin shone deathly pale. His muscles still bunched as if he were trying to lift a car by himself. He'd buried the axe blade into the metal floor all the way down to the haft — a staggering feat, one I'd have claimed impossible judging by how skinny he was. But there was the axe, inserted all intimate-like with the metal flooring, shearing into it so neatly it might've been fused there.

No one said a word. I could hear Erik breathing hard. He didn't look up. He didn't turn back to us.

Tiffany seemed at a loss as to what to do. Her eyes pleaded with me to make it right somehow. I bitterly wished I could've spared her the sight of this, but Erik was what he was. He couldn't hide it any more than she could pretend she wasn't a succubus.

Still, I didn't want her or anyone else straying too close until he got right in the head again. I had no idea how much control he had in zerker mode, whether or not the rage magic might drive him to attack us. He didn't know us well, and we certainly didn't know him well enough to risk a stupid tragedy.

I shook my head at Tiffany, held up a hand, and mouthed the word: *Wait.*

She hesitated. Anyone could read the war between competing desires on her face. My guts twisted and I suspected I might further ruin the whole ugly scene by throwing up everything I'd ever eaten in the history of me. My head pounded. My mouth felt as if it had grown a layer of sandpaper. God, what a mess.

Tiffany ran to Erik. She reached him before I could shout the warning that died on my tongue. I stumbled my sorry ass toward them, praying I could stop anything bad from happening to her, knowing I'd never make it in time.

She halted before touching him. He didn't look at her. He only stared at the axe buried in the floor. His breath rasped in and out. She set a hand on his back — gently at first, oh so gently—as if he were a soap bubble that would break if she pressed too hard. Then she whispered his name.

He looked at her. I saw the incredible pain in his eyes, that she'd seen him like this, out of control, an enraged killing machine. Guilt ate at me in acid sizzles because I hadn't been able to keep Tiffany from him as he'd asked, and the prophecy of my death was the reason he'd had to sacrifice control in the first place.

Erik started to pull away from her, but she reached out and touched his face. He froze. She said his name again. Very softly. He stood straight, staring at her as if she were the only thing in the room.

She stood on her tiptoes and kissed him, gently, on the lips. He flinched, drawing away from her. Her arms came up around him, holding him, kissing him again. His arms wrapped around her, and he pulled her tight to him. He kissed her back.

The relief that flooded through me left me weak and giddy. The danger had passed. Erik had control of himself...well, as much as a man kissing a succubus could have control of himself.

I turned to the rest of the team. Everyone was staring at Tiffany and Erik, grins all around. The relief in the air was thick enough to taste. Tiffany and Erik ignored us, lost in each other, but maybe I could carve them out a moment alone.

"What are you chuckleheads gawking at?" I demanded. "Give them some privacy. And medivac me some damn chocolate. Get it done *now*, Zero Dogs!"

They scrambled to obey.

* * *

Hanzo put an arm around my shoulder and helped me through the funhouse, but he was smart enough not to mention how heavily I leaned on him. My legs were still wobbly and my head pounded with the force of a freight-truck migraine. Still, the suffering was worth it because we'd saved the hostage. Also, I hadn't died. Letting Erik tag along had been the right choice.

True, berserkers were scarier than I'd imagined, and I'd even done the research. I still didn't know how I felt about a man who fed on his battle rage kissing Tiffany. "Ambivalent" sounded too trite for the swing between my hope and my disquiet. But I'd seen the way they'd connected back there — that understanding, that tenderness — and honestly, I didn't want to think about it anymore tonight. I was weary. I wanted to go home.

Hanzo was helping me down the metal step at the back of the funhouse when Lieutenant Stone's voice crackled in my radio headset. "Alpha Actual, this is Overwatch, do you require support, over?"

"Negative, Overwatch. Situation is locked down tight. What's the status on the hostage and the redcap?" I was worried the SWAT snipers might've shot the little Buddhist by accident, thinking him a murderous goblin psychostick instead of a hero who'd helped rescue the man.

"Hostage is receiving medical attention. Redcap suspect is in custody. What's the status on the other perps?"

"Multiple KIAs and discorporations. Primary target escaped down the rabbit hole."

"Running a hundred percent failure rate, Walker? Impressive, even for you."

I gritted my teeth, too tired to think of a witty retort. "Send in your elements to finish securing the area, over."

"Big roger on that, Overwatch out."

I tried to focus on objectives achieved — hostage saved, survival of clown-induced FPD, redcaps routed, no friendly casualties—but Stone's *shadenfreude* about the spiritmaster's second escape poisoned any triumph. Despite his size and deranged chatter, the spiritmaster's magic was some of the most powerful we'd faced, and he was cunning and slippery. Twice now we'd failed to close the book on him. We were low on EDR rounds, and so far I had no way to stop his damn Veil jumping. Worst of all, the bastard was crazy enough to tangle with us again.

I thanked Hanzo for his help, then trudged toward the police lines on my own. The only person who could've raised my spirits was Jake. Part of me harbored a deluded hope he'd push past the sawhorses and *Do Not Cross* tape and stand there grinning at me. Then he'd stride over in that lazy gait of his, walking as if he owned the world, and he'd kiss me.

The image seemed so real that I found myself scanning the crowd, the corner of my mouth already twitching into a smile. For a moment I was sure I saw him—a tall man with wide shoulders standing near a police cruiser—and my heart lurched in my chest, leaving me weak and giddy.

The man turned toward me. He wasn't Jake.

I closed my eyes until I was certain I had myself locked down again. Nothing but foolish to hold out hope for something so unlikely. I did have one helluva story to tell him when I finally saw him again. I should be content with that.

Content with that and happy to be alive.

* * *

I felt steadier after slamming energy drinks from the van and sitting for a while, enjoying the fleeting solitude. The break didn't last long enough. I set off again, hauling my carcass through the chaotic mess of police, reporters, gawkers, EMTs, and firefighters to the police cruiser with Quill in the back. I'd already given a quick After Action Report to the Commissioner, and he'd made it clear hired guns weren't welcome to participate in the police investigation. But I wanted to clear up some things about the redcap spiritmaster that bothered me. I still didn't understand how tonight's events linked me to Mistress Patel, Erik, the spiritmaster, and the prophecy of the ninth fortune cookie. I'd heard the deranged ranting the spiritmaster had inflicted on the hostage negotiator, and while crazy didn't need a reason, my rational mind still itched to uncover the pattern behind the prophecy.

Two uniforms guarded the cruiser holding Quill. Detective Miller lingered nearby with that damn coffee cup still in his hand. He watched the cops in the distance search the traveling carnival and the firefighters drench the world's first spontaneously combusting fish taco stand. For a man in charge of murder investigations Miller sure spent a helluva lot of time standing around staring at things and drinking coffee.

He noticed me coming and lifted his cup in salute, though he didn't smile. "Heard you were busy tonight, Walker."

"Yeah, things got a little heated."

"Pyromancer humor. Never gets old, does it?"

"Never. And look at that. We even left a few suspects alive for you."

"Not the ringmaster."

"Mr. Happy Boots got away."

"Again."

"What can I say? He ripped the universe a new asshole and jumped through headfirst. I sure as hell wasn't going to chase him in there."

"Above the proverbial pay grade?"

"Our contract doesn't cover interdimensional retrieval." I shrugged and glanced at the cruiser with Quill in the back. "What's gonna happen to the redcap who helped us rescue the hostage?"

He took a drink of coffee then rubbed his bottom lip with his thumb. "Multnomah County Jail."

"Jail? What the hell, Miller? He's a damn hero."

"A formality. We'll interview him, take his statement, run his background. Standard stuff. The DA's gonna want him to testify against the other goblins. Until then, he's a suspect."

"I want to be in on the interrogation."

"You know I can't allow that. This is a police matter. Besides, interrogation is an art." He waved his coffee cup at the carnival. "You don't see me charging into those shooting situations pretending I'm a SWAT guy, do you?"

"All right then, I'm calling in a marker. Remember those pixies?"

"Not the goddamn pixies again. How many times are you gonna call that in, Walker?"

I ignored him. "Remember how you needed to talk to those pixies about a certain drunken spriggan working as a Salvation Army Santa who'd been stabbed to death and buried in aluminum Christmas trees? Remember who helped you break that one open, did a little pixie liaison work? How it turned out that the fairies had killed merry spriggan Santa for his flask, then framed the pixies? And who got all the glory for solving that case, I wonder?"

"You're serious."

"Completely."

"The Commissioner would have a coronary if he found out, so I guess that means I'm in. But you only observe from behind the glass and you keep your mouth shut. No trouble. I mean it."

"Promise. And I want to watch one of the other surviving redcaps interrogated."

"You want a ham sandwich too? What the hell are you after, Walker?"

Telling him about the fortune cookie prophecy or Mistress Patel would only make me seem insane, so I didn't. "I want to know why the hell this went down. Circus ghosts bring out the cosmic existential horror in me."

He took a drink, watched me over the rim before finally answering. "Bullshit."

"I forgot to mention the pixies."

"Fine, dammit. Gawk at all the interrogations. Eat your heart out."

"I'm sure I will." I hesitated, wondering how far I could push this. "So can I go talk with Quill before you drag him downtown and grill him?"

"No."

"He helped save a man's life tonight. I want to at least tell him thanks. Everybody else around here's treating him like a serial killer. Christ, he's a Buddhist."

"And I'm Saint Miller, patron of longsuffering detectives, coffee, and Basset hounds."

"That list clearly doesn't include comedians. Look, just give me five minutes with him. I won't blow your case. Mercenary's honor. And...pixies."

"Yeah, how could I forget?" He returned to glowering at the carnival and worshiping his coffee.

I grinned and marched to the cruiser. Quill had to stretch to peer out the window at me because his eyes barely cleared the bottom edge of the window frame. I couldn't read the expression on his face when he saw me. Then again, goblins, like quantum physics, were a mystery to me.

I opened the cruiser's back door and climbed in beside him. One of the nearby uniformed cop gave me the stink-eye, but I ignored him until he decided to ignore me back. Tonight I was in no mood for power games. I did leave the door open, because I didn't want to end up locked inside and have to ask the cop to let me out. Neither did I want it to appear as if I'd been arrested.

"Hello, Captain." Quill's voice was scratchy, higher pitched than mine, but had a resonance that prevented it from sounding like a rake used to clean a bathtub. His hands were cuffed behind him. That irritated me, but it wasn't my show anymore.

"How are they treating you?" Stupid question. I'd asked it anyway.

"I'm under arrest, but Detective Miller says it's just a formality until they sort everything out."

"I told them what you did. It was very brave."

Quill shook his head. "I'm just glad Howard is safe. How is he?"

"Minor scrapes and bruises. A bit traumatized. They took him to the hospital, probably keep him under observation for a night."

"I told him I was sorry over and over. I don't know if he believed me. It's hard to read human expressions."

I smirked. "You cut him free and got him away. I'm sure he believed you."

A long pause. "So Chief Gorsh escaped then?"

"Yeah, he rabbited hard."

"The Chief…he's drawn a cloak of bad karma tight around himself, but it is still a hard thing to witness. I wished to teach him, but I failed him."

"Some people can't be taught."

"Every being can be taught. It comes down to the patience of the teacher. *Erro madacha, vlah sienveso.*"

"What is that, some Buddhist saying?"

"Vrardish, our goblin speak. Difficult to translate, but roughly it means, 'Water seeps through the hand that cups it.'"

"Surprisingly Zen for goblins."

"I adapted the original phrase a bit." Quill frowned and looked away. "Substituted 'water' for 'blood.'"

That sounded more like the goblins I knew. "I wanted to say thanks for your help tonight. And I wanted to ask...do you know a Mistress Patel?"

Quill blinked and shook his head no.

"How about Erik, the berserker you met tonight? Ever see him before? Or did your spiritmaster chief...did he have power over fortune cookies? Or, maybe was he a prophet?" Heat crept up my neck and flushed my cheeks.

"Chief Gorsh was no prophet. I'd never seen a berserker until tonight. And I'm not certain what you mean about power over fortune cookies."

"Forget it." Maybe the other goblins would know more. Quill was probably kept out of the loop of evil due to his aberrant case of pacifism and conscience.

"Captain, how did the rest of the Corvallis Boys fare? Were many of them hurt?"

"The other redcaps? Yeah, they took some casualties. The survivors were arrested. They'll do hard time in Chacaza for kidnapping. More if they're tied to any other murders." Chacaza was a maximum security prison in the wastelands of Wyoming, near Flaming Gorge, built to lock down paranormal criminals. Run by some private mega-corporation. Huge. Ugly. Prone to riots and inmate-on-inmate violence. I hoped I never saw it on anything but a television screen. Even then it was better to change the channel.

"It eases my heart to hear some survived, at least. They too earned the karma that undid them, but violence is always hard thing." Quill whispered something else.

"I didn't catch that last."

The powrie took off his cap and turned it in his hands, sliding his fingers along the edge. His fingertips turned red. "I said, may that poor salesman forgive us a thousand times. I never saw his face, but every death throws a long shadow.

People look at me and I read it in their eyes. They look at me and they see a murderer."

He closed his eyes and wiped his fingers on his robes, then gently, slowly, put his cap back on his head.

We were both silent for a time. The salesman had been killed before the Zero Dogs had been hired to go in and engage the redcaps, and yet I still felt a vague but lingering guilt for not saving him in time. Irrational, yet still…there it was. At another time I might've made an offhand joke about door-to-door salespeople to gloss over the stupid tragedy of some random salesman ending up murdered for hat dye. No one deserved that shit. But soldiers hid the horror behind the humor, because we looked at it too often. It was ugly, but sometimes it helped.

Not always, but sometimes.

Instead I stared out at the flashing lights on the ambulances. "Last mission we had — the one against you goblins at the motel, actually — some guy in the crowd started heckling me as I walked away. Calling me a murderer."

"We're all locked in suffering. I struggle with it every day. How easy it would be to hate. How easy to abhor the universe for making me a creature who needs to kill, to steal life in order to continue living. If my cap dries out I will die. But there isn't a day I don't consider letting my hat go dry and defy a universe that would ever allow such a thing as me to exist."

"If you had, there's a good chance Howard wouldn't be alive tonight."

He nodded slowly. Yet, I couldn't help but glance at his cap. He noticed the glance and his smile held no cheer.

"Pig's blood, with an apology to the pigs for the harm I cause. I'm a mockery. A sad joke. But tonight I did a little good. A little good added to a little good may someday amount to an entire ocean of good."

"You did more than a little good tonight. Don't sell yourself short. That wasn't a height joke, by the way."

He laughed. I really liked him for laughing.

"So what will you do now?" I asked.

"I'm simply trying to get through this night. The future...I suppose I'll eventually head to a monastery. I've always wanted to live in the mountains, giving my days over to meditation and study. I've lost hope that I can be a good example to my kinsmen. The weight of my failure is heavy on me. Perhaps things can't change after all."

"Before I met you, I would've sworn up and down a goblin could only deal out chaos and murder. The thought of one risking his life to save a person was a pipe dream. Now..." I shrugged. "Things changed."

He smiled at me. I smiled back.

* * *

We loaded up the technicals with all our gear and people and rolled out. We left the deserted carnival in our rearview mirrors and not a moment too soon.

The CB we used to communicate between our half-assed assault vehicles squawked to life.

"Captain, we have a problem," Gavin said. He was driving the lead truck again, the psy-ops one with the speakers mounted all over the cab, inside and out.

I strained to see what might be ahead of him on the road. We couldn't catch a break tonight. "What now?"

"The GPS can't find any directions to Funkytown."

Lipps Inc's anthem started blasting from the speakers at a disturbing volume of disco distortion. Rafe started to dance in the truck's bed, again holding onto the mounted grenade launcher with one arm to avoid falling out.

People stared.

At first I wanted to crawl into a cave, but then I started to laugh. At some point, it all became too crazy to do anything else.

CHAPTER FIFTEEN
Interrogate This!

T wo hours later I sat behind a large one-way mirror at the Multnomah County Jail and stared into the stark gray of an interrogation room as Detective Miller questioned a redcap mechanic named Valco. The powrie sat at a table, perched atop two stacked phonebooks balanced on a cheap plastic chair. He was cuffed, and a second set of cuffs locked him to one of the table's steel legs. Valco slouched, kicking his dangling feet back and forth, clinking his chain against the metal. His lawyer was Celedrael Lethlion, an Elven criminal defense attorney with an ego smaller than the state of Alaska, but only if you counted the island where you could see Russia.

Inside the viewing room, I scowled as I sipped the worst coffee I'd ever tasted and gnawed on a bagel so stale I could've used it to break up concrete. No point in complaining. I needed the caffeine and the calories. Also, I wanted to uncover any hidden connection between the fortune cookie prophecy, Mistress Patel's obscure foretelling and Erik Cantrell's arrival, the spiritmaster, and me. I had to know if the threat lingered, ready to bite me in the ass if I failed to sort it out. I'd run up against baddies before whose threat factor I'd believed combat-ineffective and degraded to the point of irrelevance, only to have them come roaring back to wreak serious vengeance. Last thing I needed was that psycho spiritmaster opening a portal into my bathroom and releasing the clown horde while I was in the shower.

"Remember the deal we made with the DA, Detective Miller," Celedrael warned, his smooth, cultured voice vibrating with an undertone of menace beneath the civility. "My client isn't guilty of murder, so courtesy would be appreciated."

Miller pushed some papers around on the table before tossing a chilly look at the defense attorney. Celedrael had wrangled a pretty deal for his client: the first degree kidnapping and third degree criminal mischief charges were dropped for charges of disturbing the peace and resisting arrest in exchange for Valco's full cooperation and guilty plea.

The officer manning the video recorder in the viewing room with me snorted. "Lawyers."

I toyed with the pen shoved through the binding coils of my notebook and grunted my agreement. Celedrael Lethlion was as difficult to miss as a peacock stranded on Utah's Salt Lake. He sported a three-piece suit and a Stetson cowboy hat the same shade of gray as the Oregon sky in January. An amethyst flashed on the brim next to a Bald Eagle feather. Bald Eagle feathers were illegal to own, but that didn't seem to have stopped him from incorporating one into his general hat ambience. His leather shoes gleamed with a perfect polish and subtly shifted color in the harsh light whenever he moved. He was blond, ageless, sporting those characteristic leaf-shaped ears, and eyes the same mottled, rotting-orange shade as Jupiter's moon Io.

"I didn't mean to chafe your client's sensitive feelings," Detective Miller said dryly. "But some of us are interested in conducting a homicide investigation and seeing justice done."

"We all want justice, detective."

Miller grinned. "Of course. But I'd hate to see your deal

with the DA fall through because your client was too bored to answer my questions."

Celedrael conferred with Valco in a low voice. Miller folded his arms across his chest and stared at the grimy fluorescent track lighting until Celedrael addressed him again. "Please proceed, Detective Miller."

Miller leaned forward again, pinning the goblin with a stare as sharp as swords. "How did you meet up with this spiritmaster guy? And does he have a real name? Something you wouldn't find on a Saturday morning cartoon?"

"Knew him as 'that asshole Gorsh,'" Valco replied. "Or 'sir Chief' if he was in hearing range. Crazy piece of work, that one. Mad as a horny badger with jock itch and the mange." The redcap whistled and shook his head. "All the time with this stupid talk about the circus. Not one of us understood more than two words in ten, and none of it made any damn difference anyhow." Valco stared at the track lighting, frowning. "And he had a boner for the word *three*. Yep...and he mentioned codpieces more than most." He shrugged.

"How'd you end up with him then?"

"Met him on the Internet. Just because I'm a goblin doesn't mean I'm not connected."

"Online..." Miller raised his eyebrows. "Like a dating site for tiny psychos?"

I snorted. The detective next to me grinned and said, "Miller loves baiting these guys."

"Uncalled for, Detective," Celedrael said, his voice reverberating with dulcet tones of elven disapproval.

Valco waved his lawyer off. "Heard worse when I was in Chacaza. Not a dating site. Try a job listing site, full of work from home offers and Nigerian real estate scams and what-have-you. Offered to hire us Corvallis Boys after someone murder-killed his last crew."

"Didn't he have ghost minions? Why hire you?"

"Ghosts don't have the concentration to set up equipment and collect tickets. 'Sides, he needed a tinkerer to run the calliope, keep that hoary rutting pipe-monster from breaking down. That was my racket. It's known I have a bit of gremlin in the family tree."

"This Gorsh and some other redcap associates were involved in the murder of Jimmy Collins, a door-to-door salesman. Yet the murder of the carnival owner, Freddy Newman, involved ghosts, not goblins. So why the switch? Circus ghosts weren't present at the motel crime scene. What changed?"

Celedrael leaned over and whispered in Valco's ear.

Valco grunted and then scowled. "That asshole Gorsh didn't have many ghosts, first off. Anything more than pulling over one or two phantoms, forget it. And he couldn't reshape them without the Ochre Calliope, not outside the spirit world anyway. When I got it running again, he started summoning spirits left and right, and then remaking them into circus-y freaky things. The calliope let him keep a bunch of ghosts this side of the Veil, more than he could shape and control otherwise."

"And you helped him by running the calliope?"

"Down economy like this? Damn right I helped him. It was a job. And I like flapjacks. With syrup. IHOP doesn't hand those angel pasties out for free, got me?"

"Why take over the carnival? Why attract attention?"

"That asshole was impatient, wanted more, and more faster. He wanted to hook his calliope up to the rides, running cable like electrical wire, mix some *nurata* and spiritmaster mojo, and have it suck in people's emotions. The fear, the thrill, the adrenaline, lust, excitement, what-have-you. Then he'd amp his little asshole self to the max to bring a whole slew of those ghost things from the spirit world. Bragged about it nonstop. *Blah, blah, blah,* bunch of incoherent yammering. But hey, I was just a wrench in a bloody red hat. Nobody asked Valco, did they?"

I scribbled a note that read: *Evil calliope machine? What happened to it?* Typical madman stuff: open portals, bring in the clowns. Was it the fifth or the sixth circle of Dante's Hell that held evil clowns? I scribbled another note: *Read The Inferno.* I stared at that for a second, then scratched it out and wrote: *Research the Inferno on Wikipedia.*

"This guy seems slippery," Miller said. "Twice he's escaped my eager little handcuffs. You know a way to pin him down?"

Valco and his lawyer conferred again.

"Oh, technically he could move across the Veil, you know," Valco continued. "Into the spirit world and whatnot, and it wasn't as easy as all that, right? It takes power, and that has to be generated. Funny thing he told me, he couldn't have escaped that motel if nobody had never attacked him. He had to wait for that electric violence, you know, that old American bullet song. Once the hammer met the anvil, he could use those sparks to tease open his little sphincter hole in the universe and shove his head in. As for stopping him?" Valco shrugged. "Grandpips knew a bit of *nurata*, claimed you could ward against portals and dimension doors. Lock 'em down, if ya like. That's all I got."

I scribbled fast on my notepad. *Double check all wards/barriers/restraining walls on Compound.* I was ninety percent certain all our spell protection was up to date, but I didn't want surprises. Past Zero Dog commanders had been known to go cheap, use cut-rate hedge wizards and uncertified freelance spellcasters, and sometimes you got what you paid for.

"So tell me how things went bad," Miller said. "I got another redcap you might know. Name's Quill. Said the Corvallis Boys started the panic at the carnival after a patrol car arrived."

Again, Celedrael whispered in Valco's ear. Valco shrugged and rattled his cuffs.

"Could be. That asshole Gorsh ice-smoked his old boss, took some government census worker hostage. The pork rinds in blue show up, the boys probably got a little nervous, hear? I wouldn't know, cuz I was busy keeping that blasted bag-pipe on wheels spitting out the ghosts."

"How did Quill get involved with you lot?"

"That asshole Gorsh brought him along, right? Seems Gorsh had some kinda thing for Quill's mother, made some promise or other. Quill always went over twitchy when we talked about murder and the like. The kind of goblin who's a bit touched, would use red food dye on his cap, if he could he get away with it. Gorsh hated the poor bastard."

Miller jotted a few notes. "There's still a few things I can't figure out, and maybe you can help clarify. Why did you demand the Zero Dogs? Why the message with the teddy bear? You *wanted* the Zero Dogs to show up. I have a hard time getting my pork rind brain around that one."

The redcap didn't answer. He only stared up at the fly-specked ceiling light. I sat on the very edge of my seat, staring at him, willing him to talk.

"You got your deal in exchange for helping us," Miller warned. "Frankly, I don't see the problem with answering a simple question."

Valco talked it over quietly with his lawyer. Miller waited them out.

"I thought taunting those mercenaries into another dust-up was fool's work," Valco finally said. "Told that asshole Gorsh right to his face he was a fool to do it. Course, I wasn't making the rules right then, and he who has the ghosts makes the rules. He wanted revenge, that's factual, you understand? But he'd sapped down the juice on the calliope bringing all those ghosties over. After all the crowd fled, he was double penetrated, to be choice with my terms. He had the start of his army, but without more power to the calliope, he could only make one of his Veil portals big enough for himself to escape through, not us, and not the ghosts he'd gone to such trouble to reshape and color so neatly between the lines."

"What's that have to do with the mercs?"

"You don't listen? That asshole Gorsh wanted the mercs to attack, so he could churn up 'three-times the energy for his infernal calliope engine' or blah, blah, wank, wank. It was *fighting* that yammering lunatic wanted. Chaos. The more the better. Who better to mix it up with than the cold-hearted killers who'd put the hurt on his boys back at the motel, right? Genuine, impeccable logic that worked out exceedingly well."

Judging from Valco's explanations, it sounded as if Gorsh had been following his own twisted plan with zero knowledge of Patel or that death prophecy. I didn't know if that made me feel better or worse. Better, because I didn't have to believe in elaborate, inexplicable conspiracies. Worse, because the universe had apparently suffered a disturbingly random and spontaneous lust for killing me.

Miller scrawled a few more lazy notes. "What made Gorsh think you'd do any better against them this time around?"

"Ghosts. This is bona fide: that milky ringmaster idiot might've been barking mad, but he had plenty of twisted ghosts at his beck and call. Better than redcaps, who barely listened to him ever, and only for the promise of blood."

"This bloody hat thing," Miller tapped the top page of the statement with one finger, "that's why Gorsh murdered Jimmy Collins? And let's not forget your boss, Freddy Newman. You dip your hat in his blood after the ghosts were through gnawing him over?"

Celedrael shook his head and sat back, smoothing his suit lapels. "I think we already covered those grounds, detective. The DA was satisfied. Let's stick to questions regarding Spiritmaster Gorsh, as we agreed. He's still at large, I believe, and a threat to the public safety."

"And I had no hand in any of it anyway," Valco continued, despite a warning glance from his lawyer. "The cappers who did are all dead, except for Quill, and turns out he's a treacherous little shin-gnawing shit. Now all my best mates are worm food, thanks to that asshole Gorsh and those pus-sucking mercenaries. Nails for all their eyes, and damn each one to hell." He laughed suddenly, and leered. "Except for that sweet-winged slut with the choice rack. Gorsh and his stainless steel codpiece had a thing for that succubus-flavored gift basket. Only thing I ever agreed with him about. I'd sip from her chalice any night."

Tiffany. My notebook burst into flames, though even that little magefire brought the weariness slamming home again, punching bone deep, forging a fiery ache in my joints. I cursed, flung the burning notebook to the floor, then stomped on it until the flames went out. It gave me something to do to other than running into the interrogation room and incinerating that wizened maggot for talking that way about my friend. The officer working the camera equipment stared at me as if I'd gone stark raving mad.

Miller pushed from his chair and leaned into Valco's face. The goblin flinched. His handcuff bracelet rattled against the table.

Miller's voice, coming to me over the speakers, sounded calm, yet Freon-level cold. "I remember a time when a gentleman could call out a disrespectful scoundrel for talk like that about a lady."

"Are you threatening my client, detective?" The lawyer

appeared ninety percent bored, ten percent amused.

"Not at all, Mr. Lethlion. Don't misunderstand my wistful reminiscing for more civil times. As an officer of the peace, I don't condone things such as, hypothetically, lowering a rude, misogynistic little shit into a blender by his balls until he repents for being an asshole. Overkill and completely disproportionate." Miller smiled sweetly. "I merely enjoy using the word *scoundrel.*"

I slowly sat again. Miller had gone up an entire level in my estimation, and he'd already been my favorite homicide detective. Never mind that he was the only one who'd even talk to me.

Valco only stared at him, wide-eyed and nervously gnawing his lip.

"Let's move on," Miller said, all business again. "You claim Gorsh wanted to be attacked to generate..." He glanced at his notes. "...energy for his 'infernal calliope machine.' All he ended up doing was running away again. So will he be back? Take another swing at revenge, maybe? Try and pull off his endgame?"

I leaned closer to the glass, barely aware I'd moved, my heart beating harder. That was one of the questions I'd begged Miller to ask. Quill had said Gorsh wanted a massive circus-flavored ghost army. Then there was the prophecy...and Jake's dream. I had to know if this was over, or if it had just begun.

Valco shrugged again. "Couldn't say, don't know, don't give a damn. He lost his doohickey of doom, so his plans are all fucked and fouled. I'll name him a urine-yellow coward for fleeing, don't get me wrong. That squid-fucker had an emergency escape plan the whole time and leaves us sad bastards behind, simply because he's given an ass-punting. Well, fuck him sideways with an ice-skate. That asshole liked to brag how no one would never get him as long as he stayed in the spirit world. How he couldn't be touched inside his personal slice of heaven. Must be nice." Valco fiddled with his handcuff bracelet. "Though he *did* have a crazy hard-on for that spicy slu—that lady with the enormous...wings." Valco coughed. "So...maybe he'll come prancing back to make her his squeeze toy. Maybe not."

Those words left me cold, but even if Gorsh still nursed some obsession with Tiffany thanks to that charm spell, I couldn't hunt him down because I had no access to the spirit world. Sarge might have arcane demon magic that could punch through interdimensional walls, but I wasn't about to risk my people looking for unpaid trouble, with no support and plenty of danger. If the spiritmaster returned, and the government or some client sent us after him again, we'd deal with him Zero Dog style. If he ended up trapped forever in the afterlife, no skin off my ass. I could return home confident that these stupid fates and prophecies and assorted bullshit had been heroically avoided. Besides, it sounded as if the police had things under control. They'd already put out a BOLO for Gorsh. After two back-to-back ass kickings, I doubted he'd show his face in Portland again. To be safe, I'd beef up the wards around the house and property, maybe invest in a few attack robots to patrol the grounds.

"Gorsh ever mention a lady named Mistress Patel?" Miller asked, revving my heart into the red zone again. Another of my questions.

"Was she in the circus?"

"No."

"Then he didn't mention her."

"What about a guy named Erik Cantrell?"

"A carny?"

"No."

"Then he didn't fucking mention him."

"He say anything about any prophecy?"

"A prophecy about the circus?"

"I get the feeling the guy had a one track mind."

"Score one for Team Bacon. If it wasn't about the thousand year circus Reich, that asshole didn't give a good goblin damn."

Miller pressed on with another line of questions, but I'd heard all I needed. No direct link existed between Mistress Patel, Erik, and the spiritmaster that I could see. Only the tenuous correlation of connections forming the spine of that prophecy. A spine we'd broken tonight.

I pocketed my charred notebook and stood to go, leaving the dregs of my coffee to be disposed of by the appropriate hazmat team. I'd just pulled open the door when the redcap said something that froze me in place.

"Tell you one thing I *do* remember," Valco said. He writhed on his seat in joy and grunted laughter. "Right at the end there, that asshole Gorsh swore the fiery merc-dog-bitch was due for the karma hammer. His words, not mine."

I turned around slowly, my blood cold as sleet. Those words could be nothing more than idle threat. Or they could be yet another shard of prophecy's broken window.

"What'd he mean by that?" Miller demanded.

"'Ghosts don't forget,' was what that he said." Valco's smirk showed a nasty edge. "'And the universe always pays back double.' That bitch burned a pretty bunch of ghosts, last I heard. Want to know where your goblin at large'll turn up, like as not? My guess, right on her front doorstep, screeching about the end of the world and packing clowns."

CHAPTER SIXTEEN
New Hires

Mercenary Wing Rv6-4 "Zero Dogs"
June 26th

Despite Valco's ominous prediction, no clowns, fire eaters, mimes, trapeze artists or contortionists—ghostly or otherwise—showed up on my doorstep in the days following the carnival battle. I paid a huge sum of money to have all the compound's spell protections updated and refreshed, preventing any unauthorized portal breaches or nefarious wormholing. Then Sarge and I reviewed our security systems for flaws. I picked out a couple of advanced AI robot weapon platforms, but the prices kept me from clicking the buy button. Even free shipping didn't help much. Instead I bought more EDR rounds and a slew of claymore mines I found on an auction site for a screaming deal.

The Ochre Calliope, the machine supercharging the spiritmaster's ghost-control, had vanished. I knew it existed from both Quill's statement and Valco's interrogation, and I'd seen photos of the hideous contraption in the police file. I only wished I'd had the chance to light that thing on fire instead of a taco stand. I managed to track it to police impound. From there it had been loaded into a tractor trailer and taken away.

"What do you mean, 'taken away?'" I'd demanded of the officer at the impound desk. "Who the hell takes away a paranormal steam organ?"

The officer had shrugged, then yawned for emphasis. "Criminal forfeiture. We offload all kinds of crazy shit."

"I thought you had to hold that stuff for evidence until there's a conviction. You didn't even have time to auction it."

He'd started clicking around on his computer, clearly torqued off by my persistence. "Another agency took custody and hauled it away and that's the *exact* point where my fuck-giving stopped."

"What agency?"

"Can't tell you. Make up your own alphabet soup acronym."

"Where'd they take it?"

"Official destination...well, look here. Says *points unknown.*"

"Can I at least see the paperwork?"

He'd laughed. "Why don't you get lost? You're interfering with police business. Class One felony."

That dead end hadn't stopped me, but the next one finished the job. My calls to the Department of Defense were transferred and transferred until they were summarily dropped. I had even less luck uncovering who had been on the phone with Hagel and changed the Commissioner's mind that night, sending us to save the hostage instead of SWAT. The mystery filled me with unease, as if some scheming faceless god behind the scenes had taken an interest in using us as his personal sword.

Meanwhile, June blazed away under a hot spell that had scorched the entire week. I'd tried to worry more about our central air conditioning costs than a phantom circus onslaught, and only ended up worrying about both at the same time. Jake had called again before he'd gone back into the field. The constant, low-grade disquiet that haunted me when he was actively deployed had dog-piled on top of my other anxieties, but I'd kept my voice cheerful. I hadn't wanted him worrying about me, and had known perfectly well he was.

I'd resolved Erik's contract status, putting his conditional employment to a vote by the rest of the team. Only one of the secret ballots had tallied negative. Gavin had later confirmed my suspicions by finding me when I'd been busy spreading Nutella on cookies and starting to rant about how I'd rue the day I hired a berserker. I'd ignored him and signed Erik to a three-month contract with option to renew. What the hell. I already rued the day I'd hired a certain bad attitude empath with zero powers of empathy.

Now it was Thursday night. The outside air still hugged the compound, warm and close even with the sun down and a thunderstorm incoming. I'd holed up in my office to attack the paperwork strategically positioned in front of the a/c vent when my stomach gave a long rumbling growl. I'd missed dinner, busy hammering away at the books and supply orders, wishing I'd hired a quartermaster or at least a half-decent bookkeeper. I turned off the computer and descended the main stairway to the kitchen in quest for food.

Midway down, the hairs on the back of my neck and arms lifted. I shivered, drawing in a gulp of cold, dry air. Something stalked me down the stairwell. I spun around, ready to deal out hurt, and stared straight into the vacant round eyes of the ghost pufferfish. It floated serene and placid, its inflated spiky body giving off a pale spectral glow. The string Quill had enchanted to use the puffer as a balloon was still tied around its tail fin.

I snatched the string and hauled the puffer over to the banister, then tied it around the post. The sea squab bobbed there, slowly drifting around on its tether, making fish faces and goggling at me.

"I don't know who brought you home," I said, although I

suspected it might've been Mai. She had a soft spot for strange animals, though I sure as hell didn't need another spirit of a restless sea creature floating amok. "And I don't want you creep-creeping around like that pervert jellyfish."

I started down the stairs again, but glanced back after a few steps. The ghost pufferfish drifted in slow circles. Crap. I couldn't leave him…her…*it* leashed there alone. That would be cruel. The puffer needed to return to Vahalla or Fólkvangr or wherever fish went to swim out the afterlife.

My stomach protested again. I wanted nothing more than to shovel down some food, maybe throw back a strong drink, and to clock out for the rest of the night, but first I had to play ghost rescue, psychopomp for an aquatic animal. I untied the string, hurried down the stairs, and raced through the back hall leading to the deck. Unfortunately, the same hall led past one entrance to the kitchen where Rafe was busy eating. He took one look at me and my spiky balloon and laughed so hard he spit yams all over the refrigerator door. Yeah. Hilarious. I took my balloonfish and flounced.

Outside, the night air smelled faintly of rain. Huge summer storm clouds massed to the north, lightning flashing in their bellies and occasional rumbling booms drifting to me across the cityscape. A relatively rare thunderstorm, far enough away that it would miss most of Portland.

As I watched the storm, something about those brooding dark clouds turned my mind back to the spiritmaster and the Fucking Prophetic Doom I'd dodged. I hated the loose ends. Quill was another loose end. The DA had declined to bring charges because of his help in saving the hostage, but I wondered where the Buddhist had gone after his release. After all, this was *his* floating fish.

Frowning, I glanced to the puffer floating beside my head and released the string. "Go on." I made shooing motions.

"Head off to the heaven that waits for inflatable fish."

The ghost pufferfish circled me twice, staring at me with those wide round eyes, and then it drifted away. It floated higher and higher, heading toward the distant storm. The glowing ball eventually resembled a wandering star before finally fading from sight. I wondered if anyone would report it as a UFO and rather hoped they did.

"Hi, Captain."

I flinched and gasped out a sound that held all the melodious qualities of an outraged bluejay. I wheeled around to find Tiffany perched on the deck railing a little ways away. Her blue eyes glowed softly in the darkness.

"I didn't mean to scare you." She bit her lip and clutched at a wing as if she thought it might tear off her back and flap away.

"Don't worry, it was nothing." A strange, hesitant tension crackled between us. My brain flailed about, searching for something to say. "Enjoying the storm?"

"I…I want to talk to you about Jake."

That made me pause, thinking I'd misheard her. I'd expected her to say Erik, not Jake. I climbed onto the railing next to her. I wished I'd brought something to drink, but I didn't want to break the moment by running inside. The electric tension told me this would be no casual chat.

"Why talk about men at all?" I asked. "All they do is throw wrenches into smooth-running machinery. Everybody's always talking about men, especially the men. Let's talk about something better instead. Like thunderstorms."

"Don't dodge." She smiled and cocked her head, then started ticking off on her fingers. "Mostly we talk about stuff catching on fire. Movies. New guns and rare ammunition. How huge our cat is getting. Food. Whether you can hide a knife inside a high heel. Queen Elizabeth the First. Why zombies

want to eat people. How elves are annoying. More about food —
"

"Fine, fine, you're right. Thunderstorms really are great though. We don't get enough lightning here."

We stared at the storm. Thunder rumbled and rolled across the city, tame by the time it reached us.

"Captain...how did you know you were in love with Jake?"

"Not going to be dissuaded, are you?"

"I'm on a mission. Zero Dogs sink their teeth in and never let go, like Gila monsters. You have to cut off our heads, pry out our fangs—"

"Okaaay, I get the point."

Tiffany grinned and settled in, her watchful silence urging me on.

"Jake. That man..." I shook my head, trying to gather the right words. "That man vexed me something wicked."

"That's how you knew?"

"There was a shade more to it than that. You sure you want to hear this? I ramble when I get sappy."

She nodded. So I told her. She knew a good deal of the story already, so I told her the abridged version of how I couldn't stand him at first, thought he threatened my command, what a pain in the ass he was, and how we'd finally come to respect each other. Then the sparks. Then the fireworks. Then the zombie killing.

"I was so happy for you," Tiffany said after I realized I'd been going on and on. She trailed a finger along the edge of her black wing. "I've been thinking a lot about Erik."

"I want you to be..." I stopped, not willing to say the word "careful." Careful sounded as if I didn't trust Erik. He'd come to Portland to help me stave off a doom prophecy, and I'd hired him as a Zero Dog. If I didn't trust him, at least to some degree, I'd be a paranoid idiot. Still, there was trust...and there was watching a good friend risk having her glass heart smashed. "I want you to take it slow."

"I don't feel like taking it slow. I'm always taking it slow and I don't have anything. Now there's something I want. Why should I torture myself with slow?"

Lightning flashed in the guts of a dark cloud, rapid strobe-light pulses. "You mind if I ask, why this guy?"

"He looked me right in the eyes."

I turned, surprised, almost amused, but not sure I could show it without hurting her feelings. So I kept my face carefully neutral.

"I'm tired, Captain," she continued. "It gets old, the way everybody looks at me."

"You mean males."

"Nobody sees me. They see a pair of…of big tits and a tight ass." She blushed and played with her wing. "Most of them anyway. People make assumptions about me—men and women—no matter how I dress. Or how I act. Even my friends do sometimes."

I looked away, wondering if I'd been guilty of that. Maybe I had been guilty, and to my shame, more than once.

Tiffany pressed on. "I can't escape expectations, and I can't escape what I am. But Erik is different."

"You sure he's different?"

She gave me a wry smile I didn't often see from her. "Oh, he's interested, but he's working really hard to not do the wrong thing. That…well, it means something to me."

"Maybe it's his berserker control. He's had practice keeping powerful instincts in check."

"All I feel is that he wouldn't use me and throw me aside. He's not like that. He's not fake. He's not acting just to get into my pants."

"You have sex with him yet?"

One thing I found endlessly irritating about my team sex demon was her ability to blush and do it prettily. She could pull this off despite being a succubus and having absolutely no reasons I could see to feel embarrassed. When *I* blushed I resembled a tomato in combat fatigues.

"We're taking it slow." She kicked her feet against the railing and stared at the city skyline crowned with storm.

"Like I said, slow is good." I smirked and nudged her with my shoulder. "I never believed those rumors about how a succubus steals souls through raging fornication."

Tiffany snorted. "A bunch of horny monks made that stuff up in the Middle Ages. We do charge up with power through...through sex." Her blush deepened. "My powers are really weak, because...well you know. I have to do things myself. That's why the redcap got away."

"Because your batteries weren't charged." We both stared at each other in solemn silence, then we burst out laughing like a couple of fourteen year olds.

When we stopped laughing, a comfortable quiet settled between us. The crackling tension had disappeared. The breeze felt good on my face, the air smelled of rain, and though I was still hungry, I felt far more easy about things than I had since I'd cracked open those fucking fortune cookies.

Tiffany broke the silence, and the problems that had retreated with our laughter crowded close again. "I know everybody's watching me and Erik. I know what people are saying—"

"People talk too damn much. Take things at whatever speed works for you, Tiffany. Really."

"Do you think he's good for me?"

The boldness of the question caught me off guard, and my answer was wary. "What do you mean?"

"You saw him. When he went berserker. He was...he was

terrifying."

He *had* been terrifying. I'd seen my share of shit, and I could handle myself well enough, but even I'd been astonished by the ferocity of his battle rage. And that was after he'd saved my ass.

Tiffany met my eyes. "Tell me the truth."

"I threatened him. After I saw what was happening between you two. I wasn't going to hire him...and then shit happened and I kept him on because he earned it." I shrugged. "I'd love it if he proved me wrong. You don't even know how much I'd love that."

"He never told me you threatened him."

"I won't apologize for it either." I couldn't read her face, had no idea what she was feeling, but I wouldn't lie to her. "He has something dangerous in him. We saw it." I took a deep breath, put my arm around her shoulder and gave her a hug. One of her wings wrapped around me and hugged me back. I leaned my head against hers and smiled. "But what did I see after that? I saw you bring him back. That means something."

"I want to believe that."

"Then believe it. It'd be easy to tell you to stay the hell away from him. Jake's mother tells him the same thing about me."

"Does not!"

"Does so. But Erik seems like the type of guy who'd rip the world apart to protect you. You know he takes duty very seriously. He never left my side that night. Not once. And it was only when we were desperate that he threw off all control and went full rage-king." I paused. "He didn't want you to see him like that."

"I know."

"Still...we don't know him that well—not yet anyway. Just... I don't know. Be certain. Get to know him before you run off to Vegas and get married at the Vampire Elvis Chapel of Rockabilly Blood."

"It didn't take you long," she said. "With Jake."

I opened my mouth to reply that we weren't married, then closed it again, because I knew what she meant and I didn't have any convincing argument to throw back. I had to trust her, and that meant I had to trust him as well. How could it be easier for me to trust him with my life than it was to trust him with my friend?

"He's a good man," Tiffany continued. "When he jumped after you into that room…when the portal cut us off…I could've kissed him, then kicked his ass. It was so stupid and so brave."

I smiled, but Gavin's words of warning about berserkers flashed through my mind, followed by the memory of Erik's uncontrolled fury, that berserker rage that made even a hardened merc like me pause. Thunder rumbled in the distance.

"Let's get back inside before it rains," I said.

She nodded. "Thanks, Captain. For everything."

We went back inside. I prayed I was right about Erik because I wanted her to be happy.

I only wanted her to be happy.

My boots thumped on the stairs as I trudged back to my office. I didn't feel hungry anymore. Tension thrummed in my shoulders. Uneasiness seeped through my guts. Something was wrong, but I couldn't pin down the source of my disquiet. Tiffany and Erik? Jake deployed on secret missions? A damn ringmaster with a possible big top-sized grudge still raving loose in the multiverse?

The pufferfish was waiting for me on the third floor landing. We stared at each other in silence. The puffer made fish lips and waved its fins.

"Oh, no. Not even. No way." I folded my arms. "I have zero use for a dead pufferfish. You can't stay."

The puffer's fins drooped. It traversed a sad circle around my head.

"I have more than enough people to look after. I don't need another headache."

The sea squab slowly drifted toward the window. Its tail twitched feebly. Its spikes seemed far less spiky.

"All right, all right. *Fine*. You can stay, dammit. I can't freaking believe this. I'm such a sucker."

The pufferfish resumed its serene circles above my head. I scowled at it. "You got a name?"

It didn't answer. Never slowed its smooth orbit.

"If you don't have a proper name, I'm gonna call you Pufferfish. Fair warning."

Pufferfish goggled at me, made fish lips, and gradually turned in the air until it floated belly up.

"Great, a smartass ghost fish. Just what I needed. God, I'm going to regret this."

CHAPTER SEVENTEEN
Exit Signs

Quill couldn't shake the haunting, skin-prickling sensation that he was being watched. He paused in the motel's dingy hallway with his mag key hovering over the electronic lock. This was the same feeling he'd experienced throughout his entire vacation in the UK, shopping in any department store, and every time he stood at the urinal at the Bowl-R-Rama. He glanced around, but the hallway was nothing more than an empty stretch of numbered green doors. He slid the card into the lock and out again. The small light flashed red and the door wouldn't open.

The sensation of being watched, of being *stalked*, grew more intense. The twinges of unease deepened to fear. He closed his eyes for a moment, trying to find his calm center and purge the fear before it consumed his ability to think clearly.

When he opened his eyes again, he found himself clutching his oilskin sack so tightly to his chest that his fingers ached and his knuckles cracked. The sack held nothing anyone would want to steal. His Tripiṭaka, a book of teachings encompassing important canons of scripture. A few extra robes. The handful of silver coins left to him after paying for the room and the taxi ride from the police station. Certainly he was grateful the DA had declined to file charges in return for his testimony, but it would've been nice if they had given him a ride to someplace decent. This motel was just as seedy as the last he'd stayed in, the ill-fated Border Inn Economy Motel, renting rooms ranging from by-the-hour to by-the-week.

Nothing to be done about it now. Existence was suffering, and he would endure in peace, grateful for what little he had. Still, that feeling of being watched...

The glowing exit sign at the end of the hall flickered and buzzed. The green light seeping from the letters reminded him of the eerie radiance from the ghost clowns. Quill shivered. Gooseflesh rippled up and down his wrinkled skin.

The exit sign flickered again and went out...which didn't make sense because he was certain emergency exit signs had both a battery backup and were hardwired into the power supply. The rest of the lights remained on and steady.

He didn't want to be alone out here anymore. He slammed the mag card into the door lock again. "Please."

The light on the lock glared red rejection.

Quill glanced at the exit sign as he tried the key card yet again. His hands shook so badly the edge of the card skittered all around the slot before finally going in. Now he was certain something was out there, lurking near the stairs and the sign. Maybe more than one thing, and definitely stalking him. Waiting until he got the door open, and then the thing would fall on him, drag him into the room and eat him with corkscrew teeth—

The terror wound tighter. Sweat ran from his gray hair and out from under his cap to sting his eyes. He swiped at his forehead with the hand holding the key card, fumbled and dropped it.

At the end of the hall, a hand wearing a blood-red glove poked out from behind the corner of the stairwell wall. A clown glove. A sly, distorted clown face peeped around the corner at him, slowly blinking one glowing eye. He could only see part of its wicked smile, but it showed enough to reveal nasty yellow teeth. Sharp teeth.

Quill couldn't suck in enough breath to scream. He gasped, in and out, a fish dying in some ugly motel hallway that reeked of mildew and old cigarettes. Beloved Buddha, how had the chief's ghosts found him already?

The electronic lock beeped and the light turned green. His heart seemed to plummet into his boots and a triumphant grin broke across his face. He turned the handle and shoved the door inward, falling into the room with his sack banging against the wall. The threadbare red and gold carpeting rug-burned his cheek, but he rolled over at once and kicked the door shut.

Something rushed at his closed door. He sensed it, didn't hear it, because the corridor remained eerily quiet. By pure reflex, he lifted his hands toward the doorway and blurted out a goblin spell. The guttural words echoed and stained the air.

The door wobbled and distorted in its frame as if it were made of taffy melting in the sun. When the final word left his lips, the door snapped back to rigid solidity, and the effect travelled along the walls of the room in opposite directions until it met again over the window. Such a powerful spell, cast unprepared, sapped his strength nearly down to nothing. His jaw ached from clenching his teeth. His arms trembled, held close against his body.

He waited, lying on the carpet in the dim motel room, panting, staring at the door. Waiting for the ghost to hit his seal. Wondering if his *petruskhmu* ward would hold true. His dexterity with goblin magic had been the main reason Chief Gorsh had tolerated his flaming pacifism, not any promise to Quill's mother as he so often liked to claim. Though most redcaps were only handy with sharp objects, Quill had delved extensively in the art before turning away to follow the precepts of the Three Jewels, searching for a better, more fulfilling enlightenment. Now *nurata* might save his life. The urge to laugh wildly seized him, threatening to spew crazed giggles into the room until he choked it down.

The hall remained silent. He stared at the door over the tops of his boots, feeling the spell's drain on his endurance seeping deeper into his muscles, the same exhausted burn a man might feel if he swam the English Channel while towing a drunken unicorn wearing orange floaties and an anchor.

His spell wailed when the ghost tried to float through the door, the sound of an air raid siren winding down. The energy that formed the spell's backbone rippled and twisted, sparking around the doorjamb.

His casting held. The ghost clown remained outside. Quill sagged on the brown carpet, heart pounding, shaking from head to toe. The chief had sent the clown for vengeance. How the chief had found him, Quill had no idea. But he did know *dukkha* — suffering, dissatisfaction, anxiety — would not triumph. He'd never let the twisted phantom take him.

A dim green glow, the same as the light from the exit sign, filtered from the crack beneath the door. Something hissed and squeaked. A green balloon began to inflate through the slim crack, expanding into the room. Quill scrambled to his feet and stumbled backward.

The balloon began to twist itself into an animal shape, making those shiver-inducing plastic screeches and squeaks until it had transformed into something he thought might be an alligator or a komodo dragon. It shuffled across the short stretch of carpet between them. Quill backed up until he bumped the wall. He sucked in air and bellowed out an ancient and crude goblin warcry. "*Vashtle shun, vossa nu Blistel Nababaah! Krag nu Lon!*" Roughly translated: *Ten times I'll splinter your shins! Crack your knees! Gnaw off your stones!*

He leapt into the air and came down on the komodo dragon/alligator balloon with both iron shod boots. The malevolent balloon animal popped. The plastic bits melted away to vapor and vanished. He could almost feel the ghost clown's consternation from the other side of the door.

He closed his eyes, wrapped his arms around himself, and tried to stop shaking. The violence of his attack on the balloon animal filled his mind with black thorns. He was no different from is brethren after all, and right now he was too afraid to even care.

The motel phone rang, blaring out a shrill, jangling cry. Quill screamed and stared at the old-fashioned push-button phone in horror. Who knew he was here? No one.

No one except the ghost clowns.

Numbly, he staggered toward the phone on the cheap, burn-scarred nightstand. His hand floated out. Closed around the receiver. Lifted it to his ear. He swallowed and his throat clicked, but he couldn't find the strength to speak a word.

"Quill," a woman said in a calm voice he didn't recognize. Her voice was steady and businesslike, and the sound quelled some of his blind panic. "I know you're in danger. Hold the phone toward the door please."

He stood there, unable to manage more than a dazed, "What?"

"Point the phone receiver toward the door, away from your ear, and yell when you've done what I ask."

For a long, horrible moment his mind blanked. He couldn't seem to process the crazy orders coming through the receiver in such a composed and collected voice. Another balloon screeched under the crack, expanding with a malicious *whoosh*, and his paralysis finally broke. He pointed the receiver toward the door and yelled, "Okay!"

Strange, shrill sounds burst from the receiver, rising and

falling in pitch, trilling like a haunted piccolo and echoing off the walls. The sound made Quill twitch and grit his teeth as if someone had pulled the old werewolf-claws-on-the-chalkboard prank. A wavering moan trembled behind the door. The balloon shot out, flying across the room and making the most absurd, embarrassing farting sound as it deflated. It landed on the ancient television and promptly melted. The shrill sounds stopped.

"Quill?" the woman asked, her voice distant because he still aimed the phone at the door with his shaking hand as if it were a gun. "Is the phantom gone?"

"Gone. How did you know about the ghost? Who *are* you?"

"Most call me Mistress Patel. You may call me Sheryl."

The room wavered and swam. A high-pitched whine echoed in his ears, growing louder as the edges of his vision grayed. He flopped down on the carpet with a tired groan and closed his eyes until the weakness in his knees passed. He only wanted a cold shower and to meditate in peace until his equilibrium returned, but these shocks kept coming.

"You wrote the *Omniphaelogos*," he whispered.

"I did." She seemed neither disconcerted nor surprised by the fear in his voice. "You must come to Minnesota."

"I don't have enough money," he explained, as if her request were perfectly normal. Only the control strengthened by his meditations kept him from screaming about how he couldn't go to Minnesota because in the last few weeks up until twenty seconds ago he'd almost been murdered by mercenaries, ghost clowns, a redcap he'd once worked for who'd gone insane, and, most recently, evil balloon animals. Also, he really didn't have enough money.

"A ticket is waiting for you at the airport," she said. "You must hurry."

He crept toward the door, bringing the phone with him,

playing out the wire, then setting the receiver on the edge of the bed and stretching the cord as far as it could go. The door loomed larger and larger in his vision. When he finally reached it, he cycled through every calming technique he knew, recited a mantra or three in his mind, listened one last time for any sounds that had clown-like attributes, and threw the door open.

Empty.

He slammed it shut again and sagged against the wall, but kept the receiver to his ear. "I have to stay in Oregon to testify. And I think redcaps were added to the No Fly list."

"Listen, Quill. You are special. You are needed. You have to come to Minnesota, and you have to do it now."

"Why?" He was so tired and drained from his spell and exhausted by the fear that he couldn't find the strength to argue.

"Because if you don't come to Minnesota, Andrea Walker will die."

CHAPTER EIGHTEEN
FPD

Mercenary Wing Rv6-4 "Zero Dogs"
June 28th

I was playing a grim hand of solitaire instead of answering email when my office phone rang. Perfect timing, since I stared yet another loss straight in the eye. I snatched up the cordless receiver without any sense of foreboding. "Zero Dogs, paranormal guns for hire. Problems solved in a variety of calibers."

The woman spoke in a crisp, all-business tone. "Captain Walker. I'm Mistress Patel. I have important information you must hear."

My little heart engine redlined like a stock car reaching a straightaway. I said nothing, my mouth dry as desert sand. Patel also stayed silent, waiting on my answer. Part of me hoped the call would drop. Another part of me wanted to help that chance along by throwing the phone out the window.

Finally I couldn't endure the quiet stand-off any longer. "I'm sorry, maybe I don't understand. We don't deal in intelligence." God only knew how true that was on every level. "So did you want something blown up? We offer attractive discounts for mayhem and destruction. Financing too."

"Don't play games. We both know why I'm calling."

"Robocall?" My mouth managed little more than a hoarse whisper. "Be sure and vote this election, rah, rah, USA?"

"The long, cold shadow still ices your path. The pyschopomps still chitter your name in my ears."

"Maybe if you dialed down the supernatural *woo-woo* a bit I might understand what the hell you're talking about."

"Most of my clients enjoy that sort of touch. Adds to the effect."

"I don't have time for bullshit," I said, ignoring the solitaire game I'd been busy losing. "So. Pyschopomps. Sounds bad. You're saying I'm still gonna die?"

"We're all going to die. Some sooner than others."

"Maybe you could be a little less cryptically obscure while you're at it."

"My visions warned me you'd be a killjoy." She took a deep breath. "I want you to come to Minneapolis and meet with me. We can stop the spiritmaster if we work together. He remains a very serious threat, and there are darker, wider shadows."

I stared at the computer screen as my heart beat too fast, the sour churn in my stomach killing any hope of appetite for the next three years. "Exactly how much danger are we talking?"

"I assume you'd prefer to continue changing oxygen into carbon dioxide? I assume you'd prefer to carry on with your Special Forces gentleman from *this* side of the Veil? Or am I wrong?"

"Way I see it, as an oracle you *already know* my answer, so I guess we can cut this conversation short."

There was a long pause. "I don't already know your answer. I called to convince you to come."

"Some psychic. I deserve a refund."

"The future keeps breaking into alternate paths. In some, you say yes. In others, you say no. In some, you're already dead, killed by ghost clowns last week."

My armpits grew damp with sweat. Nobody liked to learn that in some alternate timeline they were already dead. What would it take to be done with this dire fate and prophetic doom gig? If the clowns didn't kill me, the stress sure as hell would. "Indulge me with a little test to make sure you're not all hype."

"If you must, Captain Walker."

"Somebody with mucho political connections pulled strings and made certain we caught the carnival mission instead of SWAT. I've been burning brain cells trying to figure out who the hell that could've been and why."

"I could tell you, but how would you know if I spoke the truth or not?"

"Give me an interesting answer and I won't hang up the phone."

"Your string-puller is a certain gentleman from your governor's office who handles things the governor won't touch. From there, the intrigue snakes all the way back to Washington. It's nothing personal. There are influential people very interested in paranormal mercenaries. Private security is a multi-billion dollar industry."

Blood roared in my ears as I leaned against my desk, gritting my teeth. I kept thinking about the work we'd done for Homeland Security, how the money had been prime, but every hour it'd felt as if they'd owned us. Had that feeling ever gone away?

"I know you're trying to distract with these tests and diversions," Patel said. "Easier to dismiss me. Easier to convince yourself you aren't in danger. You may have derailed the spiritmaster's plans for his calliope machine, but he's adapted. He's consolidating power from within the spirit world. When he's strong enough, he'll invade again. Not merely with a few score of ghosts as before, but controlling a phantom army. I've foreseen that you will die first, defending your succubus friend in vain."

"So…is that all I need to know? Do I still have to fly out there for a face-to-face? Couldn't we do this over email? Or maybe video conferencing?"

"Most people I meet are more eager to save their own life."

"I don't know anybody eager to travel to Minnesota and talk about psychopomps, fucking prophetic doom or no."

"I'm sorry, did you just say…fucking prophetic doom?"

"It's a technical term. FPD for short. Feel free to borrow it."

"Thank you. Very colorful." She took a deep breath. "Now, about you coming to Minneapolis…"

The stomach-sick dread hadn't left, but my mind felt calmer and my thoughts clearer. Patel's last prophecy had been far too accurate for me to blow her off. FPD strikes again. I snatched a piece of paper from my desk and fumbled for a pen that worked. "I'm in. But we all knew that already. Give me your address."

She recited and I copied it down, wondering how much a round trip plane ticket would set me back. This would be personal business, and I couldn't write it off without tossing up a field of audit red flags.

I spun in my chair and balanced the pen on my little cactus. "One last thing. I don't know you. I've never read your book. I don't care about contacting the hamster I owned when I was six who died on that goddamn teeter-totter, an event which I'm never going to discuss with you. Yet, this is the *second* time you've gone out of your way to warn me about threats to my life. What do you want?"

"It's simple," Mistress Patel replied. "I have nothing to hide. This demented redcap with the rare power of a spiritmaster is…and please indulge my return to character…an abomination. He lures the souls of the dead, rips them from the spirit world, and reshapes their form according to his whims, forcing them to do his bidding. These are crimes I find appalling. He must be stopped before my visions come to pass."

"I don't suppose you're going to pay me to stop him?"

"Don't be such a mercenary," Mistress Patel said, and hung up.

I slammed the phone into the charging base. Then I grabbed the handset and yelled, "I *am* a mercenary!" and slammed it again. I glanced up to see Erik standing in my office doorway, watching me the way a man watches a potentially rabid raccoon rolling in garbage.

"Funny you should show up," I said, ominous cheer in my voice. "That was your good buddy Mistress Patel."

His frown deepened. "You didn't like what she had to say?"

"I'm supposed to fly to Minnesota and have my palm read or my aura stroked or my third eyebrow waxed because I'm back under the shadow of FPD."

"FPD… An acronym for doom that's fucking prophetic."

I grinned at him, disproportionately pleased that he'd remembered my pet acronym of recent days. "Exactly. I'd promote you to corporal, but I can't afford it."

He didn't smile back. "Are you going?"

"I don't have any choice. My ass is on the line."

Erik nodded, face grim, as if my ass being on the line surprised him not in the least.

"I also have to save the spirit world from that crazy little shit Gorsh. For free."

"Gorsh…the ringmaster with the codpiece?"

"The very same. Thank God it's summer in Minnesota, because I drive in snow about as well as a sea lion performs Russian ballet." It pained me to admit a flaw, but I belonged to the ranks of a good many Oregonians who sucked at driving in snow. Most believed pickup trucks and SUVs and midsize sedans had the same dependable traction on snow at any speed as did caterpillar treads on a tank.

Driving in rain, though, we had that shit down.

"I'll go with you," Erik said.

The offer made me hesitate, uncertain whether it was a good idea or not, and touched by it all the same. I could hack it on my own, and this was *my* problem, not a Zero Dog problem. True, Patel had made noises about Portland being threatened, but the city didn't pay to stop *rumors* of its imminent destruction. Only during apocalypse hour did the city coffers open.

The Zero Dogs didn't do pro bono work. I couldn't ask my people to put their lives at risk for nothing but *thank yous* and *gratitude*. Gratitude didn't fill magazines with bullets, and thank you didn't keep the a/c on.

"I appreciate the offer, Erik. I really do. But Patel didn't mention you, and besides, you played your role already…perfectly I might add, since I'm still alive. This isn't Hellfrost sanctioned work. Nobody gets paid."

When Erik spoke, it was slowly, as if each word were a struggle to drag free. "It's not about that, Captain. Because… you took me onto your team, and you trusted me. I was sent to save you, but you didn't have to do that, to bring me in, to make me part of this. And the people here…they're good people."

We stared at each other in silence. I didn't tell him that the paranoid warrior in me hadn't trusted him until *after* he'd come through in our battle with the circus-crazed goblin. I didn't regret my suspicions. He'd shown up under extremely strange circumstances. Yet, part of me felt guilty anyway, the same slow burn of shame I'd always experienced any time I received praise I hadn't earned.

He was right about one thing though. My people *were* good people. Even Gavin had his moments — rare, fleeting moments like when he'd redeemed his failure at the bouncy castle by risking his ass to help Quill cut the hostage loose. The only merc I might've quibbled over was Stefan. Then again, he was a vampire. Vampires were a different breed. Like mosquitoes or discount furniture salesmen.

"I can't pay you," I warned. "Just operating expenses. That's it."

"Money doesn't matter to me."

I watched him, not sure what to say. I admired the sentiment, but I'd stared at too many balance sheets bleeding red to feel the same.

"Better start packing then. I plan to catch the next open flight." The cost of last minute airline tickets would give me an ulcer. "Pack light. I don't want to pay baggage fees that are more than the tickets." I hesitated, meeting his eyes. "You sure about this? This isn't your fight. I'm not even sure there will be a fight. There's still hope Mistress Patel is either wrong or deranged. Or both wrong *and* deranged."

"You don't believe that."

"No," I said. "No, I don't."

* * *

I had my gear packed and ready to go in less than fifteen minutes. The entire time I was packing I kept trying to decide what to tell the rest of the Zero Dogs. I didn't want them to worry. Sarge would keep things in line for me while I was gone...well, as much as this bunch of degenerate slobs could be kept in line. And I meant that in an entirely loving way.

When I headed to my office to make the airline reservations I found the whole crew clustered around my office door, blocking the entrance. Everyone was there except for Stefan, who was sleeping off the daylight. Even the balloon dog was present, running back and forth along Rafe's broad shoulders, squeaking.

I looked them over. They stared back at me. Nobody spoke. I finally locked gazes with Erik. His face flushed, but he held my gaze without glancing away. Next to him, Tiffany clutched his hand, her mouth set with determination.

I tried a guileless smile. "Did I miss the general call for a bingo marathon or something?"

"We want to go too, Captain," Tiffany blurted. "We can help."

"Guys...this isn't a job. I'm not getting paid. This is personal business. I'm only meeting my psychic about some ESP-type things and to gossip about Nostradamus's beard and whatever. No big deal."

Sarge favored me with his best demonic *moai* statue impression. "Erik said you were in danger. Count me in."

A chorus of affirmatives rang out.

It took effort, but I slapped on my hardest, no-bullshit executive officer expression, scowling my way from face to face. "No. And that's my final order."

Tiffany flinched. Gavin snorted and fouled the air with a curse that could've killed fairies. Rafe tried out his sad puppy eyes. Identical expressions of frustrated disappointment covered the rest of the faces.

More guilt stabbed me in the gut, cold and sharp, but I gritted my teeth and ignored it because I was doing this for them. If anything, God forbid, happened to one of my people, my crew, my *friends*, on this mission it would be my fault, because this prophecy thing was *my* problem. I'd never live it down, never forgive myself. No, I'd rather do this on my own than put them at risk.

"But, Captain," Tiffany said, raising her chin and staring at me with uncharacteristic boldness. "You agreed to bring Erik."

"Erik involved himself in this when he showed up on my doorstep, sent by this mysterious woo-woo oracle from the land of the ice and snow to help save my burning bacon. This is merely phase two of that assignment, so he doesn't count."

Mai stepped forward. She appeared rather delicate and forlorn without a mutant animal in her hands. "I don't understand, Captain. Why would you leave us behind? We're strongest together."

"Mai is wise," Hanzo said. "An unyielding branch breaks under the push of a strong wind, but a forest of bamboo can hold a mountain aloft."

I chose to ignore Hanzo's pseudo Zen-salted hyperbole. "It's simple, mercs. I'm not going to put your lives at risk fighting ghost clowns and psychopathic redcaps for free. For *no* money. *Zero* compensation. That isn't what you signed on for."

I found it hard enough to send them into danger when we were contracted for a mission, even though we were professionals, and this was our job. I'd never admit that dirty secret to any of them, not even Sarge. Truth told, there were plenty of nights I lay awake in that desolate two a.m. stretch, worrying almost feverishly about each member of my team. My brain would replay scenes from past missions, sometimes giving me gruesome new endings to battles we'd fought. I'd imagine each of them leading different, safer, normal lives…well, as normal as summoners, werewolves, and demons were able to live. It was stupid, pointless self-torture, but my worries chased me on that long dark stretch of highway between midnight and dawn.

"Captain," Tiffany said quietly. "We don't care about the money."

"Yeah, fuck money!" Gavin shouted. "Wait…did I say that? Have I been drinking?"

Rafe joined in next. "Fuck money!" Balloon dog began to

hump his shoulder, doing the dirty squeak with mad abandon.

"Fuck money!" the rest of them yelled, almost as one, laughing as they shouted, but fierce too. Sarge wore a sardonic smirk. Mai danced in a circle, clapping her hands and cheering. Erik side-hugged Tiffany, who smiled like a slit-eyed angel.

Despite my attempt to maintain the hardass expression on my face, I found myself grinning like a fool. I didn't even care that my transportation costs for this joyride had just hit an exponential curve, because right now I was all about fucking the money.

And I was touched, dammit.

"Then let's pack up and move out, people," I said. "Somebody leave Stefan a note on the fridge where he keeps his blood cocktails and tell him where we went."

"We should leave him a ticket," Mai suggested. "In case he wants to come."

Everyone nodded. I doubted Stefan would want to chip in on saving my ass, not for free anyway, but in for a penny, in for another two thousand dollars in round trip airfare at specialized vampire transportation rates.

For a moment I wondered what Mistress Patel would say when I showed up with the entire crew. I had to admit, I was looking forward to seeing her reaction—and laying good odds that the famous grimoire-writing psychic would be completely surprised.

I marched into my office as everyone clustered around behind me. "All right. Let's find us a ride to Minnesota."

CHAPTER NINETEEN
The Detached God

Mercenary Wing Rv6-4 "Zero Dogs"
June 29th

T he earliest flight we could catch out of PDX was a 5:55 a.m. yawner the next morning, changing planes in Denver. I'd told everyone to pack light, but they still managed to produce a metric ton of luggage and a short ton of bitching. Sarge had grumbled about checking firearms. Hanzo had complained about checking his katana. Rafe went on and on…and *on*…about the health hazards of re-circulated airplane air, x-ray machines, and whether or not he should find a kennel for balloon dog. Meanwhile, Gavin had waxed poetic about the TSA, relying on colorful, creative, and extremely foul invective. Vampire Stefan, who had surprised me by agreeing to tag along, albeit riding asleep in cargo, had obsessed over his damask-lined mahogany coffin. He'd made us swear to encase it in bubble wrap to protect it from dings. Mai had packed the most luggage: silk and satin summoner robes, vestments, and gowns in vibrant colors and patterns. I could've purchased a small golden calf for my personal shrine with the amount of money I paid in baggage fees.

As the plane descended, I noticed Minneapolis had many

more lakes and rivers than I'd expected, all of that water still in liquid form. Never mind that it was June, I'd envisioned a city that resembled a cross between Norway and McMurdo Station in Antarctica. Skyscrapers locked in ice. Screaming winds that would freeze skin from bones. Drifts of snow larger than tidal waves. By the time we'd switched planes in Denver, I'd already imagined a frost-bound metropolis shivering under the bleak shadow of an ominous mountain range. The mountains would hold back a desolate plain of ice, riddled by cracks and chasms, with an ancient alien city trapped beneath the frozen water. Of course I'd somehow end up lost there after a three-hour tour and be eaten by carnivorous space yetis.

Luckily, reality turned out to be both far more mundane and far more hospitable. The Mississippi River wound past the city, curving and twisting, impressive even from the air. Lakes, ponds, creeks, and a great many green patches of parks and wetlands broke apart the typical big-city concrete jungle.

We spent an hour collecting our baggage, filling out forms for Gavin's lost luggage ("They 'lose' luggage to punish their most vocal critics," Gavin ranted. "They must have our house bugged."), and arranging for delivery of Stefan in his bubble-wrapped coffin to the motel where he'd sleep off the rest of the daylight while we did all the work. Finally we piled into several cabs and swung by the motel to drop off luggage and rent rooms, then arranged for several more cabs to haul us downtown.

Mistress Patel's office was on the tenth floor of an irregular, glass-fronted building, a rough cylinder with an asymmetric front that I rather liked. We had so many people that we had to ride two elevators to her floor. Rafe and Sarge insisted on being the first out the elevator, as if they were clearing a room full of hostiles instead of stepping into a posh series of executive suites. For the entire trip the Zero Dogs had been treating me as if I were, alternately, a crystal ballerina sculpture or a high-risk principal they had to protect from assassination. I tolerated it in silence. If my people wanted to feel as if they were contributing, then that was all peaches with me. The real danger lurked somewhere in the spirit world.

Mistress Patel's waiting area scored high on upscale decor. I'd expected kitsch—velvets and sable, New Age-y things, maybe tiny crystal ball snow globes for sale and Do-It-Yourself Ghost Hunting kits. Instead, the furniture was all high-end brown leather with gold accents. Sleek glass tables. A small, moss-patched fountain bubbled in the corner, clear water pouring from the top and running down in rivulets into a pool filled with oddly shaped coins. Fractal artwork hung on the walls in expensive-looking frames, and recessed lighting melted soft illumination along the floor-to-ceiling bookshelves. I recognized the haunting music piped out of ceiling speakers— Schubert's "Winterreise."

The receptionist's smooth body gleamed as if polished, a gentle wood grain adding visual texture to her brown skin, and the tufts of tiny yellow-green leaves sprouting like hair characteristic to wood nymphs and other nature fae. Wood nymphs grew themselves into human forms to better assimilate, and she was definitely female-shaped. Her eyes were dark knots of wood, each eye unique, and her hollow mouth didn't move when her voice echoed from within her chest cavity.

"Hello, how may I help you?"

Rafe was the first to reach her, all werewolf bushy eyebrows and easy charm. He'd ended up smuggling balloon dog along in his carry-on luggage. "I don't want to kennel him," he'd told me on the way to the airport. "They wouldn't understand his special needs. Besides, he's a total chick magnet."

Now balloon dog was riding on his shoulder, making excited squeaking-plastic sounds.

"We have an appointment with Mistress Patel." Rafe favored the receptionist with his bright-as-a-full-moon smile. "For Captain Andrea Walker. Probably listed under *scorching hot* or *pyromaniac*, maybe even *muy caliente*."

The receptionist was a pro, I'd give her that. She smiled back, though slowly, because her living wood body made only gradual changes to her expression. She clicked around on her screen, undisturbed by all the demons and ninjas and the girl in pastel pink summoner robes leading a rabbit on a leash who had flooded her waiting room. I seemed to be the only one keeping a wary eye on Mai's demon rabbit, a slightly different breed than I'd seen her summon before. Every so often sharp, dagger-shaped horns sprouted from the rabbit's head, its eyes flared crimson, and its fur turned the color of cinders and ash. It left little smoking rabbit prints on the carpet, and smoldering coals of rabbit crap. Then it would shift back into an innocent, normal-looking bunny, cute as babies and buttons. I shook my head. Mai and her anti-Christ bunny issues.

"Yes," the receptionist said, startling me out of my musings. "I have Captain Walker scheduled for a three-thirty appointment. We have coffee and cookies—" she nodded at Gavin, who'd already shoved half a dozen cookies into his mouth, his cheeks ballooning out like a squirrel's and crumbs dusting his goatee "—if you'd like while you wait. Mistress Patel will be ready to see you short—oh, is that balloon *alive*?"

Balloon dog had started licking its own plastic balloon crotch where its theoretical balls would've dangled if balloon dog hadn't only been a twisted shape of red, magically animated plastic. Rafe laughed and lifted balloon dog off his shoulder and set it on her desk, where it ran around dividing its attention between humping the stapler and doggy-styling the staple remover. Balloon dog apparently harbored some type of crazy sex-and-death wish.

"Oh, isn't he *adorable!*" The receptionist clapped. Her hands made the clopping sound of two wooden blocks smacked together, though her fingers seemed dexterous enough to type a helluva lot faster than I ever could.

"Yeah, isn't he?" Rafe agreed. "We saved him from some evil mimes. I'm Rafe, by the way. Would you like to see my tattoos?"

I wandered over to sit on one of the leather couches, my stomach still fluttering, and my heart thudding hard. I was too restless and nervous to put up with Rafe plying his werewolf mojo magnetism. Sometimes I wondered how long it'd be until some woman scorned came gunning for him with silver bullets.

I stood and paced, glancing at the clock. Three twenty-six. Damn. I wanted this to hurry up and be over almost as much as I dreaded meeting Patel. Waiting made me uneasy, because I'd rather be *doing* something. As an angsty, hormonal teen, nervous waiting had caused me to start a number of small, completely unintentional fires. Worse, memories of my expulsion from West Point kept circling back to haunt my mind. I vividly remembered how my stomach had twisted into sailor's knots and blood knots and my heart had beat an ominous war drum rhythm as I'd waited for the disciplinary board to review my case. The bitch of it: my expulsion had been one great big misunderstanding involving one of my best friends who'd been drunk off her ass, her dick-ish ex-boyfriend, a visiting VIP billionaire, and a fifty-caliber machine gun.

Could've happened to anybody.

I glanced at Erik and Tiffany, anything to shake my mind from this looming dread. They stood close together by the fountain, Erik holding his guitar case and Tiffany playing with the edge of one of her wings and talking to him quietly. Erik struck me as the good listener type, because he certainly didn't say much. Thinking about it, my Jake was pretty good too, except when he was watching sports, but I gave him a pass on that one. Or when I was talking about stuff I bought on sale that didn't happen to be guns, ammunition, or body armor. Or when I was talking about how someday I'd like to see an opera or Noh theater and how we needed more culture in our lives. On second thought, maybe Jake sucked at listening.

Gavin though...at least my man wasn't as bad as Gavin. He sat apart from us in a chair by the windows, scribbling in his notebook, with cookie crumbs still embedded in his goatee. He'd been one of the first to throw in to help me, which I appreciated until he'd confided how this would be prime material for his epic poem about the Zero Dogs. He'd explained how art didn't have to be true, even if he claimed it was stone fact on the book jacket. It only needed to be dramatic and explore the human condition. "So I included a verse about your tragic glue sniffing habit, Captain, and how bravely you struggle for acceptance in a world that won't love you. The existential despair of trading bullets for coin to keep food on the table. It's fucking *pathos!*"

The inner office door swung open. I stopped brooding about the poetic atrocity Gavin was cultivating and jumped right back into my nervous tension over FPD. A woman stepped out and scanned from face to face until she saw me and smiled. She had impeccable taste in clothes, with an elegant, soft gray suit and skirt, a two button suit jacket with an onyx broach on the lapel shaped in a curious spiraling pattern. The whole ensemble complimented her short stylish hair and brown skin and eyes.

"Captain Walker, I'm Sheryl Patel. Please call me Sheryl." She waved her hand dismissively and smiled. "Mistress Patel suffices for the theatrical, but it's a mouthful and I remember you prefer to be direct. Would you care to step into my office?"

Gavin muttered and scribbled in his notebook. "Nefarious

oracle's siren song, into the inner Sanctum sanctorum go!"

My smile felt plastic. Heat crept up my neck. "I'd love to," I said, far too loudly, hoping she hadn't overheard Gavin.

The entire team moved to come with me, but I held up a hand. "I'll be all right, mercs."

Sarge grumbled from where he slouched against the wall, smoking a cigarette beneath a No Smoking sign. "We'd feel better if at least one of us went with you, Captain."

"That is fine by me." The oracle flashed her bright smile at our berserker. "Erik? It might be best if you came…as you are already experienced in attending to prophecy."

Tiffany frowned and her eyes narrowed. Great, all I needed was a jealous succubus on the loose. Although my antennae twitched, wondering if Patel had received another vision where Erik's presence would be necessary.

"Fine, fine," I said before Tiffany or Sarge protested, hoping that bringing everyone along hadn't been a mistake after all. "Erik, you mind playing bodyguard for a bit longer?"

Erik shook his head and gave Tiffany's hand a squeeze. We followed Mistress Patel—who I couldn't help but think of as *Mistress Patel* and definitely not *Sheryl*—through a door and into her sanctum sanctorum. The door closed behind us without a sound.

* * *

Mistress Patel power-walked past the first door down the hallway. I glanced inside, and stopped so fast that Erik crashed into me from behind. The room was empty except for a wooden pedestal carved to resemble a tree. The pedestal held a huge open book, as big as any atlas and thick as a respectable dictionary. The pages appeared brown and delicate, the writing like neat stitches of black sewn across the page.

Mistress Patel noticed we weren't following and turned back, eyebrows raised in silent question.

I swallowed. "Is that…?"

"The *Omniphaelogos*? Yes, the original. Would you care to read?"

"I…" Did I dare? All the stories pointed to horrible endings, self-fulfilling prophecies, and fates that couldn't be avoided. Did I want to know whether Jake and I lived happily ever after? Did I want to know when I would die, or which of my people ended up killed on some future mission? Part of me burned to know, true, but far more of me was terrified. Terrified that knowing, I'd somehow *cause* those things to happen, maybe by fighting to stop them from happening in the first place.

"No." I swallowed again, feeling as though a sea urchin had caught in my throat. "No. I don't want to."

She stared at me with brown eyes, her face unreadable. "Very wise."

We continued to the end of the hall. Mistress Patel led us into a wide room, which she informed us was her "reading room." The décor in here also wasn't what I'd expected from a psychic who'd written one of the most feared tomes in history. Everything was made of wood: tables, panels, chairs. More recessed lighting filled the room with an amber glow, mixing with sunlight from large windows that displayed the skyscrapers of downtown Minneapolis. An elegant lacquered urn sat in an alcove near the door, resting on a carved pillar that was lit from below, throwing light upward onto the urn's graceful curves.

I stopped and squared off with Mistress Patel. "Before we get any further into this, I have one question—a little test of your psychic powers. What am I going to do next?"

A flash of annoyance crossed her face. "I have no idea."

I grabbed the vase and hurled it at one of the large windows as hard as I could. The vase shattered against the glass, exploding into shards that pattered to the carpet, but the window didn't break, as I'd secretly hoped.

"See *that* coming?"

Erik stared at me as if I'd not only lost my mind, but had launched every last ounce of sanity into a black hole just to be certain it had no hope of returning. I winked at him...which didn't seem to reassure him as much as expected.

Mistress Patel glared at me, then glanced at the wreckage. "My sight certainly doesn't tell me every crazed thing you're likely to do on a moment to moment basis, Captain Walker."

"Ha. What good is it then?"

She gave a longsuffering sigh, as if she'd explained this countless times before. "I don't see what's coming instant by instant. I catch glimpses of specific things, not always under my conscious control, otherwise I'd have won the lottery and retired to Costa Rica a long, long time ago. I can't use my gift as an oracle or as a death whisperer to help myself, only others."

"Ah." For a moment I felt quite foolish. "Wait. *Death whisperer*? You some kind of assassin?"

"You've heard of horse whisperers, plant whisperers, dog whisperers, and so on." Again she waved her hand in the air, a quick flutter-flutter motion. "I thought this followed in a similar vein. Perhaps the name of my future television show. At first I leaned toward *time whisperer*, but everyone is so obsessed with mortality and prophecy that I settled on death whisperer."

"Trendy." Death whisperer ranked as the stupidest title I'd heard since *spiritmaster*, but I didn't want to hurt her feelings by saying so.

"I guess we'll see after the focus group testing." Mistress Patel's smile returned, warm as ever. "Don't worry about the vase. I'll bill you for the damages. Now, please be seated. We have much to discuss and not enough time. I have someone I wish you to meet."

The wooden table she directed us to was large and round, beautifully carved, with chairs at each compass point. Erik waited until both of us had taken a seat before setting down his guitar case and sliding into a chair. He remained quiet, but his gaze was bright and active, constantly scanning the room with a mercenary's razor-sharp sense of danger.

"I don't like surprises," I warned. "Who do you want us to meet?"

She pushed a button on the intercom. "Myrrha, please ask our guest if he'll do us the honor of greeting us in my reading room."

She folded her hands and watched the door expectantly. I tensed, adrenaline burning like moonshine through my veins. Anything might come shambling, or slithering, or doing the Evil Hokey Pokey through that door.

"Be ready for anything," I warned Erik in a low voice. He glanced at me in surprise. So much for a mercenary's finely honed sense of danger.

A redcap walked through the doorway.

"It's a trap!" I grabbed the edge of the table, trying to flip it over and take cover before breaking out the pyromancy.

No one else moved. They only stared at me. The table was apparently bolted to the floor, so I strained to flip it, couldn't, and only ended up appearing rather pathetic.

"Please look again, Captain," Mistress Patel urged.

I looked again. "Oh. Hey, Quill… Good to see you."

Quill smiled shyly. He wore saffron monk robes with his hands clasped in front of him. The only thing my mind had locked on when he'd come through the door had been his height, his boots, and the crimson hat on his head. My cheeks and forehead felt as if they burned as red as that cap. I slowly sank back into my seat. Quill took the last empty chair. We all stared at each other across the table. Seconds ago I'd been ready to start demanding explanations, but Quill's appearance had thrown me off kilter.

Mistress Patel seized the initiative. "Quill has come to Minnesota to help us battle the threat from his former boss. I was given sight of a nexus of events, from which many paths split. The paths in which Quill returned and joined by our side, you and your comrades survived. Most of the time."

"*Most* of the time?"

"In the paths where Quill was already dead, or did not come here, today, you and your comrades died. Most of the time."

A chill crept through me, but I flipped Quill a casual salute. "We have to stop meeting like this, but it looks like I might owe you another one." I cut a glance at Mistress Patel. "*If* what our resident seer predicts is true, that is. Hard to tell if a dire prophecy was legit if you manage to avoid it."

"I've come to lend what aid I can to stop a greater suffering, Captain." Quill said. "Working together, the good we do will be multiplied many times."

"Great to hear. Now if Mistress Patel will fill in the details about why we had to rush to Minnesota…"

"I've been in constant contact with the spirit world beyond the Veil since you battled the spiritmaster, the redcap also known as Gorsh," Mistress Patel said. "He's biding his time behind the Veil, gathering strength, reshaping the spirits he holds in thrall, and readying for war on this dimension. When he is strong enough, he'll rip open the Veil and forth will pour horrors the like of which this world has never seen. Specters seething with chaotic malice, spreading like dark fire beneath the wolf star, a circus apocalypse even Hollywood could not imagine—"

"Wait. Like…*Ghostbusters*?" I had to admit, evil-me enjoyed seeing the unflappable Mistress Patel thrown off balance, especially after my overreaction to Quill and embarrassing failure to overturn the table. Besides, if I had to put up with this kind of interrupting smartass crap from my crew, non-stop, all mission long, I sure as hell would seize the chance to indulge when I could finally get away with it.

"I'm not sure you grasp the peril we find ourselves in. An army of twisted, enraged ghosts swarming across Portland and all its burbs and boroughs and breweries, from the trident of the Portlandia statue to the slopes of Mt. Hood—"

"I thought we agreed to drop the melodrama and hyperbole."

She gave a pained smile. "Old habits. My point stands. You don't appreciate the gravity of what I've revealed."

"And I can't get my head around why you haven't contacted the Feds. I know the Department of Defense, Homeland Security, and the state department would be interested in any potential attack. Creepy ghost clown terrorists sacking Portland would score big time agency funding and at least one piece of Patriot Act-style legislation. Besides, they have special ops units trained to deal with this stuff *and* they're tax-payer funded."

When I'd said *special ops*, an image of Jake popped into my mind unbidden, fixing me with his troublemaker smirk, his eyes full of wry good humor. My throat tightened, and I had to look at the shards of broken vase to keep my emotions locked down. This wasn't the time, wasn't the place.

"I've already contacted them," Patel said. "My request is working its way up the chain of command. They're trying to verify me and my information, and whatever else it is they require before acting."

"You'd think someone who'd created an infamous grimoire would have more pull."

Her gaze dropped to her hands, neatly folded in front of her on the table. She toyed with one of her rings. The ring was gold, etched with strange symbols that resembled eyes. "That book happened a long time ago. Forgive me if I don't give a longer explanation. Being a conduit for prophecy isn't glamorous or fun. I'd abandon it an instant if you offered me the chance."

I frowned, momentarily at a loss. I couldn't imagine giving up my pyromancy. I'd have to take a real job. Probably as a wedding planner, God save us all.

"Understand, Captain, the spiritmaster will attack long before I finally snag the attention of someone highly placed in the government with the power or agency to stop him. We both know the bureaucracy grinds slowly, but exceedingly fine."

Point to her. "So why the hell are you so determined to have us handle this? There are other soldiers of fortune. Hell, there's a group down in Chicago who aren't half bad."

"Several reasons. You're skilled and capable. You already have a connection with the spiritmaster—"

"I don't have any connection."

"Yes, you do, Captain. After your last fight. You both wielded core magic against one another in a very close space. Your auras clashed, your respective magics sparked against each other, the linked frameworks interacting. Your close contact means I can zero in on him."

"And you can't do that without me?"

"Your succubus also has a connection with him via the remnant of a failed spell. It's even stronger—"

"Leave her out of this," I said damn quick. Erik nodded, his eyes watchful, full of gray thunderstorm threat.

"I guessed that would be your choice," Patel said, "so you'll have to serve instead. The world beyond the Veil is huge beyond imagining, like nothing you've ever experienced. It's semi-sentient space, building heavens and hells according to what it believes those souls inside desire most. It's a detached, mindless god indifferently granting wishes. It's nearly impossible to find a single isolated soul in the vastness of the soul-drift without some connection."

"And when we zero him? Then what?"

"You cross the Veil and destroy him. He's a living abomination rampaging through a world of the deceased where he does not belong. He's warping it, *staining* it, and he'll return to this world and do the same."

I rubbed my temple. "You said my life is in danger, specifically. That's always been the fishhook you snag in my throat."

She nodded. "If you don't fight him there, you will fight him here — "

"Like the terrorists, right? I've heard that one before and I know how it ends."

"Do you? I've seen visions of the future. Have you? I've given a prophecy that Cridos the scribe wrote down. 'The flame dancer fighting in the rose city will drown beneath the silken tide of the master's performing horde.'"

"I'm not a goddamn flame dancer. I'm a pyromancer. I. Don't. *Dance*."

"Forgive me. The words pour out of me when I'm in a trance. I don't control what I say when the prophecy of the universal oneness has me in thrall."

Damn you, New Age-y Universe. Damn you. "Even if I wanted to help, I don't have access to the spirit world. There's no way for me to strike across this Veil. And I sure as hell ain't gonna die to score an invitation."

"I have a plan. It's simple, but far from easy. I believe you'd call it a surgical strike."

"She's not going alone," Erik said, startling me. He'd been so quiet I'd half forgotten he was there. "All of us will go with her. A Zero Dog never fights alone."

Patel smiled and spoke before I could tell Erik to tone down the gung ho and the T-shirt slogans because I hadn't promised *anything* yet, much less going alone. "I see you joined them, Erik. I'm glad. It's what I foresaw in most of the futures where Captain Walker survived."

Chilling. I still had a hard time wrapping my mind around multiverses where I was, or would shortly be, dead.

Erik nodded slowly. "Thank you for sending me.

"Thanks for sending him," I echoed. "Nobody appreciates me being alive more than me."

She nodded and leaned toward Erik. "And the other part of my prophecy for you, Erik? The lucky in love part?"

Erik blushed and shifted in his seat. I gave him the side-eye. Apparently the seer had given him an entirely different prophecy he hadn't mentioned, one filled with true love and happily-ever-afters. A small, amused smile curved my lips. Mistress Patel saw it and smiled back. Maybe I liked her, I decided. Just a little. Of course I was a total sucker for new people. I'd brought Erik onto the team after he'd shown up on my doorstep, hungry and predicting my death. I'd fallen in love with a Green Beret on our first mission. I'd…adopted a ghostly pufferfish and turned a blind eye to balloon dog.

"All right, enough mushy stuff." I slammed my fist on the table. "Back to the operational details. What's this surgical strike?"

"I've been planning for this moment for months. This room is…well, I suppose you could say it's similar to a large telescopic lens, collecting and focusing energy to a focal point. I can pierce the Veil with the oracle magic in my blood and the power in my aura. Using both you and Quill, I can identify and zoom right to the spiritmaster's dimensional axis location in the soul drift, peel back whatever reality he's constructed for himself. We invade his heaven, and you, Captain Walker, unleash the inferno. It will be the same as...what do you say? Fire in the hole. He's still alive, so he can be destroyed in the spirit world, even if the other souls of the deceased cannot. Incinerate him before he can react and we never cross the Veil, never directly set foot inside the spirit world."

"Cold blooded. We don't have up-to-date rules of engagement on this guy. I'm not sure we can legally hit him like that, no matter what he's planning. As I said, this is top government stuff. We need clearance. A contract. We can't just freelance outside the Hellfrost Group, killing people." I frowned. "Even monster people."

She sagged back in her chair, far more distressed than I would've imagined.

Quill watched the seer, his hands folded in his robes, his face serene. "She speaks truth, Mistress Patel. Killing is wrong. A vigilante killing would be worse. Doing so would injure her as deeply as she injured Chief Gorsh, but with a different shade of harm. You may have saved me from my ex-chief's ghost clown assassin, and for that I'm grateful, but I did not travel here to do evil in return."

Mistress Patel touched her forehead, then drew her hand down her face. The gesture made her seem less the inscrutable and omniscient oracle, and more the frustrated and relatable human being. "This event, and the repercussions, are far more important than you imagine. The risks. The costs. If we follow my plan, no Zero Dogs die. You slip this shadow that lies across you, and a destabilizing and chaotic menace to the word is stopped cold."

"Not without clearance. I'm sorry." And I was. It sounded like a damn good plan. Simple. Direct. Involving fire. A few of my favorite things.

"I'm sorry as well," Mistress Patel said. "Because now I'm

going to have to show you."

She seized my forearm. I had martial arts-honed reflexes, but she caught me completely by surprise. Later, I'd tell myself it was her damn outfit that made me lower my guard enough for her to grab me. She was too well-dressed. I'd pegged her as soft, but she was very quick.

My muscles tensed as I started to move—to grab her wrist and pry her hand off me—and then the world flashed-banged in glowing phosphorus white and I could see nothing.

The white brilliance died away. I stared down at my hands. I wore gloves smeared with dust, beat-to-hell body armor, full tac gear, harness, grenades, sidearm, static-hissing radio, knife. All worn and battered, all layered in brown dust and streaked with ashes. Everything had a hard, precise detail to it. No fuzzy, dreamlike sheen. This *felt* real.

The stink of char, burned rubber, and scorched plastic filled my nose, turning my stomach. Black pillars of smoke billowed slanting columns into the sky as a hot wind pushed against my face. Mistress Patel stood beside me. She was dressed exactly as she had been back in the office. Her eyes were closed, but in the center of her forehead burned a stylized eye, the kind seen on Egyptian hieroglyphics, glowing a bright electric-burner red. I stared at the eye in horrified fascination. Mistress Patel lifted her arm and pointed toward the horizon.

We stood on a rocky ledge riddled with jagged black rock. Beyond the ledge spread a valley between blasted hills, crossed by rivers that churned with dark water. The lay of the land was familiar, but I couldn't place it at first, until I realized this was the Willamette Valley, and we were on the charred slopes of Mt. Hood in the Cascade Mountains. That dark slash of river had to be the Willamette, and I spotted the thick artery of the

Columbia River. But I recognized nothing else, because there was no Portland. Another city, a twisted city, had risen in its place.

Fires burned, throwing up flames and smoke, others only smoldered, staining the air in deep charcoal grays. A vast amusement park filled the valley from slope to slope and horizon to horizon. The park was massive, staggering, cyclopean in its unbroken spread. Old style roller coasters twisted and turned, from this distance looking like marble tracks cutting back over and over in impossible curves and loops. Big top tents sprouted by the thousands. Ferris wheels blurred, spinning at insane speeds. An untold number of game booths dotted the landscape, between freak shows and grimy food stands. I saw Tilt-a-Whirls, Viking swing ships, tall metal towers and their deadfall drops, more rides than I could count. In the west, the setting sun sank into a boiling ocean of color, in searing red and burning orange and bruised purple, throwing the land into apocalyptic hues of devastation, all fire and shadow.

It took me a moment, but I finally realized this massive carnival, incestuously interbred with a circus, was abandoned and decaying slowly in the light of a sun that never seemed to finish setting. The rides were rusting or smoking, parts falling from them as they shrieked and clanked, the cars dented and hanging empty. The big top tents had faded and sagged in places, holes gaped in others. The midways stood empty, save for smoldering trash and dust devils. The booths slouched against one another like staggering drunks. Every ride, every game, abandoned, dying to rust and soot and decay. It was a circus of slow death.

I glanced at Patel again, but her real eyes remained closed, while the stylized Egyptian eye on her forehead shimmered in its hot coal reds, as if mimicking the fires I saw below us. She lifted her hand and pointed again, demanding my gaze return to the scene in the valley.

When I looked again, I understood the massive carnival megalopolis was growing. New rides pulled themselves out of thin air, metal parts appearing as if by magic and flying together. A new funhouse. A new merry-go-round. A new super loop. As soon as each ride, tent, or structure was complete, it flickered, faded, grew dilapidated and ancient-looking, the colors washed out, blackened in places as if licked by fire. A circus at the end of the world. And yet, the circus still spread relentlessly, growing like a living organism with its guts built of rusting metal and faded pennants.

My eyes watered, blurring my vision. I squinted against the smoke, staring into the uncertain light. Ghosts appeared in the midways and walked the paths between rides. Fire eaters. Clowns. Mimes. Freak show marquee members, ringmasters, trapeze artists, and jugglers. And thousands more.

No people. Only ghosts.

"What the hell is this?" I hadn't been sure I could speak in this…vision? Dream? Not until the words spilled from my lips. I barely heard myself over the hot blasts of wind.

"This is what he wants." Mistress Patel's voice resonated like a struck bell, almost painful to hear, vibrating in my mind. "This is why you must stop him."

She meant *assassinate* him. Because that was what it'd be if I ripped into his little pocket of spirit world and lit him up.

The dark mass of circus continued to spread while I stood there, wavering. I took jobs sanctioned by the Hellfrost Group, working for governments and VIPs with established rules. This was slogging into rogue territory. We might end up disavowed, branded loose cannons and hunted ourselves.

"What do you choose?" Mistress Patel's words smashed against me like an unseen wave.

"Take me back. Take me back and I'll give you your answer."

The circus vanished. The wasteland vanished. The blasting hot wind died.

I was back in Mistress Patel's office. My hands clutched the edge of the table so hard I would've sworn my fingers had crushed indentations into the surface. My breath rasped in and out of my mouth. Erik loomed over me. Worry marred his face, and his hands were raised uncertainly as if he wanted to grab me and shake me out of it but didn't quite dare.

"Your answer, Captain Walker," Mistress Patel demanded.

I looked her in the eyes and said, "No."

CHAPTER TWENTY
Motivation

Mistress Patel leaned back in her chair, watching me as if I were an untrustworthy dog loose in the Post Office. The strange stylized eye that had glowed on her forehead throughout the vision had vanished, but part of my mind still seemed to see it there, floating like the afterimage of the sun in my eyes.

"I'm at a loss for words," she said, with no trace of anger in her voice, only disappointed surprise. "I was certain you would agree to help me after you'd shared my vision."

"I *will* help you."

"I don't understand. You said *no*."

"I'm not going to assassinate him on my own, without license or approval. We don't work that way. The Department of Justice has extremely strict rules about how mercenary groups behave on U.S. soil."

"The spirit world is not U.S. soil."

"So I'll go and drag his ass back here so he can face prosecution. As it is, I'm playing dangerously close to a line—extradition by force, even if he does have a warrant out for his arrest. I'm not an officer of the law, so this is a gray area. But if he's gonna try overrunning the world with twisted circus-style ghosts then he needs to be stopped." I looked at Quill, then at

Erik. "I'm going alone."

Shock flitted across Erik's face. "Why?"

"She already mentioned how dangerous the spirit world is. Nobody here signed on for unpaid suicide missions." Most importantly, Tiffany would never forgive me if anything happened to him.

"But we all swore—"

"You guys did more than enough tagging along this far, showing your support. I can't tell you how much that means. But jumping into the land of the dead? You couldn't pay me enough to do that, even backed by a team of Navy SEALs, so that's why I'm doing it for free and going alone."

"Captain, that doesn't even make sense."

"Exactly."

Quill shifted, frowned, and cleared his throat. "Forgive my interruption, Captain. But I think you should let your people make the decision for themselves. If you wish to arrest the chief and bring him to justice for his crimes, I also offer myself to help in any way you might need."

"Thank you, Quill. And thanks for coming out here. But you've already put yourself in danger once. I can't keep asking people to risk themselves for me."

"He's right though, Captain," Erik said. "Everybody would want to help. Leaving them behind will hurt them."

I looked at him evenly. This was *my* call. If anyone had to take a fall for this, it would be me. My hands would be dirty, and I'd take full responsibility for any fallout. Either that, or I'd die screaming in the afterlife, eaten by ghost clowns, and taking full responsibility wouldn't matter very much anymore.

On second thought...only a stubborn fool jeopardized her life in the face of fucking prophetic doom and overwhelming odds. "Hey Mistress Patel, run me the numbers. What are the chances of me taking down this spiritmaster chump alone versus dragging along the rest of the team onto some Elysian playing field?"

She peered at me with her dark brown eyes, but after a moment it seemed to me as if she were looking straight through me — as if I were a window opening on a much more interesting scene. "I'd have to consult the *Omniphaelogos* again to be certain and perfectly precise, but the key is not bringing more allies. Quill is needed, I have already seen that in the ripples. The others, if they came along, would only be thrown in greater danger and make it harder for you to discover and isolate the spiritmaster."

I nodded. Good enough. Solo for me, well, except for Quill, who didn't count because he was a pacifist. It didn't thrill me to leave the Zero Dogs behind. In fact, I found the thought of charging into the underworld alone extremely disquieting. But at least I'd know my people were safe.

Erik didn't seem satisfied by Patel's answer. "Please explain, Mistress Patel."

"The moment you pass through the Veil you'd all be lost. Separated. Each of you would be scattered throughout the spirit world, trapped in your own created versions of heaven. Captain Walker will have to break through her own afterlife reality, the one her mind constructs like a dream around her. She'll have to *remember* her mission and find the spiritmaster. If she has to rescue others, the chances she'd fail and remain trapped in an afterlife reality are far, far higher."

"So what happens if I like my little personal heaven better than *this* reality?" I demanded. "Hell, what if you never have to do dishes there, and kittens follow you around singing Italian opera, and cheesecake increases both the density of synapses in your brain *and* makes you look like Angelina Jolie—"

Erik and Mistress Patel were staring at me. I shut my mouth so fast my teeth clacked together.

"There's also a chance you'll find yourself trapped in your own personal version of Hell," Mistress Patel said slowly. "A place known as the Labyrinth of Regret, where souls are purged of evil for the next cycle, paying karmic debts incurred during existence. There, the spirit world will take your nightmares and make them real."

"Sounds like a friggin party." I punched my fist into my other hand with a meaty smack. I had to go, I didn't have any choice. Pros and cons. If I went, I might be trapped and tormented by psycho clowns for my sins or locked into a heaven impossible to escape because I'd never want to leave. If I didn't go into the spirit world, Patel had warned me I'd die when the spiritmaster returned and wreaked havoc on my city with a spectral circus. At least the rest of the Zero Dogs could remain on this side of the Veil and fight the spiritmaster if I failed.

"Good thing I wore combat boots and Kevlar panties today," I said. "Hurry up and let's get this oracle mojo-hocus-pocus done before my boyfriend gets back from deployment."

"Captain," Erik said. "At least let me come with you."

"No. The decision's made." I turned to Mistress Patel. "Let's do this."

CHAPTER TWENTY-ONE
Apocalypse Carnival

This was magic I'd never seen before: an oracle (sometimes known as a professional death whisperer) wrenching open a portal through the Veil into the spirit world. Mistress Patel sat at her reading table, leaning forward with her eyes closed. She softly chanted something—a spell, a poem, a song, it contained elements of all three—that sounded half dirge, half wail. The rest of us stood behind the other chairs at the table and watched her in silence.

Erik had his axe out and twisted the haft in his hands, spinning the blade slowly. I stood ready to scorch stuff. My heart thudded a steady, heavy beat, and trickles of sweat slid down the curve of my back. Quill half hid behind the chair, seeming torn between scrambling under the table and holding his ground beside us.

A spiral of red light, a color that matched the seething sunset in Patel's carnival vision, corkscrewed out of thin air above the table. The spiraling light wavered and rippled as if it were a ribbon in the hands of a dancer, behaving like no beam of light I'd ever seen. Mistress Patel's chanting trance deepened. Her strange words came quicker, harsher. Then she leapt from her seat so forcefully that her chair toppled backward. She slapped her hands against the table and yelled incomprehensible words that stabbed my eardrums like screwdrivers.

I spat a curse and slapped my hands over my ears. I'd hoped for a quieter egress so I wouldn't draw any attention from the Zero Dogs in the waiting room and complicate my one-woman assault. Instead, Mistress Patel full-force bellowed words built mostly of consonants and animal-like grunts. Erik stepped back, hefting his axe. Quill ducked behind his chair. The portal spread open. The strange red light seeped between the spirals as if it were liquid. The spirit world light began to change, shimmering between a blistering red and a dark purple streaked with rays of black. When the beams washed across my body they felt icy cold, and my skin broke out in goose bumps. I started to shiver. Each flickering ray that touched me felt the opposite of a sunbeam. The air filled with the high-pitched grinding shriek of a plastic fork left in the garbage disposal. Vibrations shook the table and floor. The chair legs rattled and thumped.

"Get ready!" Patel yelled.

Her face appeared to have aged sixty, seventy years in bare minutes, becoming a strained mask with bruised half-circles sagging beneath her eyes and deep lines creasing her skin. The light pinned her shadow to the wall in rapid shutter-stop flashes, but her shape seemed all wrong. Her shadow flipped through a dozen changes, a hundred, becoming longer, distorting into monstrous shapes. In one shadow, her head stretched into a muzzle—a Doberman pincer melded to a human body. Another shifting shadow and she suddenly sprouted six arms. Still another, and her shadow transformed into a mass of sharp angles and blades, as if she'd become a spider made of knives.

Unsettled, I finally tore my gaze away from those unstable shadow images, and only because the portal twisted itself fully open. Calliope music blasted, echoing in my ears and mind as if the sound had somehow gnawed its way into my brain. If I never heard another calliope I would die a happy girl.

A violent wind tore through the portal, whipping and buffeting us, howling in a mad screech that didn't mask the off-key music. Unlike the twisting ribbons of cold light, the wind blew hot and dry. It stank of something strange and unpleasant—burned churros and scorched caramel corn.

Erik stood nearest the portal, clutching his enchanted axe, face grim and painted in the rippling light. I clambered onto the tabletop. *Now* I was grateful the table was bolted to the floor and didn't tip or collapse. Quill stayed behind his chair with his cap pulled down over his eyes.

The bottom edge of the portal spun in the air above the tabletop. I wanted a running jump to hurl myself through. I tried not to think about what I was about to do. I focused on the mechanics of the actions required and not my fear. Fear would only make me weak.

"That's not the soul-drift!" Mistress Patel shouted, but her voice had a strange echo to it, as if other words whispered and hissed at an ever so slight delay beneath the ones she'd shouted. Unnerving words in languages I'd never heard, laced with excitement nearing panic. "He was waiting to hijack my portal!"

Beyond the knife-sharp edges of the portal spread a world as insane as it was frenetic and sickeningly colorful. My mind reeled, and I struggled not to vomit as a massive wave of nausea churned through me. The world beyond burned in primary colors, so bright they rasped against my pupils like sandpaper. There didn't seem to be any stable ground inside the portal. Everything floated in all directions, swirling and tumbling and spinning as if caught in zero gravity. Pieces of carnival rides. Chunks of roller coaster tracks. Lost bumper cars. Floodlights on severed poles, and banks of colored bulbs that flashed as they spiraled through the air. Chunks of land spun and careened and smashed together.

I froze. No way in seven shades of hell I was jumping into that chaos. There wasn't even anything to land on. The place looked as if someone had blown up a circus in outer space. Fucking madness.

"Go!" Patel screamed. The wind whipped her black hair around her head in wild streams. Again, other incomprehensible words echoed beneath those she screamed. "Hurry! Take the fight to him. Drag him back across the Veil."

I staggered backward instead and almost fell off the table. No. I couldn't. I wouldn't last ten seconds in that nightmare.

A spectral roustabout flew out of the portal. I could see straight through him, but he quickly gained solidity on this side of the Veil. He held a huge mallet, and his striped shirt was riddled with bullet holes. He was singing about hauling stuff around and drinking his pay away, the moaning lyrics almost drowned out by the wind and the grinding calliope music.

Erik swung his axe. The roustabout ghost spun toward him, still singing, and lifted his mallet to block the attack.

The axe sheared through the mallet haft and into the ghost. The roustabout wailed and disintegrated into a splash of ectoplasm, which smacked against the table with the sound of soggy diapers hurled at a concrete wall. The goo ran onto the carpet, sparking and flashing before it began to evaporate.

More clown ghosts poured through the portal. A circus strike force. Erik battled them, slashing and hacking. One clown squirted a joke flower. The stream barely missed me and splashed the table and floor, hissing and smoking like acid. Another threw a pie that splatted against the wall. The whipped cream mutated into albino spider-things with too many legs that left little dots of cream-footprint trails. They scurried along the wood toward Quill. He yelped in disgust and dodged away, fell over his chair, and scrambled on hands and knees beneath the table.

I tried to summon my pyromancy and couldn't. I stared into the really fucked up doorway leading to Gorsh's concept of the afterlife and my magic would not respond. I stood frozen, stunned by the colors and chaos and blasting noise.

They'd attacked as if they'd expected us. They'd been lying in ambush, *waiting* –

The door to the reading room smashed open, banging against the wall so hard it busted a dent in the wood paneling. I flinched and glanced that way, dreading some new threat.

Tiffany sprinted inside. Her black wings were spread wide and one tip brushed against the wall as she ran. She cut straight for Erik, her slit eyes flashing. Her magic surged, wild, uncontrolled, and flooded the room, but the ghosts were immune. She didn't have her pistols.

Erik spun toward her, fear for her marring his face. She ran past me and reached for him.

Two ghost clowns darted toward her and seized her by the wings and snatched her away from Erik. She cried out only once as the ghosts yanked her into the portal. The last glimpse I had was of the surprise on her face.

"*No!*" So fast. It had happened so damn fast I'd had zero time to react.

Erik never said a word as he vaulted onto the table and hurled himself after Tiffany. He plunged past the portal edge and disappeared.

Everything was happening so goddamn fast that shock left me weak and unable to move, like a gut punch I'd never seen coming. I was so damn *useless*.

A ghost that had been closing in on me burst into black and purple sparks. A demon hex had exploded it to bits, leaving a burned glyph scorched against the wall. Sarge stormed further into the room, followed by the rest of the crew, but I barely registered them.

A berserker yell ripped out of my throat. My pyromancy surged back, thrumming through my body, and the air around me shimmered and filled with flashing sparks. Everything opened in a complex grid through the air that my mind could sense, a thousand canals to pour flammable vapor through then spark alight, directing it to my every whim. I ran toward the portal, bursting into flames like a meteor falling to earth.

Another spectral mime tried to stop me with an invisible wall. I shoved through both invisible wall and ghost with a crazed yell, lighting the mime on fire as I ripped through its body and plunged into the portal.

Sudden weightlessness spun me, disoriented me. The sound of grinding and crunching, shrieking wind, and calliope music all dialed up to earsplitting volume and stabbed blades of pain into my head. The strange cold light pushed against me, as if it had far more weight than physics allowed. As I sailed deeper into the portal, the light grew freezing cold. My skin ached. My eyeballs felt iced with frost.

"Trespassers!" A huge, rough voice bellowed, so loud it took my reeling brain a moment to realize it was Spiritmaster Gorsh. "Gate-crashers! You have no right to be here. Leave us alone!"

Mistress Patel's voice rang out, echoing in my head. "He won't risk fighting you in his heaven. He'll expel you into the soul-drift, try and trap you in *yours*. You must escape from the dream-gift of the detached god. It's a prison that will hold you forever if you can't shatter free. Find your friends and break them from the illusion or you will all be lost."

Here, across the Veil, I finally understood the whispered, hissing words that lingered under the English. Chilling, alien words whose meaning was clear. "*In this instant of superposition you are alive and dead. Measure and discover the truth."*

As bad as a fucking fortune cookie.

My head and shoulder smashed into a slowly tumbling wheel of fortune, knocking a grunt from me and sending me spinning off through the air in the opposite direction. The sound of the clicking arrows over the tabs seemed as loud as rain on a sheet metal roof. The sane office-world back through the portal flashed through my vision once and was gone, replaced by a wildly spinning, stomach-churning mix of too-bright colors and deafening calliope music.

Any moment I expected the spiritmaster's ghosts to swarm me, but they didn't. No sign of Tiffany or Erik. I caught a glimpse of Sarge and Rafe jumping into the portal behind me, and I tried to scream at them not to follow. No sound came from my mouth.

The light swelled. This apocalypse carnival spinning in some anti-gravity tornado suddenly smeared into blurred patterns of color. Everything went white, then black, then white again. I felt myself rushing away at incredible speed, as if I'd been tied to the back of a drag racer. I closed my eyes, trying to steady myself for the end. Confusion and terror shredded any attempt to think my way through this.

All at once, the spinning stopped. The pain and dizziness vanished. There'd been no impact. One moment I'd been spinning crazily, the next I was quiet and still, lying on something solid. I opened my eyes and found myself staring up at a tree house nestled in the heavy arms of a huge oak. Thick white clouds drifted across the deep blue of a summer sky. The air smelled of grass and wildflowers. Blades of grass tickled the skin of my neck and around my ears. They smelled of green summer.

There was only one explanation. I'd measured, and now I knew I was dead.

CHAPTER TWENTY-TWO
Slice Heaven Like Pie

I hoisted myself into a sitting position with a groan, so disoriented I could barely hold a coherent thought. No sign of the twisted amusement park or carnie ghosts and creepy clown-things.

The sun peeked through the wide oak leaves. It poured sunlight onto the ground beneath the tree, dappled and threaded with the breaching tree roots, and danced whenever the breeze shook the branches. It warmed my skin.

I stood carefully and checked myself for injuries. Not even a scrape. I still wore the jeans, combat boots, and the black and green "Friends of Cthulhu" T-shirt I'd thrown on to visit...to visit someone...

Frowning, I glanced around at the forest of oak trees, at the drifts of old brown leaves from autumns past, and I breathed in the smell of dark soil and lush greenery. My thoughts grew harder to hold and focus on. I'd been doing something...important, some mission. And...ghosts. Something to do with ghosts. But God, didn't the shade feel so cool and the breeze so pleasant? The more I struggled to remember, the more it seemed as if I'd always been here, in this quiet forest. I belonged here. All other thoughts and memories were dim. Unimportant. Past.

A ladder led up the oak's trunk to a tree house. The trap door was up, revealing a darker inside. I wondered what was up there, but idly, because I had no desire to climb and see. It was enough to know the tree house was there, waiting patiently in case I ever needed it. Strange, but the oddness of the feeling—that the tree house was there for me, or *because* of me—immediately started to not seem so weird after all, but perfectly natural. Perfectly right.

The leaves sighed under my boots as I walked—not dry enough to crunch with my tread, but sinking a bit when I put my weight down. The smell of smoke and char reached me long before I spotted the dark gray columns and hazy smears of black through the branches. I began to run toward the smoke. I felt no fear, only a hushed curiosity tugging me onward. The huge oak trees gave way to a field of high grass that rippled in the breeze, fur stroked under the hand of the wind. Ashes filled the air, drifting down in dirty snowfall.

Beyond the field rose the gentle slopes of a hill. The entire crown of the hill was on fire. The fire's crackle and roar reached me even from this distance. I squinted against the blaze of orange and yellow and the constant veil of churning smoke. In the middle of the flames stood a charred group of standing stones. Most leaned haphazardly against one another; others lay tumbled in the coals and burning grass. They must've been huge up close, as big as the side of buildings, because they appeared massive even from a mile or more away, partially obscured by the wind-whipped flames.

I watched the hill burn and thought of nothing, staring at the dancing flames as if hypnotized. Ashes still drifted gently down. The concreteness of time seemed to melt away. The fire never consumed the hill entirely, and never spread down into the fields or forest. It just burned as if self contained, feeding on some eternal jet of natural gas or another unending fuel.

The hill was closer now. I looked behind me and discovered I'd crossed more than half the field without realizing it. There, in the distance, stood the oak trees, the shade beneath their lifted arms darker than the smoke, promising relief from the sun, but I turned away, back to the fire.

The ground began to tremble. From the center of the ring of fire-wreathed stones rose a massive bird, a bird vaguely shaped like an eagle but engulfed in flames, *made* of fire. No feathers, but instead flickering, burning tongues. No eyes but blazing coals. Ecstatic joy surged through me.

The phoenix spread its fiery wings across the hill, flaming in sunset brilliance, and it loosed a shrill cry so loud it slapped me across the face with the shockwave of sound. I laughed wildly and sprinted toward the phoenix, the grass whipping against my legs, hissing as I ran. I charged up the burning hill. The smoke and heat were intense, but didn't bother me, and I had no idea why. Had I something to do with fire once, and now didn't fear it? What had happened before the tree house, before the forest?

Didn't matter. I kept running. Running into the flames, feeling the coals and the patches of raging heat under boots that didn't melt, clothes that didn't spark flame, hair that didn't catch fire. The phoenix loomed over me, big as a ten-story building, a gigantic inferno in the shape of a bird of prey.

Remember, you'll enter a dream of a dream, some voice I didn't recognize spoke in an urgent whisper. I ignored it. The words meant nothing. I had to reach the phoenix. I...I didn't know what I'd do when I reached it, but it would be sublime. Ferociously sublime.

The closest stone of the ring had toppled to the ground and lay, scorched black, in a bed of blazing coals, its shape distorted by shimmering heat. I leapt onto the fallen stone without hesitation and ran along it toward the phoenix. Smoke billowed around me. At times I could see nothing but gray and black and a steady red rain of sparks. The heat did not stop me. The smoke did not choke me. I ran into the ring of stones and, laughing, launched myself into the phoenix. As the flames engulfed me, I knew this was right. This felt perfect, felt like coming home.

Remember—

But there was nothing to remember in the fire. There was only a scream of challenge from the flame beak of the phoenix, now *my* beak, the screech coming from *my* lungs, and when I spread my wings the air currents trembled and swirled in fear of me. I launched myself upward, my wings beating hard, flames thrown everywhere below me, but I didn't care because I was climbing into the freedom of the sky.

I screeched again, wings beating furiously, climbing higher and higher. I flew. Streaked through the air, a burning meteor escaping gravity, smoke tails billowing behind me, my fires stoked hotter in exultation at this freedom. My heart might've burst if it hadn't been a searing coal in my chest and nothing more. The land was so far below me, the trees small and insignificant. The rivers glinting in the sun. The grass shifting in green and yellow waves.

Remember—

Remember nothing. I was fire. I was a star with wings. The greatest creature to sail the updrafts and glide through clouds which vanished as soon as I streaked through them.

I circled for the mountains on the distant horizon, a dim part of me thinking to melt the snow from their peaks with a heat they'd never known…and I saw the holocaust I'd left in my wake. My wings failed to beat, and dismay, cold as an icicle, stabbed into the inferno held inside.

Fire swallowed all the land behind and below me in an ocean of red and orange flames, blackened char and gray ash.

The fields burned, the trees shuddered and cracked, crowned in fire, and the rivers boiled.

I screamed with my phoenix throat, and part of me rejoiced at the thought of the world burning, and another part of me, the core Andrea part, wailed in horror at the destruction I'd caused.

Remember the dream —

And I soared higher to save the land from my flames, knowing that soon I'd reach the very edge of the abyss. Knowing I could hurl myself into it without fear, driving back its darkness with my light and throwing back its cold with my blazing heat, uncaring except in freedom and power or...or I had something to do. Something...some mission that needed me. People needed me. *My* people needed me, and as soon as I realized it, their faces started flashing through my mind with the speed of shuffled cards, over and over again.

I shot upward, tearing at the air with my wings, rocketing toward the stars. Faster, faster; I had to break free of this place. The darkening sky suddenly split, shredding into ribbons as I burst through it, igniting the atmosphere, consuming the world in flame behind me as I shot into the void.

Then, with another breath, I was plain old Andrea Walker again. Floating in darkness. My heart hammered away. Fear had me in its teeth, worrying my mind back and forth like a terrier with a rat. I drifted in nothingness, shaking so hard my teeth chattered and my hands trembled. I was lost. I'd broken my spirit world dream and now there was nothing. I was beyond the movie screen, into the back of the theater where there was no magic, no illusion. And how long would I be trapped here...floating, driven insane by all the thoughts and memories that had slammed back into my head? Forever?

How long I floated in nothingness, I couldn't say, as the fear twisted tighter and tighter inside me. A new thought came out of nowhere and hammered me, left me reeling. Patel had said the spirit world was semi-sentient—whatever that meant. Maybe I could get it to do something for me, work for me in some way, help lead me to my friends.

I had nothing else.

Patel's last warning had been about breaking free of the dream, and I'd done so, followed by a demand that I help my friends. Had that really been my personal idea of heaven? Becoming a enormous firebird and burning the universe? That heaven was pretty damn crazy when you came right out and called a spade a fucking shovel. All the same, part of it had been wicked cool: the flying, the freedom, and the green expanse of forest and fields before my tail had ignited them.

I shoved those thoughts away. It didn't matter if being a huge fiery bird flipped my switches and buttered my secret bread, because that was the past. The fear couldn't help me, so I shoved that aside as well. The dreams were all illusions and couldn't help me beat the spiritmaster...unless they somehow held the key to finding him...identifying the dreams...

The void around me erupted into billions of tiny glowing shapes swirling in every direction. Not stars—these were irregularly shaped and seemed to change in brightness and form as I watched them. I'd been in Kyoto once when the cherry blossoms were falling: drifts of petals dancing on mild breezes, fluttering in a sudden updraft, then slowly sinking. These lights brought those days back to mind with staggering force, almost pushing me back into a reality where I walked along a narrow canal again among hundreds of cherry trees, the dark water, and the fallen blossoms floating along its surface. The petal-lights fell downward—though down was a concept I only really had because the lights were moving that way—and passed beyond my sight into a unbroken shimmering glow made of seemingly infinite flurries of light. Yet, for no reason I could tell, they would at times swirl upward again and, for an instant, delay their fall while circling one another, the same as those cherry blossoms when the wind caught them. Other times groups of the falling lights seemed to dance together in complex patterns, as if aware of each other and interacting in some strange way I couldn't fathom.

C'mon, focus, dammit. It was so hard to focus. The drifting lights seemed to blank my mind, hypnotizing me with their motion. I felt that, if I watched long enough, I'd see some larger pattern hidden in the endless fall. Were these spirits? Part of the semi-sentient dimension Patel had mentioned? If so, I had friends here. I had to lock onto them, reach them somehow.

Somehow. Because there were so many of these lights, and if each one was a soul or a personal heaven, I'd never find my friends.

No. I refused to fail. Tiffany first. She'd been grabbed by those damn ghost clowns and I had to find her. The spiritmaster must be exploiting these dream traps that had shunted us off into our own isolated heavens. If he'd hurt her, nothing would save him from me.

I concentrated on Tiffany, trying to catch some sense of her here, some glimpse or brush of her aura in the infinite blizzard of falling lights. For a moment I had her…the sense of my friend, the feel of her, almost as if she stood next to me in a dark room. But I knew it was her from a million little tells, some of them so fleeting as to be nearly extrasensory. Even as my mind turned to zero her, another dark presence rose up and scattered the sense of Tiffany that I'd started to dial in on. The lights around me swirled all at once, careening in every direction. I could only float in this strange place, too disoriented to track her.

Patel had said I could zero in on the spiritmaster because our magics had tangled. I tried to locate him the same way, certain that Tiffany was trapped with him. But the same thing happened. I could feel his twisted presence in general, but when I tried to focus on it, the sensation slipped away. He knew I was here, and he must've been guarding against me.

Despair hit me, cold and inescapable as winter rain. The despair gave way to growing terror. Again I began to imagine myself trapped in this non-place forever, drifting in the snowstorm of lights, unable to escape back to the real world, unable to die, slowly going mad.

Panicking, I fought to think of something…of anything or anyone. I needed to find something concrete, someone to latch onto here, because my mind slid toward the edge, on the verge of losing it.

Quill popped into my mind. Why, I had no idea. As soon as his wrinkled goblin face formed in my mind's eye, he appeared in front of me. Here he wore no bloody red hat, but was shaved completely bald. He sat in the lotus position, of course—if he'd been jitterbugging that would've really thrown me for a loop— and a warm light the shade of lemon peels shone from his body. He smiled, and serenity radiated from him like heat.

"Quill! I found you!" I tried to speak the words aloud, but my voice didn't seem to sound anywhere but in my own head.

All the same, Quill seemed to have heard and understood the words. "We found each other, Captain Walker. Gorsh expelled us from his heaven after he captured your succubus friend. I was searching for you in the soul-drift, but Gorsh obscured your dream and hid it from me. It wasn't until I felt your mind seek mine that I could reach you."

"Where's Tiffany? He's hiding her too, isn't he?"

Quill nodded. "Gorsh obscures her, but if we can link enough minds that love her, even a spiritmaster cannot keep her hidden."

"How do I find the others?"

"That knowledge is already yours."

"Don't go all Zen on me. Just feed me the facts and fast."

His smile held the gentle amusement of a teacher watching a bright but hopelessly impatient pupil. "How did you find me?"

I'd focused all my thoughts on him, the same way I'd focused on Tiffany, sensing her aura, nearly finding her before Gorsh had hidden her from me again. "I thought of Tiffany, but Gorsh stopped me from reaching her."

"He can only do that because he trapped her in his own constructed heaven, his own detached dream. The others, who came here of their own free will, he cannot touch."

I eyed the floating redcap. I could sense he was the same creature I'd known on the other side of the Veil, but here he seemed so much more. He seemed to have weight, and yet a tranquility that soothed away the fear and confusion eating at me. "You're different here. Who are you?"

"Merely another troubled soul taking refuge in the Triple Gem. Nothing more. Nothing less."

A too-simple non-answer, but I had no time to waste pondering it.

Again I opened my mind's eye, reveling in the clarity and speed of my thoughts, and imagined Rafe. Maybe it was the lingering mental trauma of watching him perform naked jazzerbo and jazz hands. Or maybe it was the time he'd been caught in friendly fire—*my* friendly fire—when I'd been desperate to save us from being overrun by zombies. Knowing I'd hurt someone who depended on me, injured one of my friends, even accidentally, was a wound that had not healed clean. Whatever the reason, it was easy for me to sense him, the core Rafe-ness that I found both endearing and exasperating.

The space around me stretched, then warped as if viewed through a fish eye lens. Rafe suddenly felt very near to me, as if we stood close to each other inside the same lightless room, the identical feeling I'd had trying to find Tiffany. I realized I was falling, or flying through space in the same direction as the drifting cherry blossom-like lights, but it was difficult to tell for certain because of the lack of reference points.

My body spun through the drifts, brushing lights. Quill raced along beside me, sailing through the floating lights while still in the lotus position. I took strength from his utter calm. It seemed strange to think I'd once distrusted him. Here, he seemed the most solid, most centered thing in the universe.

I caught glimpses of thousands of images, shuttering like movie frames through my mind, too many and too fast to comprehend, a new onslaught every time I touched a light. I focused on Rafe, grim, relentless, and undeterred by the thousands of worlds around me, the heavens of countless souls. I had a mission to prosecute, people to save, and too much time had already passed.

One petal light in particular drew me toward it. As I closed in, the light swelled from tiny to immense, filling my vision. As it grew, I noticed the light was truly nothing like a cherry blossom at all, but something that resembled a flexible, twirling trapezoid. Some sense I couldn't describe told me this was Rafe, whatever core part of his mind that existed here free of synapses and neurons. I stopped before touching it. Quill stopped beside me.

"Touch him," Quill's thoughts came to me. "And enter."

That sounded far more intimate than I was comfortable with, but there was no backing down now. God hated the squeamish. "Will you come with me?"

"I must stay here in the soul-drift to serve as your anchor. These heavens and hells can consume you. Breaking free should be easier this time, but if I stay here, I can help bring you back if things go wrong. Ecstasy or terror, both can be dangerous to us here."

"What do I do?"

"Find him, guide him out. He may resist you, but you must make him see the truth of the illusion. As you saw the truth of the illusion."

"You sure you never worked for a fortune cookie manufacturer? The longer you're here, the more Zen you get."

He grinned. "Great, isn't it?"

I reached out and touched the flexing light-shape that my mind sensed as Rafe. The infinity world of drifting lights vanished, and I was hurled into the dream. An instant later I came to a wrenching, disorienting stop, crashing into the dreamworld with the same smashing rebound of a car hitting a concrete pylon. My mind reeled and for a moment it felt as if every thought had been shaken from my head.

Bass pulse filled my ears. When the disorientation passed, I discovered that I stood at the end of a bar inside a club. The hard beat of techno music thumped through the air. The place was packed, filled with yelling women. I barely had time to register this before I sighted Rafe on the stage with a stripper pole. There was my werewolf, swinging his hips and shaking his ass in an electric blue g-string with a smiley face dead center on his...bulge. His tattoos all shifted and changed as I stared. Some tattoos, like the pirate girl holding a flintlock pistol, danced along with him, others changed shape and design at random. Rafe was enthusiastically doing all the usual hip thrusts and gyrations that came standard with strippers. The women screamed wildly, chanting things such as "Take it off!" and "Shift, shift, shift!"

Rafe yanked off his g-string and flung it into the crowd, then began to shift back and forth from human to wolf-human hybrid rapidly and without apparent effort. The mad scramble for his g-string made me glance at the crowd again, and I noticed that the press of women around the stage were of all shapes, heights, colors, and a range of ages. One gray haired matron near the stage was yelling loudest for Rafe to "flop his way over" to her.

Ego, thy name is werewolf. Of course this was Rafe, and what the hell had I expected? Still, I didn't have time for him to end his set.

I scanned around for a way to get Rafe's attention without having to shove my way to the front of the stage. A huge, unattended sound system sat in the corner, a massive console of knobs, buttons, glowing lights, and turntables. I didn't know if my pyromancy would work in Rafe's little slice of heaven, but knowledge, or lack thereof, had never stopped me before.

I summoned and directed streams of flammable vapor around the equipment, even *inside* the equipment, and then ignited it. The sound system and DJ turntables burst into flames, but I kept careful control of the fire, cutting its fuel before anyone was hurt or the flames could spread. I didn't know whether or not the people around me were real—real as in something more than Rafe's fevered imaginings—but after the whole burn-the-world chapter of my personal heaven book, I sure as hell wouldn't chance it.

Echoes of techno bass died away. Everyone turned to stare at me. I suddenly felt as if I were trapped in one of my dreams where I showed up naked at a college auditorium to teach a graduate course in front of a bunch of people wearing those fur suits shaped like cartoon animals.

"Rafe!" I bellowed, trying to regain my equilibrium through command. "Front and center, merc! We got a job to do, ASAP! And put some damn clothes on!"

Rafe's dream-heaven shook for a moment, wobbling as if I'd just slapped a gelatin mold of Don Juan's ass cheeks. Yet, Rafe didn't seem to notice me. He yelled to the crowd, "Anyone see my g-string? No? Hey, that thing's expensive, don't *chew* on it!"

"Rafe!" I bellowed his name so loudly I would've strained my voice box in the real world. "We got a mission. Put on your soldier of fortune jockstrap and get your furry ass over here!"

Once more the world around me trembled, far more violently this time. Rafe glanced at me — actually saw and recognized me, I would've sworn it before a jury — and then the heaven construct fell apart. The images, the walls, the women, the stage, even Rafe, shook at such high speeds they blurred into streaks of meaningless color. Fear shivered in my gut. For a while I was certain my shouts had destroyed us both.

My mind reeled through undefined space filled with colors as everything shook around me. All I could think was: this is how it feels to be trapped inside an Etch A Sketch. A color Etch A Sketch. I could sense this heaven dream of Rafe's struggling to eject me, to push me back into the soul-drift as if I were a splinter lodged in some skin of unreality. I held on, determined, unrelenting.

The world suddenly stabilized, the colors shrank down into sane and defined three-dimensional shapes. The haunting song of a wolf howl echoed around me. The night sky above was full of stars, the gossamer swath of the Milky Way striping the night. No moon. A huge mountain of logs rose off to my right. Evergreens, I could smell them. They were cut, huge trunks two or three feet across, the bark black and wet as seal skin. A log pool opened in front of me with dozens more half submerged logs floating in the dark water. The surface of the water was covered by a scum of floating bark, foam, and sawdust. Several large sprinklers sucked water from the pond and sprayed long arcing streams over the top of the log pile, keeping the wood from drying out.

A wolf sat on his haunches at the top of the logs. Rafe. I didn't often see him as a full wolf. For fighting he preferred that hybrid wolfman form. His coat was thick gray and black, with scattered patches of brown. He was huge, even from this distance, bigger and thicker than a mastiff. I watched as he threw back his head and loosed another howl. The wolf song held a mournful note, seeming to ache among the cracks and crevices of the log pile, a stark, lonely sound. He kept his eyes closed and sang his song and no other wolf answered.

I climbed toward him, carefully and quietly making my way up the slick sides of the logs. My boot treads bit and scraped along the rough, wet bark. The sprinklers caught me with spray a few times, but I ignored them, concentrating on reaching Rafe. I crested the top and gazed on a silent sawmill on the other side. Beyond it, a stripe of shadow that had to be a river curved near the mill.

"Rafe," I called, focusing on him. "Rafe, it's me. Andrea."

He spun and growled low in his throat. I raised my hands, palms up to show I meant him no threat. "Rafe. It's me. Remember? Your fearless yet lovable leader."

His growl deepened and he stalked toward me along the top log, head low, tail straight out, baring his teeth. His amber eyes flashed dangerously as if they had their own inner light.

"Do you remember when I burned you?" The words popped out of my mouth though I hadn't meant to say them, and now it was too late to take them back.

His growl was near constant now. The snarl, low and menacing, made me think of a huge industrial machine. The kind that might catch hold of your clothes and rip your arm off if you strayed too close.

"I'm sorry for that, Rafe. So damn sorry. I didn't want to hurt you. But I couldn't think—I didn't see any other way to save you."

He reached me. I watched him, unwilling to move. I could taste the fear, a foul warm flood down my throat like discharge from an infected tonsil. No matter how hard I tried to swallow it away, I could still taste it.

Rafe moved very close to me, then sat on his haunches and licked my hand. He peered up at me, and I could've sworn on my grandmother's girdle that he was grinning.

Again, Rafe's heaven dream trembled, shaking with increasing violence, streaking, trying to purge me back into the soul-drift. Again I dug in my mental claws and held on with all my strength until Rafe's mind, or the semi-sentient spirit world itself, finally stopped fighting me.

We were in a beautiful saloon, with a gorgeous bar of warm polished wood. The bar mirror was aged, showing a fine pattern of cracks in the silvering, while the recessed lights poured whiskey-colored light down on the perfectly arranged bottles. Rafe sat on a barstool and smiled when I looked at him. He wore a handsomely tailored dark gray suit and gold cufflinks that flashed when they caught a beam from the lights over the bar.

I walked over to him, my boots echoing on the wood floor. There was no bartender in sight. In fact, except for Rafe, the bar was completely empty. I vaulted over the bar—something I'd always wanted to do—and scanned the top shelf before taking down the good Scotch. There were glasses to my left, but since this was heaven, I drank straight from the bottle like the barbarian daughter mama always feared she'd raised.

Rafe lifted his glass, and I caught a whiff of vodka. He leaned his elbows on the bar, and smiled, appearing genuinely happy to see me. I clinked my bottle against his glass, and we both threw back. The alcohol burn down my throat and the spread of heat in my chest was a most welcome sensation.

"Let me get this straight," I said, raising an eyebrow. "Your secret heaven dream is to dance naked to bad techno for a crowd of cheering women? That's the Valhalla of Rafe Lupo's choosing?"

He frowned. "Heaven dream? Did I die on that last mission? I always thought I'd kick off from erotic asphyxiation."

"You're not dead. Yet. We're trapped in time-space pockets of semi-sentient reality." That sounded relatively technical. He didn't seem to catch that I was talking out my ass. "That runty asshole Gorsh had some clowns grab Tiffany and drag her through a portal. So basically, we're going to kick everything's ass until we get her back and save the universe."

He grunted. "You remember Tiffany wailing on those zombies? I'm not sure she makes a good damsel in distress."

"That's an understatement. But we're here to back her up, because Zero Dogs don't get left behind." I frowned and glanced at him, unsure of what else to say, not wanting to mention his lonely howling at some abandoned sawmill and how for a few minutes I'd been convinced he would attack me.

He seemed to sense my thoughts anyway. "I didn't recognize your scent right away. I thought I was alone. This place has me a little scrambled." He took another long drink, and I joined him. Neither of us mentioned my apology.

"How much do you remember?"

"Enough. Now. But the memory is slippery. It wants to seep out of my brain again. If you left here, where ever this is, I think I'd lose it all again. Maybe right away."

So I served as some kind of reality anchor to the outside world when I broke into these dreams. Good to know.

"When I tried to track Tiffany, the spiritmaster blocked my ability to find her. I don't seem strong enough to wrestle him on his home turf—not alone. Patel and Quill hinted that if I get all the Zero Dogs together, we can use the semi-sentient nature of this dimension to help us find her."

"How can something be semi-sentient?"

"Patel has some bullshit answer, and if we drink enough, it might even make sense. Doesn't matter though. The plan will either work or it won't."

"Same as always." He turned to face me. "What was your heaven like? Were you and Captain Sanders all white picket fences and Jacuzzis and no chaffing, ever?"

I delayed by downing a healthy swig of Scotch. To tell or not to tell. I didn't want to answer—what I'd experienced seemed too private, too...weird. Of course, I'd just barged into Rafe's personal dream at a few rather delicate moments. Or at least one moment that might've been embarrassing for anyone in the universe except Rafe, who didn't seem capable of the emotion. So maybe I should share a bit. *Quid pro quo.*

"I turned into a giant bird on fire and incinerated the world."

He stared at me.

I cleared my throat. "So anyway, let's go save Tiffany. Leave your smiley face g-string, though."

A grin showed me too many teeth. "If you insist, Captain."

Now that the time was at hand, I worried I wouldn't be able to escape this place. That made little sense, as Rafe's shifting heaven had seemed to want to expel me when I'd interfered. "Hold on to your valuables. This is gonna be a trip."

He grabbed his crotch with both hands.

"That's purely metaphorical, Rafe."

"Darn."

I concentrated, focusing on what I'd done to break through my own heaven illusion and into the non-space of drifting lights. The bar around us distorted, the colors and shapes breaking into smaller and smaller shards and spinning away from us. Rafe started to flicker and distort, as if he were a three-dimensional image being stretched out of true, but I focused on him in my mind, on keeping him with me, and he snapped back to normal, joining me in the drifting lights.

"Wicked," Rafe's voice resounded in my mind. "Pink Floyd

light show meets arctic blizzard."

"You succeeded," Quill said using the telepathy here in the soul-drift. "I never doubted."

But his face told me the opposite. I couldn't blame him. I'd had plenty of doubts on my own. "I want Sarge next."

"Have Rafe concentrate with you. His mind will increase your power here. This should grow easier and easier."

Rafe sniffed at the little redcap, making me think of him in wolf form again. "How do you know all this? Have you been here before?"

"Mistress Patel has been preparing me since I came to Minnesota. She foresaw something like this, and what my role must be."

"Damn oracles," I mused. "Always with the 'I-told-you-so' smirks, and the 'Who parallel parked my universe?' T-shirts, and those smug 'Friend's don't let friends self-fulfill prophecies' bumper stickers."

Both of them stared at me. "Right-o," I continued quickly. "Rescuing Sarge. Pull up all your memories of him and concentrate. Make sure they're significant memories."

"Like the time we were in Vegas, and Sarge and Shawn crashed that Lamborghini into the Bellagio's lake with the music…and the water turned into blood like an Egyptian curse, remember that?"

"Yeah," I said, my smile feeling false. "Good times like that."

Rafe's bushy eyebrows furrowed in concentration. I brought up a memory of the first time sergeant Nathan Genna had brought Shawn to the house to meet us. Sarge had been so nervous, glowering at us as if he'd been afraid some random bit of Zero Dog chaos would drive Shawn off. Of course something *had* happened, I couldn't even remember what, but Shawn had laughed about it. And that was when I'd known, deep down, that Shawn was perfect for my grim, gun-loving demon sergeant.

Again, as we concentrated, we were drawn toward one specific drifting light, and we seemed to pass through space at high speed. This light was purple-red, perfectly spherical, and drew both of us closer. The light flared wide, filling my vision as we shot into its center, the sense of Sarge surrounded us, all pervasive, and again I slammed into another world —

—a world so different from Rafe's that both of us gaped in stunned silence.

We stood on the wide top of a massive zeppelin airship with a bitter cold wind slicing against us, eager to push us off. I fought back against the crush of fear, telling myself I wouldn't fall if I only didn't move. My boots rested on what felt like a metal frame under the silver fabric of the zeppelin's envelope, and the rumbling vibration of the four huge propeller engines buzzed in my knee joints.

Stars seemed close enough to snatch out of the air and hold cupped in our hands like fireflies. The horizon showed the last deepening purple-blue of twilight. But the sky overhead was filled with falling meteors, tens of thousands of them, burning as they sliced through the atmosphere in fire-arrow volleys. They rumbled and cracked as they fell, and the dirigible shook, the monotonous hum of its engines drowned out by the thunder. One meteor shot past so close I shied away from its blazing fireball and screaming roar.

Sarge stood with his wide back to us, twenty feet or so distant along the top of the huge airship. His hand hovered over a six-shooter slung low on his hip, his boots layered in dust, a black cowboy hat tilted low with the brim shivering in the wind.

Facing off with him was a robot. Sleek. Human-shaped, some Sci-Fi movie robot-revolution terror with its metal tinted brick red, its camera lens eyes blank, wearing a cowboy hat, boots, and another old style revolver riding on its hip.

My demon sergeant was dueling with a robot in the middle of meteor shower, which was enough to make me yearn for Rafe's perverted little slice of heaven. Rafe started for Sarge, but I held up a hand, blocking his advance. I didn't want to surprise him in the middle of this showdown and throw off his timing if there was shooting to be done.

Another meteor screamed past, missing the far edge of the zeppelin by a dozen feet, maybe less. Neither gunslinger flinched. They remained absolutely still, demon gaze locked on machine stare, waiting for some unknown signal.

Then again, I was on a tight schedule.

"Sarge!" I yelled. "Gun down that droid and come with us if you want to live!"

Sarge didn't turn, neither did he throw down, though I saw him flinch. His hand twitched.

A meteor hit the zeppelin. The flaming piece of space rock ripped into the fabric and the zeppelin's frame, striking between the two duelists. A curse slipped from my lips, soft as a sigh, and the dread churning inside me grew cold and thick. Crashes and clangs echoed from inside the airship, underscored by a roar that grew steadily louder. Sarge and the robot drew and fired, the gunshots so close they nearly overlapped. Sarge was faster and his aim perfect. His bullet caught the robot in the right eye lens, spinning it around. The six shooter flew out of its hand, and the robot toppled over, rolling along the top of the zeppelin and falling over the side.

Sarge shoved the pistol back in his holster, whirled and ran toward me and Rafe, even as the hydrogen inside the dirigible ignited and fire exploded into the twilight behind him. The zeppelin veered downward and to port. The fire moved so goddamn fast it frightened even me, disintegrating the fabric and scorching the metal frame and roaring like a hundred dragons. The whole dirigible came apart in mid air in a blaze of flames, sparks, and smoke. Sarge stayed a step ahead of the flames, but they were catching up to him fast. I sprinted toward him with my hand outstretched. Rafe ran beside me. We met as the roaring flames caught us. I grabbed Sarge's huge hand and Rafe's and we escaped the shattering dream.

Locating the other Zero Dogs grew faster the more of them I pulled back into the drift-space between worlds. Our collective mental powers amplified as we came together as a team. That wasn't to say it was ever easy dragging them from their personal heavens. Not easy, and never boring.

Mai was riding on a three-headed, winged unicorn that, I swear before Odin, appeared to be tie-dyed. Catching Mai turned out to be a prime piece of hell, because she never seemed to hear the three of us calling her. Instead, she flew her three-headed unicorn past Godzilla-sized versions of her pets that ran amok through the fields below. Crimson kittens as big as buildings with burning slit eyes and claws as long as street lights. A purple and pink marmoset sprouting far too many limbs. Ferrets as long as trains whose hair-raising squeaks boomed across the strange Dr. Seuss trees and Salvador Dali landscapes. In the distance loomed massive, wind-ravaged mountains with forbidding, jagged peaks so high they scraped at the sky, savagely weathered, the shunned slopes of archaic nightmare myth. At the top, cave mouths gaped open, and from that Stygian darkness came a single, haunting sound that echoed across the land—the chilling *whoop-whoop-whoop* of cosmic guinea pig spawn.

"This is more terrifying than the clowns!" Rafe screamed to me.

We chased her on flying jackalopes—jackrabbits the size of small horses and sprouting deer antlers—which we'd commandeered, because where the hell else would you find flying jackalopes but in Mai's cute-fevered imagination? We pursued her to a Dayglo castle that floated upside down in a sky full of shifting aurora borealis. When we finally managed to catch her, she remembered she was a Zero Dog and not, in fact, a deranged animal lover on a never-ending acid trip. When I told her about Tiffany, her face hardened into a determined scowl. She abandoned her heaven without a backward glance.

Gavin's heaven had been nothing if not predictable. He'd been street racing in some tricked out, up-armored Nissan GTR with rocket launchers, miniguns, and a supermodel riding in the passenger seat beside him. The cars were all Mad Max/Deathrace 2000-style armed to the teeth, screaming through a darkened megalopolis straight out of some dystopian cyberpunk future. Explosions. Chaos. Big screen viewers broadcast the battles to screaming fans and provided slow motion replays every time a car-slash-war machine ran down a unicycle-riding mime or crashed into a hot dog cart. Not original maybe, but points for the grand enthusiastic execution of it all. We arrived just as Gavin finished winning a race called the Megiddo Streets: World Battle Race XVII, which I read on the banners. Gavin was surrounded by adoring crowds. I saw more than my share of fawning, busty cheerleader types wearing "Team Gavin" ultra-tight T-shirts, and I could only shake my head and smirk.

Gavin didn't want to come with us.

"I'm important here, Captain," he explained. "I'm *kick-ass* here."

"Tiffany needs us. We have to save Portland from the circus. Don't be a dick." I tried to soften my tone. "Besides, I thought you always dreamed of being a writer."

"The only thing fun to write is my autograph. The rest is fucking *hard*."

Whining or no, he finally left the Team Gavin girls, his supermodel copilot, and his tricked out battle car of his own free will…and only a handful inspired threats via yours truly. As soon as we returned to the soul-drift, Quill floated beside me, radiating his pure Buddhist light—or whatever it was that let him glow here as if he were radioactive.

"Gorsh sensed me in the soul-drift." Quill's mindvoice rested easy on its core tranquility, but the glowing aura around him shifted in agitation. "He's realized what we're doing and he's trying to stop us."

"Can he attack you while we're inside one of these heaven dreams? Maybe trap us there?"

"I can sense his fear. It dominates him and twists him. I threw him back, using his own hate and fear against him. I doubt he will attack again now that he knows I am more powerful than he, at least inside the soul-drift itself. He will build his defenses inside his heaven and try to fend you off or destroy you there, where the advantage is again his."

"If you're more powerful than a spiritmaster, then kick his ass for me and get Tiffany back." I wasn't above using subcontractors if it was the most efficient way to rescue Tiffany.

"I cannot purge him from his heaven-dream—not from the soul-drift. We must go *inside* his heaven and pry him out. Collapse the dream and its defenses. The strength of hearts united can undo the damage done, free those souls caught and twisted by Gorsh, and save your friend."

Buddhists. Sometimes it felt as if you merely circled around and around the racetrack with them in some kind of eternal series of left turns. Plenty of general advice but few specifics. I turned to the rest of my crew, floating close around me. "Anybody have anything else to add? Questions. Complaints.

Apologies. Last words. Now would be the time."

"I got a question for Quill," Gavin said. "What's the sound of water on fire? Think about it. That one will *melt your brain.*"

* * *

Only Hanzo and Erik remained to be located before we full-scale assaulted Gorsh's circus dimension. In Hanzo's heaven-world, we found him fishing on a pier on a crystal-clear lake, surrounded by mountains that could've been the Alps. He lay back on the edge of the pier with his fishing pole held loosely in his hands and stared at the clouds drifting overhead. Next to him was a small, black-haired little boy, also on his back, pointing out something on one of the distant slopes. The boy's resemblance to him was undeniable. Hanzo smiled as the boy pointed, and drifts of the kid's excited chatter reached me at the end of the dock.

I made the others stay back and walked up the pier alone. Nothing so far had been as hard as walking up to Hanzo and that boy, *his* boy, with my throat burning as if I choked on the fire that had consumed the zeppelin. I'd expected Edo period Japan, samurai and war. Not this. Not a son who looked like him…and looked like Mai.

Hanzo saw me. Recognition dawned in his eyes.

"I'm sorry," I said, because I had nothing else to say. Only empty words, every one of them inadequate.

He closed his eyes for a long moment. He leaned down and kissed the boy on the top of his head. The boy smiled and stared up at him.

He gave the boy the fishing pole, stood and faced me. "Let's go, Captain."

I stood there, my hands clenched into fists. "It's not fair." A whisper. "He looks just like her."

Hanzo gave me a smile that stitched across his face in threads ready to tear from the seam. He looked past me to Mai, who waited with the others at the end of the pier. "Let's just go."

And we went.

Erik was the last.

We found him walking along an endless bridge. An ocean the gray of the Atlantic in winter spread in both directions, horizon to horizon, no land in sight. Huge black storm clouds drifted like warships through the expanse of sky. The breeze blew cold and heavy with the smell of salt. The bridge was built of dark, weathered wood, plank after plank, between pylon after pylon, stretching off into infinity in front and behind us. Erik walked, slow and steady and carrying his guitar case, dressed the same as I'd first seen him. Rumpled suit. Worn cowboy boots.

We appeared behind him, all of the Zero Dogs I'd gathered, crashing into his dream heaven, packed onto the narrow bridge. He kept walking, his boots thumping on the wood with each long stride. Except I noticed every footfall left a dark, bloody boot print behind. He'd left a trail of them stretching behind us farther than I could see.

"Erik!" I called.

He stopped, turned, and faced me. His face was haggard, coyote lean, and his eyes seemed to burn. There was no heaven here for him. I wondered if he'd fallen into some kind of hell, and the thought sent chills through me. Had *my* dreamworld been a hell and I hadn't realized?

"I can't find her, Captain," Erik said, very quietly. "She's gone."

"Tiffany's not here. You're trapped in the spirit world—a version of reality it threw together to hold you."

Gavin piped up from behind me. "As Shangri-Las go, this is

pretty lame. At least mine had supermodels and fast cars."

"Gavin, shut up," I said without turning around. "Erik, come with us. We need you to help find her. All of us, concentrating on her together, can break through the barriers hiding her."

He stared at me. His face, to someone else, might even have looked impassive, indifferent. But I could read his eyes. I saw the fury blazing inside them, the fear, but not for himself, and the twisting, intertwined desires to save Tiffany and to bring down the hammer on those who'd taken her.

"Help me find her," he whispered.

I held my hand out to him and he took it.

CHAPTER TWENTY-THREE
Roll Up! Roll Up! Roll Up!

E ven with all his power and skill in the spirit world, Gorsh couldn't hide Tiffany from us once we'd freed Erik. After we latched onto the sense of her, we immediately zeroed in on Gorsh's heaven dream in the soul-drift, and gathered around a pin-wheeling light-shape that slowly changed colors.

"He's expecting you," Quill warned. His aura blazed with a pure white radiance, a holy phosphorous flare in nimbus around him. "He'll be very strong. He's a spiritmaster and this is his turf."

"You aren't coming?" I'd expected him to want some final philosophical showdown with his old boss.

"I must stay in the soul-drift to anchor you. Otherwise Gorsh will simply eject you *en masse* back into the soul-drift."

"Any tips on dealing with Mr. Clown Fetish?"

He looked at me with an expression so serene it immediately gave me confidence. No one could appear that calm without having an infallible plan, an ace up the proverbial sleeve, a silver bullet in a very big gun.

"I have no idea," Quill said serenely.

We were so fucked.

No time for dismay. I kept my game face on as I looked at each of my crew in turn, then we linked hands, closed on the pinwheel light, and smashed straight into Gorsh's heaven like a rocket propelled grenade. One of our own had been stolen, and if she'd been hurt, there was no dimension in the multiverse that would save him from our payback.

Inside the dream, we stood on a plain of jagged volcanic rock that stretched endlessly in all directions, and no volcano in sight. A huge, stepped pyramid rose from the black rock, looming over us on the otherwise featureless world. Wind moaned and howled and brought with it the haunting sound of calliope music. God, I was so sick of the sound. I'd damn well better get a chance to melt me some calliope pipes before this was over.

The sky shone the bruised purple of twilight. A bloated sun hung high above the black plain, frozen in a solar eclipse, with a perfect white ring blazing around the sun's edge where the moon failed to fully black it from the sky. The wispy, unsteady corona danced and undulated, sea weed in a shifting current. The stars were alien, no pattern or constellation I'd ever seen, and they spun across the sky in mere minutes not hours, though, impossibly, the sun never moved. The stars streaked as the sky turned, but that burning eclipse eye hovered in place, seeming to watch us.

I stared at the stepped pyramid, my gaze traveling all the way to the top. "Oh, fuck me."

The pyramid seemed to lean toward us, at the top arc of a swing that would smash us into the rock. The structure was massive, staggering, far bigger than the physics governing stone buildings should've allowed. It vaguely resembled Mayan pyramids, except that each level was far wider and the colors were all wrong. The bottom-most step had to be a quarter mile wide before ending in fifty feet of stone wall rising to the next step. The pyramid bled primary colors across its stone body, the black rock reflecting and amplifying the sky's twilight cast until reds, blues, and yellows blazed on the stone surface.

Crowded onto every level of the pyramid, every flat surface, and stretching up toward the very top, were thousands of amusement park rides, big top tents, and vendor booths. Déjà vu had my mind reeling and my stomach sick. This was so close to the vision Patel had forced on me. Ferris Wheels flashed strange patterns of lights as they spun at insane speeds. Roller coasters screamed around tracks, clanking and clacking, and on the down slopes they wailed and shrieked like damned souls chucked into Ye Olde Lake of Fire. Merry-go-rounds blasted that damned calliope music, made incoherent by the sheer amount of competing noise. Ghost trains rattled into the darkness. Bumper cars careened around with murderous intent. Demented octopus rides lifted and dropped their cars in hypnotic rhythms. The topmost part of the pyramid was barely visible, but I could see figures moving around the lower levels — swinging trapeze, clowns, mimes, fire-eaters, strong men, bearded ladies, roustabouts, more clowns. The sheer amount of motion, from this distance, made the pyramid seem to seethe with infestation, as if lice crawled across every surface.

"Holy clown shit," Gavin said, awed. "The inter-dimensional crazy ziggurat of Circus Circus."

I pointed to the top of the pyramid. "I'm open to suggestions on how to best assault that."

I received a flood of answers from the Zero Dogs.

"Airstrikes. JDAMS. Maybe a couple of MOP GBU-57 bunker busters."

"I might be able to summon a dragocorn. A dragon unicorn that can fly us to the top while breathing napalm."

"Stealth. We shall be shadows at midnight, unseen, unheard, unsmelt —"

"Speak for yourself, Bruce Lee. I can smell Rafe from here. If only we had the moped with us. *Then* we could roll in gangsta-style, right, Hanzo?"

"Don't mock me, *baka*."

"If the princess slipper fits, ninja-boy—"

"Guys," I said. "This is the time when we all come together as a team." I took a deep breath and yelled, "*So come together as a team, goddammit!*"

Everyone gaped at me, but at least the bickering stopped.

"Great. I'm already feeling the teamwork."

As for the suggestions, I tried to sort the wheat from the chaff and came up with a shitload of chaff and negative twelve wheat. The entire time, Erik had not spoken. He stared at the top of the pyramid with his axe in his hands. The surface of the blade crackled with energy, flashing bolts of purple white. He was very still. Only his eyes glowed and crackled with the same energy of his weapon.

"I know the way," Erik said.

Everyone turned to stare at him. I tried to keep a leash on my excitement, but it was hard because I was desperate. As much fun as it might've been to slog my way up ninety-nine levels of carnival madness, battling murderous contortionists and homicidal jugglers keeping live hand grenades in the air, I simply wasn't in the fucking mood anymore.

"Spill, Erik," I said. "It can't be as bad as the moped idea."

"This is a dream world. So we dream."

I stared at him, not comprehending. "Explain."

Erik swept a hand toward the pyramid. "He created that insanity. So we create things that will let us tear it apart until we find Tiffany. We have as much power as he does."

I could foresee all manner of crazy shit happening if the Zero Dogs started manifesting aspects of our imaginations, but I had the haunting feeling that time ran short for Tiffany. Even if I killed the spiritmaster, that would be cold comfort if I lost my friend. Erik's suggestion had been the best, and possibly craziest, so far.

"All right," I said. "We use the strength of our imaginations to superpower ourselves. Good plan. Now mercs — *transform!*" I waved my arms around.

Everyone traded uncertain glances.

"Hey, Captain." Hanzo pointed toward the massive circus pyramid. "We've been noticed."

The stars still streaked across the twilight sky, unnervingly fast, and the eclipsed sun never moved. But the pyramid swarmed with ghosts, flying from the top steps, headed straight towards us. All the usual suspects we'd come to know and love, carnies of every ilk, every kind of sideshow curiosity, roustabout, circus performer, mime and clown. Too many to count, the sheer mass of them staggering, a primary-colored cloud churning around the topmost section of the stepped pyramid. The edges moved first, surging toward us like pincers that would soon clamp closed.

Screw this reimagining reality bullshit. Summoning my fire magic was far easier than in real world Earth. The usual struggle akin to trying to move acres of gelatinous flammable sludge with only my mind was nowhere to be found. The fire responded instantly, streaking out from me in a wide swath. The flames incinerated ghosts. Instead of sending bits of ectoplasm raining down like burning Jell-O, here in the spirit world the ghosts I hit flashed back to the glowing shapes populating the soul-drift and vanished, freed from Gorsh's dream and his control.

More ghosts immediately filled the gap I'd burned clear. My heart sank. Even given how much easier the summoning had been, I couldn't forge enough flame to win against the massive ghost army. I had no choice but to seize on Erik's idea, change things with creative restructuring, and I had to learn very fast.

I closed my eyes and tried forcing myself to imagine something, *anything* that could help us. Nothing came to mind. And yet…there was something else here. When I concentrated, I could sense all the intersecting lines of power, at a level beneath what could be seen, all of them interconnected, all thrumming and pulsing. When I called that power toward myself it came without struggle, so much so that I gasped in shock and delight and awe.

"This is our chance." I kept my voice low and urgent, but full of confidence. As I spoke, I looked at each of them in turn. "Didn't you ever want to be a superhero as a kid? Now, *here*, we can be anything we want. So do it. Let's go get our friend back."

I started walking toward the pyramid. I didn't glance behind me to see if my crew followed. I knew they would. Even if we had to scale the pyramid using only sporks and bailing twine, we were still going to conquer that damn carnival-shrouded stone eyesore. Fucking Prophetic Doom could kiss my mercenary ass.

The spiritmaster's circus army of ghosts had almost reached us. We charged forward as one, loosing battle yells that must've done our berserker proud. As I ran I felt myself change, and as I changed, I felt myself leave the ground, blazing with heat, ever more heat, until I flashed into flame. The edges of my vision distorted with heat shimmer and dancing fire. When I looked, I wasn't surprised to see my body had shifted into wings built of fire, a tail wreathed in flames. Yet, this time, changing into a phoenix didn't fill me with the fire-lust and power-drunk madness that it had before. I'd dreamed this. I owned this.

I streaked toward the oncoming ghost horde like a missile of flame. Faster, faster. I spread my wings so that more of the ghosts would be caught in their fire as I incinerated a huge hole in the front rank and kept driving toward the top of the pyramid. The ghosts burned as I cut through them. They flashed out of the sky in great meteor streaks as the spiritmaster's manipulations scorched away and they reverted to their true forms and escaped. Soon it seemed the ghost minions threw themselves at me in a lemming charge, as if they were eager for the fire, eager for the escape and freedom from Gorsh.

A strange creature flew on my right flank, and I almost attacked before I realized what it was. That it was a unicorn was bad enough, but it had apparently been crossbred with a dragon. Large dragon wings sprouted from the back of a beautiful Friesian horse with a flowing black mane, dragon wings and a dragon tail, and a horn sprouting from its head. The absurdly strange and strangely beautiful dragocorn banked toward me, neighing, and shot blue-white dragonfire from the tip of its horn, obliterating ghosts.

I caught sight of Sarge, back in his western gear with a huge brown duster coat and black cowboy hat, holding a Colt single-action revolver in each hand. He fired non-stop into the circus army, alternating guns, and never ran out of bullets. Every ghost he shot exploded into brilliant light no matter where his bullet hit. The tip of the cigarillo clamped between his teeth burned like a shimmering coal.

Erik led the rest of the Zero Dogs in a charge up the pyramid. He wore plate armor, something straight out of the late Medieval Era. His battleaxe sent great crescent arcs of blue energy slicing through the dancing, gibbering ranks of circus ghosts that tried to stop him. His armor shone a deep cobalt, and shards of light glinted from the surface. After a moment I realized they were stars, as if he wore the night sky for protection. Whenever a ghost did slip close enough to strike at him, the armor sucked it inside, pulling it down like water funneling into a drain until it vanished.

Rafe looked the same as ever: a werewolf enthusiastically

ripping into our enemies with teeth and claw, and on this side of the Veil they were as effective as they were against flesh and blood. Maybe Rafe believed he was already as perfect as could be.

Hanzo had turned into a death shadow, moving nearly too fast for the eye to see, a black blur with a flashing katana that sliced through any happily demented circus creature in his path. Like Rafe's teeth and claws, here Hanzo's sword hurt the ghosts, leaving gaping wounds that poured shining light as the soul imprisoned inside the twisted form escaped.

Finally I spotted Gavin at the wheel of what I could only describe as a Pirate Winnebago of Death. The whole cumbersome thing was flat black with Jolly Rogers painted all over every available surface—the classic skull and crossbones, skull and crossed swords, a skeleton spearing a red heart, too many to count—and a spike rising from the roof where a huge pirate flag fluttered and snapped. The Winnebago bristled with guns, drills, rocket launchers, and articulated robot arms fitted with circular saws. Gavin pumped his fist and the Corsair Winnebago launched into the air, plowing into the churning ghost clown mass, blasting away.

The sky lit up with thousands of explosions, streaking rivers of flame, bullets, dragonfire, the flash of insanely sharp swords. The horde of circus ghosts broke and broke hard. They fled, wailing, gibbering, scattering across the plain away from the pyramid. Triumph swelled inside me. I released the phoenix form, leaving the flames behind as I continued to fly. I loosed a victory yell that echoed back to me. The rest of my mercs took up the cry as we pressed toward the topmost structure of the pyramid. The demented little redcap held Tiffany captive there, I was certain.

The pyramid shuddered. A rending groan sounded, far louder than any thunderclap. The pyramid started to shift, shaking so badly that rides toppled and tents collapsed. About a thousand years ago I'd quipped that things could always be worse.

Sometimes I hated being right.

CHAPTER TWENTY-FOUR
Titan Born

The quake shaking the pyramid grew more violent. The rumble and roar was constant, deafening. As I watched in growing awe, the pyramid reshaped itself, breaking, changing, forging itself into a massive human shape. The impossibly mad circus pyramid became an equally impossible and equally mad towering giant. It was built of black rock and the fused parts of carnival rides, stretched swaths of bright silk tents, fluttering pennants, and broken midway booths, all set to the cacophony of a hundred competing calliopes.

The giant had a slumped head built of the topmost level of the pyramid, four eyes made from spinning searchlights, and a jagged crown formed of broken rollercoaster tracks. Its mouth was a wide Tunnel of Love entrance. Upper and lower layers of interlocking black iron spikes formed teeth inside that gaping tunnel. As I soared past, the iron spikes crashed together with a ringing clang and a drool of sparks.

The pyramid giant shouted in a voice louder and deeper than artillery fire. "You dare challenge a god?"

"Give her back!" I yelled. To my vast relief, I sounded furious and not terrified. Because the size of that monster was staggering. How the hell did you fight something that big?

The giant's iron teeth retracted, and for a moment I saw

rows of organ pipes lining its mouth and throat, the same as might be found at a merry-go-round or calliope. Then the giant sucked in a massive amount of air, a roaring, rushing vacuum that pulled me toward that gaping maw. Somewhere inside that misshapen head was Tiffany. I could sense her, the same as I could feel the rest of my Zero Dogs here in this spirit world.

"Three times 'til *never!*" the giant bellowed, the words blasted out a wall of sound that smashed against me, making my head spin and my ears ring.

The giant swung an arm as long as a runway at me. The arm was slow, but even as I twisted and dodged aside, I sensed its incredible mass as it rushed past, so close that a tornado roar of wind sent me tumbling through the air before I regained control of my flight.

The Zero Dogs attacked, nearly simultaneously, without me giving any command. They strafed the giant, they scrambled up its scrap metal legs, sabotaging as they went.

Rafe's werewolf howl resounded across the plain, punctuated by a rumbling boom as the giant took a lumbering step forward. Rafe clambered up the giant's leg, hurling and swinging from the metal struts and beams of the repurposed roller coasters and the merry-go-round horses embedded in the giant's volcanic rock skin. Gavin's Pirate Winnebago cut behind the giant, blazing away with all guns.

But it was Erik, again, that caught my eye as I wheeled back around, soaring toward the giant's searchlight eyes and meaning to blind them. I slowed in stunned amazement, seeing him *running* up the side of the giant while wearing full plate armor and wielding a huge axe as he weaved in and out of the twisted remains of the carnival rides and booths embedded in the rock. *Impossible* didn't begin to describe it, but then again, the wildly improbable seemed standard operating procedure in the spirit world. The flashing amusement park rides and the guttering fires painted him in all colors, but nothing slowed him. Erik had already reached the giant's chest. Soon he'd reach its head. I needed to keep the giant distracted so it didn't notice him until it was too late.

The giant's hand grabbed me and clenched before I could fly free. The fingers, each as thick as an industrial smoke stack, ground against each other as the fist tightened.

A jolt of pure white terror shot through me. In a second I'd be crushed to a red liquid smear. My world shrank as the ridiculously huge fingers scraped away my remaining space.

Memories of Tiffany filled my mind in rapid blinks, so fast I barely had time to identify them. Tiffany with me, walking downtown, both of us eating ice cream cones. Tiffany tricked out in her scout gear, scoping a target we were about to assault. Another image of her wrapped in her wings, peeking at me over their tops. Her laughing on the couch, laughing so hard she was crying, and some silly comedy movie on the television. Tiffany, the time she'd brought Erik out of his berserker rage. More memory images. Too many to name.

The crushing fist stopped just short of smashing my bones to powder and swung toward the giant's head. The crazy rollercoaster swoop left my stomach a few heavens behind. I caught a glimpse of that gaping tunnel mouth full of iron teeth and steam pipes. A bright, brittle moment of ice-rind fear cracked through me when I realized the giant intended to eat me.

The fist shoved me into the yawning maw. The pipes gave a huge blast of discordant sound as the giant's mouth rumbled closed. I spun through space and darkness, stunned by the blast and disoriented. I slammed into a ward that trembled like a sticky membrane. Before I could escape or catch my bearings, the membrane sucked me through and spat me into an entirely different place. I crashed to a flagstone floor and skidded to a stop.

I scrambled to my feet, realizing I'd been dumped into a great hall straight out of a Medieval castle. It was less strange than some of the things I'd seen since crossing the Veil, but I'd expected gnashing iron teeth, hoping my final act would cause the giant a terminal case of heartburn. Instead I stood in a long room with arching, twenty foot ceilings ribbed with massive timbers and dark stone walls draped with tapestries. Candles burned in iron wall sconces, long tears of tallow dripping down their sides, pools of red wax beneath them in spilled-blood puddles. A fireplace large enough to walk inside dominated the wall closest to me. Long rows of wooden tables stretched across the flagstones.

Tiffany stood on a raised dais at the far end of the hall. Gorsh stalked toward her, leering, tricked out in his white ringmaster outfit and ridiculously bulky codpiece.

"I brought your friend," Gorsh said. "Now let's three think of naughty games—"

Tiffany spun and launched a side kick that knocked him off the dais. Gorsh gasped out "Pink Brownie shite!" and toppled over a bench as he crashed to the floor.

"Tiffany!" I sprinted toward her. The sight of her alive near gut-punched me with relief.

She flashed the sweetest grin I'd ever seen, but an instant later it vanished. "Be careful, Captain! He's powerful here." She held up her hands and I noticed her wrists were bound with furry handcuffs.

I jumped onto a bench, then to a tabletop, and kept running toward the dais. Fire flared around my hands, streaming out behind me as I ran along the empty table. Gorsh flailed out from under the bench and leapt up the stairs to the dais. He threw a look back at me—half fury, half terror—then freed his red bullwhip and cracked it. The whip coiled around Tiffany's neck.

She hissed in pain, and grabbed at the taut cord. Blood-colored runes flared to life along the braided leather. She fought against the whip's pull, but couldn't free herself.

"Stand down, you blood-sipping dog of war," Gorsh snarled at me. "No closer or I'll break her lovely neck."

I slid to a stop twenty or so feet from the dais. Standing atop the table still placed me below eye-level with Gorsh. He stared down imperiously, a twisted smirk on his lips. The flames continued to dance around my hands as I cycled the magefire. "Pull that bullwhip off her neck or I'll fucking burn you down."

"A truce, then," Gorsh said. "A parley under the Moonlight Laws. I call it here, and name it thrice binding."

"Fuck your truce. I didn't jump the fucking Veil for a truce."

Gorsh jerked his arm, wrenching the whip to the side. Tiffany gasped in pain and flinched backward, but couldn't escape the charmed cord. "Agree or she'll squirm before she dies. Her slinky ghost will better appreciate my overtures."

I killed my pyrotechnics. "I agree to your truce. Get that off her."

Gorsh flicked his hand and the whip released. Tiffany stumbled against the wooden throne on the dais, rubbing her neck with her bound hands.

I kept my sniper-eyes stare locked on Gorsh, but I spoke to my friend. "Tiffany. Tell me you're not wearing a leather corset and fuzzy handcuffs."

Out of the corner of my eye I glimpsed a furious blush painting her face. "It's his idea, Captain. His heaven, his rules."

The grin I sharpened on Gorsh was all knife blade. "I'm gonna make you pay for that, dogmeat."

"You've interrupted our wedding," Gorsh said. "She's thrice claimed my heart. She's to be my blushing bride in leather."

"Well, then, consider this me speaking now and never

holding my fucking peace." My stream of fire roared at him, twisting and curling...and died an arm's length away as if the flames had hit a void with no air.

"My heaven, my rules." Gorsh's leer was nasty. "Your telekinetic tricks and feeble sparks won't work inside my giant's cranium." A huge explosion sounded outside. The iron chandeliers rattled. Hot wax spattered down. "I gut your magic here, you faithless, truce-breaking bitch."

I needed another way to hurt him if he could nullify my magefire. Luckily, I was creative. I strolled closer, crossing the distance along the plank tabletop. I needed to buy my people more time to take down the giant.

"Yeah, I broke your truce," I said. "It was a bad faith truce anyway, made under duress. Now that I burned the bullshit away, maybe you can explain what the hell this is all about."

"This isn't the hour for words. That hour is past! Enough with your feeble attempts to delay my wedding hour and avoid the hour of my wrath."

I smiled. "We freed all those souls you captured and remade, so your carnival army went bye-bye. I could've sworn those ghosts of yours were *helping* us smoke them so they could escape, which doesn't reflect well on your leadership abilities or your ultimate strategy. Fact is, I keep kicking your ass and you keep coming back. Some might call that stupid." I paused. "Actually, *everybody* would call it stupid."

Gorsh slowly coiled his whip. "Not too late, you snake-tongued pink monkey. Call off your attack dogs. Abandon my world and tell that peacefucker Quill to leave off the soul-drift forever. Not too late to call it even-up between us, go to our destinies with a wink and a curse."

"Not likely, you little son of a bitch. I'm here for my friend. While I'm at it, I'm gonna bounty-hunter your ass back to the real world. Felony charges await."

"A ringmaster of the circus eternal never suffers a—"

"Shut the fuck up. I've heard all your rants and your screeds. You and me, we're bound up in prophecy, just dogs fighting in a pit 'til this is done, and you're too damn ignorant to see it."

"Your succubus saw the size of my codpiece and cast a love spell upon me of her own free will—"

"Cast under *my* orders, so you could be arrested, charged, and face trial for your crimes. I'm just another enforcer of the system. Everything you want is pathetic and futile. A grand ghost circus? It's damn sad. But you keep hurting people anyway. That ends."

He snarled and slowly twitched his bullwhip, snaking it along the stairs. I flicked a dismissive hand at him and smiled at Tiffany. "C'mon, girlfriend. Let's fucking bounce. You know Erik will love that getup."

Tiffany hurried toward me, her hands still bound with those absurd handcuffs but she was grinning again. Her black wings spread and titled, so when she jumped from the top of the dais she glided down to the floor. Gorsh scrambled down the stairs after her, spitting a stream of weird profanities. I leapt off the table and slipped into a fighting stance. Before I could pretzel him in oh so many painful ways, Tiffany spun around and slammed him to the ground with a vicious blow of her wing. She pinned him, her wing grinding him into the flagstones. Her face was enraged.

"You picked the wrong succubus to be a victim, codpiece-breath. Now you're arrested, so stay down or I'll rip your spine through your asshole and you'll never sit upright on a toilet again!"

I circled around her, trying to get close to the ringmaster. I needed something to bind him with so he couldn't cause trouble as we left his heaven dream to collapse in on itself.

The giant shuddered violently, throwing me to my knees. My teeth clacked together, barely missing my tongue, snapping hard enough that I might've cracked them in the real world. Tiffany kept her balance using her wings to support her. I reached for her, but a great sucking force like a spaceship hull breach sent me tumbling across the flagstones away from her. An instant later a colossal *ptui!* rent the air as the stone giant spat me out, sending me careening through the membrane, past the steam pipes and iron teeth. I shot from its mouth, spinning back into the sky, surrounded by the tables and benches of the main hall. But not Tiffany.

I toppled through the air, struggling to stop my fall as the sky and ground changed places over and over again in a dizzying roll. I smashed into something, hitting hard enough to leave a crater with a crunch and screech of metal. It took me a moment to shake off the dizziness and pain and get my bearings. A pirate flag fluttered and snapped overhead. The flying Winnebago.

"You okay, Captain?" Gavin yelled from his driver's window, barely audible over the roar of wind as he sent the vehicle into a wide, swooping turn.

"She's inside!" I yelled back. "Cut that bastard's head off!"

The giant swung and stomped, trying to crush us gnats who swarmed around it, but hampered by its colossal lumbering size. It slammed its fist into its own chest, trying to mash Erik into a bloody smear. Even in his night-sky armor Erik was far too nimble and dodged the huge fist, which left a large dent and spewed a billowing cloud of black dust and a rain of circus ride debris. Erik scaled the top of the giant's chest to its rounded head. The giant goggled at him with its four searchlight eyes, lurching backward. Erik was so close it struggled to see him. Both its arms came up to grab at the berserker. Erik swung his axe.

The supercharged blade sheared through rock and metal, peeling back half the giant's rounded head and blinding two of its eyes. The giant stumbled and flailed. I launched myself back into flight, leaving the circling Winnebago behind and zooming at the giant's head. I intended to slag that son of a bitch and break Tiffany free.

Erik was already on it. Another savage sweep sliced more of the huge stone head, tearing apart its teeth and shearing away the organ pipes. Erik darted inside the tunnel mouth. I flew faster, dread spreading through me because I had no eyes on Erik anymore. I'd have no idea if he was in trouble.

A moment later the giant's entire head shuddered, a strange snapping wobble shook Gorsh's heaven dream, making the head seem to waver as if viewed distorted through water. Then the giant's head toppled backward off its massive shoulders and crashed to the ground with an earthshaking thud, breaking into rubble on the volcanic plain.

Erik stood on top of the giant's body, where its head had been, with his axe in one hand and his other arm hugging Tiffany tight to him. Tiffany was smiling like Christmas morning and like starting down the walkway to the first house on Halloween and like that instant before the first bite of Thanksgiving dinner all rolled into one.

The wheezing calliope music died in a ragged blast of notes. The endless volcanic plain broke into pieces, black rocks tearing free of the ground to shoot into the twilight sky, meteors in reverse. The alien constellations spun faster and faster until they were nothing but unbroken white streaks. The pyramid giant crumbled and fell as Tiffany glided free, still entwined with Erik, her black wings spread wide. When the giant hit the ground, the resulting earthquake ripped apart the rest of Gorsh's personal alcove in the hallway of eternity. Everything around us cracked into shards and exploded, a mirror smashed with a baseball bat, every piece a broken slice of Gorsh's heaven.

Then I was falling, and my friends falling with me.

CHAPTER TWENTY-FIVE
Egress

I plummeted out of the portal and slammed onto the conference table, bounced hard, and tumbled over a chair before coming to rest face down on the carpet. Pain made its case known before the court, and refused to be silent, despite my holding it in contempt. I grunted to myself, half laugh, half groan, because that pain-court metaphor was either brilliant or something I'd later have to blame on a concussion.

More thuds and curses sounded all around me. I rolled to a crouch. The portal still opened directly above us, like a skylight peering into the soul-drift. It made me think of *Poltergeist*. That movie had contained a goddamn evil clown too. Those fuckers were everywhere.

Mistress Patel sat in her chair, hands neatly folded in her lap. She watched us with a nonchalance I found rather irritating, considering we'd just fought our way through the spirit world then swan-dived into her conference room. The majority of the Zero Dogs had thumped off the table and fallen to the floor or had ended up in undignified heaps, but not Erik. He stood on the table in his dark suit, and gently set Tiffany down beside him. Then he pulled her close and kissed her.

A cheer went up all around me. I joined in, whooping so loud I almost yelled out a lung. Then I glanced my crew over, carefully counting my people and their limbs. All present and accounted for, thank God, and everyone had returned to normal. Or at least as close to normal as Zero Dogs ever came. And no, that joke never grew old.

Tiffany stood beside Erik, her black wings spread as she beamed her bright smile around at us. I couldn't help but grin back. Seeing her safe sent a surge of relief rushing through me, so powerful it left me giddy.

Spiritmaster Gorsh, no longer a pyramid-carnival-skinned Godzilla, had tumbled beneath the conference table. He rolled out from beneath it, jumped on a chair, onto the table, and lunged at Tiffany. Curses and snarls poured from his lips in one drooling string of anger.

Tiffany punched him in the face. Nose shot, dead center. The punch sent the redcap staggering, and he clutched his nose and shrieked. Blood dripped onto his white ringmaster uniform, coordinating nicely with the color of his hat.

"That was for giving clowns a bad name." Tiffany's slit-pupils had narrowed with fury. "Clowning has a long, proud history and you twisted it into something horrible. Clowns make people laugh. They have tiny trained dogs and they save cowboys. And all those circus performers, they just want to give people a good show. You wanted to terrify people, but carnivals and circuses and amusement parks are for people to have *fun*. You tried to ruin that, and that makes *you* the monster. And your codpiece is fucking *miniscule!*"

The spiritmaster sneered and spit blood. "You know nothing about the grand histories of the circus, you big-titted cow—"

Erik moved with amazing speed and caught Gorsh by the throat. He lifted the bloody spiritmaster with one arm, muscles bulging, and in his other hand, the enchanted axe crackled with energy that seemed alive, twisting around his blade in snake-eating-tail patterns. Slowly, the blade swung to rest against the side of the spiritmaster's neck.

"No one insults her." Erik's voice was little more than a harsh whisper. "No one hurts her. No one takes her from me. No one and never."

The spiritmaster tried to say something else, but Erik's hand crushed the words before they escaped his throat.

"I'm open to opinions on what we should do with this asshat," I said, keeping my tone relatively neutral.

"Let Erik terminate his command," Sarge replied with a shrug. The spiritmaster made the gulping squawk of a man who'd swallowed an entire hardboiled egg.

"We could dress him like a clown and lock him in a tiny car," Rafe suggested. "A very tiny car. With a very pissed off wolverine."

Gavin raised an eyebrow. "So you enjoy dressing men like clowns, eh, dogface? Kinky and yet totally disturbing. Especially when you throw in wolverines."

"Hey, Gavin, I just wanted to say: fuck you. And I mean it."

"Yeah, yeah. Been there, bought the T-shirt, took the cell phone pics and posted them on the Internet. Me, I say we accidently run him over with a snowplow. Or maybe we shove him ass-first into a jet engine."

"We could test the edge of my katana on his neck," Hanzo suggested, because apparently they didn't teach the Hippocratic Oath at ninja medical school. "Mount his head on a torii gate for the crows to peck out his eyes."

The spiritmaster made whimpering noises. Take away his ghost clowns and the guy was as hard as vanilla pudding. If he hadn't transformed from a pyramid of carnival death into a stone-wrapped giant I might've been embarrassed to have fought him in the first place.

"How about we switch his brain with one of my furry

friends? Then he'll not lack for love, just because snuggle deprivation has driven him to evil."

I stared at Mai. "What the hell are you even talking about?"

"Trying to be creative, Captain."

"Well, stop. You're creeping me out."

She fidgeted a little, clearly disappointed. I was going to have to keep a better eye on that girl. The rabid animal lovers always snapped first.

Erik remained quiet, focused on choking the spiritmaster. The spiritmaster flailed, clutched at the hand clamped on his throat, and made noises like a kinked garden hose.

"Um. Erik. Hate to interrupt your chance to slowly strangle that asshat to death...but you're *slowly strangling him to death* and we haven't decided his fate yet."

Erik took his time about responding. Finally, he eased up a little, enough that the spiritmaster ceased turning purple.

I glanced at Tiffany, searching her face for a hint of how she was doing. She'd been kidnapped by the spiritmaster, compelled to wear fuzzy handcuffs and a leather corset, and almost forced to marry him in the spirit world. I fought to keep a handle on my red desire to hurt the bastard. True, it appeared as if she'd beaten the shit out of him the entire time she'd been captured, but if I learned he'd done anything to her, I doubted my ability to show restraint, and I doubted my ability to hold the other Zero Dogs in check. More, I doubted how hard I'd even try.

But Tiffany still smiled and eyed Erik as if she wanted to kiss him again, except that his hands were full, one with an axe, the other crushing a throat. The handcuffs and corset had vanished when we'd left Gorsh's heaven dream, leaving Tiffany back in her sensible fatigues. I was about to ask her what *she* thought we should do with the spiritmaster, when Mistress Patel spoke softly.

"I have a solution," the oracle said. "It will be in line with his karmic debt and will stop him from threatening the world again, but will not stain our souls with his murder."

"Let's hear it." While it might seem easier to let Erik lop off the guy's head, now that the battle was over and he was clearly defeated and Tiffany seemed unharmed…well, as I'd said earlier, we might be mercs, but we weren't cold-blooded executioners. I preferred to believe we were firmly in the white hat section of the good guy/bad guy paradigm, though some whites were dingier than others.

"It would be best if I show you." Patel turned to Sarge and me. "Captain Walker. Sergeant Genna. Will you help me finish this?"

God, all I really wanted was a drink and a shower and Jake—Jake more than anything—but I nodded anyway. "What do you have in mind?"

"We take him back to the spirit world. I'll anchor us in the soul-drift and we'll yield him unto his punishment."

"Maybe I'm a little fuzzy on current events, but didn't we just tear shit up all through the spirit world to kick his ass *out*? Won't he be supercharged again, maybe escape?"

"I shall keep him powerless," Patel said. "As long as he is held within the circle of my influence he won't be able to flee or control spirits."

"Or we could just haul him back to Oregon, hand him over to the authorities for trial."

"Your victory won't be complete until we settle this. I've seen possible futures, watched them unfold as I awaited your return. Even if Gorsh is arrested and convicted of murder there is no guarantee that Chacaza prison will hold him forever. His ability to forge portals makes him too dangerous. If you don't follow my advice you'll end up fighting him again and again and again until you finally lose."

We locked gazes. I was exhausted and done with this whole dirty business, but I nodded anyway. "Fine. Let's finish this shit."

"One moment please, Captain," Quill said in a quiet voice. "I'd like to speak with him first."

Gorsh sneered and spat a gob of bloody slime that barely missed Quill's boots. "Swallow your tongue, Judas-boots. I don't want to hear your bleating. A weeping shame my ghosts never ate you hollow. And your mother used to squeal like a hamster when I was after her. Keep that in your mind forever."

Erik made as if to pound Gorsh into silence, but Quill, his face impassive, held up his hand and the berserker subsided.

"I forgive you, Chief," Quill said. "I pardon every wrong you've done me. I forgive you for your failings. I'm sorry I couldn't lead you to enlightenment, which is the one thing I wished. Now the suffering you've caused has boomeranged on you, and you must pay the price for the harm of your own deeds."

Gorsh began to curse and yell again, but Quill only bowed, turned on his heel, and left the room without another word.

* * *

It didn't take long for Sarge and me to follow Mistress Patel through the portal, both of us dragging Gorsh between us. In the soul-drift, Mistress Patel shone with a blazing icy-white radiance all around her body, but her face was blank—empty and featureless except for one large brown eye in the center of her forehead. Strange shadows flickered in random directions from her, though there was no strong light source to cast them. Large shadows. Distorted, writhing shadows that moved when she didn't.

Spiritmaster Gorsh had lapsed into sullen silence. He no longer tried to flee. Sarge and I kept a tight hold on him as we floated in the drift.

"Let's hear the solution." I didn't think I was going to enjoy this, not at all, but I wanted it over with.

Despite having no visible mouth, Mistress Patel had no trouble forming words. "There's a labyrinthine dimension here—"

The spiritmaster made a sudden lunge, twisting and cursing. Sarge and I yanked him back. Gorsh thrashed again, filled with a desperate strength that nearly broke him free. We barely held on.

"Just kill me you three gutless shit-chewing cowards," he spat. "Kill me and get it over and done."

"The Labyrinth of Regrets," Mistress Patel continued, as if Gorsh hadn't spoken. "It is a kind of Hell, in a way and from a certain point of view. A type of…forced rehabilitation. It can't be changed the way the heavens here can be changed, with desire, imagination, and the whim of the mind." She swept a hand and spoke words that I didn't understand—harsh words that crunched and ground like someone stomping on light bulbs.

Another doorway unfolded before us, an opening in the soul-drift that unfurled like origami in reverse. Inside, a black-stone maze stretched as far as I could see, built into spiraling towers and plummeting into pits, and everywhere were walls and intersections and dead ends. The Labyrinth of Regrets twisted beneath strange stars I'd never seen before.

I started to second guess myself. The spiritmaster hurled himself backward again, breaking out of my grip. Sarge grappled with him. Gorsh fought like a wounded badger. He almost wrenched free of Sarge's grip. I moved to stop him, and he swung a fist at my head, snarling. I barely dodged aside. He bit at my hand and just missed taking off the tip of my pinkie finger.

We shoved him forward, mostly to be free of his violent thrashing and non-stop curses. He tumbled through the portal, falling end over end into the labyrinth. He hit one of the maze's towering black walls and fell inside. Looking down from the portal, we could see him crouching in the darkness. He peered around frantically.

That's when I spotted the clowns. They poured out of the walls, appearing from nowhere and nothing and floating toward the spiritmaster. He tried to command them. They only giggled and kept on coming. Gorsh screamed and ran. The clowns gave merry chase.

"How long will he be trapped there?" I felt increasingly uneasy. Maybe the spiritmaster had been right. Maybe flat out killing him would've been kinder.

"Until he purges his evil karma and atones for his sins. Then he'll find the center of the labyrinth and a door that will lead him back to this world or another like it, but only if he is changed to his core. Otherwise the door will not open."

"What happens if the clowns get him?"

"The ghosts are in his mind. They cannot truly harm him, but he can't realize that until he overcomes his fear and hatred and lust for power."

Sarge grunted. "Too easy."

But I didn't know if I agreed. I thought it would be pretty fucking horrible to be chased through a never-ending maze by a bunch of giggling, insane clowns laughing for my blood. I met Patel's gaze...or the disconcerting gaze of her one brown eye in the center of her forehead. "You're a cruel woman."

She blinked her eye, but I would've sworn she smiled, despite having no mouth. "Am I? Perhaps I show the greatest mercy."

The next instant a portal opened around us, swallowed us, and the soul-drift vanished as if it had never been.

CHAPTER TWENTY-SIX
Back in Minneapolis

The rest of the Zero Dogs headed for the parking lot to hook up with cabs and make the best of our remaining time in Minneapolis before we flew back to Portland tomorrow. They were talking about visiting some sculpture garden with a gigantic bent spoon and a huge cherry and then hitting a pub hard.

I lingered in the trashed reading room for a moment alone with Mistress Patel. We faced each other, standing on opposite sides of the conference table. The portal to the spirit world had collapsed after we'd jumped out. I wondered again if I'd done the right thing, tossing the spiritmaster into the Labyrinth of Regret. Hell, even the name didn't sit right with me. I thought Labyrinth of Lamentation had a better ring to it.

Then again, Gorsh had helped murder two people, kidnapped Tiffany, tormented Quill, and nearly killed us all. Maybe I needed more scar tissue for my bleeding heart.

I set my hands on the table and leaned toward Mistress Patel. "You manipulated all of this. The entire time, shutting off sections of the maze so the dogs ran the way you wanted."

"Yes. And…no. I controlled nothing the spiritmaster did. As for the Zero Dogs…your free will was never constrained. You made the choices. I just improved the contrast, so the picture would be clearer."

"A bunch of blah, blah, blah. Were there ever any real prophecies? Or were those more lies and manipulations?" Fury made me stand up straight again and clench my fists, and yet I felt exhausted at the same time. I just wanted to go home...but Jake wouldn't be there, so what was the point?

"The prophecies were real," Mistress Patel said. "They set everything in motion. Nothing I did, I did lightly or callously. An oracle's nights are sleepless."

"What about us? We were nothing more than a sword to you."

"If you think of yourself as a sword, don't be outraged when someone swings you like a sword."

"Quippy. Self-serving, but quippy."

She shrugged. "You're determined to be angry at me. I can't do anything about that, and I'm sorry for it. But think of it this way—we're all called to be something, to do something with our lives. Some never achieve this calling. Other people search their entire lives and never find what it was they were meant to do. And still others do what they were meant to do, whether that be something as simple as loving a significant other with all their soul, or being a good parent and raising a child, or leading armies, or—my favorite—refusing to give up their seat on the bus and shuffle to the back. Any of these things, even the smallest, contains the potential to change the fate of nations. Perhaps the smallest have the best chance. Many an avalanche started with a single loose pebble."

"So the sword should be happy with its lot."

"No oracle has ever seen a future where swords weren't necessary."

"That's pretty damn grim."

"It is what it is. You fight for justice and to protect the innocent."

I shook my head. "I fight for money."

"Let's not start lying to each other. No blood-money mercenary would've jumped into the spirit world after her friends. Erik chased the woman he loves. You jumped after her because of love, a different love, but still powerful. Your men and women all followed you for the same reason."

I didn't have anything to say, so I kept silent. A knot burned in my throat, and it was hard to swallow. She might've pushed and nudged us into doing what she'd wanted, all to thwart the vision of the future she'd showed me, but I could look into her eyes and see she believed what she'd done had been right.

"Just ask me outright next time," I finally said. "A girl likes to be asked."

She smiled. "Perhaps I will."

"And dedicate your next book to me. It'd better be something impressive—at least as good as the *Necronomicon*."

She arched an eyebrow. "No one will envy you for your name trapped within the grim tomes I unleash upon the world."

"Fine. Your first born kid, if it's a girl, name her Andrea Queen of the Phoenixes. Queen of the Phoenixes can be her middle name, I suppose. If it's a boy—"

"I can't promise that. In fact, I think the answer's closer to *not on your life*."

"Worth a shot anyway. Don't ever call me. Not even if you have visions of my death. I don't fucking want to know."

My combat boots thumped on her plush carpet as I left her office. She watched me go, I could feel her gaze burning into me, all her eyes, even the sometimes invisible third one.

But I never looked back.

* * *

Home. The Zero Dog compound. I never thought it had

looked quite so beautiful, all lit up with floodlights underneath a cloudy Oregon night. Bomb craters, crashed jet skis, even the plastic zombie lawn gnome sculptures dangling by their feet from the trees as a warning to the undead. This was our place. This was *my* place.

Stefan's coffin had arrived on an earlier flight and had already been delivered to the house, so he was up and waited for us on the front steps. The rest of the Zero Dogs marched inside, but Stefan motioned me off to the side.

"What's up, Stefan?" I asked, perhaps a little clipped, because I was damn tired after the long flight and the whole interdimensional war with the crazy redcap thing. The *free* war with the crazy redcap, because we hadn't made a dime risking our asses. Far as I was concerned, Portland, maybe even the world, owed me big time.

Vampire Stefan appeared genuinely distressed. When he spoke, his voice was restrained but urgent. "Captain. A word. I beg you."

"What's wrong? I just bought a month's supply of Type O Negative."

He shook his head, dismissing my words. "I know it's not always...pleasant...having a vampire under your roof. I understand I am not always...the easiest creature to be around." He frowned and stared up at the clouds. "But I am part of this team. I'm a Zero Dog. And for all of my comrades to go with you to fight by your side...and to leave me at the motel lost in the sleep of the dead while you battled a spiritmaster... Captain, I'm sorry I wasn't there for you."

I stared at him. Was this the same Stefan who ran nearly empty washing machine loads half filled with color-safe bleach because he didn't want any of our filth on his evening wear and smoker's jackets? The same vampire who carried his own travel-sized battery operated air filter so he didn't have to smell all the dirty humans, succubus musk, foul demons, and horny lupines?

My surprise seemed to distress him further. "I'm part of this team. You were in danger, and you should've allowed me the chance to help you, like the others. It's not fair that you all went off and left me, it's not…good sport. Please. I am daylight challenged. Don't leave me behind on a mission again, not when someone here is in danger. Give me a chance, at least."

I took a moment to collect myself. This, I hadn't expected. "I'm sorry, Stefan. I didn't even think… I mean, it was daylight, and I never thought we'd see action at Patel's office. But I would've waited if I'd have known it meant that much to you." I'd been surprised that everyone had agreed to tag along for no money in the first place, but the concept of Stefan doing anything selfless was mindboggling to me. Pleasantly mindboggling.

"Thank you, Captain. That's all I ask. They care about you, and so do I, and it's not fair they get the honor of helping you while I, due to my own condition of being sunlight disabled, do not."

He left me, wandering off to help with the luggage. Yes. I said *help* with the luggage.

I tromped inside to get a beer and head up to my room, wondering if I hadn't fallen into an alternate dimension when I'd come back from the soul-drift. It had been a long, *long* couple of days.

There was no beer in the fridge. Gavin and Rafe had probably chugged every last bottle. I cursed and trudged up the steps to my room. God, I was exhausted, just weary to the core. I entered the code on my room's digital lock and stepped inside, eager to shut the door on the world and revel in some peace and quiet.

I nearly tripped over the two-gallon milk jug set on the

foyer floor. An entire line of milk jugs marched down the hallway leading to the living room, interspaced with fat red candles. The candle flames flickered and danced, making the shadows of milk containers writhe all across the walls and ceiling.

What the hell?

I stalked down the hall, ghost-quiet, heart hammering and adrenaline in my veins. I cleared the corner and there was Jake, sitting on the couch, reading a book about Saladin and Richard the Lionheart, surrounded by more candles and gallons of milk. All percentages. Two percent, one percent, skim, whole milk, fortified with vitamin D, and next to him on the table, two beers in a bowl of ice. Jake looked up at me when I entered and he smiled. My heart did happy little electro-shock jags in my chest, and I had a hard time breathing.

"Andrea. I missed the hell out of you."

"You're back," I said. Stupidly.

He nodded. He had the grace not to make fun of my obvious statement.

"What...?" I started, so many thoughts crashing around in my head, so many wild emotions sparking and flashing through me, that it was impossible to focus on just one. "What are all these milk jugs?"

His grin widened into cat-ate-the-goldfish territory. "You asked me to pick up some milk on the way home from work. Well, I'm home, and I didn't know what kind of milk you wanted, so I bought them all."

I laughed. I stood there laughing, wondering how I'd ever tell him the crazy events I'd just survived, and laughing until he stood up, grinning, walked over to me and took me in his arms. He kissed me. A perfect kiss. And I kissed him back.

A perfect kiss.

EPILOGUE

Mercenary Wing Rv6-4 "Zero Dogs"
The Zero Dog Compound

As for the other Zero Dogs, well, it was the usual crazy shenanigans in the days following the defeat of Gorsh the redcap spiritmaster. Some things never changed.

For an entire week Stefan Dalca decided that, in addition to being secret Romanian aristocracy, he was also an exiled Emperor and Eternal Champion trapped in the wrong dimension. He informed me, straight-faced, that his newly revealed status qualified him for a higher pay grade. I replied, straight-faced, that when he was able to summon Dukes of Hell or found a respectable sword, he'd get his damn raise and more besides.

And that was the end of that subject.

Balloon dog came home with us from Minnesota. Rafe set about trying to teach him to fetch boxes of condoms by color. After a misunderstanding involving a poodle-shaped piñata in a party supply store, I ordered Rafe to keep balloon dog out of public spaces forever. Meanwhile, Squeegee the mutant housecat destroyed another industrial-sized scratching post—a 55 gallon drum wrapped in heavy duty carpeting—and got into some catnip Rafe had brought onto the premises, in violation of house rules. She shredded a couch and obliterated two end tables before vomiting on the second floor landing. Vomit which I promptly stepped in while wearing socks and heading down to the kitchen for a midnight snack. Pufferfish decided to stick around, materializing in the game room and rolling around on the pool table when it wasn't busy making fish lips at itself in the washroom mirror and disturbing our clients. Ghosts.

Mai joined one of those programs that brought pets to the elderly to enhance their quality of life and extend the lifespan of senior citizens. She happily summoned various fluffy abominations and drove them to Assisted Living Facilities. Those red kitten-esque things. Silver canine creatures that resembled French Bulldogs with six legs and glowing purple eyes. Freakish-looking ferret monsters. I had an ominous feeling from the get go, but her pets were a wild hit. The elderly adored those grotesque little monsters and looked forward to her arrival all week. The world was clearly mad.

Hanzo declared he'd joined the True Pure Land School of Shin Buddhism. He got drunk with Rafe one Friday night and ended up getting the kanji for ninja tattooed on his shoulder. I thought the ink job pretty damn cool looking, and told him so. Even Mai complimented him, and Hanzo blushed so red that for a moment I worried he'd spontaneously combust. Better than Rafe, though, who'd had the image of Tim Curry as Pennywise the clown tattooed on his left calve. When he was sober again, I asked Rafe how many of his hot dates would enjoy seeing the big daddy of all creepy clowns on his body. He'd only grinned and told me that was why he'd had the image tattooed on the *back* of his leg, not, say, on his *hip* where it might distract from certain enjoyable endeavors.

I walked away holding my head to stop it from exploding.

Gavin finished Part One of his epic poem called "Die

Tragische Geschichte von Fremden Hunden." None of the other Zero Dogs were particularly thrilled with Gavin's portrayal of them in verse. I made him read the sections pertaining to yours truly. I came off like a psychotic pyromaniac with tyrannical delusions of grandeur and a secret drinking problem. But I escaped relatively lightly compared to Rafe, whom Gavin made out to be a male prostitute trading in sexual commerce with lonely widows and people into the freakier side of the kink scale in order to finance his dream of world tour competition in hot dog eating contests. Or Stefan, whom Gavin claimed was actually Rasputin's illegitimate offspring, raised by the Roma, turned by a vampire with dentures, who then traveled the Oregon Trail and ended up working as a bartender in a seedy Portland vampire nightclub. Gavin duly celebrated the completion of Epic Poem Part One by binge drinking and announcing he was going to marry a woman from the Ukraine he'd met over the Internet.

Rafe, in addition to the drunken tattoo episode, started dating an aerobics instructor named Honey that he met at the gym two weeks to the day after Nikki dumped him. Apparently Nikki was a fan of phone psychics, and Monsieur Philippe, that damn psychic from New Jersey, had told her Rafe wasn't her destined mate after all. Also, she really didn't appreciate his Pennywise the clown tattoo. Rafe had taken it in admirable stride. Although we had our own gym at the Zero Dog compound, Rafe had calmly assured me he needed more eye candy from the aerobics class as well as a steady supply of excessively expensive vitamin-enhanced water.

Same old Rafe.

Sarge took a vacation and traveled to Aspen with Shawn for a week of skiing. In light of recent events, I suggested he swing through Vegas and spend some time gambling at the Circus Circus casino. Sarge called me a wise-ass breeder and departed thoroughly unamused. My best ideas were seldom appreciated.

Erik stayed on with us. I made him a formal offer, grateful for his role in helping me avoid FPD and a tragic death. He formally accepted. We both knew he mostly did it to be near Tiffany. Erik still lugged his axe in a guitar case, tromping around in his black cowboy boots and looking grim when he wasn't with her.

Quill flew back to Portland with us. I put him up at the compound for a few weeks as he tried to decide what was next for him. He spent a good deal of time walking the grounds alone. One day I found him mediating on the edge of a bomb crater. We sat together for awhile in silence, listening to the birds, to the distant sounds of traffic and jets. I finally asked him what his plans were going forward.

"A monastery perhaps. I have a lot to learn."

"You were pretty shit hot and squared away in the soul-drift. I was impressed."

He blushed and stared past his iron-shod boots into the bomb crater. I let the silence play out for awhile, then said, "I was talking the situation over with the rest of the crew. They agreed we could use our own personal Yoda."

Quill glanced at me with something like excitement dipped in holy terror. "I will not use violence, Captain. I refuse to harm another living being." He took his cap off and held it loose in his hands, staring at it. It left red prints on his fingers. "This bloody cap is a curse. I won't deepen the stain."

"You wouldn't see combat. That's a promise. I was thinking more like...like a spiritual advisor. Also, I pay top dollar for donated blood—*freely given* human blood—for our vampire. If you stay with us, you wouldn't have to worry about using pig's blood or anything violent to keep your cap wet."

"Why, Captain? Why offer this to me?"

"Maybe I could use a little voice of reason on my shoulder. I think I accidently burned my good angel to death once when I was drunk and pissed off."

He gaped at me. "You killed...?"

"That was a joke, Quill. But I'm serious about finding a place for you, if you want one." The goblin had shattered a bunch of my stereotypes, and maybe I owed him for more than I cared to admit. "Regulations say we can have a chaplain. Regulations don't say what religion that chaplain has to be."

"Captain, I may not approve of some of the methods the Zero Dogs use. There could be conflict between us. I will speak my mind."

"Unfortunately I'm used to that kind of thing." To be honest, and despite my words, Sarge and I had been the least enthusiastic about bringing Quill onto the team. It wasn't as if we didn't like the goblin, but he had spoken the truth just now. The life of a mercenary didn't line up well with the precepts of Buddhism. Even if Quill agreed to stay, I wondered how long he would last. "I expect you to be a pain in my ass. And maybe I'll regret this. But maybe it'd be good to have someone around to push back on some of our...entrenched ways of thinking. Maybe blowing shit up should be option B instead of always option A." I grinned and slapped him on the back. "Who am I kidding? I'll never believe that. But think about my offer. Let me know when you decide. No pressure."

Two days later, Quill agreed. The Zero Dogs had a new chaplain slash spiritual advisor in a completely non-combat role.

Jake and I...well, we did what any two lovers did when finally back in each other's arms. I'd missed him something awful, and judging from the time he spent with me, Jake had missed me much the same. He only had two weeks furlough and I intended to exercise, exploit, and indulge every moment of it. What can I say? I'm chock full of mercenary greed.

It was long after one such marathon "exercising" session, well after the house had fallen quiet, and deep into the wee hours of the night that I woke up feeling something tickling my bare foot.

"Stop that," I mumbled to Jake. My sleep-addled brain certain he was screwing around, trying to wake me up for more screwing around.

With a sweeping chill, I realized Jake was lying *beside* me, snoring softly. Very slowly I opened my eyes. The room was dark, but moonlight painted silver stripes on my bed and bureau, streaming through the blinds, past the decorative curtains I'd put up when some fit of home decorating madness had seized me.

A glowing pale pink jellyfish hovered in the air above the end of the bed. The jellyfish bell pulsed as it floated. Thin tentacles dangled around my right foot, caressing it.

I cried out in disgust and jerked my foot away. I summoned magefire, directing flows of flammable vapor and igniting it with a blistering curse. The ghost jellyfish vanished an instant before my stream of flame could incinerate it.

Sacre motherfucking *bleu*, I was gonna destroy that creepy foot-molesting ghost jellyfish if I had to burn down the entire mansion to do it.

"Hey, babe, quick question," Jake asked in a sleepy voice from beside me. "Why are the drapes on fire?"

Son of a *bitch*.

THE ZERO DOG KENNEL
Message Board Reader Comments

"First Post!!" posted by Pr3matureEjacko1o

"It was missing something. Needs more rhesus monkeys." posted by mkanimber23

"Nothing to see here. +1" posted by PostCountHound

"This book didn't have enough hawt sexxors. No centaur girl humping. And it haz teh bad smellz. EPIC FAIL!" posted by PwnUpr0nwrytr

"Where was that scene with the goat and the fish? That's why I read it and it was totally missing. Disappointing." posted by Wildlife Lover

"Call me when the author learns how to write a coherent sentence." posted by StrunkWhyte

"Hot Russian women want you today! Click Here For Love Now!" posted by RooskieLuv4U!

"Reading this book felt like listening to the local gamer geek jacked up on four energy drinks. The country is doomed." posted by MayanSecretMath12

"Nerf clowns now!" posted by xUberOldSchoolx

"Attention all disappointed readers! If you want a better story, go read Patricia Briggs. Her werewolves totally make me squee!" posted by JelloGirlCindy

"The author was on crack. True story." posted by InvestiGativeJoe

"I just came for the chickens." posted by RandomNoob

"OMG I LOVED IT AND CAN'T WAIT FOR THE NEXT ONE IF IT COMES OUT SOON I'LL LOVE YOU ALL YOU ROCK I LOVE CLOWN CARS AND SMALL ANIMALS!" posted by PinkCottonCandy15

"Turn off your caps key, assclown!" posted by B&Bailey

"Reads like being trapped in the mind of a schizophrenic geek living in his mother's basement and babbling in a forum for 72 hours straight. The horror. The horror...." posted by ConradJ

"The cake is a lie!" posted by TurretNumber3

"That meme is played out, fool." posted by Netcop666

"I pity the fool, fool!" posted by HawkMyMo

"No. Just... No." posted by Netcop666

"What kind of a hack switches from 1st to 3rd person point of view in the middle of the story?" posted by LeoPurist

"Enlarge your Penis NOW! Add 6 or 8 inches! She'll never want to leave your bed again!" posted by EngorgeYourSwords6969

"Kittens fucking hate spammers! Kittens FTW!" posted by Spammers2Die

"God hates kittenz!" posted by navybluegray

"Pwned!!" posted by QuakesterNails

"OFN. Evil clowns were done best by Stephen King. Everyone else is merely a sorry little also-ran, wannabe, inconsequential regurgitater of now tired tropes. Recommend the author get a plot wheel and his head out of his ass and try and fumble his way to something halfway original." posted by EWallaceKongLives

"A wannabe Terry Pratchett. Trust me, this bloody over-caffeinated Yank is no Terry Pratchett." posted by Wellesleykicked@ss

"Zombies vs ghost clowns! Who will be the deadliest monster?" posted by Legend44

"Cheerleaders vs French Maids!" posted by trollosky

"French Maids. Feather dusters *own* pom poms." posted by Sockpuppetry424

"Pigs." posted by 4reason::voice4

"Pigs vs Bacon!" posted by animalfarm235711

"Bacon vs Chuck Norris!" posted by ReturnOfTheDragon

"You're an idiot. Thank God you found a home on the Internet." posted by Bollox

"Mods are AWOL. Spam Ponies FTW!" posted by pOny2theTah

"Still light years behind the relevant meme curve." Netcop666

"All members not insulting the author or discussing the failures of these books will be permanently banned." posted by Modabee4

<This post has been deleted by the Author> posted by Eraser81

"OMFG! Enuf already!" posted by dittoditto

"OMFG! Enuf already!" posted by dittoditto

"My Grandmother could write better than this and she has a glass eye, gout and Tourette's. Too much pop culture B.S. Tries too hard to be funny. Ends up being bloated prose spitting random curse words." posted by TommyGilles

"Relentlessly snide, snarky & sneering. Killed the humor for me. Like watching mean girls if they were piranha shapeshifters. Catty teenage werepiranhas from Hell." posted by RooseveltsCow01

"Reading this felt like being slapped in the genitals with a dead fish." posted by NorthAdams

"I'm with RandomNoob." posted by Bndwgn2

"Men write romance like eunuchs fuck." posted by Origen

<This post has been deleted by the Moderator> posted by =HALMod=

"Makes me yearn for the good old fashioned book burnings of my youth." posted by G.Savonarola

"Hax!" posted by Casemancer

<Members of the forum don't feel this post adds to the discussion>

"Trainwreck. Don't break your epeen, buddy." posted by AllYourBaseAreBelongToUs

"Another tired internet meme! O_O" posted by Netcop666

"No U!" posted by quippieG

"Free the puppies!" posted by VNvet-astic

"nO wai! GTFO! Teh foam iz toothpaste!" posted by HoBoyError!

"Ur rong noobslice! Ghost Clownz eat Ur face!" posted by WTFO209b

THIS THREAD HAS BEEN LOCKED BY THE MODERATOR. Have a Nice Day. =) posted by =HALMod=

ACKNOWLEDGEMENTS

A special thank you to the excellent human beings who were patient and kind enough to beta read this novel: Matt M, Devin Harnois, and Robyn Bachar. Your suggestions vastly improved the story.

Another sincere thank you to my editor, Matt Dale, who asked all the hard questions.

~ ABOUT THE AUTHOR ~

Keith Melton is a fantasy author and part time were-sloth.

Discover more about Keith Melton here

Website: http://keithmelton.wordpress.com/

Twitter: http://twitter.com/KeithMelton99

Facebook: http://www.facebook.com/pages/Keith-Melton/199082863480486

~ AVAILABLE NOW ~

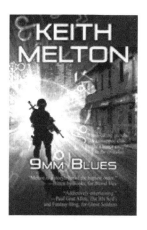

9mm Blues
Thorn Knights Book One
Keith Melton

Flesh-eating ghouls. A kidnapped child. A knight's honor caught in the crossfire...

Christopher Hill is a knight in the Order of the Thorn — the sacred order of soldiers armed with submachine guns, swords, and magic. Their mission is simple: destroy the ancient, profane evils that prey upon humanity.

But that mission becomes far more complicated when a young boy is kidnapped by flesh-eating ghouls, turning a routine search-and-destroy mission into a nightmare standoff. Barricaded inside a run-down house, the ghouls gain a deadly upper hand, and while the body count rises, Hill finds himself caught in a power struggle within the order that puts his life, and his honor, at risk, and threatens both the mission and the boy Hill has vowed to see home safe, no matter what...

Made in United States
Orlando, FL
27 March 2025